TESTING THE LIMITS

KATE LANCE

SEA
BOOKS
PRESS
seabooks.net

Print ISBN: 978-0-9872113-5-4
Ebook ISBN: 978-0-9872113-7-8

Published by Seabooks Press
seabooks.net

A catalogue record for this
work is available from the
National Library of Australia

BY THE SAME AUTHOR

Fiction

Harbour of Secrets
Embers at Midnight
Silver Highways
Atomic Sea (As CM Lance)
The Turning Tide (As CM Lance)

Non-Fiction

Alan Villiers: Voyager of the Winds
Redbill: From Pearls to Peace

To Donna Karp and Jane Keany

Contents

PART I: FAIR WINDS

2. Eliza: Freddy's Four-Master

My father, Samuel Lee, was a passenger on the steamer *Koombana* when it disappeared in a cyclone off Western Australia, just a few weeks before the *Titanic* was lost.

I was not even five, but I still remember his deep voice and how safe I felt when he swung me up to his warm shoulder. I remember a wonderful scent, uniquely his, of spices and tobacco and sun-dried clothing.

I remember my mother's grief, too. A great beauty named Rosa, with creamy skin and red-gold curls, she had chosen to elope with my father and make her life with him.

She could have had any man in Melbourne, my aunt Lucy said, but she wanted only my father Sam, who was kind and wise and handsome. Of course it caused something of a scandal, because Sam Lee, born of an English father and a Chinese mother, was not a white man.

Still, my parents found a haven for themselves in Broome, the famous pearling port in Australia's north-west, notorious for its Asian sailors and informal way of life. A place where mixed marriages—while hardly encouraged—were at least tolerated.

I was born in Broome and nowhere else on earth compares. I remember aqua-glass waters and ember-red soils and seagulls mewling in an amethyst sky. I remember sun-dried clothing and spices and tobacco.

Before *Koombana*.

After *Koombana*, my mother, brother and I went to live in the gunmetal chill of Perth, fifteen hundred miles to the south.

In Perth my playmates called me a quarter-caste, a chow, a quadroon, and expected me to be ashamed of my dead father. Ashamed of myself. I could not comprehend their malice, but I did not weep. Since my father died I had not wept.

The Great War began when I was six. We are but a far-flung post of the Empire, our teacher declared, but we know our *duty*. The happy young men marched away and their parents' faces became old, first with anxiety and then with grief.

The neighbourhood boys said the Hun didn't just kill babies, they roasted and ate them. They did terrible things to women too but the boys weren't sure what, only that they were shameful. I didn't understand, then, that terrible things happen to women all the time.

My mother's grief eased, perhaps sooner than one might have expected, and Captain Gideon Meade entered our lives. He had met Mama years before when she sailed from England with her sister Lucy, and now he was master of a great steamship. I could never call my stepfather *Papa*, although he wanted me to. The very thought made my throat clench in rage and anguish.

Gideon Meade was not a good man. He made Mama weep and, although he was kind to my small brother Pete, he was not kind to me. He would pinch me and slap me and tell me I deserved it. I had no idea why.

Still, I did not cry.

The Great War brought us one relief: Gideon Meade went away to Britain to do something very important (he said) at the War Office, and our lives became easier. Then the war ended and I turned eleven, and he returned to our pretty house in Perth.

That did not make Mama very happy, nor me. When no one else was around Gideon started hugging me, and touching me and hurting me when I resisted him. I hated it. I hated him.

Joy at the armistice was brief: the influenza epidemic began. First the mother of a friend died, then someone's brother.

Even one of the girls in my class started coughing one day and went home and we never saw her again.

Mama's sister Lucy was a nurse, and I worried for her when she went to work at the quarantine station, looking after the soldiers returning from Europe. She did not become ill, but when we saw her again she was thin and very quiet.

By then Gideon was drinking too much and would yell at Mama in their bedroom. They separated and he moved to an expensive hotel, but that did not save him from collapsing in the final wave of the epidemic. Lucy nursed him, but he died.

Another of my aunts—beautiful Izabel—grieved terribly at his funeral, but I was glad, so glad, Gideon was gone.

Mama, who clearly enjoyed being a wife, married Anton McKee when I was twelve, and a new life began. Papa Anton was easy to love, as he was calm and grey-bearded and never hit anyone. I was happy to become Eliza McKee and forget I once had to carry the name of Meade.

Papa Anton used to be Mama's painting teacher and now they were well-known artists, holding exhibitions or working in their studio at our house in Victoria Park. My brother Pete and I would amuse ourselves with reading and playing in the reserve and sailing our dinghy on the nearby Swan River.

I liked books about secrets, ciphers and spies, but most of all I liked reading about windjammers, the great steel sailing ships that carry the Australian grain harvest over the ocean to Europe. Oh, how I loved to dream about life on those deepwater barques!

But Pete wasn't interested in the sea—he preferred books about the Air Service Boys and yearned for his own Sopwith Camel. He taught himself Morse code and made me learn it too so we could tap messages back and forth. I didn't mind because it could come in handy if I were ever on a ship.

Despite his passion for the air, Pete also loved growing things. I'd tease him that gardeners weren't allowed to become pilots, but he'd just give me a fresh carrot or tomato and grin. Everyone called Pete a charmer and he certainly was.

Not so me. Gideon used to mutter 'nasty little bint' and twist my wrist. My teachers called me a fidget because I learnt quickly and became bored just as quickly. My schoolmates said I was cold-hearted because I didn't let anyone know when I was hurt or sad or angry. (That, of course, is what used to infuriate Gideon the most.)

Dr Freud's famous theories on repression were reported often in the newspapers, and they always made me smile. I hardly needed him to tell me my reserve had its roots in those long-ago, painful memories.

But while Dr Freud might not have approved, I came to enjoy my coolness, my distance, my clear secret gaze.

We would visit Broome in the wintertime, and in summer my aunt Lucy and uncle Danny would bring their two children to stay with us in Perth.

Lucy has the kindest of grey eyes, and Danny, curly-haired and Irish, would call me Lizzie Lee and make jokes with a straight face. I'd try to keep a straight face too.

Danny had been a good friend of my father Sam's when they were young officers together on the square-riggers (so I probably don't need Dr Freud to tell me why I love sailing ships, either).

Lucy and Danny would play their violins together—they call them fiddles—and the music would make me want to dance or, sometimes, cry. But I never did.

Lucy was especially close to my grandmother Min-lu, Sam's mother. They'd known each other for years, ever since my parents eloped to Broome.

I loved Nanna as much as I did Lucy, although I didn't see her as often because she spent half her time in London. Nanna was tiny and dignified and spoke perfect English.

Her charcoal-grey hair was swept up with golden combs, her clothes were from Paris couturiers and her gems were set by the jewellers of Amsterdam. When she visited my school even the nastiest of my classmates quailed before her level gaze.

Once a girl whispered, 'She must be an *Empress!*' and the others nodded in awe. Sadly their awe never lasted very long.

Mama was often very busy but Lucy always had time for me. One day in my bedroom, gazing into the mirror as Lucy brushed my hair, I said, 'I *hate* my hair.'

Lucy smiled. 'Heavens, why, darling?'

'A girl in my class calls me a Chink. If my hair were red like Mama's she wouldn't say that.'

Lucy stopped smiling. 'What a horrid child. Your hair is lovely, Eliza. It's wavy and thick and the prettiest shade of mahogany.'

'But I *am* a Chink, Lucy. I'm a quarter-caste.'

'Darling, those are just names. Yes, your father was part-Chinese and some people don't like that, but who cares? Sam Lee was the kindest and cleverest of men. Remember, Min-lu always says wealth trumps race, and she should know.'

'But my skin isn't milk-pale like Mama's and everyone says how beautiful she is.'

'Your skin is like silk, Eliza. But remember, child, there are many ways of being beautiful and most have nothing at all to do with looks. Come on, let's walk down to the river and watch the yachts.'

I never felt lonely when Lucy was around. She loved sailing ships as much as I did. She even had her own boat, a lugger named *Sparrow*.

Japanese and Malay men would take it to sea for her and go diving for pearlshell. Whenever we visited Broome I'd watch it for hours, skimming like a white sea-bird on the turquoise bay.

At school I stoically ignored the spite. It turned out that I was good at mathematics, so I helped my unpleasant classmates with their geometry and algebra, and when Mama won an art competition and the story was in all the newspapers, I found myself briefly popular.

Over time, other new girls arrived to be the latest blood sport, and at last I was unremarkable and unremarked. That suited me.

When I was sixteen something exciting happened at last! My aunt Izabel came to Australia for a visit. She was the aunt who had so surprised me with her grief at the funeral of my stepfather Gideon Meade (nobody else was grieving).

Izabel had gone to live in London and now, five years later, she was a startlingly beautiful stage actress. She wore furs slung around her shoulders and short sequinned gowns, and her pictures in the paper and a brief outing to my school gave me another pleasing burst of popularity.

Eyes sooty, mouth voluptuous, hair adorably bobbed, Aunt Izabel was glamorous beyond imagination. Born of Min-lu's later marriage to a Portuguese man, Izabel and her sister Filipa were younger half-siblings to my father Sam.

A Portuguese father is all well and good, but to account for Izabel's exotic looks—and of course pander to prejudice—she invented a Gypsy mother, now also conveniently deceased. Only her immediate family knew the truth, but Izabel was so lovely I doubt the dukes and counts and barons who vied for her hand at the stage door were much interested in her real heritage.

Izabel came to dinner at our house. She gave me a strongly scented bottle of perfume and charmed Pete and Papa Anton, although I had the feeling Mama didn't like her very much.

After she returned to London, posed prettily on an ocean liner, my life subsided into its usual slog of lessons and exams. Then one day, amazingly, the dull wasteland of school ended.

An obligatory coming-out season followed but nobody paid me much attention. I'm not giggly and I don't paint my eyes or wear short skirts like Izabel. And I still like being unremarkable.

Now, at twenty-one, I'm fed up with *everything*. Despite a certain aptitude—I excelled in mathematics at school—I don't want to go to university like Pete, who's studying engineering. I don't want to get married and have babies, or write racy novels about lust in the desert, or be a secretary, a teacher, an artist or a nurse.

I don't know what I want.

I go to parties and dance and kiss drunken young men, but never settle on a single beau. Some, too persistent, remind me of Gideon Meade and I keep my distance. The thought of actually marrying one of those foolish boys and living with him fills me with despair.

One humid day, reading a womens' journal in the sitting room, I'm overwhelmed with a wave of fury with myself and my boring life. I hurl the magazine across the room and it just misses Liam coming through the door.

Liam is my younger cousin. He lives here and studies art with Mama and Anton. 'Not too keen on the latest hairstyles, then?' he says, knowing perfectly well this will irritate me.

I've never cut my long hair into a fashionable bob, so Pete often makes tedious jokes about the titian-haired temptresses of Victorian art, women who could hardly be less like my own small, dark self.

Mama's own mother was an artists' model of that era, immortalised in the famous canvas *Ophelia Drifting* which hangs, Mama says, in London's National Gallery.

I shake my head and say, 'Just *bored*.'

'Come and sit for me, then,' says Liam. 'I want to do some figure work and need a model.'

I raise an eyebrow in what I hope is a sophisticated manner.

'A *naked* model?' I say.

'No, just a person. You'll do. Come out to my studio.'

I can't be bothered to argue so I follow him. We're not alone in the house, of course—Liam's studio is across from my parents' and I can hear them murmuring. He sits me in an armchair and arranges my legs and arms as coolly as a doctor.

He turns my shoulder slightly, drapes my hair along it, then goes to his easel and begins sketching quickly with a paintbrush. I gaze at my cousin as he works.

Liam came to a school open day recently with my parents because he wanted to see some of the famous old paintings in the chapel. The other girls fluttered and flirted and whispered he was a *sexy sheik*, but he just smiled.

Of course he's no longer an annoying little boy like Pete, but for the first time I notice he's grown into his own self in a way that's quite different from my dancing partners.

Is Liam a sexy sheik? The strong bones of his face suit him, his skin glows with health, his dark hair shines, and his shoulders move pleasingly beneath his shirt as he paints.

Frowning in concentration, his eyes shift from my body to the painting and back again. He looks at me and through me, seeing something that's partly myself and partly his own vision.

His hands are large and supple and I think of those clever hands touching my waist, my breasts, as deftly as he turns his paintbrush. I'm surprised at the instant pang of pleasure. It's curious that such a simple idea—his hands on me—could cause such a response. Again. My face flushes.

'Hot isn't it? Want a break?' Liam says.

'Yes. Let me see.'

I stand beside him at the canvas. It's not what I expected.

The forms are strong, the colours intense, magenta and turquoise—nothing at all like the beige dress I'm wearing. It doesn't look like a woman at first, but then it does, with narrow sinuous lines and a sense of something poised, hopeful, waiting.

Liam gazes at the painting smiling slightly, his eyelashes curved like the corners of his mouth. I turn towards him, my body alert, sensitive, aligned with his. He pushes a fall of my hair back, his eyes curious.

To my own surprise I reach out and touch his wrists, thoughtless with daring, and run my hands along the cords of his forearms to the shift of his shoulders. Barely breathing, I lift my head and return the confident gaze of his eyes.

Mama walks in saying, 'I'm out of burnt sienna, Liam, do—'

I drop my hands.

Mama looks at the canvas. 'Oh, that's nice. Do you like it, Eliza?'

'Yes,' I say and turn and leave.

'He's not even my *real* cousin, Mama. He's only a cousin by marriage, and nothing happened, it was just a stupid moment. You should see the octopuses—octopi—I have to deal with at parties. They're the menace to my purity, not *Liam*.'

'I'm not saying he's a menace to anyone's purity, darling. I expect you're more of a menace to him. But you're bored, that's obvious. You need to see a bit of the world. I only suggested you should visit your grandparents.'

'They're in *England*.'

'You went there with Lucy, when you were—what—twelve?'

'I was *eleven*, Mama.'

'You liked it then well enough. Why not go again? Min-lu and Freddy would love to see you and I'm sure Izabel would introduce you to some fascinating people—'

I take a deep breath. I don't know what I want. Yes I do. I want that pang of pleasure again. I want to find out what would happen if my hands moved to the sides of that sculpted head and I brought that mouth down to mine and ...

'It's winter over there now,' interrupts my infuriating mother.

'But you could be there for spring. So lovely, London in spring, and the art galleries, Eliza—what a treat!'

I groan. I don't want art galleries. I want—something. Oh, I just *want*.

Liam avoids me and I avoid him. His parents Lucy and Danny arrive and seem to think spring in Britain is a wonderful idea. Even their young children do. Seven-year-old Mikey says I should visit the lions at London Zoo and Anna thinks Buckingham Palace is the place to go. I remain unconvinced.

Then over dinner one evening, Lucy says, 'Eliza, I've had an idea. I telegraphed Freddy to check, and he thinks it's possible as long as you get moving immediately.'

'What's possible?' I say, pushing a few peas around my plate with the fork.

'Freddy's four-master is sailing soon from South Australia. You could go too.'

I look up, startled. '*Go*? On *Inverley*?'

Deepwater ships have always been important to my family. Mama's father was a captain, and my father Sam and uncle Danny were both Masters in Sail. When I was eleven, just after the Great War, I went to England with Lucy, Pete and my grandmother Min-lu, and during that trip two extraordinary things happened that drew me even deeper into the world of ships—*Inverley* and Freddy.

Inverley was a magnificent four-masted barque we visited at the London docks, her figurehead a lady holding a sheaf of green lilies. Her master made us very welcome.

Captain Nilsen had been a shipmate of my father's and knew Mama and Lucy from the old days, when they were girls sailing to Australia. When it was time for us to leave England, Lucy sailed home on *Inverley* while the rest of us had to go on the boring old steamer.

I was bitterly envious of my aunt's experience, although by then I knew my childhood dreams were merely fantasies. Windjammers may appear glamorous, but in truth they are hard, rough, dangerous worlds.

So that was *Inverley*. And Freddy?

Freddy Havers was an old man, a friend of my grandmother's from long ago in Hong Kong. He had a big white moustache and blushed a lot, especially when looking at Nanna. He took us around the countryside and to Ireland, where he had an estate.

One day Nanna sat Pete and me down and explained that Freddy was actually the father of Sam Lee. He was our own *grandfather*, a shadowy figure I'd always assumed had died years ago. Nanna said they had loved each other when young but were forced to separate, so she'd raised their child Sam by herself.

Of course I didn't understand how agonising her predicament must have been—to my girlish self it sounded romantic.

Freddy and Min-lu had gone on in life to marry other people, but now they were both alone and it was clear they would never again let themselves be parted.

They had a big wedding, which I liked (I wore a blue dress), but most of all I liked my new Granddad, who would speak to me as if I were a grown-up.

It turned out that Freddy's father was a Sir or a Lord or something, but if anyone ever asked he'd laugh and say he was just a second son making his own way in the world.

Best of all, my two new enthusiasms came together after the wedding, when Granddad Freddy bought into the ownership of the marvellous four-masted barque *Inverley*.

It was a wise business decision for the time, but I think he also did it in memory of his lost son's sailing days.

So today, along with a dozen other barques, *Inverley* loads grain from South Australia every year and carries it to Europe. The vessel that makes the fastest passage gets a trophy and wins what the papers call the 'Grain Race.'

Inverley, sadly, has never distinguished herself in this (or any other) way, but Granddad just smiles and says since they all go different routes at different times it's not precisely what he'd call a contest.

Yet whatever it is, Freddy's four-master is loading grain right now and leaving soon for Europe—and if I hurry I can go with her. I'd believed my childhood sailing dreams were long forgotten, and I know perfectly well this is a ploy to get me away to London, but none of that matters. Packing begins.

A few days later I walk into the kitchen and Liam is making tea. He looks up. 'Want a cup?'

I shake my head and put a plate in the sink and stand there awkwardly, gazing out at the garden and our play-house beneath the trees. I recall my eight-year-old self insisting Pete and Liam take 'tea' there with my dolls. How embarrassing.

'I'm sorry, Eliza,' Liam says. 'I didn't mean this to happen.'

'Oh, I'm *delighted* to go. Simply delighted. London in spring will be so, so ...'

'Delightful?' he says, suppressing a grin.

I sigh. 'Look, I'm sorry, too. I didn't mean *Mama*—'

I run out of words and shrug. He sets down the tea. 'Have some, anyway. Better than that vile concoction you used to make Pete and me drink. What *was* that stuff?'

'Grass clippings and water.'

'Thought as much.'

'Why did you put up with it?'

'We admired you,' says Liam. 'You were rather a fierce, definite child. You always knew what you wanted. Pete was too—him with his aeroplanes, you with your ships. I only ever thought about colours and shadows and shapes. I always felt *indefinite* that way.'

I'm astonished. 'But you seemed so certain of yourself.'

'Perhaps we're none of us as we appear, Lizzie.'

My old nickname makes my throat ache and I say, 'I'll miss you, Liam.'

'No you won't, not in the slightest. You'll have a wonderful time, brace-hauling and keel-hauling and over-hauling and whatever else it is you'll have to haul.'

I laugh. 'My goodness, so I shall!' I hesitate. 'But this won't be a problem for you with Mama? Sometimes she's so straight-laced.'

'I doubt she'll throw me out for trying to seduce her daughter.'

'But surely you weren't.' I turn, deliberately graceful, and meet his eyes. 'Were you?'

'Of course I was.' He kisses me briefly on the mouth, then steps back.

I'm disappointed. 'Oh. Is that all?'

'Has to be. We're going our different ways, Lizzie. I've decided what I want at last—and it turns out it's colours and shadows and shapes after all.'

He smiles and tucks a wave of my hair behind my ear. 'But you're embarking on your great ship and you don't need me. You don't need anyone.'

3. Pete: To Port Lincoln

Lord, what a pain in the neck Eliza's departure is. I stay right out of it, spend as much time at the oval as I can, but it's impossible to avoid. Wet-weather gear, cold-weather gear, hot-weather gear, ad nauseum. Boring old sailing ships are the only topic of conversation at every meal.

I've never understood the affection my otherwise clever sister has always held for those inefficient anachronisms. They look dashing enough on the horizon: you might imagine fine timbers, clouds of canvas, a rakish master and brave men who've sailed the seven seas.

But up close—what a disappointment! Rusty steel hulls, patched sails, tubby captains in old suits, crews of hard-faced Scandinavians. No speed, no glamour, just plodding grain warehouses.

Even my Aunt Lucy, a sensible woman in most respects, once sailed on such a vessel, and the name *Inverley* has bored and irritated me most of my days. And it's certainly driving me right around the bend at the moment.

Then they inform me of the ultimate indignity: it's me they expect to chaperone Eliza to South Australia to put her on that stupid boat. *Me!* My team has matches lined up all summer and I'm lead batsman, but expressing my indignation gets me precisely nowhere.

Aunt Lucy and her brood are on the way back to Broome, Mama and Anton have yet another exhibition coming up, and even bloody Liam just laughs when I suggest he take my place. So I'm stuck with it, and in mid-February 1929 Eliza and I depart Perth, with all the usual tedious farewells at the station.

The first leg of the trip is to Kalgoorlie via the Eastern Goldfields Railway. Eliza isn't what you'd call chatty and I don't have much in the way of small talk either, but time passes pleasantly enough.

We reach Kalgoorlie late that evening, then there's a bit of fuss changing over to the Port Augusta train on the wider-gauge Trans-Australian Railway. (We studied the gauge problem in Engineering Standards, and I rather enjoy seeing the odd situation in real life.)

Eliza and I have separate sleeper carriages and I'm glad of that. I'm still not very comfortable with my body and the way it thrusts me into embarrassing situations with a mind of its own.

I sleep well, and after breakfast Eliza and I sit in the lounge car and watch the passing scenery. It's quite extraordinary at first, with scattered scrub and red stony soil to the flat horizon, but soon becomes dull in its sameness. The waiter brings us morning tea.

I say, buttering a scone, 'No second thoughts, Sis? You're remarkably quiet.'

'About the passage?' Eliza says. 'No, but I'm thinking about everyone I'm leaving behind. When I come back you'll all be different.'

'I doubt it. Not me.'

'Yes you will, Pete. You'll have graduated and be assembling dull machines by then.'

'I've told you a hundred times that's not what engineers do.'

'Well, you'll never be my little brother again.'

I think for a moment. 'You're right, you know. For once.'

She gives me a wary look. 'Oh?'

'This'll be my second year at university and I'll be out in a couple more. And who knows when you'll come back? London in spring, *et cetera*.' That makes her smile.

I lean forward. 'But I won't be an engineer, even though everyone else thinks I will.'

'What, then?'

'I'm going to be a pilot,' I say, finishing my scone.

'I thought you'd given up on that idea.'

'Mama would get so cross whenever I said it so I stopped. But I didn't stop thinking about it.'

'Oh, my goodness, Pete! What if you crash?'

'What if you sink?'

'Ships have been sailing for thousands of years, but *aeroplanes?*' she says. 'They're so new and dangerous.'

'But safer all the time. Remember, Smithy flew the whole Pacific Ocean last year. It's a great time for aviation, and Australia needs trained airmen. Who knows what enemies we'll face one day?'

'The British Empire will protect us,' Eliza says firmly. 'And everyone swore there'd never be another war, not after the last one.'

I shrug. 'I don't really care about that anyway. I just want to fly.'

'Well, I suppose that horrid motorcycle of yours is more dangerous than any aeroplane,' she says. 'And you haven't killed yourself on that yet, not for want of trying.'

'Don't be so rude about my bike. Norton Big Four, for God's sake, one of the finest.'

Eliza gazes at me. 'You always seem so biddable, Pete, yet you're really as stubborn as the proverbial mule.'

'But you'll always be my determined big sister. Nothing will really change.'

'Definite? Fierce? *Determined?*' She shakes her head. 'I'm hearing far too much lately about what a harpy I am.'

'Doesn't make you a harpy,' I say. 'You just have to be determined *quietly*, that's all.'

'Remember when I'd make you and Liam drink tea with my dolls in the play-house?'

'Don't think so. Did you really?'

She looks at me, half-smiling. 'Yes, I did.' Then she says, 'And do you remember our father at all, our real father, Sam Lee?'

'No. I wasn't even two when he died. How could—?' I stop. 'Funny. Now you mention it I do have a sense of ... someone lifting me up as if I were flying. Do you think that was him?'

'Yes, he used to do that with you. Oh, I wish he hadn't died. I wish *Gideon* hadn't ...'

'Steady on, Sis. Gideon wasn't that bad. You always say he was such a monster but he was good to us. I was dashed proud of him being captain of that steamship too.'

'Good to you, maybe. He used to make Mama cry.'

'She'd cry about everything,' I say. 'Women are like that.'

'No they're *not*, Pete! And she only cried when he hurt her.'

'Where's the proof? I didn't see it.'

'I saw it and felt it too.' Eliza bites her lip. 'I've never told anyone this before—but Gideon used to hurt me sometimes, as well.' She swallows. 'And he used to ... touch me. Touch me where he shouldn't.'

'Good God!' I shake my head in disbelief. 'Eliza, he was a master mariner, he worked for the *government*. Someone like that couldn't, wouldn't—'

She lifts her eyes and looks at me. 'He did, Pete.'

I'm horrified but I believe her without question. Eliza has never lied to me, never in her life.

'Good God, Sis, that's awful.' I stare at her. 'He didn't—*ravish* you, did he?' I can't think of another way to put it.

She shakes her head. 'No. But it was still frightening. He was so powerful and if I'd said anything who'd have believed me?'

'Oh, Lizzie. I'm sorry I didn't understand this before.'

'I'm not sure I understand it even now.' She sighs. 'Anyway, apart from the odd bad dream I've almost forgotten it. But I'm glad you believe me, Pete. I thought you'd be shocked.'

'Me? Man of the world, you know.'

For some reason she laughs.

We have dinner then sleep, the train rolling on into the night, and finally next morning we stop at Port Augusta. We're woken beforehand to take breakfast, then we alight and I'm glad to see the car we'd arranged waiting for us. The driver seems a nice bloke, although someone chattier would have been a relief. We still have over two hundred miles to go before Port Lincoln and it'll take most of the day. I groan to myself.

Soon we're motoring southwards to Eliza's blessed ship. We pass through smoky Whyalla without stopping, then after a hundred or so tedious miles we take a break for an early lunch at Cowell, a town on the Spencer Gulf.

The hotel is a handsome old building near the water and the sandwiches are good. One of the waitresses is pretty too, and she smiles at me rather thrillingly when no one else is looking. Regrettably we don't stay very long.

Next leg is an interminable seventy miles through scrub to a small place with long white beaches called Tumby Bay. We have some very welcome afternoon tea at a hotel, but sadly the waitresses there don't smile much.

Thirty miles to go, dear Lord, but finally we crest a rise and can see the harbour of Port Lincoln. Before us is a long island offshore and several jetties leading out to sea. But what astonishes me—*me*, who's so blasé about this whole project—are the three enormous sailing ships at the longest jetty, their spiky yards and masts like a vision from another century.

'My God,' I say, sitting forward. 'You're going on one of *those*? Golly, Sis. Are you sure you'll be safe?'

She nods firmly, staring at the ships, but she looks stunned.

'Glad you're so sure about it all. Now, what do we do?'

'Um, register at the hotel, I suppose,' says Eliza. 'Then see the Harbourmaster and get a message to *Inverley*'s captain to say I've arrived. They're sailing tomorrow.'

We stop on the foreshore outside the Grand Hotel and I pay the driver and arrange for his return. Across the road is a broad strip of trees and sand, where people are picnicking and swimming in the afternoon sun.

A woman at the hotel shows us to our rooms upstairs. They're small but lead onto a veranda with a fine view of the harbour and the ships at the jetty, perhaps half a mile distant.

'Rather basic,' I say. 'Still, you'll recall this as unadulterated luxury after a few days at sea.'

Eliza digs me ungently in the ribs.

We ask the woman at the desk for directions and find the Harbourmaster's office not far from the jetty. He's a middle-aged man with a grey moustache, who glances at Eliza from under his eyebrows when she asks him to send a note to the captain of *Inverley*.

'A *girl* passenger?' He shakes his head, looking at her light cotton dress. 'I can't imagine what your parents—well, I hope you've got something more suitable than *that* to wear, miss. You'll need—'

'Cold-weather gear, wet-weather gear, yes, we know,' I say. 'She's ready for any occasion.'

Eliza hands him the envelope and says straight-faced, 'You're very kind, Captain.'

I hear him mutter 'Flibbertigibbet,' as we leave.

We stand on the shore and gaze at the handsome old craft, with their great steel hulls sweeping from pointed bows to massive sterns. Tall spiky masts are outlined against the sky, with spars as bare as winter branches touched by a frosty haze of rigging.

Enough of the poetry, lad, I tell myself. They're nothing more than absurd anachronisms in this age of oil and hydrodynamic vessels. Yet it's strangely difficult to look away.

'Which one's your boat, Lizzie?'

'Ship, not boat. And *barque*, to be precise.'

I laugh. 'Who cares?'

'The crews whose lives are easier with fore-and-aft sails on the jigger, that's who.'

I roll my eyes. 'Double-Dutch, Sis. So which blessed *barque* is your famous *Inverley*?'

'There,' she says, pointing. 'See the four-master at the end, in front of *Herzogin Cecilie*?'

'Hair-tso *what*?'

'Honestly, Pete. The magnificent white one, named for the Duchess Cecilie. Won the Grain Race last year. Probably the most famous sailing ship in the world. Ring a bell?'

I shake my head. 'Magnificent? Rusty and worn out, I reckon. But cripes, it's a big brute.'

'Over three hundred feet long.'

'Really? Good God. I suppose you know all about the one on the far side of the jetty too?'

'Yes, that's *Olivebank*. Rather lovely, but not as fine as *Inverley*.'

I can see its name, but for some reason she calls it *Oh-leever-bahnk*. I suppose that's how the foreigners say it.

'Next you'll be telling me they've all got personalities,' I say.

'Well, they certainly have different characteristics from their structures and cargoes and ballasting. I suppose knowing how to work them together is what makes a good captain.'

'Just a matter of engineering, *I'd* have thought.'

'Plus a lifetime of experience,' she says dryly, shading her eyes and gazing at the sea. 'Oh, look, there's another barque out in the offing.'

'Don't be absurd, Lizzie,' I say. 'The offing's not a *place*. It means an event is about to occur.'

She laughs. 'The offing *is* a place, a real place, you ludicrous landlubber. It's the most distant waters you can see from the shore.'

'Ah.'

'And it's where I'm going, Pete,' she says, in awe. 'Tomorrow.'

We rest in the hot, dozy afternoon then meet in the empty dining room, where the menu is limited and a small electric fan beats uselessly against the heat. At least our drinks, beer for me and shandy for my sister, are pleasantly cold.

The door from the street opens and three people come in, a fair middle-aged couple and a younger man. The woman is well-dressed, the older man solid and distinguished.

He says to Eliza, 'You are Miss McKee, yes? I received your note. I am Captain Mattias Nilsen and this is my wife, Maria.'

'Captain Nilsen, welcome!' says Eliza. 'My brother, Pete McKee. And—?'

'This is Mr Harry Bell, able seaman. He is Australian too.' The captain chuckles. 'We are a very cosmopolitan ship, Miss McKee.'

'Please sit down,' she says. 'And do call me Eliza. Do you remember we met in London when I was a child? You showed us over *Inverley* then.'

'How could I forget?' he says gallantly. 'What a curious little girl. You said I was a lucky captain to have such a fine ship.'

'It's wonderful to meet again,' she says. 'And Mrs Nilsen, I'm so glad you'll be on board.'

They sit down while Mr Bell goes to the bar to get drinks.

'Have you sailed often?' I ask Mrs Nilsen. She's blonde and rather fine-looking.

'Yes, indeed. I like to sail with Mattias. This is now my fourth passage.'

'My wife is a very good sailor,' he says, and they beam at each other.

All right, I think, if she can do it I suppose Eliza will survive.

'And how is your uncle, Mr Whelan?' asks Captain Nilsen. 'He was third mate on *Willowmere* when I was just a deck boy. Good sailor, but always playing that noisy fiddle.'

'Yes, he and Lucy are very well,' Eliza says.

'Ah, Lucy.' He smiles. 'I never forget her as a child, in the rigging like a monkey. The men were so shocked, they did not know such a thing was possible for a girl.'

'Do you remember our father, Sam Lee?' I ask the captain, suddenly curious.

'Ah, Mr Lee, second mate. A very fine man. Quiet, but we always jump to do what he says.'

There's a silence, then Mr Bell arrives with a tray of drinks and sits down beside me. We hold out our glasses and Eliza says, 'To *Inverley*,' and Captain Nilsen is pleased. He and Eliza start chatting about something nautical so I say to Bell, 'Australian, are you? From around here?'

'No. Newcastle, north of Sydney.'

'How on earth did you come to be working on a foreign four-master?'

He's a light-haired chap in his mid-twenties, well-built like most sailors. I wouldn't care to go up against him in a fight.

'I stowed away,' he says. 'But they took me on as crew because they were short-handed.'

'Stowed away?' I smile. 'Must have been a great adventure.'

'Not really, it's fairly common. If you work hard the masters don't mind as much as they pretend to. Last year there was even a woman stowaway on *Herzogin Cecilie*.'

'Good God, on *Herzogin Cecilie*?' I say smoothly, as if today wasn't the first time I'd heard the ludicrous name. 'A woman of ill-repute, I expect.'

'No, I met her once. A music teacher, very innocent.'

I chuckle. 'Probably not quite so innocent by the time they reached England.'

He smiles politely. 'Finnish sailing ships are dull and respectable. Passengers and women don't usually mix with the crew.'

I'm finding him a little dull and respectable myself so turn back to the others. Sadly, the conversation still seems stuck in the groove of wet-weather gear and the like, so I'm glad when Captain Nilsen drains his glass and says, 'Well, young Eliza. Mr Bell will meet you here at nine in the morning. He'll help with your luggage and bring you out to the ship.'

They rise, and after farewells the three of them leave.

'Golly, Sis,' I say, 'I hope you know what you're getting into.'

'I think so. Oh, Pete, how extraordinary! My last night on shore for months.'

Later, over quite a good steak, I say, 'Tell me again why these ships are sailed by Finns? Whatever happened to the British merchant fleet, or the French or Germans, for God's sake?'

'They've all given up sail,' she says. 'Sold their vessels cheaply after the Great War to anyone who'd take them off their hands. In this case, the wily Ålanders.'

'Orlanders? I thought we were talking about Finns?'

'From the Åland Islands in the Baltic Sea—once owned by Sweden, now Finland. Swedish-speaking, fiercely independent and the finest sailors in Europe. Clever enough to make a profit with these sailing ships when no one else can.'

I shake my head. 'You're quite mad you know, Lizzie. You love dancing and parties! You should be finding a nice fellow to settle down with, not going on old boats with gloomy blokes from obscure Baltic islands.'

'I'm not a fool, Pete,' she says. 'I know the trip will be uncomfortable, perhaps even dangerous, but I've *got* to escape this tedious, limited life. Maybe I'll settle down one day, but no matter what, I'm going.'

I gaze at her fondly. 'Done my best, old girl, can't change your mind. I give up.'

Next morning we wait beside Eliza's luggage. Even in the veranda's shade it's hot and I'm sweating beneath my coat.

My sister looks cooler than I feel, her long dark hair tied back under a neat cloche hat.

She's wearing a blouse and beach pants that are apparently all the go from Paris. At least they'll be the soul of respectability for wherever and whatever it is she'll soon be clambering over.

In the dusty haze towards the jetty I can see rail-wagons laden with bags of wheat and barley. 'Does that railway go all the way out to the end of the jetty?' I ask, curious about the weights the timbers have endured over the years. 'Hope it's safe.'

I think briefly about getting out a piece of paper and trying to calculate the forces involved, then decide it's too much like an exercise one of my tutors is still waiting for me to submit.

'The rails do, but not the steam-engines. Draught horses pull the wagons along the jetty, then the lumpers load the bags into the holds of the ship.'

'Ouch. Makes my back ache just thinking about it. Are they nearly finished now?'

'Yes. Captain Nilsen said we sail this afternoon.' Unusually, her voice wavers a little.

In the haze I see movement near the jetty, then a wagon starts towards us. After about ten minutes the plodding horse arrives, hauling a group of five wharfies and the man we met last night, Harry Bell, lying down with his hat over his face. The lumpers jump out and nod, looking curiously at Eliza, then proceed into the pub.

Bell lets down the wagon's tail-gate and slides off. 'Morning,' he says.

He glances at Eliza's luggage then picks up the heavy trunk as if it's a briefcase and places it in the wagon. I put her smaller bag beside it.

Eliza turns to me. 'Darling Pete. Give everyone my love, and have a good trip home on the train. I'm sorry you had to miss your cricket match.'

I hug her tightly. 'You have a wonderful time, Sis. Be *careful.*'

She nods and whispers, 'I will.'

I step towards the waiting man and shake his hand. 'Thank you, Mr Bell. I hope you have fair winds and—oh, cripes, what is it, Lizzie?'

'Fair winds and following seas, you goose,' she says, laughing. 'Well, then, let's go. Bye, Pete.' She sits on the edge of the wagon and swings her legs inside.

Bell climbs up, refastens the tail-gate and sits. The wagon-driver says, 'Giddy-up.'

I watch until they're lost in the shimmering haze, the spiky silhouettes of the four-masters beyond them. I sigh and shake my head and return to the hotel. I can hear the lumpers carousing in the bar—at nine o'clock in the morning, for God's sake!

At least the car is picking me up soon to return to Port Augusta. It'll be another long day but anywhere is better than this dreary hole. And perhaps I'll see that smiling waitress at Cowell again.

4. Eliza: We Sail

The patient horse plods along the road to the jetty.

'Is the grain all loaded now?' I ask Mr Bell.

'Mostly.' He gazes ahead.

'Thank you for coming to get me. You must have to get a lot done before sailing.'

'Yes.'

I try again. 'Have you shipped with Captain Nilsen before?'

'Two passages.'

'Is the crew as cosmopolitan as he says?'

'Yes.'

His voice is deeply pleasant, but sparkling conversation is clearly not his forte.

'Do many of the men speak English?'

He glances at me with cool grey eyes. 'No. Why I got the job.'

'Job of ... oh.' Me.

The silence lasts until we reach the jetty. We get out, then Mr Bell opens a gate in the side of a wagon on the rail lines. We put my luggage in the wagon and sit on a small pile of grain bags as another patient horse hauls us out along the jetty.

As we slowly trundle along, I gaze at great white *Herzogin Cecilie* to our left. She was once a German training-ship and magnificently set up, but now her figurehead of sweet-faced Duchess Cecilie is thick with layers of cracked paint.

Then we pass *Olivebank* on the right. Like *Inverley*, she's painted black and her figurehead is pretty too, but not (I think loyally) as lovely as *Inverley*'s, whose lady holds a sheaf of lilies. Finally my ship looms large, her name and home port, *Mariehamn*, in white letters across her steel stern.

'She's deeply-laden. How much grain is she carrying?' I glance at Mr Bell.

'Four and a half thousand tons. Fifty thousand bags.'

We stop, and once we get out a group of lumpers reach in for the last of the cargo. Mr Bell and I proceed to the gangway with my luggage. The lumpers wave to us as we pass and one calls out, 'Bon voyage, dearie!' Were it humanly possible, Mr Bell's eyes become even frostier.

Captain and Mrs Nilsen are waiting at the top of the gangway. They shake my hand and welcome me. Mr Bell sets my trunk down and disappears into a crowd of sailors. They all seem very young and aren't in any sort of uniform, just light rag-tag garments suited to the heat.

Mrs Nilsen says, 'Come with us to saloon now, Eliza.'

I want to stay on that vast deck and watch what's happening, but I follow them towards the stern, trailed by a red-headed lad carrying my trunk. Before us is the high poop deck, topped with the charthouse and a great double wheel at the stern. Beneath the deck is a steel door. We step over the raised sill into a corridor with cabins set on both sides.

At the end of the corridor is the elegant saloon, lit by a domed skylight and panelled in timber. Leather armchairs are set around a table where a dark-haired man is reading a book and smoking. He looks up, stubs out his cigarette and rises to greet me. 'Our valiant young lady has arrived at last. Welcome aboard, Miss McKee.'

Captain Nilsen clears his throat and says, 'This is Mr Malory, also a passenger.'

'Do call me Felix. We can hardly stand on ceremony throughout the perilous straits ahead.'

'I do not wish for any perilous straits ahead, thank you sir,' says Captain Nilsen, and for the first time I see the steel beneath his joviality.

'Eliza, I show you cabin,' says Mrs Nilsen.

It's a small room off the corridor, a high bunk along one wall with drawers beneath, and a chair, desk and wash-stand along the other. My luggage is lying on the bunk and through the porthole I can glimpse Port Lincoln.

For an instant I yearn to be back on land, safe in familiar surroundings. Then I scold myself for feeling as if I've just arrived at a new school.

'Thank you so much, Mrs Nilsen. This will be very comfortable, I'm sure.'

We return to the saloon where the steward has set out an elegant tea. Captain Nilsen goes to the deck while Mr Malory chats to Mrs Nilsen and me. He's a good-looking man, with a cleft chin and intense blue eyes beneath dark brows, but I make it clear I have not the slightest intention of calling him by his Christian name. He is older than me (I learn later he is thirty-one), and seems the height of sophistication.

After tea I put my clothes in the drawers beneath my bunk, then the silent red-headed lad takes the bags away to be stored. Along the corridor is a bathroom with a small bath and basin and, I'm grateful to see, a water closet. Refreshed, I ask Mrs Nilsen if I may go on deck to watch our preparations for sea.

'Of course. I show you the way.' She takes me up a narrow flight of internal stairs, a companionway. Off the landing at the top is the charthouse, with a desk and a wall of shelves holding rolled-up charts. Another steel door leads us out to the poop deck. Mrs Nilsen takes me to the fore railing and I can only gaze, stunned.

I thought I had an understanding of sailing ships, but I can hardly take in what I'm seeing. *Inverley* is no dear little three-masted barque, the sort so common in picture-books, but a massive, steel-hulled four-master, and everything about her is on such an extraordinary *scale*.

Behind us is the smallest of her masts and before us loom the other three, soaring hundreds of feet over our heads. They're anchored by ranks of steel cables, each as thick as my wrist. Half a dozen men are high on a yard-arm doing something to a sail, their feet braced on a line that swings and moves as they do. From here it looks as fragile as a sewing thread.

In front of us is a deckhouse and towards the bow, a larger one. Mrs Nilsen points. 'You see deckhouse, Eliza? Cook's galley and bunks for day-men—sailmaker, carpenter, bosun. And big one has donkey-engine and foc's'l, quarters for the crew.'

Steel cables lead to winches for lifting, lowering and turning the yards—the main yard must be nearly one hundred feet wide. Swathes of rope drape in every direction, ending in coils along the sides, the bulwarks, of the ship. It is almost impossible to believe anyone could understand what all those ropes do!

The men aloft undo the ties on the sails, clamber down the ratlines to the deck, then run to the next mast and climb again. My breath catches as they scamper so casually, leaning back to climb over and up onto the platform at each masthead, without a care in the world.

On the solid deck so far below them, others (including Mr Bell) are hammering timbers over layers of canvas to secure a gigantic hatch cover. They set steel bars across the timbers and anchor them to bolts on the decks. Naturally I've read of the dangers that require such precautions, but for the first time I feel a chill of anxiety.

A whistle shrieks, the signal for sailors to start releasing the lines holding us to the jetty. Other men haul on mysterious ropes, and I hear the crackle of canvas and look up. The limp sails are filling with air, becoming round and taut.

Silently we begin to move. Slowly at first, and then faster, our tons of steel and timber and grain begin slipping through the water to a distant splashing at the bow. I grip the railing in front of me, my heart thudding, almost unable to breathe.

Captain Nilsen comes over and smiles at his wife, saying with satisfaction, 'We sail.'

Felix Malory joins us as well. 'What a sight, Miss McKee, eh?'

I murmur politely, my mind a jumble of amazement. The day is sunny, the wind from behind, and our passage has begun.

For the next three or four months we'll be out of sight of all land. The ship has a small radio receiver but no transmitter, so no one will know where we are or how we fare. Our survival depends entirely upon *Inverley*'s seaworthiness and the skills of her young crew.

I shiver. I hope it's from joy.

Some time later the red-headed lad comes up to me and squeaks, '*Kapten*,' pointing at the charthouse, then dashes away. Inside the charthouse Captain Nilsen is sitting at the table with a document in front of him.

'We must get you signed on, Eliza. Please put your signature on the Ship's Articles, there.'

'I am to be part of the crew?'

'It is not legal to carry passengers as such. Everyone on board must sign the Articles, and those without sea time must be rated as *jungman*, deckboy.'

'My goodness, I'm allowed to be a *deckboy*?' I scribble my signature.

The captain chuckles. 'In name only. Of course you do not have to—'

'But I'd *like* to. At least learn a little and help when I can.'

'Ah, you are truly Lucy's niece,' he says, nodding. 'Indeed, there are many small jobs you may help with. We have brass to polish, timber to paint, decks to be cleaned. I will put you in the starboard watch under the second mate, Mr Pölönen. He speaks some English.'

'When do I begin?'

'Tomorrow. The off-duty officers usually eat with us, so this evening you will meet Mr Pölönen at dinner. You may rest tonight, then tomorrow we will see how well you like to be a *jungman*.' His smile is kindly, but I suddenly wonder what I've signed up for.

Dinner is in the mess-room near the saloon, not a large space, but the table is set with linen and good silver and china. Captain Nilsen takes the head of the table, his wife opposite. Felix Malory, amiable and amusing, is seated across from me, the second mate beside him.

Mr Pölönen turns out to be a stocky brown-haired young man, with a gold tooth that twinkles whenever he smiles: which is fairly often, as his English appears to be rather more limited than Captain Nilsen had indicated.

To my surprise, unfriendly Mr Bell enters the room and sits beside me in the only empty chair. I wonder why he isn't eating in the crew mess. He's not an officer, only an able seaman, and going on this morning's performance he's certainly not here to charm the passengers.

The steward serves us mushroom soup and Mr Malory remarks how tasty it is.

'We are very lucky,' says Mrs Nilsen. 'We have fine cook. He bakes bread every day.'

'Simple fare,' says Captain Nilsen. 'Yet you will not go hungry on my ship, no indeed.'

'But how can this possibly be the true Cape Horn experience without hard tack and weevils?' says Mr Malory, smiling.

Mrs Nilsen laughs politely but Captain Nilsen frowns.

Mr Bell says, 'There'll be hardships enough ahead. Wouldn't go asking for any more.'

Mr Malory gazes at him. 'Of course, times have changed on modern vessels and we should all be grateful. No oppression of the crew either. Fair democracy reigns triumphant.'

'A ship cannot be a *democracy*, Mr Malory,' says Mrs Nilsen.

'*Kapten* is always in charge. I do not understand.'

'Oh, I *must* apologise. Of course, the captain is the ultimate authority. I'm merely referring to your laudable practice of supping with the deckhands.'

Beside me, Mr Bell returns Mr Malory's stare. His lean face is expressionless but I have the odd sense he is amused.

'Mr Bell is not a deckhand,' says Captain Nilsen.

'Heavens, I am putting my foot in it tonight,' says Mr Malory with a short laugh. 'When you introduced us earlier I thought you said he was an able seaman. A deckhand.'

'I fear you misunderstand. Mr Bell is *matros*, able seaman, because he has sea time. You and Miss McKee are deckboys because you do not. But you are all passengers.'

Mr Malory flushes and Mr Bell eats his soup. Mr Pölönen smiles his innocent golden smile and the steward brings the main course which, we hasten to agree, looks delicious.

After dinner Mrs Nilsen, Mr Malory and I walk on the poop deck beneath the crescent moon and a river of stars. The breeze is mild as we sail on Spencer Gulf towards the ocean. Light gleams from scattered farmhouses ashore, but otherwise the horizon is dark.

How wonderful to be on a ship! I breathe the night air with contentment.

Next morning I awaken to delicious scents of bacon and eggs from the mess-room. We're sailing on rougher seas now, and by the time I get to breakfast the food seems a lot less attractive. I eat just a small piece of toast and climb the stairs to the deck, where the last of the land is slipping quickly behind us.

Captain Nilsen says, 'Kangaroo Island, Eliza. Say your farewells to Australia.'

As we reach the open sea the movement of the ship becomes livelier and I begin to regret even that small piece of toast. I return to my bunk, a bucket on the floor beside me.

This morning I will not be joining the starboard watch.

Mrs Nilsen says I will suffer for only a few days, until my body adjusts to *Inverley*'s motion. She brings me tea but I can only moan, and wish I were anywhere in the world but on a ship.

Two days later breakfast again smells enticing. It's cold now, and I tie my hair back and put on dungarees and a woollen jumper. I wonder if the captain has decided yet if we're to sail east past stormy Cape Horn, or more slowly west, via Africa's Cape of Good Hope.

'*Kapten*, have you chosen our route to England?' I ask him at the table.

'Indeed. The winds are better for Cape Horn.'

'How thrilling!'

Captain Nilsen shakes his head. 'Ah, *jungman*, you may yet regret those words. Finish your coffee, then I will introduce you to the starboard watch.'

He takes me to the bow and leaves me with Mr Pölönen and the nine men of my watch. Eight of them stare, snicker or scowl at me. The ninth, Mr Bell, gazes out to sea.

Mr Pölönen smiles and says, 'Pigs, Miss.'

Behind him are the pigs in their enclosure. Mrs Nilsen had mentioned the ship carries nine chickens for eggs, five pigs for meat and three rat-catching cats, but I hadn't realised what that might mean in terms of daily maintenance. Unfortunately it's all too obvious in the surrounding reek; not quite what I'd envisaged as the life of a sailor.

Mr Pölönen says, 'Like farm, yes?'

My brother and I used to go for holidays to Aunt Filipa's horse farm, so I'm used to the basics of animal husbandry. I nod and pick up a broom and bucket. Mr Pölönen addresses the men in the common lingo of the ship—Swedish with snippets of Finnish and English—and they go to other jobs, leaving me and the red-haired deckboy with the task of cleaning the pigsty.

The lad is probably all of fifteen and can't look me in the face. We slosh water around and use the brooms to push the mess out through the washports, while the pigs serenely contemplate us. When we've done our best I stand back and say, 'Good, yes?' to the lad.

He blushes beneath his freckles and says, '*Ja*,' then flees.

I follow him to Mr Pölönen, who's with some men who are chipping rust off a deckhouse. He looks worried at the sight of me and says, 'Pigs good?'

'Pigs good,' I say. He finds some rags and kerosene and takes me to the poop deck to polish the brasswork. He says, 'Cleverly and carefully, yes?'

That's the most he's said so far, so I take it as encouragement and set to work. The hardest part is the brass on the compasses —the large standard one at the fore of the poop deck, and the two steering compasses, one each side of the great ship's wheel.

The helmsman pays me no attention as I polish, which I'm glad to see. If his concentration should ever fail then the ship might broach: turn sideways to the wind and, in severe weather, capsize. The thought of broaching terrifies me.

Finally the watch ends and I'm glad to stop and have lunch with Mrs Nilsen. 'For now, while sea is quiet, cleaning and painting must be done,' she says. 'When storms come men must work sails, no time for other jobs.'

On deck later I'm surprised she calls this a quiet sea (it looks worryingly energetic to me), and the wind in the rigging is making the most eerie noises: a deep bass thrumming, a range of moaning tones and dozens of high fluty whistlings. It's almost like music.

Dinner that evening is quiet. Mr Malory is absent, still seasick in his cabin. Then the second mate blows his whistle and my watch goes back on duty. The men haul lines to adjust the sails and turn the winches to angle the yards to the wind. Various ropes are thrust at me and I hold on and haul with the others—

yank, pause, yank, pause, to a rhythm chanted by Mr Pölönen.

At midnight this long tiring day is over. *Kapten* says I'm not to attend the four a.m. watch with the others, so I don't have to work again until after lunch tomorrow. Thank God.

Next morning after breakfast Captain Nilsen shows me our course on the chart. We're almost past Tasmania and heading towards the open seas south of New Zealand, where the constant winds will push us east towards Cape Horn.

My task today is to clean the chicken coop on top of the small deckhouse, and the best that can be said of it is that it's not as awful as the pigpen. After that, Mr Pölönen hands me a tin of black grease and sets me to rubbing it onto various wires.

Some of my watchmates are nearby chipping rust, half-working and half-contemplating me and whispering to each other. Mr Bell is painting the bulwark not far away. I'm enjoying the crisp breeze and blue sky and don't notice one of the men coming closer. Later I find out he's a twenty-year old German named Karl.

'Girl on ship *unlucky*, you must go away, *flicka*,' he says. 'But in trousers, so maybe not girl?' He squeezes my breast painfully and snickers, 'Oh, *girl*, after all!'

I jerk backwards, spilling drops of black grease onto the clean timber deck.

'You in trouble now,' Karl says, shaking his head. '*Bad* deckboy.'

Some of the men laugh as Karl saunters back to his job, while others look shocked.

Mr Pölönen hurries over and stares at the deck in dismay. 'Not cleverly or carefully, Miss.'

I gasp. 'It wasn't *my* fault—'

'Don't argue with an officer,' Mr Bell says. He takes a turpentine rag and rubs at the marks, and they become lighter. 'We can holystone the deck later.'

My jaw clenched I say, 'I'm very sorry, Mr Pölönen.'

He nods sadly. As he leaves he points at the German boy and a couple of his friends and says, 'You. Pigs.' They stare at me with dislike and go to clean the sty.

Mr Bell returns to his painting, then says quietly, 'Miss McKee, you really shouldn't be playing at sailor like this. You heard them, women on ships are unlucky. It's not magic, they're just a distraction—but an instant's distraction here can kill somebody.'

'Then they shouldn't let themselves get so damned *distracted*.' I'm furious, but I don't cry.

He turns and gazes coolly at me. 'Why not simply enjoy the life of a passenger?'

'I don't want to be a passenger, I want to *do* things.'

He puts down his brush and says, 'All right, come and meet the sailmaker. He can always use a hand.'

'You think because I'm a girl all I can do is *sew*?'

'You think sailmaking is just sewing?' Mr Bell laughs. 'You really do need to meet the sailmaker.'

He leads me to the sail locker, beneath the poop deck, and introduces me to Mr Hendriksson. He's a round-faced, middle-aged man who gazes at me over his glasses then smiles, reminding me a little of a goblin. My fury eases.

Mr Bell leaves and Mr Hendriksson fits a leather pad, a palm, onto my hand. He shows me the stitch he wants, then sets me to joining two small pieces of canvas. After a time he says, 'I have daughter, twenty-t'ree, she *never* want to go on ship. How you like being *jungman*, Eliza?'

'It's not very easy, Mr Hendriksson.'

'When too hard, you come here and help me.' He smiles. 'Still much work but I have warm stove, better than cold deck, *hey*?'

'Thank you, I will.'

It's hard to wrestle the large curved needle through the fabric, but Mr Hendriksson shows me how to use an awl to punch holes in the canvas, which makes it easier.

Later that night, rubbing balm into my aching hands, I feel glad I've made at least one friend among the crew.

Next day a wan Mr Malory, recovered from his seasickness, comes to breakfast. We tell him about the ship's progress, and Mrs Nilsen says what a hard worker I am. Captain Nilsen asks him jovially if he plans to take up his own place in the port watch today.

Mr Malory flinches. 'I certainly shall *not*. And I cannot imagine for the life of me what Miss McKee thinks she's doing, wearing men's clothing and associating with the dregs of humanity. No good will come of it.'

I sit astonished, a forkful of egg halfway to my mouth.

'Those *dregs*, sir, are the men who will take you safely across the world,' says Captain Nilsen stiffly. He excuses himself and goes above. Mrs Nilsen collects several plates, and also leaves.

'What a thing to say, Mr Malory!' I cannot stop myself. 'You haven't been around since we left port and you don't know any of the crew. I think you should apologise to the captain.'

'I hardly see why,' he says. 'You're not going to pretend they're a bunch of fine Oxford-educated chappies, are you? They're clearly of the lowest type.'

'I'd suggest you keep your opinions to yourself, Malory,' says Mr Bell. 'As captain said, our lives are in the crew's hands and most of them are hard-working lads.'

'Ah, Bell—the Bolshevik emerges at last! Thought as much, given your passion for the proletariat life. But don't expect *me* to labour beside you in delight. I, at least, know my place.'

Mr Bell gazes at him, shrugs, takes his plate and leaves.

I realise a nerve under Mr Malory's right eye is twitching and his hand trembling. How odd. It wasn't a pleasant argument but hardly ugly enough to cause such distress. I feel embarrassed for him and stand to leave, then sit again.

'Mr Malory, I do apologise for speaking rudely, but since we're to be together for some months, undergoing all sort of hardships, perhaps we should be more circumspect in our language. At least until we are better acquainted.'

There is silence then he lifts his head, his eyes strangely remote. 'Miss McKee, you are correct. My words were immoderate and I shall apologise to all concerned. I should explain I am in some ... physical distress. An injury that would prevent me from working beside the men. I spoke from a position of humiliation rather than dislike.'

'I'm very sorry to hear that. I hope your injury improves.'

He smiles mirthlessly. 'If it hasn't healed in eleven years I doubt there's much room for improvement. No, it was a shattered hip-bone and I'm stuck with it. However, I do apologise for my bitter words. I expect this bout of seasickness has done little for my temper either.'

'Probably not. Thank heavens that particular trial is over.'

'Indeed.' He hesitates. 'But tell me, Miss McKee, do you truly enjoy getting about in such extraordinary garb?'

'Yes, of course,' I say. 'And if you'd worn dresses all your life you'd love dungarees too.'

'Still—I cannot believe my eyes—is that a *knife* you wear on your hip?'

'We must all carry them. They help with small jobs and we must be able to cut lines instantly in extreme circumstances, it might save the ship.'

He raises an eyebrow dubiously. 'You?'

I laugh. 'I doubt it, but the knife is required so I shall wear it.'

'Yet working with such—dare I say ruffians? What would your mother think?'

'My mother's own sister would work beside me if she could. And the men are not ruffians, well, not all. You must let me introduce you to the sailmaker, Mr Hendriksson. He's very kind.'

Mr Malory smiles. 'And should I meet this paragon of the sailmaker's art, will you forgive me my rudeness?'

'Let us see that new leaf turned over first,' I say lightly.

5. Pete: Her Long Eyelashes

Eliza's boat—ship—*barque*, for God's sake—will be sailing this afternoon and then she'll be away on her silly adventure. Once she's trundled out of sight with boring Mr Bell, the car picks me up, and I must say I'm glad to leave Port Lincoln behind me in the dust.

At Cowell, the pretty waitress smiles at me again but then I realise she smiles at everyone. I feel a bit let down and insist we depart promptly for Port Augusta, although I'll have to hang around for hours at the station. When we arrive I pay off the driver and go to the waiting room.

I pour a cup of tea and sigh. I hadn't really expected to have a chance to say, kiss the waitress, but … it would have been nice to try. It seems so easy for other boys. They tell me Perth is teeming with willing hussies, but I never run into any of them.

A second cup. I'd have preferred a beer but I don't want to leave the station and lose my way back. The lads laugh at my poor sense of direction but I tell myself that's only on the ground. In the air? I'd be all right.

Anyway, all the best pilots—even Kingsford Smith himself—have their own navigators, co-pilots and radio-men. Gosh, that magnificent Pacific crossing! How did he do it? And what about the record-breaking Melbourne to Perth last August?

I smile. Probably the best day of my whole life.

I'd ridden my Norton out to Maylands aerodrome early because the papers were predicting crowds, but it turned out someone had royally screwed up and hadn't allowed for the time difference between Perth and Melbourne.

So just as I was parking the motorcycle I saw the plane

approaching, two hours ahead of schedule!

In a few moments they were down, smooth as silk. Smithy and Ulm helped their crew out then staggered to the hangar to meet a gaggle of astonished, unprepared officials.

I even managed to get a good look at *Southern Cross* later, before a policeman chased me away. Those three radial engines, the silver wings as wide as a highway, that blue Fokker chassis twice the height of a man—what a bird!

And what a pilot. Such a down-to-earth bloke, with his leather coat and goggles, cigarette and cocky grin. He's irresistible to women—half the girls I know want to marry Smithy, and I'm not sure the others'd even wait for a wedding.

I wonder what being married is like, really. Must be nice to have someone there all the time, someone you can actually go to bed with whenever you want. What an idea.

Then I mentally shake myself. Can't leap into matrimony just yet, my lad. You've got plans to be a man about town. Escort beautiful women to the cinema, wave to them from the cricket pitch as you score sixes, thrill them by doing loop-the-loops in your aeroplane. Light their cigarettes as they glance up at you through their long eyelashes …

'Excuse me, I'm all out. May I?'

I lift my head, a little peeved at the interruption to my reverie. An older gentleman from the table next to me is pointing at my box of matches on the table.

'Yes, of course.' I light his cigarette. He takes a puff then turns to his companion. 'Darling?'

She nods and opens a small silver case. I stand and lean over and light her cigarette as she glances up at me through her long eyelashes.

And that's how I meet Laura.

It turns out that the older man is her father, and they're also taking the train to Perth. I can't believe my luck!

We chat over the dinner table as the train chuffs through the evening and I don't make a fool of myself.

Laura is a blonde, with high cheekbones, grey eyes and the softest-looking mouth. She's eighteen too, my own age, and the good fortune simply keeps multiplying: her father Cyril is a prosperous art dealer in Perth and knows my parents well.

When I go to my sleeping berth that night I lie awake for hours. Laura's mouth is the most enchanting thing I've ever seen and the swell of her breasts under her fine knit sweater is the stuff of fantasy.

Next morning I stare anxiously into the shaving mirror. Will she like me? I know I have a certain charm (Eliza's mocked me about it for years). I know where I sit among my mates—I'm no Adonis but I'm not one of the plug-uglies either.

I wash the soap off my face and brush back my hair, and look at my profile, left and right. Should I grow a moustache, perhaps? Bit late for that now. Does she like brown eyes? Hope so. At least I'm tall and muscular, in a rangy sort of way. I got our grandfather Freddy's big build while poor old Lizzie is almost as tiny as Min-lu.

But of course there's the matter that so exercises my sister— our Oriental grandmother. Eliza got a rough trot about it from the nasty little minxes at her school, but the boys at mine didn't give a toss about anyone's background. Sport was the only serious qualifier and I excelled: I worked very hard to make certain of that.

In any case, among the students we had a couple of African princes, three young Maharajahs, four sons of Italian nobles and a nephew of the Japanese Emperor, so I was pretty small fry in the non-white stakes compared to them. My mates say I look like one of the Wops, anyway.

Will Laura care about that? I take a breath. Let's find out.

By the time we reach Perth we're great friends. I like Laura's father Cyril—he's sly and witty, especially about the art world whose doings so consume my parents—and it goes without saying I like Laura who, it appears, has no qualms at all about my ancestry.

We make arrangements for dinner at their house the following week and I float homewards on a cloud of ecstatic lust. When the great evening arrives, again I don't disgrace myself. Laura's mother likes me. I dress well, speak wisely and discuss my studies as if all I dream of is to become a sensible and well-paid young engineer.

I relegate my passion for flying to an 'interest.' Yes, I say, flying might one day be a fine sport to indulge in. After I'm making a good living and able to support the family I, ahem, hope to enjoy one day. Laura likes that.

Oh, Laura likes a lot of things.

We go out to cinemas and nightclubs and dance and drink cocktails. She lets me hug her and, one glorious night, kiss that soft mouth. It's everything I ever dreamt of and more. As the weeks go by there are greater liberties too. I explore the swelling glories beneath those knit sweaters, happier than I've ever been in my life. Of course I'm not permitted the final, extraordinary, liberty. That must wait, says Laura, with coyly downcast eyes.

I start working like a demon at my studies. I'll graduate with honours I tell myself, and become the prosperous young man who might one day make this angel my wife.

My *wife*.

In April 1929 Smithy, Ulm and their crew crash in Western Australia on the way to England and aren't rescued for weeks. Two of their mates searching for them go down and die horribly in the desert.

Some people whisper it was all a publicity stunt. I don't believe that, but the whole thing leaves a bit of a bad taste. Besides, I tell myself, I'm not interested in flying anymore. Just a year and a half to go and I'll graduate and become everything Laura wants.

My mother and Anton hold a dinner party with Laura's family, something of an event because they rarely leave their studio. I wear a new suit and Mama looks her usual fine self, despite the green paint under her fingernails. Grey-bearded Anton is always dignified, but tonight he's as outgoing as I've ever seen him.

And good old Liam is there too. I can hardly believe it: when not at his easel he usually prefers the pub. Mind you, he doesn't bother with a suit, in fact, I doubt he even has one. An open-necked white shirt—can you believe it? At least his trousers are clean and he's behaving himself. He appears strong and reliable (far from the case) and I'm proud of my cousin.

The food is excellent too—our cook's been with us for years—and the wine superb. We're all smiling at one of Cyril's wry observations and I look around at my darling Laura to enjoy the moment with her.

And she's gazing spellbound at Liam, darkly handsome Liam. The maiden's dream, I used to tell him mockingly, Perth's answer to Lord Byron, and he'd grab me in a wrestling hold (which I'd get out of pretty easily) and we'd laugh together.

But he's not laughing tonight. He's returning her gaze.

And that's how I lose Laura.

Of course I drink, I'm blotto most days. I stop going to lectures. Soon I'm being scolded by my tutors, told to just get over it. Why, this happened to them too, old chap, but a man simply gets on with the job. Just a woman, for God's sake. Plenty of fish! And so on.

My mates are sympathetic at first, but once I stop going to cricket practice they start to see me as a lost cause. A woman?

Thought he had a bit more backbone than that, they mutter.

Then Liam loses interest.

Laura comes to see me, weeping. I keep my distance in the armchair. I think, stupid cow—he always does that. He doesn't care, not really. Maybe he wanted to paint your bloody ankles or something and once he has, he's done with you.

'He adored my hands,' she sobs. 'Sketched them over and over.'

Hands then, but not *you*, Laura, he never loved you. Not the way I did.

'Can you forgive me, Pete darling?' she asks. 'It was just a moment of madness and I've come to my senses. I see what a fool I've been.'

Can I forgive her? It's been a tad longer than a moment, old girl. Try seven weeks, three days and some half-a-dozen agonising hours.

'Did you sleep with him, Laura?'

'Of course not.'

The flush on her neck tells me the truth. Odd how much you can understand about someone when they've broken your heart. '*Forgive* me, darling,' she says. 'It's you I really love.'

I take out a cigarette and offer her one. I light my own then lean over and light hers. She looks up at me through her long, rather soggy, eyelashes.

'Of course, sweetheart. We'll say no more about it.'

'Oh, Pete. You'll never regret it. I'll make you so happy!'

Yes, you will, I think. Who needs a waitress when you've got a guilty woman at hand?

I smile and she stands and throws her arms around my neck. I run my palms over her tits and narrow waist and soft arse. I pull her hard against me so she can't pretend she doesn't know what's pressing against her belly.

This time there'll be no coy talk of waiting. Yes, Laura, you'll make me very happy indeed.

6. Eliza: Deckboy Elias

On deck next morning, I'm surprised to find two of my watchmates have just finished cleaning and sanding the timbers where I'd spilt the black grease. One is my freckled friend from the pigsty and the other, I remember, stood back and didn't join in the German boy's mockery.

The red-haired lad says, 'Rolf,' pointing at himself, then the other boy, 'Niilo.' Niilo is dark and wiry and smiles shyly.

'Eliza,' I say. 'Thank you. *Tack.*' I know that much Swedish.

'We call you *Elias* now,' says Rolf. 'Must have boy's name to be in our watch.'

'Good,' I say. 'I'm very happy to become Elias.'

Mr Pölönen arrives, looking pleased at the sight of the clean deck. 'Painting now,' he says.

We get pots of grey paint from the store-room and set to work on the bulwarks. While daubing away in the sunlight I have plenty of time to admire the ocean slipping by below.

Out here the water isn't the teal or aqua of coastal seas, but the violet-blues known only to deepwater sailors, the slowly shifting glints of sapphire and amethyst and lapis-lazuli.

I'm mentally comparing the sea's beauty to my mother's best earrings (the sea is prettier), when I realise the light is fading and the blues are becoming greys. Rolf calls out, 'We stop now,' and I close my paint-pot and see the clouds that were distant ten minutes ago are now rolling dark above us.

Then the wind hits, howling, and the ship lurches. Men on deck haul lines to shorten the sails, while those aloft try desperately to secure them. As I turn I see Mr Malory, standing in the doorway of the corridor watching the mayhem.

Suddenly two sails blow out with loud bangs, one after the other, and he falls backwards. Was he struck by flying debris?

I run and reach him as he's pulling himself to his feet. 'Are you all right? Did something hit you?' I yell over the noise of the storm.

He stares at me, his eyes enormous. 'No. No. Go *away*.'

I don't know what to do—he's staggering—then I hear three shrill whistles, the signal of an emergency, all hands on deck.

'*Go!*' yells Mr Malory.

I run to help haul on the lines to furl the remaining sails before they also blow out. The ship leans over from the pressure of the wind, but as the sails are taken in the angle of the deck slowly eases, thank God.

The stormfront passes and we start the job of sending down the tattered canvas and bending—attaching—heavy storm sails. I help by dragging heaps of torn fabric to the sail locker.

'Lucky, Eliza, hey?' says Mr Hendriksson.

'*Lucky?*'

'Lucky the fair-weather sails are up so they blow out. Maybe we broach if storm sails are set.' He chuckles. 'Lucky for me too. Must change over to storm sails soon, so today we get some canvas up and no complaining.'

'But Mr Hendriksson, you said we might *broach* with the storm sails. What if another squall hits us like that?'

'Better be damn good sailors then, hey?' He shrugs, smiling. 'Must have storm sails for Cape Horn, Eliza. Must be careful too.'

At last the emergency is over and our watch stands down. I'm wet through so I change into fresh clothes and rub my hair half-dry, then go to dinner. Mr Malory is seated already. He has his own supply of spirits, permitted for passengers, and a half-empty glass is in front of him.

He's pale, his eyes forbidding. I feel he doesn't want me to say anything about his fall so I don't.

'Eliza my dear, are you all right?' says Maria Nilsen (we're now on informal terms). 'You work too hard. Perhaps you should not go out in such conditions.'

'But that's when most help is needed, Maria,' I say. 'I'm careful and stay on deck, I have no interest in climbing aloft.'

'Of course not,' she says. 'Who on earth *would*?'

Mr Bell smiles slightly, while the first mate, gloomy-browed Mr Larsson, says nothing, as usual. Captain Nilsen enters and the steward begins serving dinner.

'Will we see more weather like that?' I ask *Kapten*.

'More and worse, much worse.' He smiles. 'Good practice, yes? Mr Larsson, I noticed some men who must try harder.'

'I hope you do not mean our Mr Bell,' says Maria. 'Look at his poor hands. How will work in London with hands like that?'

Mr Bell's well-washed, callused hands are oozing blood here and there from wire cuts. He takes out a clean handkerchief and dabs at the lacerations.

'Sorry. Don't want to stain your tablecloth.'

Maria clicks her tongue sympathetically. 'You must take better care of yourself, Harry. Your noble calling demands it, after all.'

Heavens I think, is he a priest? Might explain the remoteness.

Mr Malory says lazily, '*Noble* calling, Bell? From deckhand to Admiral, is it?'

Mr Bell gazes at him deadpan. Again I sense his amusement.

Maria says, 'Admiral—indeed not, Mr Malory! He would have to join the Navy to be an Admiral. No, Mr Bell is a *doctor*.'

Malory laughs. 'Is that what he told you?' His voice is slurred. 'Gracious, from windjammer to Harley Street, a most mysterious leap. Of imagination, I expect.'

'Mr Malory, please keep a civil tongue in your head,' says Captain Nilsen. 'We have known Mr Bell since he first sailed with us as a lad.'

He smiles at Maria. 'As a foolish young stowaway I should say.'

Maria says, 'He studies to be doctor in London, then comes out with us last year to see his family. Now he goes back.'

'There is no mystery,' says *Kapten*, chuckling, 'except why Mr Bell works so hard and does not put his feet up in a deckchair.'

'A *doctor?*' says Mr Malory. 'Prove it, Bell.'

'No.'

'Thought as much.' Mr Malory smiles unpleasantly. 'Quite the fantasy life, old man.'

Mr Bell says, 'It's really none of your business, Malory.'

'Worming your way into Captain Nilsen's good books with a pack of *lies*? Trying to impress Miss McKee with your *noble* calling? I'd say that's my business. Could affect the safe running of the ship and we wouldn't want *that*.'

I realised, belatedly, he must have had several drinks before he even came to the table. 'Please, Mr Malory, you had a bad fall today,' I say. 'Perhaps you need to rest.'

'It wasn't a fall,' says Mr Bell, looking up. 'He threw himself down at the noise of the sails blowing out. He's suffering neurasthenia from the war. Shellshock. No shame in it, Malory, but don't take it out on everyone else.'

Mr Malory pushes his chair back, his face white, the nerve jumping beneath his eye. He swallows, then turns and leaves.

'That was a little harsh, Mr Bell,' I say.

He looks at me, considering, then turns. 'Yes. I'm sorry for upsetting him, Maria. I should have been more thoughtful.'

'No, Harry,' she says. 'He is unkind man and does not know when to stop.'

Next day I'm not on watch till the early afternoon so I stay longer in my bunk with its narrow, warm mattress. When I get up only Mr Malory is at breakfast, the others have finished.

I say 'Good morning,' and sit down with a bowl of porridge.

'Please, no pleasantries,' he says, rubbing his face. 'My behaviour yesterday was inexcusable.'

'It was. But is it true? You suffer from shellshock?'

He nods. 'I was wounded in—terrible circumstances—shortly before the war's end. I lived, but that has never brought me much comfort, although many have informed me it should.'

'Can't the doctors help you?'

'I've seen the best in Europe, Miss McKee, and they've helped me greatly. On shore I'm hale and hearty and you'd never know I'd been ill.' He laughs bitterly. 'On shore I'm trusted, a man of some consequence. Here, I'm sick and weak and can't stop myself cringing—'

'Mr Malory, please don't torment yourself. I'm weak here too and worse—seen as a source of bad luck! Some of the crew already insist I caused yesterday's squall.'

He smiles a little and indicates a book open beside him. 'The war correspondent Philip Gibb wrote of men like me: *They were subject to queer moods, queer tempers, fits of profound depression alternating with a restless desire for pleasure. Many of them were easily moved to passion when they lost control of themselves. Many were bitter in their speech, violent in opinion, frightening.*'

He sighs. 'And there you have it.'

'At least you understand your own predicament,' I say. 'Please don't disparage yourself. It's so easy to do when you feel yourself the butt of unkindness.'

He looks at me, puzzled. 'You speak with an air of experience, but I cannot for the life of me image you as the butt of anyone's unkindness. How could that be?'

I hesitate, then take a breath. 'One of my grandmothers is a Chinese woman, Mr Malory. Such a thing does not go unpunished in this world, even at the best of girls' schools.'

'Really? About your grandmother, I mean. I see no trace—ah yes, your skin is so very fine—but that is all. Well, I'm quite certain when you stop hiding behind that bulwark of hair and dungarees you'll emerge a most engaging young lady, and you may then say to hell with your harridan classmates.'

I laugh. 'And I expect when we're back on *terra firma* you'll emerge once again as a man of some consequence.'

He smiles ruefully. 'So I pray.'

'What is it you actually do on shore, Mr Malory?'

'I'm a barrister, Miss McKee, a member of Lincoln's Inn.'

'That sounds most impressive. So what on earth is a barrister doing on an old grain barque in the Southern Ocean?'

'Far too many boyhood fantasies, I expect,' he says ruefully. 'I was a great reader of sailing tales as a child.'

'Oh, me too!'

'I was recently involved in a legal inquiry in Adelaide so I thought I'd take a relaxing trip home on a sailing vessel.' He looks around and raises his hands in mock despair. 'It's not exactly what I'd imagined.'

'No, it's not. How could we possibly know what it would be like? But we should accept it and enjoy what comes to us, no matter what.'

His blue eyes are warm. 'You are a kind young lady.'

'I've never been called kind before. More usually fierce.'

'I can see that too.' He hesitates for a moment. 'At the risk of returning to unpleasant topics, I must urge you to remain on your guard with Mr Bell. I do not trust him.'

'Perhaps, like yourself, there are things he prefers not to tell the whole world upon superficial acquaintance.'

'Perhaps, but please be cautious … Eliza.'

'I shall. Thank you—Felix.'

Felix Malory makes his surprisingly sincere apologies to everyone and civility returns to the passenger quarters. The weather turns freezing and the saloon with its heating stove becomes our refuge.

As time passes we become easier with each other, learning things we might never have suspected.

Maria possesses a beautiful singing voice, Harry Bell loves sketching scenes of shipboard life and Felix once took an undergraduate course in Japanese. I also speak a little Broome Japanese, so we have fun with simple conversations, laughing at each other's mistakes.

One day Captain Nilsen shows me how to use the sextant to discover our latitude. He's surprised I understand geometry and can do the calculations easily, and is even more surprised when I explain they teach mathematics to girls in Australia.

I do as much on my watch as possible. Of course I don't go aloft, and once when I took a turn at the wheel (to the contempt of the German boy, Karl) I was quickly relieved because I couldn't control it. I'm also forbidden to report to work during the hours after midnight, presumably to preserve my virtue.

The preparations that so amused my brother pay off and I rug myself up in the cold most satisfactorily. I'm called Elias and grudgingly accepted by my watchmates. Even the help of a girl, a bad-luck *flicka*, eases the grind for everyone else, including such ghastly duties as cleaning the heads. I tell myself firmly that toilets are no worse than stables, but sometimes they are.

A couple of weeks out of port and *Inverley* is making an excellent ten or twelve knots under full sail, rolling along magnificently, covering nearly two hundred miles every day. We rig lifelines and nets along the bulwarks to stop anyone being washed overboard in high seas. The carpenter and cook go to the bow to kill one of the pigs for food, stunning it with a hammer then bleeding it. I'm sorry for the pig, but not at all sorry to have fresh meat for dinner.

Despite our good progress I'm aware of a tension in the air. The mates are wary, and *Kapten* seems always to be listening for something no one else can hear. Puzzled, I ask him why, as he stands braced, his old oilskin coat flapping in the drizzle.

'This is strange weather, *jungman* Elias,' he says. 'Often by now we are fighting storms, the men working hard, learning what they must know to survive. But this? Too quiet. The men are getting lazy.'

Personally, I wouldn't mind a bit of excitement. My watch has been been chipping rust in the forepeak, coughing in the dust, illuminated only by sooty lanterns.

I force myself to keep going despite suffering tempting visions of the warmth of the saloon: my rightful place as Felix says, rather too often, in his dreadful Japanese.

Next day everything changes. Squalls of sleet sweep in, the barometer plummets and the sleet becomes hail. Tons of green water swirl deep over the deck, more beautiful and more terrifying than I ever imagined.

The helm is protected by a shelter, but the two men now at the wheel have to fight for their footing.

By evening the seas around us are dark hills, foam whipping in ghostly sheets before the wind. *Inverley* rolls and lurches and falls into troughs and rises again to the peaks, down and up and down again.

I tell myself these massive ships are designed to survive such conditions—as long as the raised poop, and its vital helm and compasses, stays above the maelstrom.

There are three men struggling to hold the wheel now.

That evening I'm in the charthouse with the captain, Mr Pölönen and Harry Bell. Despite the din we hear the explosion as a sail blows out. As we look up a massive wave swamps the ship and I must grab the edge of the table to remain upright.

Another thundering wave follows, and *Inverley* shudders and seems to halt in her way. Very slowly I feel her begin to rise from the torrent, but before she is free an enormous third wave collapses upon us.

It swamps the deck and water pours into the chartroom and down to the quarters below. Mr Pölönen swears, '*Sataan!*' and races out with the rest of us following.

First mate Mr Larsson is helping the men at the wheel, bellowing, '*Kompass, kompass!*'

With horror I realise we've lost both of the steering compasses. One has simply been smashed away, while the lamp of the other is extinguished, making it unreadable in the gloom. Without them we cannot keep the ship on course, keep her from turning side-on to the gale.

Keep her from broaching.

Mr Pölönen runs to the charthouse for another lamp but it blows out. He tries lighting it again, the captain helping him, without success. Fifty feet away, near the front of the poop deck, I can just see the third, standard, compass. Is that one still lit, could it be used?

But it's hidden by the charthouse and the helmsmen couldn't hear someone yelling directions in this storm. Still, perhaps two people in relay could signal! My heart pounding, I catch Harry Bell's eye and point at the standard compass and he seems to understand. He speaks quickly to the mate, who nods.

Harry calls, 'Come on!' and moves forward, and I follow. He braces himself by the standard compass and I cling to a handhold on the corner of the charthouse. There's just enough light to see his hand pointing to port and I relay the signal to the mate, who roars to the helmsmen. Harry points again, I signal again, and slowly the helmsmen correct our course.

The ship shudders with every thundering wave and the rain is deafening. The torn sails whip at the rigging, loose timber blocks swing like pendulums, and broken lines lash against the steel masts, setting off explosions of sparks like fireworks. After what seems a very long time, I see Mr Pölönen finally get a working lamp into the binnacle.

I yell to Harry, 'They've done it!'

He grins and we work our way back to the others. The captain looks at me and shakes his head in mock despair. He points to the companionway.

'Below, *jungman*.'

Below, water is sloshing from side to side over all the floor. Maria, the steward and the cook are mopping it up but it's a slow job. To my surprise even Felix is helping, carrying full buckets out to empty them.

'My God, Eliza,' says Maria. 'You are soaked! Go and change.'

My rain hat is dangling down my back and I realise water is trickling beneath my oilskins. I shiver and go to my cabin to change. After cleaning up most of the water we sit at the saloon table drinking coffee, while the ship wallows onwards.

One squall blows out the last remaining sail and Felix flinches, then takes a deep breath and smiles a little. 'Almost getting used to it by now.'

Harry comes below to get the captain's bottle of brandy so the men on deck can have a tot to warm them through the freezing night. Before he leaves he says to Maria, 'I'll try to get *Kapten* to rest soon, we seem to have things under control.'

She nods and sighs, her face pale, and looks at me. 'It is time you rest too, Eliza. Will be much work to do tomorrow.'

She is correct.

The cook's galley is a mess, the firepans drenched, food flung everywhere. Three of the nine chickens have drowned (poor chooks), but the pigs are safe and so are two of the barque's cats. The third, as unfriendly a beast as you'd ever meet, was swept away. I hope it didn't suffer.

The saloon and messroom and cabins are wet and chilly and already smell of mildew. The crew foc's'l was swamped. Red-haired Rolf's camera is gone, quiet Niilo's few books are pulp and several men have lost clothes overboard.

They have little enough warm gear at the best of times so I offer them some of my largest woollen jumpers. After initial jibes that they're probably lacy or beribboned, the sober-hued garments are deemed acceptable.

They call themselves men, but I understand now the crew is made up of boys. Even the officers, apart from *Kapten* and the sailmaker, are absurdly young. They never stop working, their fingers blue, their faces bearded and growing weather-aged. I help whenever possible, surprised at my own increasing strength, but I cannot match their courage.

We left port five weeks ago and we're sailing now at the freezing cold latitude of fifty degrees south. There are one thousand miles to go before we even approach the perils of Cape Horn.

7. Harry: The Vigil

'Harry?' says Maria Nilsen tentatively at my cabin door. She starts coughing and when the spasm has passed she says, 'I am sweating every night but I feel so cold. Will you take my temperature?'

I get the stethoscope and thermometer from my medical bag and discover Maria has a fever, her chest congested.

'You should go to bed for a few days,' I say.

She smiles. 'No, Harry, I am all right. Who will keep the saloon tidy if I go to bed?'

'Maria, I must insist. Please.'

She's silent for a moment then nods. I think she's glad to be forced to rest. But two days later her temperature is still rising and she shows no improvement. It worries me.

Eliza McKee and I are on watch that morning. I don't much want to, but I take the girl aside and say, 'I have a favour to ask.'

'Oh?' she says, her eyes surprised.

'Someone should be with Maria. I'm needed on deck, the weather's getting worse. Will you stay with her?'

'Of course.'

We both know that in conditions like this my strength is more useful to the watch than hers. Still, I've come to respect how hard she works, never avoiding a duty no matter how distasteful for a girl, even cleaning those foul heads.

'You'll tell Mr Pölönen where I am?' she says. 'I don't want him to think I'm shirking.'

I nod. 'Please take Maria's temperature every half hour and keep her cool with damp cloths. We must reduce the fever. Come and get me if she seems to deteriorate.'

After a godawful few hours on deck the watch changes over and I return. Eliza says she's been sponging Maria and keeping a moist handkerchief on her forehead as she sleeps.

I pull up another chair and take Maria's pulse and temperature and listen to her heart and lungs. The pyrexia is worse, she's congested, having difficulty breathing, and shivering convulsively. I fold the stethoscope and sigh to myself. When I look up Eliza is gazing at me, her eyebrows raised.

I shake my head slightly and say, 'Go and eat. I'll watch her this afternoon.'

'I'll come straight back,' she says. She returns with a sandwich for me and a bowl of hot water infused with peppermint tea-leaves for Maria: I'm impressed, that treatment hadn't occurred to me.

We help Maria lean over the bowl, a towel on her head, taking in the aromatic steam. When she lies down again she's breathing more easily, but I wonder for how long.

Eliza insists I take a rest before the next watch. I'm bloody exhausted after this morning, so I agree and go to my bunk.

When I return to Maria's sickbed Captain Nilsen is just leaving the cabin, his eyes concerned. 'Do not report for duty tonight, Harry,' he says. 'I want you here.'

I suggest to Eliza she goes to dinner but she says, 'I've already had something. Felix came and relieved me earlier for half an hour.'

'Felix? But he keeps whinging that Maria's coughing irritates his nerves.'

'Odd isn't it?' she says. 'But I'm touched he's helping out now.'

'Well, I suppose even he's capable of fellow feeling,' I say doubtfully.

At first Malory put my teeth on edge. It wasn't the shellshock, I've known plenty of good men who've had to deal with that.

But he's got such a ludicrous air of entitlement it's almost amusing. Although his politics, rather to the right of Genghis Khan, certainly aren't.

I take Maria's temperature and it's risen again despite our efforts. She's shivering, her teeth chattering. She manages to sip some water then falls asleep again.

'I feel such a knot in my chest,' Eliza says quietly. 'Maria is so kind and I do like her.'

'You sound surprised. I'd have thought you liked most people.'

'Not necessarily,' she says, an odd note in her voice. Interesting. She's an amiable child but I've seen moments of ferocity. Elusive too: thoughts fly like quicksilver over her face.

'So who is it you're not fond of?' I ask lightly.

'Oh, someone who's dead. And my watchmate Karl.'

'Well, you certainly wouldn't be alone in that.'

At perhaps nine in the evening Maria groans and starts coughing very heavily. We help her lean over to open her lungs. I hold a small towel to her mouth and see there are streaks of blood among the mucus. After a long time she lies back, exhausted.

I fold the towel and say, 'I'll just throw this over the side.'

Eliza appears curious I'd jettison one of our small supply of towels but doesn't comment. When I come back, Maria is asleep.

I say quietly, 'While she's so ill I want you to be very careful. Wash your hands continually and don't be in any closer contact with her than is necessary.'

'Of course. I don't want to infect her.'

'No, it's not her in danger, it's you. There's always the possibility she has tuberculosis.'

Eliza stares at me. '*Consumption*? But that has no cure.'

'I'm simply being cautious. She's always had a weak chest: on our last voyage she had bronchitis. I doubt she'll be able to go to sea again, conditions are simply too harsh.'

'That will break her heart. And Captain Nilsen's.'

'Her death would be the more heartbreaking,' I say realistically. 'In any case, please be careful. Once she stops coughing the threat will be much less.'

The girl goes to scrub her hands in the bathroom, then makes us some tea. We sit drinking it beside Maria as the evening passes.

After a time Eliza yawns. She's dressed in the paint-spattered overalls she wears on watch, her long hair tied back with string. She's thin and small and has circles under her eyes.

'You should go now and rest,' I say.

'I will.' She glances at me. 'Is she starting to breathe more easily, perhaps?'

I take Maria's temperature. 'Yes, she's a little cooler. Perhaps we're getting past the crisis point.'

Eliza sighs in relief. Her narrow hands are callused, her nails as short as a labourer's. The crew call her Elias and she answers serenely to a boy's name.

I think, ashamed, I really *cannot* go on blaming every female in the world for bloody Charlotte and her misdeeds, and take a breath. 'Eliza. I wanted to say—to apologise, I mean. To you. I was rude, stupidly rude when you first came to the ship. I'm very sorry.'

She grins. 'Heavens, you weren't *that* bad, I've known much worse. My brother when he was fifteen, for instance, and cranky all the time. You'd hardly register on his scale.'

That makes me laugh and I'm surprised at how light-hearted I suddenly feel.

Eliza gazes at me in the lamplight. 'Harry, would you tell me something?'

'Of course.'

'It puzzles me you're a trained doctor, yet you work as a sailor. I know Maria and the captain joke about it but you must admit it's odd. Surely a doctor can afford to travel by steamer?'

'I suppose it is odd, but I wasn't always a doctor.'

I sit back in my chair. 'My parents emigrated from Edinburgh to Newcastle, New South Wales—both of them teachers, not much money, but I always hoped to do medicine. An uncle left a bequest to pay for my studies in London, but it wasn't enough to get me there as well. No one would give me a job on a ship so I stowed away on *Inverley* and worked my passage.'

'Why London—why not Australia?'

'My uncle had lost a child to malaria, and London is a global centre for tropical medicine.'

'Ah. But you're a doctor now, so why aren't you more prosperous?'

'Well, after graduating I practised at an East End clinic—not quite the path to riches. You'll have heard Malory mock me for my Bolshevik tendencies, but he probably has a point.'

A smile flits in her eyes.

'Lack of money didn't seem to matter at the time, but eighteen months ago my father became ill and I desperately needed to get home.' (And get away from Charlotte, who also had a lot to do with my poverty. Oh God, don't even *think* about that faithless cow.) I collect myself.

'I saw in the paper *Inverley* was leaving for Australia, and *Kapten* kindly took me on again.'

'That was fortunate. And is your father now recovered?'

'No. He died soon after I arrived.' I swallow and stare at the floor: the words are still unreal.

'I'm so sorry.' I look up to meet her eyes, such an odd shade of amber in the lamplight.

I clear my throat. 'I stayed at home for a time, unemployed, helping my mother and sister, then a few months ago I was offered a position in London. If I don't take it up soon I'll lose it.'

'So once again you must work your way aboard *Inverley* across the seven seas.'

'But now I'm rated as *matros*, able seaman. Could come in handy if medicine doesn't pan out.'

'*Matros* Bell? Oh, yes. Far more impressive than Doctor.'

Maria murmurs and turns on her side. Eliza rises and pulls the blanket over her shoulder.

When she sits again I say, 'And you? Where are you bound?'

She shakes her head. 'Haven't the faintest idea. I love being here and being part of the watch, part of something greater than myself. But what can a girl like me do?'

'You could do anything you set your mind to. You're a most determined young woman.'

Eliza laughs. 'Determined, fierce, definite, so everyone tells me —but that's not what I feel.'

'What do you feel?'

She hesitates. 'I *want*. I want something but I don't know what it is. But I will not … I will not simply marry. I will not settle for a man, any man, only because he's available.'

Unusual. Don't all females want a blind, stupid meal-ticket? Stop it, this girl isn't Charlotte.

'You could be a business-woman,' I say. 'I hear that's the done thing nowadays.'

'Nowadays? My own grandmother proved herself in business before I was even born.'

That reminds me of some gossip. 'The boys say your grandfather actually part-owns this vessel. Is that true?'

'Yes, he's one of the shareholders.'

'Aha! There it is,' I say. 'I can see the headlines: *Shy Perth Girl Becomes Global Shipping Magnate*. What do you reckon?'

She laughs. 'I like it! But shy? You may be the first person ever to call me that.'

I feel Maria's forehead and listen with the stethoscope. Her temperature has fallen and her breathing is almost even again.

'Reserved, then?' I say. 'You keep a great deal hidden, Eliza. But Maria has good reason to thank you. As do I.'

8. Pete: Crazy Lady

My affair with Laura unfolds pleasurably, my parents are pleased with me, and my tutors are glad I've returned to the fold. But one morning I wake up and think: No more. I've had enough of being studious and charming and well-behaved.

Laura is still asleep, face-down beside me, her honey-coloured hair in adorable disarray over those soft pink shoulders. We went to a party at one of her friend's houses yesterday evening and sleeping here together all night long was a real treat.

Laura's society-column mates don't much interest me. Of course I like a drink and a party as much as anyone else but their vapid chit-chat sometimes drives me mad.

Still, we've been surprisingly content. In my heart I haven't forgiven her, but she's amiable and even passionate once she stops pretending to be a 'good' girl.

My cousin Liam and I patched up our friendship, though it will probably never be quite the same. I know he can't help his effect on women.

He acts as if each is the only one in the world, when all he really cares about is the shadow on a collarbone or the colour of an earlobe or the curve of a foot.

He even managed to turn sensible Eliza's head, although come to think of it, sailing away on that old ship wasn't very sensible of my sister.

I get out of bed and stand naked at the window, looking out at a vista of lawn and garden and trees, the Swan River flowing beyond. The gums along the river banks are scented and glorious, and I think a little guiltily of how I've neglected my beloved garden at home.

I've never quite reconciled my delight in the unfolding of life from the earth with my desire to fly as far above that earth as possible. Eliza's always teased me about it, and I can't make much sense of it either—and now this fascination with women has come over me like a madness. Sometimes I don't know who I am.

But now, on this lovely morning, the air smelling deliciously of cut grass, I stretch and feel so many possibilities, intoxicating possibilities, lie ahead of me if only I have the courage to reach out and take them.

Without noticing it I've come to a decision. I don't know how Laura or my parents will feel, but I've grown tired of pleasing everyone else. I'm going out to Maylands today, to the airfield on that great slow river before me, and I'm going to learn how to fly.

I park the Norton at the rear of the hangar, where a large sign reads *West Australian Airways Limited*. Kingsford Smith himself used to be one of their pilots! They've just started a service with four big Hercules flying out of this very aerodrome.

And Smithy's got a new company too, Australian National Airways. Round-trip flights, Sydney to Brisbane or Sydney to Melbourne, just nine pounds a ticket. Perhaps I'll even fly for them one day ...

More important things first, I tell myself sternly. I read the small sign again: *Quinn Aviation—Joy-flights—Lessons—Enquire Within*.

I take a deep breath and walk around to the front of the hangar, my leather helmet under my arm. Unfortunately none of the Hercules are parked there today, but I can see a two-seater to one side, an old de Havilland Moth with its engine cowling open, a mechanic leaning into it. He swears as he drops a spanner.

'Good morning,' I say. He scowls.

'I'd like to take flying lessons with Quinn Aviation. Can you tell me—'

'Bill. Office.' He nods his head towards the hanger.

I walk through the wide doors, blinking in the dimness. Windowed offices run along a wall, but only one seems to have someone inside, so I knock and enter. A secretary is leafing through a pile of papers on the desk. She glances up with a scowl akin to the mechanic's.

'Ah—Is Bill here?' I say. 'I'd like to enquire about taking flying lessons.'

The secretary looks at me in dislike. Her short copper-coloured hair is surprisingly messy.

'Course you would,' she says. 'Everyone's a flyboy nowadays.'

'Um, is Mr Quinn here?'

'No,' she says, gazing at me with narrow green eyes.

'I'd like to find out—'

The secretary rubs her eye sockets with the heels of her palms and runs her fingers through her hair. When she looks up again she's even more unkempt than before. She sighs heavily.

'I'm sorry,' I say, utterly confused. 'Is there a problem?'

'Just a couple of fucking rich boys think it's hilarious to pay for their lessons with a bouncing cheque, that's all.'

I sit down abruptly in a chair, dropping my helmet. I have *never* heard a woman say that word before. 'Um, well,' I say. 'I can pay cash if you like.'

The woman rests her chin on her hand and gazes at me, expressionless. A long silence. I glance around, worried there's something I've missed, but there isn't. She must be crazy.

I try once more. 'Look, I just want to see Bill about some lessons. Seriously.'

She shakes her head, eyes closed, then stands and holds out her hand, her face hard.

'I'm Bill Quinn. Billie.'

I shake automatically and sit down again. Of course everyone knows of the famous aviatrixes—Earhart, Johnson, Miller—but I've never heard of any Billie Quinn.

'You're the instructor?' I say. 'The, ah, flying instructor?'

'That'd be right.' Her voice wavers and she stares out the window.

Suddenly it's all too much. I do *not* want to learn to fly with some demented, foul-mouthed woman. I want a teacher like Smithy. Confident, wise, experienced. Male.

I stand up. 'Perhaps I should come back another time.'

I leave without the slightest intention of ever coming back. I reach the bike before I remember my helmet. Damn. I retrace my steps. The mechanic glares at me again as I pass.

I open the office door saying, 'Sorry. Left my—'

The woman is crying.

Oh, God. I stand there, not knowing what to do. Finally I say, 'Are you … all right?' I curse myself because she obviously isn't.

'Yes,' she says, teeth gritted.

I get out my handkerchief, thankfully clean. 'Here.'

She takes it and turns away, blows her nose and mops her eyes. I bend down to get my helmet and when I stand up she's staring at me. Her nose is red and her hair sticking out.

'Cash, did you say?'

'Ah, look—I'm not sure—'

Her mouth twists. 'Yeah. Who'd go flying with a woman? Might have a tantrum up there. Lose an earring or something.'

'It's not that,' I say, although it is.

'Look, kid, I'm a qualified, highly experienced pilot. Can even teach dabblers like you.'

'I'm not a dabbler! I've wanted to fly since I was a kid.'

'Yeah? Not much more than a kid now. What, fifteen?'

'I'm eighteen,' I say, suddenly annoyed. 'And you know what? I've just decided I don't want lessons from you because you're completely *crazy*.'

She looks at me then smiles. Not pleasantly. 'Have you got one pound?' she says.

I mentally calculate the contents of my wallet and say, 'Yes.'

'All right, come on. Oh, money first.' She holds out her hand.

Dazed, I give her the note, wondering what on earth I'm doing.

She pushes open the office door and yells, 'Fuel the Moth, Frank.'

'What?'

She looks at me, eyebrows raised. 'Coming for a joy-flight with the crazy lady?'

'Holy *Jesus*,' I say as I lower myself to the ground. My knees are shaking and I have to clutch the side of the cockpit.

'Yeah,' says Billie Quinn and heads back to the office. I follow. Frank scowls at me as I pass. Billie leans back in her chair with her arms behind her head and says, 'Always feel better after a few loops.'

'A *few*?'

She smiles. 'Got to enjoy myself when someone else is paying.'

She sits up, pulls a writing pad towards her and taps a pen on it in a business-like manner.

'Okay, kid. What's your name?'

'Peter McKee.'

'How many lessons do you want? I can get you to licence standard with, say, twenty hours. If you're good enough.'

'Twenty would be fine.'

She jots down a few figures. 'That'll be three pounds per hour, sixty pounds total.'

'Oh.' I have less than thirty pounds in the bank.

'Oh? You mean you're not so rich after all?'

'I've got savings,' I say. 'They'd cover—well, ten hours or so.'

'Ten it is then, cash up front. But I won't let you go for your licence if you're not ready.'

I say pointedly, 'You sure you'll be in business long enough anyway? Sounds to me like your finances are a bit strained.'

'Yeah, too many bludgers.' She hesitates. 'We had a second plane but ... it crashed yesterday near Mandurah.'

'Was the pilot all right?'

'No.' Billie's face is very still.

'Gosh. I'm sorry.'

'Goes with the territory, kid.'

I nod. 'Hey, I've got a suggestion. You stop calling me *kid* and I'll stop calling you *crazy*.'

She shakes her head. 'Nah. Fits.'

Laura will still be at her friend's house so I ride back in a state of —well, I'm not sure what. Ecstasy. Terror. Astonishment. I think of that final barrel roll the madwoman did, the moment I was convinced I was going to die. *And I didn't care.*

I laugh aloud and gun the bike, sunlight flickering through the branches above the road, everything green and golden and streaming past in a mad blur. And I don't care.

When I pull up I can see Laura lying on a deckchair with a cocktail in her hand, even though it's barely noon. Her mate John, whose parents own the house, is sitting beside her.

A couple of people are playing tennis with a handful of others watching. I can hear thwacks of balls and grunts of effort, and the occasional 'Well done,' or 'Oh, bad luck.'

I walk towards Laura through the warm, grassy-scented air. John is leaning towards her murmuring something. She smiles to herself and I know exactly what that smile means.

'Hello, Laura,' I say. 'Morning, John.'

'Morning, mate,' he says. 'You're out early. Been for a spin?'

'Yeah.'

Laura glances up at me through her long eyelashes.

'Darling. Got some news for you,' I say. And I don't care.

Telling Mama and Anton about my change of direction is a little more difficult. I wait until dinner so my euphoria has subsided a little and I can marshal my arguments.

It's a beautiful summer evening, the perfect close to that perfect day. Our house looks onto a reserve with great shady Moreton Bay figs, and the windows are wide open, curtains billowing softly in the breeze off the river. The cook has made a simple meal of chops and vegetables, and Anton produces one of his excellent bottles of white wine.

'Let's toast your mother,' says Anton. 'She completed a canvas today that, well,' he shakes his head, 'is extraordinary, my dear. I'm so proud of you.'

Mama looks at him affectionately as we raise our glasses. Since joining our family Anton has been the haven my mother needed after being widowed, then married to that bastard Gideon Meade. (My view of our late stepfather has changed a lot since Eliza confided in me.)

'Um, I've got some news to celebrate too,' I say.

Liam grins. 'You? Hit a six again? Hardly news, Pete.'

'No, not cricket. I, well—' I shrug. 'I went up in a plane today. My God, it was …' I sigh with pleasure. 'Anyway, I'm going to take flying lessons.'

So much for my carefully marshalled arguments. There's a long silence.

'No,' Mama says. 'It's too dangerous, Peter. The paper said one crashed just yesterday at Mandurah. Dear God, the pilot was burnt to a crisp. *No*. You're too young.'

'What about your degree?' asks Anton. 'It would be a great distraction, Peter.'

'Well, that's it, you see. I can use the experience for my honours project, engineering aeronautics.' I have no idea if this is even slightly plausible but it sounds good.

Liam muses, 'I wonder what the light's like up there,' and I know he's on my side.

'Well, if it's useful to your course …' says Anton.

'Planes are getting safer all the time, new models, new engines,' I say. 'And my instructor, um, Bill Quinn, is highly experienced.'

'You can't afford it,' says Mama. 'And I won't give you a penny.' She stands and leaves.

Later, in my room, I hear a knock. My mother enters and sits silently on the bed beside me. I put my arm around her and remember how often she's comforted me: the disappointments, the scraped knees, the time I broke my wrist.

'I'll be careful,' I say gently. 'I won't take risks. I've *got* to do it, Mama, you know I've always wanted to fly, always.'

Her breath catches. 'I thought you'd grow out of it, like all little boys. Oh, my baby.'

She draws back and looks searchingly into my face.

I gaze at her lovely eyes, her fair skin, her soft red-gold hair so unlike the fiery spikes of my soon-to-be instructor. My instructor already, I think in surprise. I seem to have learnt a lot today, although I'm not quite sure what.

'I *will* take care, I promise, Mama.'

She nods and wipes her eyes. 'Your father Sam left money in trust for you children, for when you're twenty-one, of course.' She takes a long breath. 'I'll release some of it, one hundred pounds. Will that be enough?'

'Yes! *Thank* you, Mama.'

'He'd have wanted you to do it. So brave, such a fine man, I loved him utterly. I've never—' She stops, and after a moment smiles a little. 'You remind me of him, darling. Not so much looks, though you have his shoulders, his height—no, it's the stubbornness.' She suddenly laughs. 'My God, the *stubbornness*. Your whole life you've wanted this and you've never wavered for a moment. My boy.'

9. Eliza: Stockholm Tar

Aboard *Inverley* my particular friends are Rolf and Niilo. After work we often find a quiet corner and chat and share pieces of cake I smuggle away from the passengers' well-stocked mess.

I'm becoming fond of slim dark Niilo and dream of kissing him, but of course privacy is almost impossible on a ship. In any case I haven't the slightest idea if he returns my fondness.

Dear Maria leaves her sick-bed but doesn't return to her previous bustling self, so I take over her tasks in the living quarters.

That's hardly a sacrifice. The deck is now as grim a place as anywhere on earth, and my admiration for the crew only grows as they meet storm after storm with stoic endurance.

The days are short and dark. Our ship plunges forward, powered by the few sails we dare carry. Sometimes I stand at the bow, looking out to the limitless horizon, and think: we're no more than specks of life clinging to this great steel creature, rising and falling and rising again. The restless inky water and the cosy saloon are the only true boundaries of our world.

Storms come and go as if they'll never end. Fog surrounds us and hides the sun, so we can't even use the sextant to be sure of our position. We know that land—Cape Horn—is not far away but we cannot see it, and land unseen is the greatest possible threat.

But one day birds are skimming the waves around us, albatrosses and mollymawks, storm petrels and shags and pigeons that flutter in the rigging. Captain Nilsen, alert as a greyhound, stands listening and watching, yet still we dash along at twelve knots as if we're in the open sea.

Then at midday the lookout reports to him and he smiles. In the hazy distance a squat island is emerging, snow on its peak. 'There, *jungman* Elias,' he says. 'Cape Horn. We are lucky, it is rarely visible.' He clears his throat. 'You will please go below and tell Maria. Perhaps she would like to see it too.' *For the last time* is unsaid.

I help Maria up the companionway and onto the deck beside the captain, where she holds his arm for balance. 'Ah, *Kap Horn*,' she whispers and they smile into each others' eyes.

After that pivotal day we're no longer 'running our easting down,' as the boys say. We leave the Cape behind and head north-east. Another pig dies to feed us but is much appreciated. A week later we're hardly warm, but at least we're less cold, and we're set to scrubbing the teak-work with sand and caustic soda to remove the varnish before repainting, a nasty job.

At noon another storm rushes over us. A sail blows out and all hands hurry into the rigging to furl the canvas and lower it with pulleys. (Not me. I'm told to stay on deck and keep sanding the teak-work.) The rolled-up replacement is carried on the shoulders of ten men: even when dry the sail weighs the best part of a ton.

When the storm blew up my starboard watch was about to be relieved, but we work beside the port watch to replace the sail, and after a brief meal go back on duty again. Much Swedish and Finnish swearing goes on (in which I gleefully join) but we all know it must be so.

The ship comes first.

That is the last of the Cape Horn storms. The sun emerges and the waves glint cornflower blue. I put my woollen things away and wear cotton shirts under my dungarees. The boys dress only in singlets and shorts, and I find the sight of their muscled arms and legs pleasantly disturbing.

Niilo, especially, is beautiful to me. Somehow I understand he finds me as desirable as I find him, but we're never alone.

The days grow warmer, Easter arrives and with it a short holiday. The grinding round of maintenance is briefly put aside and the boys lie in the sun or play cards or carve model ships that sell well on shore and supplement their meagre pay.

Most of them shave off their beards now we've left Cape Horn behind, and the carpenter, *timmerman* Frederik, cuts their hair. He jokingly threatens to snip my long pony-tail, and I laugh with the others and pretend to ward him off with my knife.

Maria is stronger now and no longer coughing. One night we walk on the deck in the starlight, the ripples of the wake tumbling with green phosphorescence, eerie and mesmerising.

'I will miss this,' says Maria. 'My sisters think I am mad to sail with my husband and even more mad to tell them light comes out of the water.'

'How many sisters do you have?' I say.

'Three. All are married to sea captains but do not sail with them. They work their farms and manage everything while their husbands are away.'

'Will you work your farm now too?'

She nods. 'Perhaps I will get better there.'

'Perhaps you can have a baby too,' I say lightly.

Maria is suddenly still. 'I cannot have baby. I lose three already before they are born.'

'Oh, *no*. Maria, I'm so terribly sorry.'

She shakes her head. 'It is God's will.' She turns to me. 'Eliza, you are like my own child, you even help me when I am sick. This has been a happy voyage for me.'

'You've been so kind to me too. *Tack så mycket*, Maria.' Thank you very much.

She smiles. '*Tack så mycket*, Eliza.'

One calm day I'm allowed to go aloft for the first time and it's not as frightening as I'd expected. My body understands the ship now and even when I'm out on a yard, my feet braced on the footrope and my hands busy, I move with the swaying and have no time to think about the great distance to the solid deck below.

Today I'm aloft helping overhaul the buntlines that stop the ropes from fraying the sails. I smile as I remember Liam's list of things I'd be doing—*brace-hauling and keel-hauling and over-hauling*. I rarely think of him now, which is probably just what my mother had hoped.

Yet I doubt she imagined I'd meet a boy like Niilo instead. In a dark corner of the deck yesterday evening he kissed me at last, and untied my long hair and ran his fingers through it, murmuring with pleasure. I sigh: such delight.

I quickly concentrate on the job again, remembering Harry's words. An instant's distraction here can kill somebody, and he's right. I've seen many small accidents occur, even when people are being careful.

Back on deck, freckled Rolf and I are applying a mixture of tar and linseed oil to some ropes to preserve them against the salt air. It's sticky black stuff called Stockholm tar, used all over the ship. Rolf goes to the store-room to get us another can.

I hear a noise and look around. Oh no, it's German Karl, who still loathes me.

'Working hard?' he asks. 'Girls should work hard. In the kitchen and the *bedroom*.'

He snickers and comes closer. I back away but he hems me against the bulwark.

'You like kissing, *flicka?*' His breath is awful.

'Go away,' I say firmly. It's broad daylight and others aren't far, but no one is in sight. *Rolf, come back.* My throat tightens.

'I seen you last night, you know,' he says slyly. 'You kiss dumb Niilo. You fuck him too?'

'*Stop* it, Karl. Not funny.'

My heart is hammering. What if he touches me? I drop the paintbrush into the tar-pot to free one hand, images of Gideon Meade flashing through my mind. Karl reaches out and painfully squeezes my breast. I scream with rage, grab the knife from my hip scabbard and hold it against his throat.

'*Stop now or I will kill you.*'

Karl's eyes widen in fear as he sees how serious I am. His hands come up defensively and hit the tar-pot. The thick, sticky contents splash onto my neck and hair. I freeze in shock as he runs away. I stand there, black tar dripping, and think, thank God we spread canvas earlier to protect the deck.

Rolf, returning with a fresh can in his hand, stares at the fleeing Karl then me, his mouth open in amazement. 'Elias! *Karl* do this?'

'*Yes,*' I say, outraged. Everyone knows Stockholm tar is almost impossible to get off anything it touches. I suddenly feel sick. The stuff is all through my hair.

Rolf finds a cloth and wipes some off, but it's hopeless. He says sadly, 'I get *timmerman?*'

I slowly nod.

Frederik the carpenter cuts off my hair. I do not cry.

Living with a mother of great beauty, there's no room for vanity in my heart. I'm quick-witted and capable, but not vain. Yet since the day my aunt Lucy called my hair *wavy and thick and the prettiest shade of mahogany*, it's been my single small joy.

Now I look in the cabin mirror and gasp as if I've been struck in the belly.

Timmerman did his best, but he had no idea how to do even a simple feminine bob. Before, when the waves of my hair fell almost to my waist, the central parting had a gentle old-fashioned air, but now it's as severe as a spinster's.

The ragged ends dangle somewhere between my ears and shoulders, one side a little longer than the other. I look like a starving Victorian orphan. Not the winsome sort, either: it'd be straight off to the poorhouse for me. I laugh a little hysterically and put my hands over my face.

The news has spread quickly and Maria is outside my cabin. 'Eliza, child, come now to the bathroom. I tell cook to boil hot water for you.'

Maria insists on washing my hair herself over the basin, the water turning black. She rinses it several times then rubs it with a towel, which goes grey. She combs the hair this way and that, frowning, and ruffles it with her fingers as it dries in the warm air.

In the mirror I no longer see a starving orphan, more a startled emu. Be grateful, I chide myself, at least much of the tar is out. Maria stands beside me as we gaze into the mirror.

'Perhaps,' she says hesitantly, 'I have nice scarves, Eliza. Good to cover hair.'

A bubble of laughter begins in my chest. Maria is surprised then starts laughing too, and soon we cannot stop. For the rest of the passage, she and I simply have to murmur *nice scarves* to set ourselves off again. Finally we calm down and wipe our eyes.

'Thank you, Maria. It's much better, truly.' I sigh. 'It will be cool on my neck when we're in the tropics. I'm certain I'll come to accept it.'

It takes resolve to sit at the dinner-table that evening. Captain Nilsen, clearly tutored by Maria to be diplomatic, says gruffly, 'Now you can be a very modern girl.'

Felix gazes at me. 'Rather dramatic and Isidora Duncan-ish, but you'd better avoid automobiles and long scarves in future.'

Maria says, 'And nice scarves too, Eliza,' and we giggle.

'The starboard boys are muttering threats against Karl,' says Harry. 'He's making himself very scarce indeed.'

I'm puzzled. 'Why would they care?'

'You're part of their watch, one of their own. An attack on you is an attack on them.'

'It was an accident, Harry, not really Karl's fault.'

He gazes at me. 'We'd better spread the word, then.'

We don't spread it quickly enough and Karl turned up with a bloody nose next day. Rolf has a split lip, Niilo a bruised cheek and stocky Artur—a boy I thought barely tolerated my existence —has a black eye.

I explain firmly I don't want Karl to be in any more trouble, but I'm greatly impressed at their courage and care for me. Little Rolf takes on something of a swagger for the rest of the week.

After that, Karl won't meet my eyes and moves away if I come near. He's widely disliked as well, and probably from the anxiety of looking over his shoulder all the time his face breaks out in disfiguring boils: fair exchange for my own loss.

And Niilo? He satisfied his male sense of honour by fighting Karl, but that was between them. Between us? As days go by he no longer gazes at my hair, and I realise I am no longer desirable to him without that marker of femininity.

I'm hurt, but say nothing and pretend I never kissed him and pressed against him in the dark. Or wondered what life might be like as a sea captain's wife on an Ålands farm.

Now we're becalmed in the stinking hot tropics, desperate to catch the trade winds. I try to remember the Cape Horn cold but it's quite beyond me. We barely sleep in the heat and everyone is bad-tempered. We drift, we chip at rusty metal and repaint it, we take down the Cape Horn canvas and bend the old fair-weather sails.

The ship passes the equator. I'm the only one who hasn't crossed the Line before, but there's no question of dunking me and daubing me with tar, as usually happens to unfortunate first-timers. Karl, especially, flinches at the word *tar*.

We still have a small ceremony. An unconvincing King Neptune (Mr Pölönen in a rope wig) and his consort Amphitrite (Rolf in a longer wig) potter around the deck with a gaggle of courtiers and present me with a parchment of welcome to Neptune's realm.

But despite such distractions time drags unendurably: the same heat, the same faces, the same work.

Then one glorious day the trade winds arrive. The sky becomes blue and perfect, the sails fill with air and we start to move; four knots, six knots, ten *amazing* knots, as the rigging sings with the music of the ship.

We paint brace-winches and bollards in crisp white, and sew sails from reams of canvas laid out on the deck, attaching metal eyes and loops and rope reinforcement along the edges.

Felix lies in a hammock, becoming tanned from the sun, and grows a narrow moustache that makes him look like Douglas Fairbanks. I call him the Black Pirate and he likes that.

He's become a much easier travelling companion since he and Harry reached some sort of truce around Cape Horn. Now they sit together on deck, Felix smoking and Harry sketching the life of the ship, as he loves to do.

In the soft dusk the boys bring a wind-up gramophone out to the foc's'l head and we listen over and over to the few records they possess, sentimental Swedish tunes. And we watch the moon rising and the stars wavering in the dark endless sky.

Despite the glorious weather we know what lies ahead, and over the following days we change the sails back to the heavy storm canvas.

All too soon the rains come rushing in and suddenly we're cold, *förbannat* cold, after so much heat. But now we're only a few weeks away from port and anticipation hangs over everything we do.

Yesterday little freckled Rolf and I were tarring some lines together when he declared he would marry me when he grew up, because no one else would want a woman with hair like mine, especially one who wears dungarees. I solemnly thanked him. Harry was sketching us at the time and caught my eye, and we both smiled.

Now I smile again, seeing Rolf scurrying up the rigging with five of the other boys. I'm on deck helping raise a sail and Mr Pölönen is chanting the usual rhythm, but we barely need it. By now it's second nature.

And then, as we're coiling the ropes, a squeal as sharp as a seagull's makes me look up. A dark shape is falling, a flailing shape. It's over in a gasp of incredulity, a thud on the deck. We run forward, Harry getting to him first, feeling for a pulse.

I kneel beside busy little Rolf, now appallingly still. His eyes are half-open, gazing at nothing. His mouth is askew, not upturned in its usual grin. A red puddle seeps onto the deck from his head and rivulets dribble this way and that with the rolling of the ship.

We are silent and Harry shakes his head. 'Get *Kapten*,' he says.

The captain is already hurrying towards us. He stops and rubs his forehead, staring. By now the crew who were on the yard with Rolf have dashed down to the deck, and stand there as horrified as the rest of us.

Niilo, shaking, says, 'He is laughing, beside me. He changes handhold and slips. I grab his shirt but he *falls*.'

Someone sobs.

'Back to work,' says *Kapten*. 'The ship does not sail itself. Go.'

The boys disperse, looking behind them. Mr Hendriksson hurries along the deck, a pile of soft old canvas in his arms, murmuring to himself at the pathetic sight. He sets a layer of fabric on the deck, then he and Harry lift the small body onto it. Mr Hendriksson folds the canvas and carries Rolf away to sew him into his shroud.

I rise trembling to my feet. '*Jungman* Elias,' says Captain Nilsen. 'Go and tell Maria what has happened, and stay with her.'

I go. I do not want to be on that deck, with its ragged puddle of blood, a moment longer.

Later I sit in my cabin, my head aching. I think of Rolf, vivid and alive. Rolf, dead and blank-faced. His blushes and ruffled red hair, his small kindnesses when everyone was so hostile, his christening me 'Elias' to help me fit in. He was barely fifteen, although he told them he was seventeen when he signed on. Just a child, a good-hearted child.

And I cannot weep for him.

Dinnertime has the small comfort of company, but the captain is gloomy, Maria's eyes are swollen and Felix is on his third or fourth drink. Harry is not there.

'Did he have a family?' I ask Maria tentatively.

She sighs. 'A widowed mother. He was the only son. I tell her —' she swallows. 'I tell her I will take care of him.' Her breath catches and she stands and leaves the room.

Felix says, 'Damned shame, but the men know the risks. Their job, after all.'

'Dear *God*, Felix,' I say. 'At least try to pretend to be sorry.'

'I am,' he says. 'But being sorry didn't help at the Front and it won't help now.' He gets up and leaves the room unsteadily.

The captain says, 'Good night,' and follows Maria to their cabin. I sit over a cup of tea, unable to think.

Harry comes in and gets his plate from the sideboard where the steward has left it. The food is cold by now but he eats a little, then pushes it away. I pour him some tea.

'Where were you?' I ask.

'Oh, sitting with a few of the boys. Explaining that Rolf felt nothing when he fell.'

'I heard him cry out.'

'He wouldn't have known what was happening, not really.' Harry looks at me, and I wonder why I ever thought his gentle grey eyes were frosty. 'How are you feeling?'

'Oh …' I shrug. 'I don't know. My head aches.'

'I'll give you a powder for that.' He hesitates. 'Eliza, you're as white as a sheet.'

Surprising myself, I say, 'Harry, I cannot cry.'

'That's shock. You'll know some relief later, tears always help.'

'But I haven't wept since I was a tiny child. Since my father died,' I whisper. 'Rolf was my friend, my first friend on this ship, and I cannot cry for him. I cannot cry for anyone.'

'Not even for yourself?'

I shake my head. 'Least of all for myself.'

He sits back, gazing at me. After a time he says, 'I'll give you a sleeping-draught, Eliza. God knows, you need the rest.'

We bury Rolf at sea. The sailmaker has sewn him into a shockingly tiny bundle, a flag with the blue cross of Finland on top. The captain says prayers, then the bundle is tilted over the side and slides away and disappears.

Not so our memories.

We holystone the deck where Rolf lay, but no matter how often we try, a ghost of the stain remains. We have nightmares. Artur says one night when he heard the mate's whistle he saw a pale form rise to go to its duty.

No one sleeps in Rolf's bunk, of course. More than ever I see how young the sailors are, just boys calling themselves men.

It's almost a relief when the storms return with furious headwinds and we have something to do. We tack back and forth but it's a slow, hard business.

We're only four hundred miles from Falmouth now, *Kapten* says. Then the winds turn and at long last they're from behind.

A few nights later we see the Bishops Rock light near the Isles of Scilly: less than one hundred miles to go. Seagulls cry around us and squat ugly cargo vessels throb past in the distance.

We tidy the deck and harbour-stow the sails neatly against the yards. Orders are no longer roared at us by the mates, they simply say what is needed. We know what to do.

The last evening before landfall I stand with Harry watching the light on the distant coast as we pass. Scents of meadow grasses fill the air. It's June now and I've almost missed spring in London (sorry Mama), but soon I'll see the great city in summer.

'What will you do when we arrive?' I say.

We've all been asking this of each other. Most of my watchmates are planning to get drunk and find themselves a *real* girl they say, looking askance at my paint-stained dungarees.

'Research at the School of Hygiene and Tropical Medicine. It's all I've ever wanted to do.'

'But I thought you worked in an East End clinic after you graduated,' I say. 'Why didn't you do your beloved tropical medicine then?'

'Ah.'

'Ah?'

'For a time there I had very strong political opinions.' Harry sighs. 'I wanted to dedicate myself to the ills of the working class and help bring about a socialist revolution.'

'My goodness. So Felix was right to call you a Bolshevik?'

He smiles. 'Probably.'

'But you don't believe in that now?'

'Well, yes, I still do. The world is cruelly unfair, and the poor bear the brunt, despite what people like Felix prefer to think.'

'He's convinced you're hiding something from us. Was that it?'

Harry is silent for a moment then shrugs ruefully. 'There was a woman named Charlotte, the daughter of a socialist philosopher in London. In some ways—and I'm more ashamed of this than you can imagine—I took on my Bolshevik quest to impress her.'

'And what happened?'

'She played me for a fool. Ran through all my savings then dumped me.'

'So that's why you were a poor doctor. Oh, penniless, I mean. You're a very good doctor.'

'Thank you,' he says, amused.

'Still, that's not such a *terrible* secret.'

Harry hesitates. 'It's a stupid thing to be ashamed of, but you see, it led to such sad consequences. If I'd had the money to take a steamer home I would have had more time with my father before he died—I might even have found a treatment for him. But because I lost my head I failed, him and my mother both.'

'No, *matros*, it's not your fault some silly woman wasted your money. You mustn't be bitter.'

'That's not what I feel in my heart, *jungman*, and it'll be a bloody long time before I give that away again.' He laughs shortly. 'And you? Is a life with young Niilo in your future?'

'Sadly no. He discovered he could not love me without my bountiful tresses.'

'Well that's certainly his loss. But now all you have to do is find a man who adores—'

'Stockholm tar? A startled emu, perhaps?'

'I was going to say, a man who adores a brave woman.' He can't restrain his grin. 'And a man who knows a good hairdresser too, of course.'

'*Dra åt helvete*,' I say. Go to hell. Then Mr Pölönen calls us to take in a sail.

In early June 1929 we reach Falmouth. We furl the canvas and let down the clanking anchor half a mile off land. We've taken one hundred and seventeen days on our passage. As the winner of the Grain Race usually comes in at around ninety days, it certainly won't be us.

The captain is rowed ashore to telegraph our safe arrival to the owners while the boys stare longingly at the town. Soon, I think, our calm shipboard life will be overwhelmed by a world unknown for months. Anything might have happened: earthquakes, volcanoes, plagues!

Then *Kapten* brings back some newspapers and nothing much has changed. Just the usual gangsters in Chicago, goings-on in Russia, battles in China, debt in Germany and half-a-dozen dictators, pacts and rebellions. The financial world is booming too, and everyone is buying, selling or gossiping about stocks.

If only any of it mattered as much as our ship.

Our orders arrive—port of discharge, Cardiff, South Wales. We raise the anchor and in less than two days make our way to Barry Docks. A tugboat eases us against the wharf and we tie up for the first time in almost four long months. I feel a great stillness.

The gangway is lowered and customs men come on board, and immigration officials and doctors and agents and brokers and stevedores. My watchmates stand back wide-eyed, as suddenly strangers are milling everywhere on our clean deck.

Our precious deck.

A few hours later I stand waiting in a crumpled dress, no longer part of my watch, just a useless *flicka* once again. I've given my wet-weather gear away to the boys for their next passage around the Horn, and my luggage is stacked nearby.

I remember the day we sailed, the day small freckled Rolf took my empty bags away to be stowed for the passage. *I promise you, Rolf, Elias will never forget you.* For some reason my throat hurts quite a lot.

Felix is waiting impatiently beside me, moustachioed, tanned and dashing. Harry is leaning against the stays, a hat on the back of his head. He starts a new drawing in his sketchbook but then stops and simply stares the length of *Inverley*, as if he's trying to memorise every beautiful line of her. Just like me.

He catches my eye and I shrug ruefully, and he nods, smiling. In a panic I think, how can I possibly leave this life behind? Leave my friends, my ship? What will I *do*?

My heart pounds and my eyes sting.

A limousine drives onto the wharf and stops. Granddad Freddy and Aunt Izabel get out, followed by my grandmother Min-lu, a dear small figure in an elegant coat, who looks up and waves. My throat swells and I run down the gangway and fling myself into the comfort of her arms.

And then at last I cry.

10. Izabel: What Fun

Dear Lord, how *tedious*, just to pick up that child I barely remember from my trip to Australia—when was it, five, six years ago? I think I gave her a half-used bottle of perfume the Baron flew in from Paris especially for me. I didn't much like it.

But I do remember the rather delightful man I met on the passage home, and the publicity that got me a wonderful part in *The Spring of Lady Smithers*, so I suppose it was all worth it.

We step out of the limousine and a scruffy girl runs down the gangplank into the arms of my mother. I stroll closer to the big boat or ship or whatever it is, and realise there might be possibilities in the day after all.

Young men who take my breath away are lounging about everywhere. Blond, tanned, muscular—wall-to-wall heaven. Then I notice a dark-haired man in a suit, clearly not one of the Viking crew. He's standing back, smoking and watching me. Well, of course I'm used to *that*.

But there's such intensity in his gaze, eyebrows drawn down over the bluest of eyes, fine moustache, chiselled jaw. He could be a matinee idol, one with a bit of substance to him, and I'm instantly certain he's no poof, not like my rather disappointing leading man in *Britannia on Parade*.

Amid hubbub the captain and his mousey wife are coming down the gangplank and shaking hands with everyone. Freddy and the captain are old friends—he's reminisced about it all the way from Kensington to Cardiff—but I paid him no attention.

He's such a bore. I know he's my brother Sam's father but *really* I haven't the faintest idea what Min-lu sees in him. Even at their age they can't keep their hands off each other. Ghastly.

I'm aware Mr Matinee Idol is coming down the gangway too. He's limping a little, rather touchingly: perhaps he's a war hero. I gaze calmly everywhere but at him until he's beside me.

'How do you do?' he says in a cultured voice. 'You must be the famous Miss Peres. I'm Felix Malory, one of the passengers who sailed with your niece.'

He holds out his hand like a gentleman and I offer mine most daintily. He kisses it and I feel a bolt of lust. Oh, yes.

'How do you do, Mr Malory? I hope it was a pleasant voyage.'

'A most exciting passage, thank you.'

He's still holding my hand but I withdraw it. Slowly.

My mother has her arm around the girl and is presenting her to me. 'Izabel, you remember Eliza, of course?'

Wearing a wrinkled dress that's horribly out of date, Eliza peers at me through clumps of hair. I can't imagine why anyone would let themselves appear in public like that.

She kisses me on the cheek. 'Hello, Aunt Izabel.'

'Oh, darling. Just call me Izabel. You're all grown up now.'

She's such a thin little thing it's hard to tell, but I know she must be, she's only seven years younger than me.

A forgettable man in a hat is introduced too, then more chit-chat. Suddenly it seems farewells are being made. I don't want to walk away without making sure I see this delightful Felix Malory again, so I say, 'Min-lu, I've had such a marvellous idea.'

She turns to me. Of course I never call her Mother in public and if anyone asks, she's my darling old nanny who's married up in the world.

'We took that suite at the hotel for two days,' I say. 'Why don't we have a party tomorrow evening to thank everyone for bringing Eliza safely over the sea to us?'

She can hardly say no to that. It's all arranged, and we'll send the car to the ship (or is it a boat?) tomorrow evening to collect captain, spouse, Mr Forgettable-in-a-hat, and the delicious, smouldering, divine Mr Malory. What *fun*.

In the car on the way back to the hotel I finally have to ask, 'Eliza, darling, did something—*happen* to your lovely hair?'

'It got covered in Stockholm tar and had to be cut off.'

Covered in *what*? 'I'll get my maid to see what she can do.'

'Thank you, Izabel,' the girl says. She starts chatting away to Min-lu and Freddy about the voyage. I don't much care, I'm just remembering the feel of his fingers—and lips—on my hand. The vibrations of the car over the rough street make me move my hips a little, rather pleasantly, against the car seat.

Tomorrow.

Back at the hotel I ring my agent in London, Rupert Grimstone himself, of course. I'm his most famous client.

'Darling,' I say. 'I'm stuck here in medieval Cardiff, of all places, but wanted to check in case you'd sent word to my flat. Have you heard anything about *Cowgirl on Broadway*?'

I'm playing it cool but my heart is thumping. I want that part so badly. Dusty, the jazz-singing cowgirl, could catapult me from the London stage into the booming world of Hollywood talkies. I have the voice for it, everyone says so.

'Izabel darling, I was *just* about to get in touch. Congratulations, Miss *Dusty*!'

'Oh my *God*, Rupert, really?'

'Of course. I never doubted it for a moment.' Yes you did you old fraud, I think, but that doesn't matter, I have the part!

'Now you must sign the contracts of course,' he says. 'When will you be back?'

'A few days. Oh, Rupert, what *fun*! Thank you, darling, for all your hard work.'

An exaggeration of course. He certainly threw himself into the wining and dining, but it was me who did the real work, practising song-and-dance routines for the auditions till my feet bled. And the 'audition' as well with that awful producer. Ugh.

But I've done it, I'm acting in a *talkie* and with Jack Brandon too! The city girl's Gary Cooper they call him—just as likeable but *so* much smoother. He's not really my type but we'll see what happens. Or will we? Suddenly Jack Brandon doesn't seem very interesting: no man does but Felix Malory. I shiver with pleasure.

At dinner I announce the wonderful news about my talkie and everyone raises their glasses. I'm feeling generous and tell Eliza, 'Penfold will trim your hair. I have a dress you can have for the party too—Penfold will take it in—and some shoes. Our feet are the same size.' (Eliza's are larger but she'll just have to suffer to be beautiful.)

Of course it's a good deed but really, I just don't want such a plain little presence spoiling my party. Then Eliza, Min-lu and Freddy start going on about an array of family members I can hardly recall, but I hear a familiar name and my scalp prickles.

Lucy? Of course, I'd forgotten that Lucy is Eliza's aunt. The bitch Lucy who'd let the love of my life die and even told me to my face he'd refused to go to hospital! As if *that* was likely in the middle of the flu epidemic.

No, little nurse Lucy simply let my darling Gideon die. Didn't lift a finger. Perhaps she was jealous. After all, she was a dried-up old maid compared to me at eighteen.

I was Gideon's *kittikins*, perfect and sweet a peach, he'd always say. Of course, I know now he wasn't the most considerate of lovers ... but oh, if we'd had more time! We'd have been so happy together, the two of us with our own darling child.

I only ever saw my mother cry twice: when Sam died, and the day I told her I was pregnant and would keep the baby. She whispered, 'It's desperately hard to raise a child by yourself, Izabel. The cruelty, the attacks. My dear, I *cannot* let that happen to you.' It's for the best she said, and really, she was right.

It all hurt rather a lot though, and the recovery was slow and gruesome—we had to tell everyone I'd had appendicitis. But soon after I ran off to London and my wonderful new life, and of course that would have been impossible with a baby in tow.

Still, I could never forgive Lucy.

Once I said, Lucy *killed* Gideon, and my mother slapped me for the first and only in my life. 'You have no *idea*, you foolish child, what that dreadful man *did*, how much he hurt us, how his stupidity caused Sam's death—'

She broke off then and left the room.

Well, I know *all* about that. Gideon explained it was a tragic misunderstanding, no one's fault. Sam was his oldest friend and he suffered terribly.

I was just a child then, and Gideon went on to marry the widow, Eliza's mother—that red-headed tart who loves to swan around playing the great artist. She broke his heart when she left him, Gideon said, kissing me.

It's odd what you forget over time. What with my marvellous career and all the darling men who pamper me I don't often think about Gideon now. Recently it was ten years since he died and (I recall with a pang) I didn't even notice the anniversary.

Now this scruffy girl has brought it all back—but then, she also brought Felix Malory into my life, so I might forgive her. I smile and pretend I'm interested in the chit-chat, but I can only think about tomorrow.

Tomorrow.

Eliza stands shyly in front of me and I say, 'Darling, you have *eyes!*' and she laughs.

Penfold is quite the grooming marvel. I say so and she does her bashful routine, hoping for some time off or extra money or something.

Eliza is actually quite pretty, I see with surprise. Penfold has given her a stylish bob, lightly ruffled on her forehead and around her chin. She has a fringe of eyelashes so dark I doubt she'll ever need mascara and her eyes are a nice shade of amber.

Her mouth isn't bad either—a little lipstick will be perfect—and all in all I feel rather pleased with myself. Clever old Penfold: maybe she can have Sunday afternoon off.

'And did you like the dress?'

'Oh, it's just *beautiful*, Izabel, thank you. I had some good clothes in my luggage but I don't think the sea air did much for them.'

I smile and bite back a comment on her outdated wardrobe. 'Penfold will help you get ready later and do your make-up.'

'Make-up?'

'Of course, darling. My God, it's nineteen twenty-*nine*. No sane women goes without make-up at night. Or day, come to think of it.'

'That will be lovely, thank you Penfold,' she says.

Don't go giving her ideas, I think. She already imagines she's a cut above lady's maid.

'Very well, Eliza, I'll see you tonight,' I say. 'Penfold, draw my bath, please.'

Tonight.

11. Eliza: Shipmates

Pretty dresses are always fun, but I've never had anything like *this*. Moss-green chiffon scattered with tiny bronze beads, the dress plunges daringly at the back. It's fitted to my thighs, then falls into long pointed layers that drift when I move.

My hair is not just beautifully cut (oh, *thank* you, Penfold) but the dark waves shimmer with reddish lights. My eyes sparkle, my lips are rosy and small diamonds cascades from my ears, a gift from Min-lu. Izabel's beaded shoes, although tight, are the finishing touch.

When I enter the sitting room of our suite, Nanna says, 'Oh, child,' and hugs me. Granddad chuckles and says, 'Where's our little matelot got to, then?' and hands me a glass of champagne.

'*Very* nice, darling,' says Izabel, sitting on the sofa, smoking.

'Oh, Izabel, you look amazing!' I say.

She's wearing a silver dress, far more daring than mine. Sequins glitter like her dark eyes, a white orchid sits above her ear, and diamonds sparkle in fine chains over her bosom.

There's a knock at the door and Granddad welcomes Captain Nilsen, Maria and Harry. The captain is in his uniform, Maria is wearing a pretty floral dress and Harry looks as formal as I've ever seen him. Greeting are exchanged, and glasses filled and handed around.

'Is that a *tie*?' I ask Harry. 'From the bottom of your sea-bag?'

'From the finest purveyors of haberdashery in Cardiff I'll have you know. And what on earth's happened to your hair? I'd grown fond of the asymmetry and faint scent of turpentine.'

'Penfold, a genius of grooming, happened to my hair. Isn't it wonderful?' I ask, laughing.

'Yes, it is,' says Harry. 'I bet Niilo's going to be sorry now.'

'That's *exactly* what I was thinking. Here, have a canapé. Where's Felix?'

'At a hotel somewhere, didn't want to stay on the ship any longer.'

'Why am I not surprised?' I turn to Maria and we hug. 'How lovely! The blue in your dress is the same as your eyes.'

'Oh, little Eliza, you are so pretty tonight!' she says.

'*Jungman* Elias,' says the captain firmly. 'You realise you have not signed off the ship's Articles yet? I can put you in irons, you know.'

'Does *Inverley* have irons, *Kapten*?' I say. 'I've never seen them.'

'Sadly, we have none.' He chuckles. 'So I shall just have another drink. *Skål!*'

There's a knock at the door and Felix joins us, rakishly handsome in an evening suit. Izabel rises from the sofa like a dancer in the Arabian Nights, and offers him her hand. He kisses it and they look into each other's eyes.

I have to glance away, the sheer intensity of it makes me blush. I've never seen such a thing between virtual strangers before.

The evening is a joy. We eat and drink and laugh together— Maria and the Captain, Min-lu and Freddy, Izabel and Felix, and Harry and me. That's a rather neat pattern of partnerships, I think, a little sozzled, as I wriggle Izabel's uncomfortable shoes off my feet.

Harry and me? Not very likely! I gaze at him as he talks to Freddy—something about the ship I expect, from the movement of his hands. Of course he's a nice-looking man, fair, well-built, easy to talk to. And his smile, so rare at first, now comes often to his lean, intelligent face.

But I can't imagine Harry as my partner, not the way I'd dreamt of Niilo. He's too old for a start—well, only twenty-seven, but he seems older—and he's certainly duller. No, Harry's not for me.

But there's someone ahead, I know in my heart, someone thrilling. Someone who'll look at me the way Felix looks at Izabel. They're out on the balcony, smoking and murmuring, their heads close together.

Izabel laughs, her lovely throat and bosom gleaming, while handsome Felix leans on the railing, grinning, fully the man of consequence he said he'd be off the ship.

How beautiful they are.

Inverley's grain is unloaded and taken away to become bread and pies and beer. She's leaving soon for her home port in the Åland Islands, where she'll be made ready to go out to Australia again in just a few months.

Freddy's chauffeur drives me back to the docks to say goodbye. For the last time I sit in the saloon and drink coffee with Maria and Captain Nilsen.

The captain says, grinning, 'You know, *jungman*, if you sign on for the next voyage I will rate you ordinary seaman.'

'Tempting offer, *Kapten*, but I don't want to go home yet.'

'One day, you will visit us, Eliza?' says Maria. 'I will show you everything. Please come.'

'If I can, Maria. I'd love to see the Ålands. One day.'

'The Western Harbour is a very good anchorage,' says Captain Nilsen. 'All the sailing ships are there in the summer.' He turns, smiling, to his wife. 'Home, Maria. Soon we will be home on the farm and I will sleep all night.'

I much enjoy the effect I have on my old watchmates. Among the teasing and amazement it's gratifying to see Niilo recognise, chagrined, that short hair can be perfectly feminine, while stocky Artur declares he is in love with me and will marry me when he's twenty-one.

Karl skulks in the background. I say, 'I hope your skin improves soon, Karl,' and he dashes away red-faced.

It's unkind of me, but he tormented so many of us. In any case I'm giddy with delight at my own prettiness.

Artur says, 'You know, Elias, Karl is in love with you for very long time.'

'Karl? Funny way of showing it.'

'German. What you expect?' shrugs Artur from the world-weary heights of his seventeen years.

Mr Pölönen smiles, his gold tooth twinkling. 'Go cleverly and carefully, *jungman*.'

I thank him with '*Tack så mycket*, Mr Pölönen,' and he smiles again, but that's probably at my pronunciation. I have belatedly realised that not only does he speak more English than he allowed, like most Åland ships' officers he's probably fluent in Swedish, Finnish and German as well.

I feel ashamed that I, with my Broome Japanese, schoolgirl French and smattering of Swedish curses, could ever have regarded the verbal skills of my shipmates with scorn. And despite their boyish crudity (which taught me more about anatomy and human behaviour than I'd ever imagined possible), almost all treated me with kindness.

I gaze around the deck and cannot believe *Inverley* will soon be sailing without me. I sigh, but I already know from small Rolf's fate there is no turning back. I stop at the sail locker to farewell Mr Hendriksson, then as I'm about to go ashore I see Harry.

'Still here?' I say. 'Surely there's dozens of patients with malaria and yellow jack and dengue fever just desperate for you to come and sort them out.'

'Working aboard for a day or two longer, *jungman*, then I'll take the train to London. But I expect to find microscopes waiting for me there, not patients.'

'Is that really what you want, *matros*—boring old microscopes? What about people?'

He smiles. 'What I do with microscopes will help many more people than if I sit by bedsides.'

A thought strikes me. 'Oh, Harry, I wanted to tell you I can *cry* now, I'm free of that strange restriction. It's almost absurd—my eyes prickle at every little thing.'

'I'm glad for you. Everyone needs to be able to cry.'

'Did you cry when your father died?'

He gazes at me for a moment, then nods.

'Perhaps we'll meet again one day,' I say. 'I hope we'll always be friends.'

'Better than friends, Eliza,' he says, half-smiling. 'We'll always be shipmates.'

That pleases me and I step forward and kiss him on the cheek.

'Goodbye then, shipmate,' I say. 'Fair winds and following seas.'

Izabel and Felix hire a car and drive up to London by themselves. My grandparents and I take the slow route with Penfold the maid and chauffeur Spencer, and stop for a few days at Granddad's farm on the South Downs. It's just as it was on the trip when when I was eleven: rolling green hills, linens scented with lavender and glowing coals in the fireplace, but I find it hard to sleep without the sense of a ship rolling beneath me.

Today Granddad and Spencer are out in a field and Penfold is helping the cook—that's not her job but she's a kind woman. I wander aimlessly around the farm sheds, then go inside, make up a tea-tray and take it to Min-lu. She puts her sewing aside and pours the tea.

'How are you feeling today, darling?'

'Well, a week ago I was furling sails—and now? I'm actually a little bit lost, Nanna.'

'But you need the rest,' she says, handing me a teacup. 'You must have worked so hard. Darling, you've got calluses and muscles. Muscles!'

'I *know*,' I say, pleased. 'And by the end I could even handle the wheel too.'

'Not precisely what I meant,' she says. 'But, child, I'm so happy you're here. Four years is too long to be apart.'

'I've missed you terribly, Nanna. I didn't even realise that till I saw you again.'

'You've grown up, darling.'

'I think most of it happened over the last four months,' I say lightly, though it's true.

'Now what would you like to do when we get to London?' She takes a sip of tea.

'I'm under orders from my little cousins to visit Buckingham Palace and the lions at the Zoo.'

'Wonderful.' Min-lu puts her teacup down. 'What else?'

'I'm under another set of orders from Mama and Anton to visit various art galleries.'

'Lovely. But what do *you* want to do, Eliza?'

'I don't know.' I shrug. 'Visit the tourist spots, I suppose.' My eyes suddenly sting. 'Nanna, it's very strange. I've been busy for so long and now I'm lost. I keep expecting the second mate to pop up and set me to work.'

'Heavens, what a tyrant.'

'Oh, not at all! I *loved* being part of my watch and using my wits and strength and working with the others, all of us looking after the ship. It was satisfying.'

'Then we must find you something else to do that's satisfying.' She gazes at me. 'You know, you're rather like Lucy, always needing to be busy, but she was a trusting child. I feel you've known something more of the world, darling, and it's left you a little unhappy.'

I nod, a lump in my throat. After a time I say, 'I told you what happened to Rolf, and that was awful enough. But the last few nights I've had some bad dreams. About something else.'

After a silence she says, 'Eliza?'

'I didn't say a word to *anyone* my whole life, Nanna, then I told Pete before I left home …'

After a silence she says, 'Tell me.'

I take a breath. 'Do you remember Gideon Meade, my stepfather before Papa Anton?'

She goes very still. 'I certainly do.'

'When I was young he used to beat me and molest me.' I look up and shake my head. 'No, he didn't rape me. But sometimes I have nightmares, and I've had a few lately.' I try to smile. 'Just getting used to being a landlubber again, that's all.'

(After the informal crudity of the starboard watch, at last I know what happened to me and what, even worse, might have happened. I'm so grateful they gave me the language for it.)

Nanna is silent.

Finally she says, 'I had thought I understood the depravity of that man and still he shocks me. Oh, my *dear*.'

Nanna takes me to visit a doctor in London, a psychiatrist, and over months we talk together. He's a kindly presence, and simply telling him about Rolf comforts me. Then slowly he helps me uncover and confront the memories of my childhood ill-treatment.

Recalling Gideon's hands upon me is far from pleasant, but a piece of some great puzzle falls into place the day I recognise it was not his lust but his *cruelty*, his erratic, casual violence towards me, that inflicted the deepest of my wounds.

The doctor guides me gently towards an easier perspective on those long-ago events, and my nightmares recede and after a time, finally disappear. Despite—or perhaps because of—this time of introspection, London starts to fascinate me.

I live with my grandparents and Izabel in a tall house in Kensington, an exclusive neighbourhood where a many-storied residence like ours is much envied. To someone from a country where most homes sprawl over just one or two levels, it's quite a novelty.

We're always going up and down stairs to the dining room, the library, the sitting room, the bedrooms, and it keeps me as fit as on a ship.

I say Izabel lives with us but that's something of a formality, as she spends most of her time with Felix Malory. She's also busy with preparations for her talking film, which sounds terribly exciting.

She dashes in for supper and tells us the latest on the plans, clothes, scripts, actors, then dashes out again for some event at which she's photographed for the newspapers. Felix is always there by her side, christened the 'Barrister Beau' by the press. They're the darlings of London society.

Nanna and I visit the the obligatory Zoo and Palace and tourist sights, and I send lots of postcards home to prove it. One unforgettable day we go to the National Gallery to see *Ophelia Drifting*, the famous painting of Mama and Lucy's mother, Annabel.

Veiled only by her long auburn hair and a scattering of wildflowers, this Ophelia's eyes are not shut: lovely Annabel's gaze is direct and amused. The canvas caused a scandal in its day.

'Sadly I never met her,' says Nanna. 'She died of pneumonia just after the family arrived in Australia. It was a terrible time for the girls, especially Lucy.'

'She told me once you'd saved her life her after her mother died.'

'Did she? Dear child. She was grieving and lost in all the fuss when Sam and Rosa eloped, but she was always brave, another daughter to me.'

I gaze at the painted Annabel, the grandmother I'd never known. 'She has Mama's colouring but her eyes remind me of Lucy. They seem to be smiling, even though she's not.'

'Your mouth is like hers though, darling. You know, you've become rather beautiful.'

I hug the small, kind woman beside me. 'Then that must be my *father's* Lee ancestry coming out, Nanna.'

She stands straight-backed and smiles, but I see a glint of the tears that well up whenever we speak of her son.

My twenty-second birthday arrives in November 1929, and soon it's Christmas. The snow wafts lightly, exquisitely through the air, nothing at all like the spiteful sleet of Cape Horn.

We receive cards from my family, and from Maria Nilsen on her Ålands farm. She says the captain and *Inverley* sailed three months ago for South Australia, and soon they'll be loading grain again, there in that unimaginable heat.

In London we have crackling fires, holly wreaths, a candle-lit tree and a traditional dinner. I've never been happier.

PART II: THE LEE SHORE

12. Pete: An Evil-Tempered Earhart

'Johnson's landed!' Billie yells and I come into the office and read the newspaper over her shoulder, keeping my grease-covered hands out of the way.

I read aloud, '*24 May 1930: Today in Darwin, the largest concourse of people and cars ever seen here assembled to welcome intrepid girl flyer, Amy Johnson.*'

'Girl flyer,' scoffs Billie. 'She's twenty-six, for Christ's sake, older than me.'

'How long? Oh yeah, Nineteen days, London to Darwin, sixteen stops. Incredible.'

'Wouldn't have used a Gipsy Moth myself,' says Billie. 'Something bigger I reckon.'

'Well, if someone gave us a new Gipsy Moth I wouldn't say no.'

'Too bloody right. How's that repair going?'

'Badly. Parts are simply worn out—expensive parts.' I sigh.

'Haven't you got classes today, kid?'

'Just going.' In the small bathroom at the back of the hangar I scrub the grease off my hands with Solvol, say 'See you later,' and get on my motorcycle.

As I bump along the dirt road and lean my weight round the corners and slow down in the traffic near the city, I think how complicated life has become, as I rush between home, university and the airfield.

I miss Laura—or I miss sex with Laura—but I'm glad I don't have a girlfriend now. I couldn't possibly keep up this punishing routine with a social life as well. But I'm happy, so happy. Though I still call her *crazy lady* Billie isn't nearly as crazy as I first thought.

The day we met she was in shock from the loss of the company's second pilot and plane. With her it's hard to know what hit her hardest, but she'd been almost sick with grief.

Her company was in worse straits than I imagined and my fees for the full training course, thanks to Mama, saved it from the creditors.

Billie gave me twelve dual lessons then let me go solo. I nearly killed myself that first landing, but I've improved now, though it's a slow business.

She's a hard taskmaster but I just acknowledge she's a brilliant pilot, better than I could ever be. Even Frank the mechanic smiles at me now, or at least he's stopped glaring.

My university course is handy too because I can get small parts mended in our machine lab; while my tutors are simply delighted at my renewed interest in mechanical, electrical and aeronautical engineering.

Yet Quinn Aviation still isn't doing well. Competitors are starting up all the time, with better planes and more capital. Billie gets the occasional student but has no chance of saving for a new training plane. At five hundred pounds or so the latest Gipsy Moth is relatively cheap, but it's still beyond her reach.

She talks to bank managers and friends, follows fruitless leads and sells almost everything of value she has, but can't raise the money. Her family won't help either. They were appalled at her taking up a flying career after they sent her to an exclusive girls' school.

I t turns out she went to the same school as Eliza. That makes Billie a few years my senior so I sometimes call her an old lady. It doesn't seem to bother her. She says after the bitches in her class nothing can ever get under her skin again.

Billie herself, tall and slim, is like a copper-haired Amelia Earhart: a sarcastic, scowling, evil-tempered Earhart. She holds several flying records—fastest between Perth and Adelaide, that sort of thing—but she doesn't talk about it except when trying to get new business.

No matter how cranky she is on the ground, she's calm and patient in the air, teaching me over and over what I need to know. But basically she thinks I'm an idiot, and *kid* is about the kindest thing she's ever said.

Still, she's a bit of a mystery. Sometimes I wonder if she's one of those Sapphic women, the sort who only make love to other women, but I have no idea how that's done without a man's tackle in the equation and if I dare think about it when she's around I go red.

My theory seems to be upheld by her ridiculously short hair. Surely no real woman would put up with that coppery mess? Still, her skin is fine and fair (under the smudges of grease) and I thought women of that sort had coarse skin and moustaches. Don't they?

Despite my time with Laura I don't know much, and despite diffident enquiries among my friends they don't either. But one cricketing mate has what he says are some racy Edwardian postcards.

The women have long winsome ringlets with flowers dotted here and there, and they're plump and solid of thigh. I'm used to the current style of lissom young cuties, and these women look old-fashioned and not the slightest bit racy.

But they seem to be doing things with their fingers—and mouths. *Really?* Was that what Sapphists did?

It all seems a bit complicated. With Laura I just, you know, did it. She always said she liked it, although now I recall she'd sometimes be a bit grumpy afterwards.

Once she hinted she'd have liked it to last longer. I don't know how that's even possible, but maybe this fingers-and-mouth trick would help. Oh well, too late now. Perhaps I can try with my next girlfriend.

I smile. When I've finished my degree, when I have my flying licence, of course I'll get a new girlfriend. Maybe a dark-eyed brunette this time. My cricketing mate says they're more passionate.

13. Izabel: Quota Quickie

Rupert gives me the ghastly news early in 1930, and I flee to the sitting room hoping no one will disturb me, but Eliza is there, reading the paper.

I can't hide the fact I've been crying and she says quickly, 'I'll get you a cup of tea, Izabel.'

'No, gin and it, please, darling,' I say, and sit in an armchair away from the light.

She pours me a gin and vermouth—I've taught her a lot over the last few months—hands it to me and sits down again.

'Izabel, what's wrong?'

I take a slug and pause, then say shortly, 'He's sold me out completely, the bastard.'

'Who?'

'Bloody Rupert Grimstone, that's who. My so-called agent.'

'What's on earth's happened?'

I laugh bitterly. 'My picture, the role of a lifetime. I'm not going to America now. They've decided to make the film here in London, not in *Hollywood*.' I can't suppress my sob.

'But you'll still be the star, won't you?'

'Instead of Dusty the cowgirl on Broadway, I'll be Doris the secretary from Wootten Bassett—or worse! Oh, yes, I'll still get to sing but who'll watch me? People want to see films from Hollywood, not *quota* quickies.'

She understands. I've explained how a certain percentage of movies shown in British cinemas must also have been filmed here. It means the studios make cheap movies in London to meet their quota, and put their *real* money into Hollywood.

The phone rings and Eliza answers. 'Editor of which paper?'

She lifts her eyebrows at me and I shake my head.

She says, 'I'm afraid Miss Peres is not available at the moment.'

I can hear an awful gravelly voice. 'Well we've heard her new film's going to be a quota quickie and she won't be going to Hollywood after all. Any comment?'

I stare at Eliza in horror, tears stinging again.

'No, I'm afraid that's quite incorrect,' she says. 'Miss Peres *demanded* the movie be made here. She prefers working with British crews, a condition of her contract.' Eliza lowers her voice. 'And of course she doesn't want to leave her Barrister Beau, you understand. They begged her to do the film in Hollywood but she's the star and had the last word. You may quote me on that. Anonymously.'

'Good story,' the editor rasps. 'Thanks, girlie. Who are you, again?'

'Miss Peres' personal assistant,' Eliza says. 'She's actually out celebrating at the moment, delighted to show her support for the British film industry in this way.'

The man chortles. 'No need to gild the lily, girlie. Good story anyway. Cheers.'

Eliza hangs up and I stare at her. 'That was *brilliant*, darling! I almost believed it myself.'

She laughs. 'Well you'd better get Rupert to issue a press release pretty quickly to applaud your principled stance in support of British cinema.'

'No, really, darling. That was wonderful.' I gaze at her. 'My God. I never knew until now how much I need a personal assistant. Would you like a job, Eliza?'

'*Me?* There's plenty of well-trained young women out there who'd jump at the chance.'

'Yes,' I say, eyes narrowing as I light a cigarette. 'But I don't know many who could come up with such a plausible—and *flattering*—story on the fly like that. I'm terribly impressed.'

'Heavens,' she says. 'I don't think ...'

Time to pull out all the stops.

I sigh. 'It's hard to admit, Eliza, but I'm in rather a *lonely* position in this cut-throat industry. It would be so comforting to have family with me, someone I trust.' I go to the window and turn, mischievous. 'And filming is just thrilling, darling, you'd *adore* it. Please say you will, Eliza. You see, I *need* you.'

Good, that works.

I go out in the evening with Felix to even more flashing light-bulbs than usual. Rupert issues his press release, and editorials fill the papers approving of my commitment to the British film industry.

'You look different in this one,' Eliza says, puzzled, holding up a studio portrait of me leaning wistfully against a Grecian column with an armful of flowers. We're sitting in the library, sorting through piles of old photos and clippings to bring my scrapbooks up to date.

'Do I? Oh, yes, that was taken just after I came to London,' I say. 'Before the op.'

'Op?'

'You know. The eyes, the nose.'

Eliza looks at me, then the photo, then me again.

'Oh, *honestly*, darling,' I say. 'A nick at the corners of my eyelids to open them up, make them rounder. The tip of my nose narrowed, the bridge built up a little. Marvellous surgeon, such useful experience from the war.'

'Izabel, you had an operation on your *face?*' she says. 'But you were already so beautiful. Why on earth would you do that?'

'Dear God, are you really that naïve, Eliza? Do you think I'd get a part, any part at all, if people know I'm half-Chinese? The story about my Gypsy blood only goes so far. I've got to *look* completely European.' I run my fingers lightly over my face. 'And now I do. Wasn't much fun, but certainly necessary.'

'But you shouldn't have to do that to get work, you're a wonderful actress.'

I laugh shortly. 'What kind of world are you *living* in, dear? Certainly not this one.' I light a cigarette and gaze at her, considering. 'You know, you're very lucky to be only quarter-caste, Eliza, it barely shows.'

'Didn't stop them bullying me at school.'

'That's because the little bitches *knew*. But no one here knows anything about me, I make certain of that. And *look* at the rubbish in those clippings! Only some of it came from me. The papers'll write anything, they don't care if it's true or not.'

'Yes—this one says you're an orphaned Greek heiress, and that one an Albanian princess.' Eliza laughs. 'And here, a White Russian countess from Manchuria!'

'And the more famous I get, the more the studios need me to make them money. No one can say a word because it'll upset their own applecarts.'

She thinks for a moment. 'But you live here with Min-lu, doesn't that give it away?'

'Well, it wouldn't be good for my image to live alone.' I laugh. 'Still playing virgins, after all. So she's my dear old nanny, *everyone* knows that.'

'But it's denying your own past. What about you, Izabel, the *real* you? Min-lu's daughter—'

'She's Chinese,' I say flatly. 'And I'm not. That's the real me.'

Eliza looks oddly lost. 'Then what am I?'

'Not the foggiest, darling. Hand me that clipping.'

The script and music arrives for the quota quickie, now renamed *West End Winnie*.

'God. Could be worse, I suppose,' I say. 'Let's see.'

Eliza sits with me in the drawing room and we read the script. I make my usual careful notes in a leather-bound diary.

Eliza is surprised and I say, 'I know it's startling, dear, but I actually take my work rather seriously. Read the summary again, please.'

'*Winnie is a rising young singer. Her beloved Johnny goes to fight in the Great War and is reported missing in action, believed killed. Winnie mourns in a song.*'

I go to the piano and play the chords, humming the poignant melody. 'That's rather good.'

'*Winnie is heartbroken but her cruel agent Basil forces her back to the stage.*'

'Bloody Rupert could play cruel Basil and he wouldn't even have to learn the lines,' I say. 'But "Welcome Back, Winnie" isn't too bad.'

'*Winnie becomes a West End star. She doesn't know Johnny has survived, disabled.*'

'That just means he gets to limp picturesquely with a cane until the final song and dance.'

'*Basil tells Johnny that Winnie is engaged to a wealthy man. Johnny knows he can never compete and should just forget her. Then he saves an adorable child from being hit by a car and the child's rich grandfather rewards him with a legacy.*'

'The kid could be ghastly. Still, "You're My New Best Friend" is amusing.'

'*Johnny goes to the stage door to see Winnie from afar for the last time. Her hat flies off in a gust of wind, Johnny saves it and the lovers' eyes meet. Johnny discovers Winnie is not engaged after all.*'

'Cue grand finale,' I say at the piano, playing the cheerful chords. 'And, my God, I think that one's a winner, too.'

I sit quietly for a moment then look at the girl. 'This might be *good*, even as a quickie.' I shiver. 'Oh darling. Suddenly I'm terrified. Come on, help me start learning it now.'

And, again to Eliza's surprise, we stay up till late that night, and quite a few nights afterwards, until I've memorised every line.

Filming begins in July 1930. Spencer drives us from Kensington to Borehamwood in North London. I'm feeling a little nervous, my fingers drumming lightly on the seat leather. Still, I know I look impressive.

I'm wearing my sable stole and gold silk Vionnet, and Penfold has lightened my hair a touch and cut it into flattering waves at my chin.

Eliza looks every bit the modern assistant, in a stylish suit of fine blue tweed, with a narrow belt and kick pleats. 'We'll be meeting Jack Brandon today, won't we?' she says. (She has a small crush on my co-star.) 'His eyes always seem so amused, as if he knows everything about a woman's pleasure. And those shoulders ...'

'Yes. I *do* hope he hasn't got bad breath.' I say. I'll have to warn her. God forbid she gets taken in by a bloody *actor*.

We arrive at the group of buildings. The largest, emblazoned British International Pictures, is where the sound stages are. We stop outside the smaller building, with the offices, studio restaurant and film laboratories.

'I played a small role here once,' I say. '*Last Curtain Call*, heroine's best friend, *ghastly* wardrobe. So don't be surprised if I greet people as if they're my oldest chums. Remember, darling, that's how it is on set. We love each other—until it's over.'

We enter a sound stage and I gasp. 'Roger! Oh, what fun. Eliza, this is the director, Roger Trent, a dear old friend.'

Roger is middle-aged now but he's still got that gleam in his eye. Sorry, sweetheart, not this time. I've got my gorgeous Felix.

'Roger, this is my assistant, Eliza. Well, where do we begin?'

'Over here, darling, your chair of course. Let's have a chat.'

Roger points to the set chairs, one of which says *Izabel Peres* in pleasingly large letters, beside an empty one marked *Jack Brandon*.

Roger introduces me to the cast—pompous Cecil Boston (rich grandfather), admiring Joan Ferris (best friend), smooth Jasper Vaughan (evil agent) and steely-eyed young Mickey Mason (adorable child).

Jack Brandon arrives. He's short but his grin is friendly enough. He shakes everyone's hands and I can see Eliza is disappointed there's no swoonworthy meeting of eyes.

Roger discusses the schedule—four weeks for rehearsal, shooting and recording. Jack Brandon looks surprised and Jasper says, 'Roger, old chap, isn't that a bit tight?'

'Better than most and we've got to stick to it. Now, I'd like to run through the first scenes, then we'll break for costume fittings. After lunch we'll have a dress rehearsal, then see if we can get something in the can by this evening.'

Jack Brandon's eyebrows go up at that and he catches my eye. I shrug a little and he gives me his famous lop-sided grin. I don't find it quite as charming as the movie magazines do.

'All right then, Izabel and Jack, let's hear it,' says Roger.

We start reading. Soldier Johnny is bidding farewell to young singer Winnie, then agent Basil entices her onto the stage, encouraged by best friend Joan.

I was worried Jack Brandon wouldn't be prepared, but he's put in the work, thank God. We run through the scenes three times, with occasional interruptions from Roger, then sing a romantic duet, accompanied on the piano by a young chap in spectacles.

'Good work,' says Roger. 'Costume fittings now, everyone.'

'Ah, morning tea?' asks Cecil hesitantly.

'It'll have to be on the go, old boy,' says Roger. Cecil sighs.

Eliza follow me to the wardrobe department, wide-eyed. Joan and I try on various outfits, pinned, discussed, changed. We twirl, sit, bend and stand to the dresser's directions, amid a running commentary on the patterns, the colours, the fits.

'All right,' says the dresser. 'Off to lunch now, ladies. These'll be ready for the first scenes.'

We eat in the studio restaurant but don't linger as we have to get back to the sound stage, with all its complications of positions, movements, lights up, lights down, microphones and cameras. We rehearse the scenes several times then break for a cup of tea and the costumes. The makeup girl refreshes my face, a dresser adjusts my gown and we take our places again.

'Quiet,' calls the stage manager. Roger says calmly, 'Action.'

We get through a good half page, then Roger stops and has the cameras moved slightly, the lights adjusted. My feet hurt.

Action. Stop. Rearrangement. Action. Take. Stop. Rearrangement. Action. Slowly a few scenes are assembled to Roger's satisfaction. At the end Jack and I perform a duet to the piano which will be overdubbed later by an orchestra.

'Thank you, everyone,' says Roger. 'See you nine a.m. tomorrow. Sharp.'

In the car on the way home I lie back, my eyes shut.

Eliza says in awe, 'Just *watching* you felt like an eight-hour shift aboard a sailing ship. You were amazing, Izabel.'

I smile. 'Shh, darling. Buggered.'

14. Eliza: At Last

'How did today go?' says Min-lu over dinner. (Izabel has gone out to the theatre with Felix. I don't know how she has the energy.)

'It was fascinating,' I say. 'And they all seem so good at their jobs. But why was the film downgraded to a quota quickie in the first place?'

'They probably had less funding because of the stock market,' Granddad says, and smiles at my puzzlement. 'You *did* hear about that small unpleasantness last year, Eliza?'

'I saw something in the papers, but doesn't the market always goes up and down?'

'Well, it went up for too long, and now it's coming down,' says Min-lu. 'And a great deal more brutally than anyone expected.'

'Will it affect your investments?' I ask. 'And *Inverley*?'

'We've diversified,' says Granddad. 'And *Inverley* will be safe, the world always needs grain. I think we'll survive.' He nods towards Min-lu. 'Of course it was your grandmother who realised the stock market had become a mania and we needed to get out.'

'Freddy's being modest, Eliza,' says Min-lu. 'We both saw the danger.'

'Now Min-lu is being modest, my dear. She's got the fiercest eye for business I ever encountered. I'm a fortunate man.'

I gaze at them both affectionately. It was hardly business that had brought them together when they were young, or rekindled their passion when they met again in their middle years. Oh, I think, to have a love like that.

To have a love at all.

Next morning Izabel is clear-eyed and energetic, and hurries us away after a quick breakfast.

'Everyone worked so hard yesterday,' I say. 'I thought filming would be more leisurely.'

'Yes. Most people assume it's a picnic, but it takes effort, concentration and the patience of a saint,' says Izabel dryly. 'Sometimes I barely know myself on set.'

During this morning's scenes I'm amazed again at the result of lighting and make-up and acting. Izabel's glamour is now naïve and girlish, and sophisticated Jack Brandon has become an ardent young soldier, his American drawl crisply English.

I'm kept busy looking after Izabel's belongings and bringing her cups of tea. Between scenes she likes to sit quietly in a corner with her eyes closed and have me gently rub her shoulders.

'I'm not entirely happy how that last one went,' she murmurs. 'What do you think?'

'When Winnie was worried about Johnny?'

'Mmm. It felt, I don't know, not quite right.'

I hesitate. 'Perhaps it was a little as if you were on stage, Izabel, trying to reach the furthest seats. But that might not be necessary here. Filming seems so intimate.'

'You mean I should tone it down a bit, darling?'

'Um, possibly.'

I'm not sure how she'll take my suggestion, but when they re-do the scene she's more subtle, her character's fears held back until the moment at the end when you see her eyes.

'*Bravo*, Izabel,' says Roger. 'That was marvellous. Look, I know we're up against the schedule, but tomorrow I'd like to reshoot a few of yesterday's scenes—I want that *restraint* again, it works beautifully. What do you think?'

The cast murmurs in approval and Izabel smiles, relieved.

After lunch they shoot Johnny's supposed death against grey-painted scenery and mounds of papier-mache trenches. Jack Brandon's brave young man is surprisingly touching and he too has started bringing an effective restraint to his performance.

I spend a lot of the time being called to the office telephone to handle Izabel's calls and appointments and taking messages from her agent Rupert (who isn't at all as beastly as Izabel says, but rather amusing).

After tea comes a scene where Winnie is receiving the terrible news Johnny is missing, believed dead. Roger is walking Izabel, Joan and the telegraph boy through their moves and I decide it's a good moment to go to the bathroom.

When I get back I lean against the wall at the rear near some scenery flats. While Roger speaks to the actors there's a low hum of chatter as lights are moved and cameras and microphones organised. I hear two men murmuring behind the flats.

'She was a bloody cow in *Last Curtain Call*.'

Oh? I think. Wasn't that the movie my aunt played the best friend in?

'Yeah. Heard she's a complete bitch,' says a familiar drawl.

'But she always fucks her leading man so you're on easy street, old chap.'

My God, they're talking about *Izabel*. I feel fury spark through my body and step forward to see them. It isn't the language—my education in the starboard watch left me inured to that—it's the unkindness, the casual brutality of people who hardly know her.

'How *dare* you,' I say in a low voice. 'She's working her heart out for this film and that's all you can say about her?'

One man—the piano player—looks at me in horror and darts away. The other is Jack Brandon, his hands in his pockets. His grin fades to dismay.

'Oh, honey, I'm sorry. Just boys' locker-room talk. We all know Izabel's a real hard worker. And a little thing like you shouldn't be hearing language like that.'

He reaches out and caresses my neck. 'Look, gorgeous, don't be cross with me—'

I grab his hand and twist the thumb in a move that red-haired Rolf once taught me, saying solemnly, *Will save you from bad man one day, Elias.*

Jack Brandon gasps in pain and cradles his hand. 'Are you *insane?*' he whispers.

'Yes. I'm a complete bitch.' I turn and leave.

On the way home in the car that evening Izabel isn't as tired as she was on the first night. She's pleased at their progress and excited at her new, restrained style of performing.

After we've chatted for a time I ask her, 'So what do you think of Jack Brandon now?'

'Hmm, competent, quite good sometimes. Easy to play off, doesn't try to hog the scenes.'

'Do you find him attractive?'

Izabel stretches a little and sighs contentedly. 'No, after Felix I don't find anyone else very attractive.' She looks at me suddenly. 'Why, do you?'

'God, no.'

'Oh darling, has he made a pass at you *already?* It's a professional hazard, I'm afraid.'

'No. I just don't like him.'

'Well, I do hope his sprain doesn't affect filming.'

That afternoon I'd waited anxiously for Jack Brandon to have me thrown off the set. Instead I was astonished to hear him tell everyone he'd tripped and sprained his thumb. While it was being bandaged by the studio nurse he looked across at me and nodded with a wry smile.

Of course I don't find him attractive.

Before we leave the house next morning there's a delivery of flowers, not for Izabel as usual, but for me.

They're blue, the shade of blue of my tweed suit. I open the card, puzzled. It says, *Will you teach me judo? In awe, Jack.*

In the car Izabel says, 'God knows it's flattering but please be careful, Eliza. He's only here for a few weeks, remember.'

'It's all right, he won't turn my head,' I say. 'I couldn't care less.'

'Why judo?' she says. 'Oh my God, was it *you* hurt his hand?'

'Mmm.'

'He's my leading man, please don't cripple him.' She looks at me. 'Did he attack you?'

'No,' I laugh. 'No, I attacked him.'

'Eliza, tell me *exactly* what happened.'

'He was talking to someone and I didn't like what they were saying. Or how.'

'Ah. About me,' she says flatly.

'But then he called me a little thing and touched me. So I twisted his thumb.'

Izabel squeals with laughter. 'What *fun*, I'm so proud of you. But don't do it again.'

'Of course I won't, Izabel!'

'God, *actors*. But I mean it, darling. Stay away from him.'

They re-shoot the earlier scenes and both Izabel and Jack play their parts subtly, and everyone applauds after their touching farewell.

Then the first rehearsal in the afternoon is Winnie's build-up to her break-through West End performance. I'm watching admiringly—Izabel really is an excellent actress—then I realise Jack Brandon has come up beside me.

He takes my arm, whispers 'Shh,' and gently steers me outside the sound stage. I feel ashamed of having mistreated someone so important to Izabel's career.

'Look, I'm sorry, truly, Mr Brandon,' I say. 'You took me by surprise and I over-reacted. I really am sorry.'

'So did you like them?'

'Them?'

He shakes his head in mock dismay. 'The *flowers*, honey. Did you like them?'

'Well yes, of course. They're beautiful.'

'And I matched them to your suit.'

'I noticed. That's odd, most men wouldn't think of that.'

'Ah, but I'm not most men, gorgeous.'

I'd walked right into that one. 'Anyway,' I say. 'I really do apologise, Mr Brandon. Is your hand all right today? I hope it's not hurting too much.'

'Hurts like hell, honey. Hurts like *hell*.'

I say, 'Oh,' and he laughs. 'No, it's fine. Wasn't much fun at the time but not too bad today. But, hey, I'm impressed. Seriously. How does a little thing like you learn a judo move like that?'

'If you stop calling me a little thing—'

He holds his hands up in surrender. 'You got it.'

'Well … a friend taught me. A friend on a sailing ship.'

He looks at me, eyebrows raised.

'Young Rolf. He died in a fall. He was only fifteen.' My eyes prickle.

'Oh Jesus, I'm sorry, didn't mean to—'

'No, no,' I say. 'Really. It's all right.'

He produces his handkerchief and I take it gratefully.

'A sailing ship, you say? What rig?'

I'm surprised. Most people nowadays aren't interested in sail configurations.

'Four-masted barque.'

He looks at me silently and finally says, 'You were on a *four-master*?' Then he smiles. 'Oh, I get it, you were a passenger.'

'No. Crew. I started as a passenger but then worked in the starboard watch.'

'Holy Jesus.'

'What?'

'Me too. Port watch. About eight years ago now, before all this.' He nods at the sound stage.

'You were on a four-master?'

'God's truth, honey.'

'You can stop calling me honey, too.'

'What do I call you, then?'

'Eliza.'

He grins. 'Well, Eliza, I sailed on *Lawhill* in 1922.'

'*Lawhill*?'

'You know her?'

'Poor, bald-headed *Lawhill*. Who doesn't know her?'

He laughs. 'Enough, she's a fine old thing. What about you?'

'*Inverley*,' I say. 'Last year.'

He looks surprised. '*Inverley*? Wow.' Then he grins again. 'Must have been a pretty easy passage. Honey.'

I take a breath then realise he's teasing me.

'No,' I say. 'Not easy. The usual.'

'The usual.' After a moment he says quietly, 'Never anything usual on a sailing ship.'

'No.'

We gaze at each other, and someone calls, 'Mr Brandon?' from the sound studio.

'Your cue, I think.'

'Yeah. Good talking to you, Eliza.'

'I was down and out in Australia in 1922, and don't ask me why because it involved too much rum and I'd rather not think about it, so I signed on *Lawhill*. They needed crew and I had plenty of experience. Or so I told them.'

I shift my head on his shoulder and gaze at his face as he speaks, the black eyelashes, the warm hazel eyes, the dark brown hair falling over his forehead.

'Bound for Queenstown on the Good Hope route, but we had to put in for repairs at Cape Town. So a hundred and twenty-three days all up. Total disaster. What about you?'

'An entirely respectable one hundred and seventeen days, thank you.'

'That's *awful.*' He laughs. 'You didn't even have the excuse of repairs, either.'

'It was pretty hard work anyway.'

'Tellin' *me*, honey.'

I like it now when he calls me honey.

We're at his hotel. Of course I can't take him back to my grandparents' and I certainly don't want Izabel to know either. Despite all her warnings, I haven't been able to hold back.

At twenty-two I want to *know*, I want to be rid of my old-maid virginity. And I want Jack.

That afternoon he took my hand and drew me behind the scenery and kissed me. Then we went out for dinner but never made it to the restaurant.

He simply told the driver to take us to his hotel and kissed me again and again, until I grew dizzy as the streetlights flickered past the car.

His eyes that promised so much? Oh yes, he kept that promise. After the first small discomfort of initiation he gave me pleasure, more than my maidenly fantasies, more than I ever imagined was possible.

Now I cling to his broad shoulders, his narrow hips, I welcome his mouth of such sweet daring, his mouth at home in places I'd never dreamt could be permitted, could be welcomed, could be so utterly *relished.*

And in return there's the thrill of my own daring, my own wickedness, my own wanton mouth on him. *Oh,* how I enjoy his pleasure. And how I enjoy my own.

I don't recall, over those weeks, how I ate, dressed, spoke. All I remember are the veins on the backs of his brown hands. The dark curled hair, shocking and intimate, in his armpits, his groin. The scent of his sweat. The heat of his climax. The oblivion of mine.

He's thirty-one and the Great War ended, thank God, just before his regiment was to leave for Europe. I love to hear the stories of his childhood on a farm, and I love his gentle humour, and best of all I love that we share the same joy in the sea.

Of course Izabel realises and she's furious. She lifts my chin and looks at my kiss-bruised lips, my intoxicated eyes, and says, 'You stupid child. You poor, *stupid* child.'

I cannot fathom why she'd say such a thing.

Jack watches me from across the room the same way Felix looks at Izabel, and I think, yes, at *last*. A smile touches his lips as if he can't believe his luck at finding me, possessing me.

And why not? I know how beautiful I've become.

I can see it in the mirror, in the faces of the men who gaze at me as I pass. My winged eyebrows, my amber eyes, my full lips, my lithe body—my lithe *clever* body. The wardrobe ladies sigh and say I remind them of wicked, lovely Louise Brooks.

Every day's filming goes surprisingly well. Izabel's character is passionate, touching, inspirational, and Jack brings such poignant depths to his scenes of loss and redemption I see hardened floor crew wiping their eyes.

And every night brings me desire and joy and the certainty that the promise of my life is being fulfilled.

To my surprise the day arrives when we reach the last scene of *West End Winnie*. Johnny's eyes meet Winnie's, he sees her hand bears no engagement ring, they fly into each other's arms and the notes of the final duet rise ecstatic.

'And … *cut*,' says Roger. 'My God, that's a take. Well *done*, Izabel, Jack, magnificent job. I think we've got something very special here.' Everyone bursts into applause. 'Now, the farewell party's at my place tonight, so I'll see you all there to celebrate.'

That evening I wear a dress of crimson silk velvet. Diamantes sparkle on the straps and the belt around my tiny waist.

It's flatteringly low at the front, shockingly low at the back, and falls in bias-cut layers to the ground. When I show it to Izabel it makes even her envious.

'Wish I'd seen that before you, darling. More suited to my colouring, don't you think?'

I laugh. 'You know quite well you'll look lovely in anything.'

Izabel shrugs. 'Suppose I'll have to make do with the Schiaparelli rag.'

That evening she's going directly to Roger's party after a meeting with her agent, so Felix is picking me up in his car. I'm looking forward to a chat as I haven't seen him for some time.

'*Kon'nichiwa, otame-san*,' he greets me in his awful Japanese when I open our front door, then grins wolfishly. 'But perhaps it should be *wakai josei*, not *otame*, what do you think?'

'*Kon'nichiwa*, Felix.' Yes, I think, I'm a young woman now, no longer a maiden.

'My goodness, you do look smashing,' he says, as we get into the car. 'And I hear you've been cutting a swathe through Hollywood royalty.'

'Perhaps.' I smile. 'And you, Felix? Is life at Lincoln's Inn as exciting as Cape Horn?'

'Sadly not at all, although it's certainly more lucrative.'

'You're feeling—better—now?'

'My God, yes,' he says. 'I told you once I was back on land I'd be fine, and I certainly am. But I'm more than fine now I've met Izabel.'

'A match made in heaven.'

'Don't you laugh, young Eliza. When Cupid's arrow hits the bullseye there's not a lot you can do but acquiesce gracefully. As I'm sure you know perfectly well.'

'I think I may. And what are your plans?'

We stop at a red light and he says, 'As you know I was swept off my feet when I met Izabel. Couldn't believe she'd take a shine to me. Simple chap, fresh from the sea.'

'Simple chap! Come on, Felix. You're well-connected, you belong to an Inn of Court and you're a handsome devil to boot. How could she resist?'

He laughs. 'Well my wildest dreams do seem to have come to fruition, and I'll tell you a secret, you cheeky young thing. I'm talking to a chap in Hatton Garden about setting a stone with a ludicrous number of carats into a handsome ring—but don't you tell Izabel, it's a surprise.'

'No, I won't. How wonderful, Felix, I'm happy for you both.'

'It'll be you next, my girl.'

'Perhaps,' I say, affecting doubt, while my heart is incandescent with certainty.

When we get to Roger's house Izabel arrives at the same time, so I leave them nuzzling each other and go looking for Jack. Oddly, I can't find him anywhere.

I greet people who've become friends, actors and crew, but Jack isn't in the garden or the greenhouse, the library, the sitting-room or the kitchen. I even check the bedrooms, but all I discover are two extras guiltily kissing.

I ask Roger, puzzled, 'Did Jack say when he'd get here tonight?'

'Ah, not really, but he wanted me to give you a letter. Come to my study.'

Roger hands me an envelope and I flush with pleasure at the sight of the strong handwriting I know so well. Roger politely leaves the room and shuts the door. I sit down and read.

An aeon later, when I grasp that the darkness around me will exist no matter what I do, I put the letter in my evening bag and leave the room.

Izabel comes over and gently takes my arm. She'd tried to warn me, of course she had.

'Remember, that's how it is on set. We love each other—until it's over.'

'Let's go home now, darling,' she says.

'But it's your party,' I say. 'Your party to celebrate your film with …'

And I realise there is a world out there where Jack Brandon movies are in every cinema. Where *West End Winnie* posters are pasted onto walls and shops and telegraph poles. Where I will be confronted, for years to come, with images of the man who was once the warm breathing centre of my universe.

The man who has left me.

15. Pete: Shutting Up Shop

In early 1931 I go to see *West End Winnie* with my cricketing mates and they all agree my aunt Izabel is the bee's knees. When they were making the film Eliza's letters were full of chit-chat about the leading man, Jack somebody. I expect she had a crush on him, but can't for the life of me see why.

At Quinn Aviation a stroke of luck comes Billie's way at last. A friend of a friend suggests someone to contact, a small businessman who's looking for an investment, and she arranges to see him one evening. He's going to pick her up at the airfield and take her to dinner.

'Careful he doesn't make a pass at you,' I say.

'He'd regret it.'

He probably would too. For such a slim woman Billie has powerful arms—cockpit controls are not light and she has to wrestle them for hours at a time.

That afternoon she goes home to get ready. She lives just a five-minute bicycle ride away, in a shack on a small vegetable farm owned by the mechanic Frank and his wife.

I stay in the office working on the plans for my honours project, a small plane I'm designing to test some recent theories. The topic startled my tutors but they approve of anything that engages my enthusiasm.

Billie and Frank have shared their ideas too and we've argued over engines and aerodynamics for weeks, fruitfully and pleasurably.

In the evening I hear Billie's bicycle crunching over the gravel outside, followed by the unfamiliar tapping of high-heeled shoes as she enters the office, gazing defiantly.

I'm so surprised I can't speak for a moment, then say, 'My goodness. You really want that investment, don't you?'

'Shut up, kid.'

She isn't glamorous in any usual sense, no satin or glitter, but for Billie it's an astonishing departure. A dress, for starters. A trim dress in a sort of green that goes with her eyes, high heels, stockings and a handbag (she usually carries a shoulder satchel). She's washed her short coppery hair too and done something to make it look pretty good.

'Is that?—my God it *is*—you're wearing *lipstick*.'

'I swear I'm going to hit you with a spanner.'

'You'll get grease on yourself.'

She groans. 'Come on, Pete, you know how desperate we are. If I play the nice girl I might have a better chance. Being myself hasn't worked out very well so far.'

'Sorry, Billie.' I grin. 'Hey, I could almost fancy you myself if you weren't so ancient.'

She clips me over the ear, which really hurts. Just then we hear a car pull up and she stares at me in momentary panic.

'You look *great*,' I say honestly. 'You'll knock him out.'

A few moments later a man comes to the door. 'You must be Miss Billie Quinn.'

She restrains herself from saying, 'Well, it's hardly flyboy over there,' and smiles. 'Mr Davidson. Lovely to meet you.'

They chat briefly. Billie introduces me as her Head of Engineering, which I rather like, and says she's sorry the Head of Maintenance can't be there as he's on a study tour (Frank's wife has dragged him off to a family wedding for a few days).

Will this Mr Davidson be the one to help Billie out of her financial hole? He looks prosperous enough—good suit, silk handkerchief, shiny shoes—but for some reason he puts my back up.

He's a used-car salesman so I suppose that's it, but if he bankrolls Billie I don't care what sort of creep he is.

She takes her coat and handbag and they leave. I return to my technical drawings and the pages of calculations in my workbook. A few hours later I yawn—I expect Billie will return soon for her bicycle.

I'll probably stay here and sleep on the couch, as I often do when I'm too tired to ride the Norton home. We share the hangar now with a few other small companies, so I enjoy the quiet when I'm alone.

I love the dawn at the airfield, mist on the river, magpies warbling from the trees, planes parked serenely in rows, tools on the workbench smelling of oil—everything so full of ingenuity and energy and *potential.*

I hear a car pull up, and after a time a door slams, then the car takes off with a screech. I wait for the tap-tap of Billie's shoes in the hangar.

She's probably gazing at the clear sky as she often does—nothing to do with navigation, she simply loves looking at the stars—and I go out to meet her, hoping for good news.

She isn't out the front of the hangar or at the side. Puzzled, I walk towards the road at the back and meet her around the corner. It's dark and I can't see very well.

'Was the dinner okay?' I say.

There's silence then I hear a sound, a single sob.

'Billie?'

She puts out an arm as if to ward me off. I dash forward and catch her as her knees give way, and she groans as I help her limp back to the office. In the light my hair prickles with horror.

I lower her carefully onto the couch and she gasps. Her nose is bleeding, her face red with welts. Her dress is torn, her arms bruised, her knees bleeding and one ankle is swollen.

'Jesus, what *happened?*'

'Whiskey,' she whispers. I pour her a tot of the whiskey we keep for medicinal purposes and the occasional celebration, and she grabs the glass and gulps it all.

I go to the washroom and soak a towel with warm water. She takes it and buries her face in it, saying, 'Jeez, that hurts.'

'*How*, Billie? What happened?'

'That bastard told me to suck his cock and I said I wouldn't, so he hit me. A lot. The first thump nearly knocked me out, I couldn't fight back.'

'But your knees, your ankle?'

'Jumped from the car and fell over. Twisted my ankle in these *fucking* heels.'

'Come on, we've got to get you to a doctor.'

'No. It's too late.'

'We'll wake someone up.'

'No. I can't *afford* it, Pete.' She shakes her head. 'It looks bad but the worst is my ankle, and that's not broken, just twisted.'

She wipes her face again and winces. 'I'll be all right. I just need to sleep.'

'You could stay here on the couch.'

'No, I want to go home.' Her voice shakes slightly.

'Would you be all right riding pillion on my motorbike? I'll take you.'

She saved her handbag but had to leave her coat behind in Davidson's car, so I find an old jumper in a cupboard and she gingerly pulls it over her torn dress. I'd kill that shit if I could get my hands on him.

I help her out and onto the bike, and drive slowly, carefully, as she directs me along the dirt road to her little place on Frank's farm. We pass the dark farmhouse, then pull up outside a timber shack.

Inside she lights the lamps and says, 'Got to go to the bathroom. Make a cuppa?'

There's running water in the kitchen sink so the place isn't as primitive as it first seems. The stove still has a few embers so I get it going and boil the kettle. I take the tea into the small sitting room and build the fire up there too.

Billie comes back wearing flannelette pyjamas and a man's woollen dressing-gown. She eases herself down on the sofa and gives me a bandage and says, 'Strap up my ankle?'

I do so, then she pulls on thick socks and sits back with a sigh. I pass her a cup of tea.

'I don't *get* it, Billie,' I say. 'Why would he *do* this? I mean, yeah, he wanted sex and no one likes to be turned down, but every man's got to accept that when it happens.'

She shakes her head. 'I felt him—I don't know—getting colder, *angrier*, whenever I mentioned the company, my flying records, my plans. But he kept saying how much he'd love to back such an enterprising girl, all that crap. I believed him. I wanted to believe him.'

'Billie, it's not your fault. *He* did this.'

'When he was hitting me he kept snarling, *Think you're so fuckin' smart, girlie? Think you're better than me, bitch? Think you're braver? You're nothing but a—*' She stops and shrugs. 'You know what he said. I could have taken my vocabulary to a whole new level if I hadn't been so busy protecting my eyes.'

'Jesus, this is unbelievable. We'll go straight to the police tomorrow and charge the bastard and get him thrown in gaol.'

'Good idea, kid, except his name isn't Davidson. I noticed when he wrote the cheque at the restaurant, but couldn't see what it was. I have no idea where he works or lives and our friend who suggested him hardly knows him. So the police won't have much to go on.'

She puts her face in her hands. 'And I'm just so *tired*, Pete. Tired of trying to keep the business going, tired of men like that —so *many* men like that—who hate me for pushing the limits. For being a woman who flies.'

She looks up, her eyes anxious. 'When we passed the farm I stupidly blabbed how I live down that road. He knows where to find me now, and Frank's away.'

'I'll stay here tonight. On the couch.'

She closes her eyes briefly and says, 'Thanks.' Then she grins as much as her poor face will allow. 'But it's all right, you can sleep in my bed. I'll be safe.'

'How do you know?'

'Haven't got your licence yet, and you need my report to get it. You'll behave.'

I sleep comfortably enough in my clothes and there's plenty of room in Billie's double bed. She groans when she turns over but seems to get some rest.

When I wake up, sunlight is coming through the curtains and I feel content. My arms are around a delicious breathing body and I snuggle and sigh with pleasure.

'What the fuck do you think you're doing? And stop pushing that *object* against me right now.'

'Oh. Oh, sorry, Billie. I thought you were—'

Who did I think she was? Idiot. This is crazy lady Billie, older than me and only interested in doing things with hands and mouths and other women …

'Stop it, kid. That's even worse,' she says, but it sounds like she's smiling.

I pull my hips away from that nice warm arse and turn on my back. 'Sorry, just habit. I know you're not interested in men—'

'And how do you know that, flyboy?'

'Well. Just assumed. Thought you liked, um, women.'

She laughs, then turns towards me.

'Oh,' I say. 'Your poor face,' and gently touch a bruised cheek.

'How are my eyes?'

'Red, and one of them's sort of purple around the socket. It'll get better soon. I had something like that once from football.'

'Did you? Guess kids heal quickly.'

'Come on, Billie. You know I'll be twenty-one soon.' An amazing thought hits me.

'My God, I've just had a *wonderful* idea.'

'Better not involve my body.'

'No, *listen*,' I say. 'I'm going to be twenty-one in six months. I inherit some money then—and *I* could buy a new plane for the company.'

'What, you'd be an investor?'

'Why not? I could be a partner, you wouldn't have to do it all by yourself anymore. I had no idea what I was going to do after graduating—but this, my God, I'd *kill* to do this!'

She says slowly, 'So I'd get money and a business partner without having to dress up again?'

'You don't have to—but you looked really nice, Billie. Whatever you want.'

'Your parents will think I seduced you.'

'Not if you wear your overalls and hair like you usually do.'

She laughs. 'True. But we don't have six months, mate. I'm going to have to close down in a few weeks, once you've got your licence. Then it's all over.'

'Shut down?'

She nods. 'Ow. I need aspirin.'

I get her a glass of water and some aspirin, then sit on the side of the bed as she takes it.

'Okay,' I say. 'How about this? When you're not so red and purple we'll have dinner with my parents, explain everything and try to get my money released earlier than November.'

'Why don't we go while I'm still red and purple then they can be sure I didn't seduce you.'

'Great!' I say.

'And just for the record, kid, I actually do like men.'

'Yeah?' I say hopefully.

'The operative word is men, not boys. Strictly business with us, Pete.'

I sit down and explain to Mama and Anton that the Bill Quinn I've been flying with is actually a Billie and I'd like her to come to dinner with us. It's rather awkward, probably because I've been misleading them for, oh, eighteen months now.

I assure them there's nothing romantic going on but Mama says coolly, 'You've spent rather a lot of nights at the airfield, Peter,' so I suspect she doesn't quite believe me.

Then I say Billie recently had an accident, but unfortunately Mama assumes it was in an aeroplane, so I have to expand on how a potential investor turned out to be a maniac as well, and when we spoke to the police we found they weren't much interested in trying to trace him.

By the end I'm not entirely convinced I've prepared them as well as I'd hoped.

On the night of the dinner Billie doesn't wear her overalls. She's in neat trousers and a blouse and jacket, and her hair is clean and reasonably tidy. Definitely no lipstick, but at least the whites of her eyes aren't scarlet anymore.

Mama and Anton are always good hosts and greet her warmly. It's in her favour she was at school with Eliza and soon we're all chatting happily over the first course.

I'm amazed at how civilised the foul-mouthed crazy lady can be in polite company. I can see Liam is entranced by the line of her long neck.

He starts to do his Lord Byron smoulder and Billie, *magnificent* woman, simply ignores him. While we're chatting about her business I decide it's the right time to strike.

'Mama, Anton, you know how dedicated I am to flying.'

'Indeed we do,' says my mother dryly. 'More potatoes, Billie?'

'And you know I'll be twenty-one in November.'

'Heavens,' says Mama. 'Twenty-one. It seems just yesterday you were my baby.'

'Hasn't changed much,' says Billie. (Everyone laughs at that more than I feel it deserves.)

'Well,' I say firmly. 'I want to invest in Billie's company and help develop the business.'

'I'm encouraged to hear you're looking to the future, Pete,' says Anton.

'That's very enterprising of you, darling,' says my mother.

'But I want to do it *now*, Mama. The company will have to close if we can't get some funds within a couple of weeks and we need a new plane as soon as possible.'

'Ah,' she says. 'You mean you'd like your legacy today, Peter, not at your majority?'

'My father would have wanted it, you said yourself when you gave me money for lessons.'

'That was only a hundred pounds, darling, this is rather more.'

'What do you think, Billie?' asks Anton.

She hesitates. 'Well, I have exactly the same concerns as you. Pete is terribly young, he has no idea what he wants to do with his life, he doesn't know anything about business and he over-glamorises the work I do.'

'*Billie?*'

'It's true, kid. The aviation business is going downhill. People don't have the money for frivolities like flying lessons. I expect only the biggest companies will survive the next few years. Minnows like me will soon disappear. You'd be throwing good money after bad.'

'That's *my* decision. And I reckon with new planes, a new direction, we could ride out these hard times and make something of the company.'

'Planes?' she says, laughing. 'What, more than one?'

'Why not? Billie, I thought you were on my side, I thought you *wanted* this.' My chest hurts.

'No, Pete. Fact is, I'm worn out. Let's get you licensed, then I'll close up shop.'

'But what will you *do*?' All I can see is Billie.

'Sleep in.' She smiles wryly. 'Become a secretary. Who knows?'

'What about Frank? It'll break his heart.'

'Frank can get a job tomorrow with any company and they'd be lucky to have him. No, the time has come to stop—for me, anyway. Once you're licensed you can still fly.'

'But I want to fly with *you*.'

Billie's eyes are so green, so gentle.

'No, Pete.'

16. Eliza: Golden Charlotte

After Jack leaves me I stay in bed crying. I can't stop. When I'm up I sit curled on the sofa, watching the clouds through the window, wondering what they look like where Jack is. Where he is without me. I try to read but nothing makes sense. My grandparents and the psychiatrist say time will ease the pain but I don't believe them.

Of course I've given up my job as Izabel's assistant—I couldn't bear to be in her world now. She takes on a series of harassed young women instead, necessary because *West End Winnie* is the hit of 1931. Izabel is acclaimed a star.

One day I pick up the paper to see a photo of Jack with his arm around Joan Ferris, the girl who played Winnie's best friend. I wonder if he was romancing her at the same time as me. Perhaps it was her he went to see on the night of Roger's party. I groan and go back to my room.

In a bitter contrast to the years I could not cry, my tears well up without end. Of course they're tears for my father's death, my bitter schooldays, Gideon's cruelty too. But my heart, my poor wounded heart, had believed this love affair would lead me to a life of joy where those past sorrows would be forgotten.

I groan again, this time with shame at my naïvety. Where is brave Elias now?

Izabel knocks on the door and comes in. She sits on the side of my bed, hands me an embroidered handkerchief and shakes her head. 'You're going to have to come to grips with it eventually, darling.'

'I will, just not yet.'

'Something I thought I'd better ask,' she says. 'Did he use protection with you?'

'Protection?'

'A French letter, a sheath, you know.'

'Oh. Yes he did.'

'Thank God for that. One less thing to worry about.' She looks at me fondly. 'It happens to all of us, Eliza. I had someone like that too, my very first lover. Heavens, I'd never even kissed a man before him. You think you'll never recover but it gets better, believe me.'

'Did he leave you too?'

'In a way.' She sighs. 'He died.'

'Oh, *Izabel*, I'm so sorry!'

'At least I know he didn't want to leave me,' she says with a crooked smile.

'Was there anyone here to help you?'

'Oh, it wasn't *here*, it was in Perth. You were even at the funeral, a child of course. But that's how I learnt that losing someone can cut so very deeply.'

'But ... but I've only ever been to one funeral in Perth,' I say. 'My *stepfather*?'

'They were planning to divorce anyway, not a lot of love in that marriage.' She shrugs. 'Still, I suppose Lucy's little finger in the pie saved your mother the expense.'

'*Lucy*?'

'Lucy killed him,' says Izabel, her face hard.

I'm bewildered. 'But Gideon died of *influenza*. Lucy nursed him, she tried to save him.'

'Makes a good story, doesn't it? No, Eliza. The truth is she let him die. I don't understand why. Perhaps he rejected her and she wanted her revenge.'

'Izabel, that's simply not possible.'

'She didn't bother taking him to hospital when there was a

chance. Oh, no. She stayed with him—in a *hotel* room—and just let him die.'

'I can't believe it.'

'That's because you still think the best of people, darling. But I'll never forgive her. She destroyed my hopes of a life with Gideon.' She touches her waist. 'A life with our baby.'

'*Baby?*'

'Oh, I found out I was pregnant afterwards. Had to have an op to end it and was sick for rather a long time.' She clears her throat. 'Pretty grim all round.'

I take her hand. 'I'm so *sorry* you had to go through that, Izabel. I didn't like Gideon much, but how I wish you'd been able to marry and have your baby and be happy together.'

After a few moments she says huskily, 'Thank you, darling. I think I'll just …'

She stands and leaves. I'm glad, because I might have been tempted to tell her the horrible things Gideon did to me, and on top of everything else she's suffered that would be too cruel.

But what a *revelation*! How old were they? Gideon died at thirty-eight (he always insisted we children celebrate his birthday) and in early 1919 Izabel was—eighteen? I recalculate and it's true.

Gideon was more than twice her age, mature and experienced, and she had never even kissed a man. While not unheard of, it still shocks me.

But even more shocking, how could Izabel believe my gentle aunt Lucy had let Gideon *die*? Of course she wasn't fond of him, very few people were.

I think of the few times she spoke of him, and recall one evening at the dinner table. At the sound of his name an odd expression came over her face, one that puzzled me even then. What did it mean?

Dislike, certainly. Regret, but of course a nurse would regret losing a patient. But was there something else?

She'd looked at her husband Danny and he at her, a mutual communion. Was Danny's gaze one of sympathy?

And Lucy's, could it possibly have been—*guilt*?

Next morning I make a tray of tea and take it into the library, where I know Min-lu will be working on her accounts. She looks up at me, pleased, light glinting on her golden combs and neat glasses. 'Oh darling, how lovely.'

I sit down beside her. 'How's business going, Nanna?'

Since her days in Broome, Nanna has run a small company called Pearlshell Ltd, selling high-quality mother-of-pearl to the jewellery trade.

She takes her glasses off. I think she's pleased I'm at least pretending an interest in something apart from my broken heart.

'Rather poorly, I'm afraid, darling. This awful Depression just won't end, and the bottom is dropping out of the pearlshell market. Freddy and I are all right so far but it's a battle, and we're doing well compared to many of our friends.'

She closes her account book and looks at me a little expectantly.

I hand her a teacup. 'Nanna, there's something I want to ask you about.'

'You can ask me anything, Eliza.' I know that's true.

'Izabel told me she was once … very fond of Gideon Meade.'

Min-lu sits up straight. 'That is so, but you do not have to be euphemistic for my sake. They were lovers.'

'Did you know at the time?'

'Looking back I recall she was behaving oddly, but then that's Izabel.' She smiles. 'An actress in the making, even then.'

'She told me Lucy had simply *let* Gideon die of influenza. How could she even imagine a thing like that?'

There's a long silence then Min-lu says, 'Because it's true.'

'Nanna?'

'Eliza, Gideon was a monster. A man of substance, fine-looking, well-regarded, and a monster in his arrogance, his stupidity, his deceit. Dear God, his *deceit*.'

She twists her glasses in her fingers. 'He tried to blackmail Lucy into sleeping with him at his hotel. She could see he was sick, but he hated hospitals. He begged her to nurse him there instead, so she did. And he died.'

'Would he have died anyway in a hospital?'

'Lucy was an experienced nurse and believed he was beyond help. She sat with him to the end, as she did for many others. She wishes she'd done more, even for that creature, but I am glad, *so* glad she did not. However Lucy is kinder than me and still suffers a little, I fear.'

Nanna puts down her glasses. 'Gideon's actions led to Sam's death, and of course, now I know about his unforgivable behaviour towards you, Eliza, I am even happier he is dead.'

'But how ... how did he cause my father's *death*?'

'Sam was in Perth, booked on a steamer to Broome, but Gideon got into one of his usual stupid sordid messes and begged for help. Sam, bless his heart, stayed behind for Gideon's sake, then sailed on the next scheduled ship. That, of course, was the one lost in the cyclone.'

'Oh, *Nanna*. I had no idea!'

'It's not something we often spoke of, and never in front of you children.' She sighs. 'It's been nearly twenty years since we lost my boy, and I still think of him every day. How I wish you'd had a chance to grow up with him.'

I shake my head in amazement. 'Does Izabel know?'

'Gideon told her a pack of lies, simply a misunderstanding, no responsibility of his. Poor child, she was with him so briefly she's retained all her illusions. Had they lived a life together she'd probably loathe him by now as much as the rest of us.'

'And also, she says she was ...'

'Pregnant? Yes. But I would *not* let that fiend ruin her life from beyond the grave. I found her a sympathetic doctor. Eliza, she was barely eighteen.'

'Oh, poor *Izabel*.' I look up. 'Nanna—I thought if I told her what Gideon did to *me* it would be like letting him hurt her all over again. So I've decided I won't say anything about it.'

My grandmother gazes at me. 'Are you certain, darling? Secrets are heavy things to bear.'

'What good could it do?'

She squeezes my hand. 'That's kind of you. Sometimes I worry about Izabel—she's strong in so many ways but vulnerable too, treading rather a fine line between fantasy and reality.'

'That's true,' I say, smiling.

Nanna says, 'Well! What an interesting morning.'

'My goodness, yes. It's strange to see everything I thought I knew about my family so upended, but at least it's stopped me thinking ...'

She nods. 'Then we must find more to occupy your mind, child.' She opens her account book again. 'Perhaps you'd care to help me with this?'

I know Min-lu doesn't need the slightest assistance from anyone, but I'm good with numbers and always fascinated by her clever techniques. As we work she tells me about the deepening economic depression. What it will mean for *Inverley*? Freddy thinks the ship is safe from financial woes, but from Min-lu's words it's hard to imagine anything being safe.

And when we stop for lunch I realise with gratitude I haven't thought about Jack for hours.

Spring arrives, and the blossoms give me a faint sense of hope. One afternoon Izabel and Felix arrive at the house in a flurry of excitement. Izabel holds out her hand with a large diamond ring, and says laughing, 'Felix has asked me to *marry* him.'

'Min-lu, Freddy—only with your blessing, of course,' says Felix. 'Hope you don't mind me butting into the family circle like this.'

'Mind?' says Min-lu. 'How *wonderful*! Oh, darling—' She hugs Izabel. Freddy shakes Felix's hand and I kiss Izabel and congratulate them too. Freddy pours champagne and they're so happy my heart aches for them.

Well, for myself really.

Preparations for the wedding soon dominate our lives but I have no objection to that. I adore the distraction of silks and laces and flowers, dressmakers and milliners, services and receptions and honeymoons. I'm to be one of Izabel's bridesmaids, and the others will be women she knows from the acting world.

'Have to be sensible, darling,' she tells me. 'They'll owe me a favour and who knows how useful that might be.'

I realise Izabel doesn't have any close friends—everyone is a potential rival. But then, I don't have many women friends either—and I can hardly blame professional rivalry for that. Perhaps my unhappy schooldays suggest I'm not very good at friendship.

Izabel and I are sitting in the library one day going through the guest list, when I see a familiar name.

'Harry Bell! You're inviting Harry?'

'Felix's idea—I barely remember him, but apparently he was there when we met in Cardiff.' He eyes narrow dreamily. 'Of course, the only thing I could see then was Felix.' She looks at me. 'It's all right isn't it, he's not some uncouth sailor?'

'No, Harry's a doctor, a medical researcher. It'll be lovely to see him again.'

'Marvellous,' she says, lighting a cigarette. 'Eliza, there's something else I need to talk to you about. You do understand, this wedding isn't just about Felix and me. I have to think ahead, think about what might be useful for my career.'

I smile, familiar now with Izabel's brutally pragmatic streak.

She glances at me. 'I need to invite someone to the wedding you may not wish to see—'

I don't understand for a moment, then say, 'You can't mean— Izabel, *no!*'

'Jack's my co-star and our agents are already in talks about a big movie. We've got *it*, darling, people love seeing us together. So I must have him there for the publicity.'

'But what about *me?*'

'You'll just have to buck up, Eliza. You can't keep wafting around the place forever like some Victorian wraith.'

I say bitterly, 'How long did it take you to stop wafting around after Gideon died, Izabel?'

She blinks. 'Years, but I put on a brave face. As must you.'

'I can't. I *won't.*' I leave the room.

Izabel gets her way of course, she always does. She says how *jealous* Jack will be to see me looking so glamorous. She'll pair me with a *gorgeous* groomsman. I'll be so busy helping her I won't have to talk to him—indeed, I won't even see him for the seething *multitude* of guests.

She wears me down. We both know how much I want to show him how wrong he was to discard me. How beautiful I am, how far out of his reach I am.

How I do not mourn him for even a moment.

The dresses, oh God, the *dresses*. Izabel's is ivory silk charmeuse that flows like quicksilver over every curve of her body and pools in ripples at her feet. The bridesmaid's dresses are equally exquisite, in the palest coral silk like the interior of a seashell, a shade that suits me to perfection.

The wedding will be held on a summer afternoon at Salisbury Cathedral and Felix's parents have a country house nearby where our wedding party will stay.

As Izabel's 'Gypsy' mother is supposedly deceased, Min-lu and Freddy have been invited simply as family friends.

On the great day I'm helping Min-lu with her dress, a sapphire blue gown with a complicated row of tiny buttons up the back.

'Does it ever hurt, Nanna, the way Izabel denies you?' I ask, doing up the last of the buttons. 'How she pretends you're not really her mother?'

'It used to, but not now.' She adjusts the gold combs in her charcoal grey hair and gazes back at me from the mirror. 'It's sad. Izabel never knew my brave parents and has no heritage, poor child.' Nanna turns, smiling. 'But oh, how happy I am she's reached contentment at last. So let us enjoy this lovely day, my darling.'

I go to my room to bathe and dress. Well, undress, really. The fluid fabric of the gowns demands we wear no underclothing other than feather-light chiffon knickers. They're wide-legged, open to caresses, and I shiver with pleasure putting them on.

An image of Jack flashes into my mind, smiling, slowly removing my panties, kissing my thighs, going higher and sweeter and deeper and *between*.

Oh, you bastard, I don't want to remember you anymore! I want someone to make me forget. Someone like Angus, the groomsman who's been paired with me, a Scot, auburn and broad-shouldered, with a ready grin and wicked eyes.

We met at dinner last night and he's certainly as gorgeous as Izabel promised. As the silk dress slithers over my shoulders and caresses my breasts and ripples to the floor, I think, oh yes, *please*.

I ring for Penfold. She does my make-up and fixes a cluster of perfumed gardenias to one side of my hair, brushed into glossy dark waves falling below my shoulders.

'You look like a princess, Miss, a princess.'

'Oh, Penfold—it's your doing really. Now, I'd better run and see how Izabel's going.'

Disciplined by years of wardrobe and make-up sessions, Izabel is going surprisingly well, sipping a glass of champagne as a hairdresser fits her veil. The other bridesmaids are laughing and chatting and smoking. I don't know any of them very well so I just sit and wait.

Izabel catches my eye in the mirror and winks. What *fun*.

The cathedral is beautiful, with elegant arches and glowing stained glass. Sheaves of flowers—roses, lilies, orange blossoms—perfume the air like incense. As I follow Izabel down the aisle to the chords of the Wedding March, I glance around quickly, but no sign of Jack.

Rupert Grimstone is giving Izabel away. How appropriate, she said, my agent's *always* keen to give me away, especially when there's a lousy contract in the offing. Still, she smiles at him adoringly and most guests have no idea that the tall, distinguished man is not a relative.

My job is to concentrate on Izabel, her veil, her train, her bouquet: but her heartfelt vows to Felix almost bring me to tears. Felix himself looks dashing, his blue eyes fierce with emotion, and I hope they'll always love each other as they do today.

We pose for photographers outside the cathedral, then in a hail of rice climb into the cars. As we drive back to the country house my attractive groomsman partner, Angus, proves to be delightful company. The newlyweds mingle with the guests in the gardens, kissing, chatting and drinking, while dinner is being set up in the grand hall.

Angus goes inside to help sort out arrangements and, gazing around, I see Harry Bell's fair hair through the crowd. I catch his eye and wave. He comes towards me, a woman with him, and we lightly hug. I'm surprised at how pleased I am to see his thoughtful face.

'My goodness, Harry, you've bought *another* tie. When will this mad extravagance ever end?'

'Ah, but I had to—the moths ate the old one. Eliza, let me introduce Charlotte Fischer.'

Interesting. Is this the same Charlotte he mentioned on *Inverley*, the woman who ran through all his money and left him? She's a pretty blonde in a blue dress, the colour of her amused eyes, and for some reason I like her immediately.

'It's wonderful to meet you, Eliza!' she says. 'I've heard so much about the voyage and Elias the brave deckboy—but you're such a dear little thing. I thought you were ten feet tall with enormous muscles. Harry, you've quite deceived me!'

'But that's how I always think of her,' says Harry mildly. 'You're looking well, I must say.'

'Oh, you too,' I say. 'How's research going? Still microscopes?'

'Still microscopes, or interesting things we see in microscopes.'

'It's a miracle I was even able to drag him away from the lab for this wedding,' says Charlotte. 'I had to rip the white coat off him in the car.'

A waiter brings us champagne and we chat happily. Charlotte seems fun and Harry is in high spirits. Charlotte particularly admires the wedding gowns, and I tell her about Izabel's dress, cut by a master couturier and taking half a dozen seamstresses four months to sew.

'My God, it's so magnificent I'd believe that too,' she says. 'And silk satin, I think? But, oh dear, we mustn't bore Harry with his girlish nonsense.'

'I admire any fine craftsmanship,' Harry says. 'And sewing isn't always women's work—Eliza knows how much I respected our sailmaker, Mr Hendriksson.'

'What a lovely man he was!' I say. 'Once he told me how a friend of his sewed a new mainsail in just two weeks and said, "You know how big is that, *hey*? T'ree *t'ousand* square feet. In fourteen days. Im-*possible*."'

'That's him exactly,' says Harry, laughing. 'You learnt something after all in the sail locker.'

'Just *something*? How unkind of you, Harry. I learnt so much! Round stitch, flat stitch, herringbone, leech ropes, cringles and grommets. And I've still got the calluses to prove it.'

Charlotte smiles. 'I can't even *imagine* sewing things on such a scale. I spend all my time drumming languages into the minds of bored young ladies and that's hard enough.'

'Are you a teacher, Charlotte?' I ask.

'Part-time, at a horribly posh school. Drives my father crazy.'

'Heavens, why?'

'He's a socialist philosopher—rather famous, Harry tells me.' She gazes teasingly at him. 'When we met, Harry thought I was a socialist too, and tried to impress me with good works. Luckily for him I'm awfully shallow.'

Harry smiles but I remember his pained words about his 'Bolshevik quest.' I change the topic, complimenting Charlotte on her gold brooch, a silhouette of a galloping horse.

'My favourite piece,' she says, touching it. 'I *adore* horse racing, it's simply thrilling.'

Just then a woman passes and waves at her.

'Heavens, there's someone I know and I *do* need to catch up,' says Charlotte. 'But Eliza, I've so enjoyed chatting. Would you care to meet for afternoon tea one day, the Dorchester, perhaps?'

'Of course,' I say, pleased. 'Harry, do you have a piece of paper?'

I tell him our telephone number and he jots it down.

'I'll be back in a minute—' Charlotte says, and disappears into the crowd.

17. Harry: Desire

Eliza turns to me, a rather nice scent wafting from the flowers in her dark hair.

'What a lovely woman,' she says. 'Far too good for the likes of you. So is *that* the Charlotte you mentioned on the ship? How did you get back together again?'

I nod. 'I'll tell you all about it one day. She's rather … persuasive.'

'And you enjoyed being persuaded, I suspect.'

I smile. 'Afraid so. But it's going well the second time around, I think.'

'I'm glad for you.' We're quiet for a moment then Eliza says, 'And do you ever hear of anyone from *Inverley*? It seems a lifetime away now.'

'Well, Niilo's become third mate on *Olivebank*.'

'Third on *Olivebank*? Good on him.'

Eliza says it the way the Ålanders do, *Oh-leever-bahnk*. I love the sound of it.

'And Artur?' she asks.

'Still on *Inverley* and studying for his ticket.'

'How on earth do you know all this?'

'I've kept in touch with Maria Nilsen—we write every now and then.'

'Oh,' Eliza says. 'Last Christmas she sent me a card but I was feeling … low, and didn't reply. But now I certainly shall. Is she well?'

'Better than on the voyage, but not fully recovered yet.'

'I *do* feel such a beast for not replying, Harry. Maria was so good to me.'

'That's not like you. You must have been low indeed.'

'I was. A man, of course,' Eliza says lightly.

'Not surprising. It's usually men—or women—take us to our unhappiest moments.'

She laughs, 'Heavens, isn't that true—' She stops, shocked.

'Eliza, *honey*,' says a bloke in a flashy suit. 'How're you *doing*? My gosh, you looked so pretty in the church. Some smart fella's going to get you up in front of the altar any day now.'

I think she's going to faint. I want to hit the loud-mouthed bastard, but he shoves his hand at me and somehow the polite response takes over. 'Jack Brandon, at your service, sir,' he says with what he imagines is charm.

'Harry Bell.'

'And you're Eliza's new beau? Great girl, eh?'

Eliza is trembling. I realise her irises are dilated with—what— fear? Desire? Is this the man who brought her so 'low'?

'No, Harry's a friend from *Inverley*,' she says, her voice steady.

'*Inverley*? My gosh,' Brandon says. 'I was on a four-master too. Starboard watch on *l'Avenir*.'

'You told me it was the port watch,' says Eliza. 'On *Lawhill*.'

'That sense of humour of yours, honey, just *slays* me.' He smirks confidingly. 'The two of us've been best buddies since *West End Winnie*.'

Eliza winces slightly and I remain deliberately unimpressed.

'You know,' he says. 'The big box-office hit. I played the lead.'

'Izabel played the lead,' says Eliza. 'Not you.'

Brandon smiles a little uncertainly. 'Hey, look, here's someone else you know from the film. You remember *Joan*, don't you?'

A woman with too much make-up simpers, 'Of *course* she remembers me.'

Eliza says nothing but sways and I ready myself to catch her.

Joan says, 'And you wouldn't *believe* it, Jack was so touched by that romantic ceremony he's just *proposed*! Look!' she says with a squeal, holding out her hand wearing a showy ring.

Oh Christ, I've got to get her away from these absolute shits right now. But Eliza stands very straight and says, 'I must go.'

Her eyes flash to me and I see her anguish, her desperation, her rage. 'Another time,' she says and turns and leaves.

Jack Brandon stares after her like a spoilt child losing a toy.

'*Well*. That's not very polite,' says Joan. 'So, Harry, did you enjoy the wedding?'

'Until a moment ago,' I say and walk away.

I can see Eliza moving through the crowd ahead of me but can't catch up. Then she reaches a big auburn-haired fellow, a groomsman, puts her hand on his arm and whispers in his ear. He looks at her, pleased and surprised. She walks away without a glance and he follows her.

I see them go inside the house. I stop, uncertain. From his expression I know perfectly well what she said to him and if a woman said that to me I'd follow her too.

Young Eliza has grown up. Still, it's none of my business.

A waiter goes by and I grab another drink. I wonder where Charlotte is. I feel a bit concerned at the thought of her having tea with Eliza. Charlotte's so ... plausible.

So who *was* that bastard? An actor he says, but he's surprisingly short. I'd actually heard of *West End Winnie*—Charlotte saw it and raved about the stars—so when I got an invitation to the marriage of Felix Malory to the amazing Izabel Peres there was no getting out of it.

I must say I was surprised to get that invitation from Felix. On the ship at first we rubbed each other up the wrong way, but over time, and as long as we stayed off politics, we got on well enough. Still, I'd never have expected him to invite me to his wedding.

But perhaps he doesn't have many other friends. Felix is so ambitious under the smoothness and so insecure beneath the class privilege, it probably doesn't inspire closeness.

And then there's the neurasthenia, the shellshock. How much

does the lovely Izabel know? Does she have the faintest idea there's no real healing of such wounds?

Even Eliza, who's been on the sharp end of his vicious tongue, probably doesn't suspect how deep it runs. I expect she thinks it all went away when he reached land, back in his own familiar world.

Unlikely. Felix is a good-looking, well-educated, highly-respected man, and he has nothing but fear at his core.

Some time later we're summoned to the wedding dinner. I look around for Charlotte but still can't see her. Then Eliza appears. Her shimmering gown has creases, her irises are dilated, her lips are swollen and she smiles like someone drugged.

I recognise the look: I know myself what it is to put up with almost anything to find that sweet annihilation again.

'You should take your seat, Harry,' she says, her voice distant. 'The entrées are arriving.'

'Eliza, are you all *right*?' I say helplessly.

She's silent, her head bowed. I gaze at her cloud of dark hair with its cluster of white flowers. They're fixed to a comb, a little askew, and without thinking I ease it gently back into place.

'I try, Harry,' she whispers. 'I really do try, but I can't quite get my bearings.'

'Heading for a lee shore, perhaps?'

'Getting off one, I hope—but oh, it's such a bitter beat against the wind.' Eliza smiles wryly. 'You know, we're probably the only people here who understand how hard that is.'

'But wasn't that stupid Yank in the starboard watch?' I say. 'On *l'Avenir*, no less.'

'Really? And there was me fancying it was the port watch on *Lawhill*.'

We gaze deadpan at each other, then start laughing.

After a time she takes a deep breath. 'Heavens, we'd better go in.' She gazes at me and I can see a glint of tears. 'I'm so terribly glad you came, Harry.'

'I'm glad I came too, despite my dashed plans for a day with some glass slides.'

'Glass slides now—not microscopes?'

'Ah, going up in the world, you see.'

She's silent for a moment then says, 'Will you dance with me later, *matros*?'

'I've got two left feet, *jungman*, but I'll do my best.'

Two weeks later Charlotte drops by my flat after taking tea with Eliza at the Dorchester. I'd been concentrating on some rather interesting results on avian *Plasmodium* life cycles, but Charlotte flings her arms around my neck and kisses me.

'Lab-coat man,' she murmurs.

'Mmm, you smell good.'

'That's all the dear little cakes I've been eating, not my perfume.'

'You'd make a million if you bottled—' I stop because she's kissing me again. Things take their inevitable course and we end up in bed. I think fleetingly, don't forget that reference to the reticuloendothelial system, then think no more.

Afterwards I get up and make us both a cup of tea and bring it back to bed. This is always my favourite time with her, when she's relaxed and free of her demons.

'So how was your afternoon?' I ask.

Charlotte curls against my thigh as I lean back on the pillow. 'What a sweetie that girl is. She makes me feel terribly maternal, as if she needs protecting.'

'There was a chap at the other end of Eliza's knife once who wouldn't have said that.'

She laughs. 'You know what I mean, you awful pedant.'

She rolls onto her back and stretches. I lean down and kiss her shoulder, my face buried in her soft fair hair. Her scent of sweat and sex is like a drug, and I fleetingly recall Eliza's face at the wedding, flushed with desire.

'It's Saturday tomorrow,' Charlotte says casually. 'Might pop over to Ascot for a flutter.'

Oh God. I sit up on one elbow and stare at her innocent expression.

'Darling,' I say, 'You can't afford it.'

'Oh, Papa's given me a little cash. For my birthday.'

'But you already owe the bookie—'

'Papa took care of that,' she says coolly. 'It was peanuts.'

'Charlotte, it was two hundred *pounds*. You can't just throw money away. My God, that's more than my annual stipend.'

'Well, you'd be richer if you took a real job, not *research*. You could work in Harley Street if you wanted. My friend's husband there makes thousands of pounds a year.'

'But you knew perfectly well I was planning a career in research when we met again,' I say, one arm over my eyes. I don't want to do this anymore.

'I simply couldn't resist you, darling. I had to come back.'

To my surprise that's true. Charlotte feels desire for me in a way that we both find quite mysterious. Sadly, out of bed, she finds me as dull as ditchwater. She's younger, twenty-two to my twenty-nine, so I suppose it's no surprise she wants more excitement than I can provide.

I sigh. 'I just don't know, Charlotte. Perhaps—perhaps we shouldn't have started again. Should have learnt our lesson first time around—'

She's silent and I hear a change in her breathing. She throws back the bedcovers and stands, naked, and even from the depths of our quarrel I think, Christ she's magnificent, the sway of her breasts, the narrow waist, the supple hips.

She opens her handbag and throws an envelope onto the bed. '*There*. The money Papa gave me. I won't gamble it, Harry, I promise.'

She's said that so often before. Along with all the times she's said she hasn't been drinking when she can hardly keep herself upright. I like a drink myself, but not that way.

'Charlotte,' I say, feeling hopeless. 'I know you get bored and restless, but you've got your job, you love films, theatre. I just don't understand why you're so *unhappy.*'

She sits on the bed. 'Not unhappy, Harry, truly, it's more I'm *anxious.* I can't help it, especially when my bloody mother starts going on about my godless ways. It only eases when I'm risking everything on a bet—and oh, the thrill of it when I win!'

'But isn't that sort of thing ... unusual in a woman?'

She shakes her head. 'Plenty of other women gamble. I know, I meet them at the track.'

'Perhaps a psychiatrist might be able to help?'

'Funny you mention that. Little Eliza's been seeing one of those.'

'Whatever for?'

'She didn't go into details—man trouble, I gather. But she says he helped her. Perhaps *that's* what I should do.'

'Well, you've got the money your father gave you—'

'What a marvellous idea, darling. Yes I will, I'll go and see someone.'

She puts the envelope back in her handbag, gets under the bedclothes again and nestles against me. I close my eyes in relief.

'Harry,' she whispers. 'There's something I need to tell you.'

I can feel her head move as she gazes at me and I open my eyes again.

'Actually, I've been so anxious for a reason.' She takes a breath. 'I'm ... well. Harry, I'm going to have a baby.'

I feel a rush of amazement and delight. 'A *baby*? Charlotte, *really*? Are you sure? My God, that's marvellous!'

'But aren't you angry with me?'

'Angry? About a *baby*?' I kiss her. 'Oh, love.'

'I'm sorry I've been so difficult, Harry. I've been worried, you see.'

'Worried? But that's *wonderful* news!' Joy lights up my whole being—nothing matters, nothing compared to this, and I laugh aloud. 'But you do realise, my darling, we'll have to get ourselves hitched as soon as possible.'

She smiles slowly. 'Are you asking?'

'Damned right I am.'

'Very well. I'm accepting.'

Two weeks later we marry at the Registry Office. It isn't a large affair—Charlotte's parents (her mother sour-faced), some friends and workmates, and Eliza and her boyfriend Angus, the groomsman from the wedding. I'd have asked Felix and Izabel too, but they're still away on their wedding cruise.

We have lunch at a pub afterwards and it turns into a pleasantly riotous afternoon. That evening Charlotte and I take the train to Brighton for a honeymoon at a sea-front hotel.

Autumn is coming on, but it's fun getting rugged up against the wind and walking along the beach laughing at absurd names for our baby. We eat fish and chips out of newspaper, and visit antique shops and browse the second-hand books. Charlotte hardly drinks at all too, which is a relief.

We return to London refreshed and happy. We go looking for a larger flat and find a place in Bayswater, grubby but with good-sized rooms and big windows. We scrub and repaint and shop for second-hand furniture, and after a few weeks of labour our place is more than comfortable.

Sometimes I worry about Charlotte's anxiety coming back, and wonder if it was all my fault because of our long, uncertain courtship.

But she's probably right when she ascribes it to her difficult mother. The day we showed her parents the new flat, Otto laughed and said it reminded him of his youth in Vienna, but Ilse sneered, her face ugly with disapproval.

Charlotte became very quiet, then after losing an absurd sum at the track (I later discovered) she returned to her sunny self. The poor woman swings painfully between her pious mother's *hausfrau* demands and her father's free-thinking beliefs. I know Ilse refused to speak to her for months when she took her teaching job, while her father—unwisely—keeps on bailing her out of her financial messes.

I've known Otto, a bearded academic, for years. At the wedding he said, 'Harry, we almost lost her at birth. Ilse nearly died too and she has always found it difficult ... well, she is too strict with my darling girl, while I fear I am not strict enough. But I trust you, as a son, to to care for her now.'

For myself I love Otto as a father, and I told him I'd do anything to make Charlotte happy.

Now, coming home in the dusk, I sometimes pause outside our flat and gaze at the glow of the lamps and firelight through the curtains. I feel as if Charlotte and I have found the safe harbour we both so desperately needed, and I damn myself for a fool for not asking her to marry me years ago.

18. Eliza: The Ruby Ring

My brother Pete writes me ecstatic letters about his new flying life and I'm charmed to read about his instructor, a girl I remember well from school. Billie Quinn was a byword for insolence, sarcasm and disobedience. I admired her, but she terrified me.

As thin as me but a head taller, Billie was sophisticated and scowling under a mop of red hair. Half the girls loathed her, the rest had crushes. In her final year she was expelled for truancy, but I heard whispers too of some saucy misdeed.

Then just after Izabel's wedding, Pete writes to tell me his heroine has closed her business down. He got his licence before the end but that doesn't seem to comfort him much.

> *Billie's moved and I don't know how to contact her. So I just keep on at uni—the only good thing is my project, the little plane we designed. This year'll soon be over but don't know what I'll do then. Maybe I'll come and visit you, I'm fed up to the back teeth here.*

Poor old Pete. I write back saying it's all a matter of time. After Izabel's wedding I'm so much happier—seeing Jack Brandon with new eyes was such a release. I now spend my time with Angus, the groomsman, enjoying theatre and parties and bed together. I tell him I don't want to take it seriously, but gradually realise he does. That isn't my concern I decide, he's an adult.

Another source of happiness is my growing friendship with Charlotte. I went to her small wedding with Harry Bell, and afterwards in the pub, Harry, his lean, clever face so happy, sat with his arm around her.

Just before they left to catch the train for their honeymoon I noticed Harry gently touch her belly as they smiled at each other. Ah, that's why the wedding happened so quickly. But how lovely for them. He'll make a wonderful father.

One night on *Inverley* Harry and I had been chatting about families, and he said he hoped one day to have lots of children. I said that sounded like my idea of hell. 'No kids, no husband, and neither just for the sake of it.'

He said, 'Ah, *jungman*. You'll have to become a *kapten* one day.'

'What on earth does that Delphic prophecy mean?'

He grinned. 'Not the faintest idea, but it sounded profound, didn't it? Perhaps—we all have to grow older, take responsibility for others, and it's usually via husbands, wives, children.'

'Well, we'll see about that, *matros*.'

It's Christmas Eve and I'm curled on a settee before the fire, sipping a brandy. Angus is away visiting family but I don't mind. Lately I'm starting to feel a little stifled when we're together.

'This is my third Christmas here,' I say to my grandparents. 'I can hardly believe it—two and a half years in London.'

'Do you miss Australia, darling?' asks Min-lu.

'A little, but I'd like to see something of Europe first. In fact, there *is* one place I'd love to go—the Åland Islands. Maria's often invited me to stay with them.' (Maria Nilsen and I write to each other regularly now.)

'Too infernally cold at the moment,' says Freddy wryly. 'Knew a chap who touched a ship's rail in winter in Mariehamn and left a chunk of his hand behind.'

'Goodness. Have you ever been there, Granddad?'

'No, but I've always wanted to go. In fact I've started to suspect some of my fellow *Inverley* shareholders haven't been very forthcoming regarding certain expenses, so it might be worth a visit when it's warmer.'

'The Baltic in summer?' says Min-lu. 'Sounds lovely.'

'As it happens, Eliza,' says Freddy, 'I seem to have too many irons in the fire at the moment, and need someone to help me manage my ownership of *Inverley*. It's not a large job but needs a close eye on the details. I don't suppose you'd care to give me a hand with it, my dear?'

'Of course I would!'

'You'd learn rather a lot,' says Min-lu. 'It could come in handy for your own future.'

'Heavens, you had this all planned out, didn't you, Nanna?'

She smiles.

Early in the new year of 1932 I meet Charlotte for tea at the Dorchester, as we often do. She's flushed and happy, her blonde hair set off by the prettiest little hat. It's been three months since her wedding and I'm happily anticipating the announcement of her pregnancy any day.

I enjoy Charlotte's company so much. We don't chat about anything profound but it's lovely to be understood by a woman close to my own age. I'm actually a year or two older, but in my eyes she's the more mature.

For a start she's married, which seems terribly grown-up even if it is only to my old shipmate Harry. And she was raised in a house of politics and philosophy, a haven for refugees from European revolutions and counter-revolutions. To me it sounds intriguingly sophisticated, but Charlotte says her mother was an evil-tempered scold and she's glad to be out of it.

Despite that I think she's still dependent on her father's financial support. Harry's income in his research post is minimal and, although she still has her teaching job, Charlotte often mentions money worries. I know she has an odd fondness for betting on horse races, but can't imagine that being an expensive hobby.

I sometimes feel a little guilty, as I'm supported by my relatives and have my own small income from my father's estate, so now and then I buy Charlotte perfume or an elegant dress or a small piece of jewellery she admires.

I'll often buy us a bottle of good champagne too because I know how much she likes it. Of course I like it too, but not as much as Charlotte does. Sometimes we even get into a second bottle, though usually she has to finish it. It never seems to affect her.

Today I say teasingly (we're on the second bottle), 'You'll have to cut back a bit on the old bubbly when—you know—'

'Know what?' she asks, laughing.

'Oh, *Charlotte*. The baby, of course.'

'What makes you think I'm having a baby?'

'I thought—oh, I'm sorry, darling,' I say, flustered. 'I had the impression from your wedding day you might have been in a bit of a hurry, that's all.'

She gurgles in delight. 'You are *so* perceptive, sweetie. Actually, I did tell Harry I was expecting—he needed a bit of a prod to get around to popping the question. Later I said it was just a false alarm. In fact, I find the limitations of motherhood rather daunting, so I'm doing my best to avoid it for now.'

'Oh. But how does Harry feel about that?'

She shrugs. 'He says he'll do anything to make me happy.'

She empties her glass and waves at the waiter to refill it. When he's gone she says, '*Mutti* will be pleased, though. She thinks any woman who's pregnant has announced to the world she's a whore. And if it's outside the bounds of holy matrimony—well, you'd think Satan and his minions had manifested before her.'

'Heavens. That's rather extreme in this day and age.'

Charlotte's mobile face is still as she gazes unseeing. '*Mutti* used to beat me with a cane when I was little, and call me names. She can't beat me now, but still the names … I thought if I were married she'd stop, but she never does.'

She laughs. 'But what do I care? Give me enough champers and horses and I don't give a damn what she thinks.'

'Charlotte, I'm so sorry. I could see at your wedding she was—disapproving—but I had no idea she was that unkind to you.'

She shrugs, then sits forward. 'Eliza, sweetie, don't think I haven't noticed what an absolute angel you are to me, always. I wanted to give you something to say thank you.'

'But I love buying little things—'

She shakes her head and says, 'I *insist*,' and hands me a small box. I open it and see an antique ring, with a small glowing ruby set in filigreed gold.

'Oh, that's just *beautiful*. How kind of you, Charlotte!' I slip it on my middle finger, where it fits perfectly.

'It was my darling grandmother's, so it's very special to me,' she says. 'And one day when Harry's got a real job, I'll buy *you* lots of champagne and we'll pick all the winners and get simply blotto!'

She laughs and spills a little of her drink. 'Silly old me.'

With her clever blue eyes and wry, generous mouth, Charlotte is such a delight to know. How lucky I am to have such a friend.

Harry lands that 'real job' at last, a promotion with a handsome pay increase, and he and Charlotte hold a small party at their flat to celebrate.

That evening I go alone. Angus and I have finally parted ways. We'd come close to it before but this time I was adamant. I would not marry him. He said he hoped I'd die an old maid. I said I already was an old maid, being all of twenty-four. He said I could hardly claim to be a maid due to my whorish behaviour. And so on.

Now I feel relief, and a little regret too. But I don't love him. I tell myself it's the right thing to do and the right time to do it, and sigh.

Still, spring has arrived, and I walk beneath the ruffled blossoms in Hyde Park to Harry and Charlotte's place, welcoming in the lamplight. I don't know the other guests and as Charlotte passes around the drinks she murmurs, 'Sorry, it's a collection of crashing *bores* from Harry's institute.'

But I don't find them boring at all. They chat about theatre and music and books, and a female scientist tells me about her recent thrilling expedition to the Amazon. Several of the professors have their own amusing tales of travel in odd parts of the world, and when I mention my approaching Ålands trip, two say they've been to Finland and love the place.

I notice Charlotte is gazing at the fire, left out of the conversation, so I move to sit beside her and say, 'How's your new life as a lady of leisure?'

'Well, it was certainly fun seeing the headmaster's face when I simply walked out on the school.' She takes a drink and sighs. 'But things are a little dull without work—and sweetie, I doubt you ever imagined you'd hear me say *that*! Harry's always so busy in his silly laboratory, and he's just getting more boring by the day. Perhaps I'll take up flower-arranging.'

We laugh and I help her hand around trays of canapés.

Later in the evening, someone asks Harry about his grain ship voyages and he calls me into the conversation. It's good to talk over old times, although I'm a little surprised when asked about the presence of *Anopheles* on four-masters (they turn out to be mosquitoes). By then we've all drunk enough for that to seem a simply hilarious idea.

Then one man gets a far-away expression and says, 'But as an infection vector for *P. falciparum* that's not actually implausible …' and wanders away to murmur to someone else, their heads bent over a note pad on which they take turns busily scribbling diagrams.

Harry nudges me and says, 'You realise the one on the left's a Nobel Prize winner? You may have started something big.'

Charlotte smiles. 'Look, darling, it's been hours and it's time to start winding up. I've got a bit of a headache and want to go to bed. Let's do the coffee now.'

'I can give Harry a hand,' I say. 'You go and rest, Charlotte.'

'Oh, you absolute *angel*.' She disappears upstairs.

'Right,' says Harry as I follow him into the kitchen. 'Cups and saucers are over in that cupboard. We'll need a few biscuits too, professors always have sweet tooths. Or is it teeth?'

'Sweet teeth? Doesn't sound right.'

He fills the kettle and sets it on the stove, and we sit at the table waiting for it to boil.

'What a lovely night,' I say. 'Such interesting people.'

'I think so too,' he says. 'Though they're pretty cut-throat in funding meetings.'

'Even the nice lady scientist?'

'*Especially* the nice lady scientist.'

I laugh, then say, 'There's something I wanted to ask you about, *matros*, something medical. Remember the influenza epidemic thirteen years ago?'

'Of course. I was just seventeen and a good friend died. A dreadful time.'

'I wanted to know, Harry—if patients were nursed at home rather than at a hospital, did it make any difference to their survival?'

'Interesting question.' He thinks for a moment. 'Well, today we know the flu is caused by a virus, but they didn't know that then, so they tried all sorts of odd remedies. In the end only bed-rest and nursing care helped—a little—but patients didn't need hospitals for that. So no, I don't think it made any real difference.'

'Ah.'

He looks at me. 'Ah?'

'Well—I know someone who feels guilty, because someone else had the flu but she didn't send him to hospital and then he died.'

'Eliza?' His eyes are concerned. 'Not you?'

'Oh no. My aunt, a nurse—and it was my stepfather who died.'

'I remember on *Inverley* you mentioned disliking someone, and I hear that note in your voice again. The aunt or the stepfather?'

'The stepfather,' I say. 'I adore the aunt, and she's been worried for years because she didn't force him to go to hospital.'

'Then she should stop worrying this very minute, *jungman*.'

'Good,' I say with relief and tuck a lock of hair behind my ear.

Harry smiles. 'That's a nice ring. Charlotte's got one just like it.'

'Beautiful, isn't it?' I hold out my hand to admire the ruby. 'In fact, this *is* Charlotte's ring, she gave it to me. I was so touched, it used to belong to her grandmother.'

'Actually,' he says slowly, 'the ring belonged to *my* grandmother. I gave it to Charlotte.'

'Oh, I must have misunderstood,' I say, puzzled. 'Here, take it back.'

I tug at the ring but Harry stops my hand. 'Please—no. I'd rather you had it, Eliza. My granny was dark-haired too and it suits you.'

'But it was a gift to your *wife*.'

He shakes his head. 'Keep it.' He smiles briefly. 'I know—if I ever have a daughter you can give it to her instead.'

'That's a lovely thought but I can't possibly—'

He takes a breath. 'If it goes back to Charlotte she'll just pawn it.'

'*Pawn* it?'

'Yes. She's taken to pawning her jewellery lately.'

'Oh, God. Are your finances that bad?'

'No, our finances are excellent,' says Harry. 'I just won't let Charlotte gamble away our savings, but she has to pay the bookies somehow. Her father's given her thousands of pounds and I have too, but it's not enough.'

He rubs his face. 'Christ, it's *never* enough. I'm at my wit's end. It's a terrible sickness, but no one has the faintest idea how to treat it.'

'I'm so sorry, Harry. I knew she liked betting, but had no idea it was such a problem.'

He sighs. 'I'd hoped marriage would give her some stability but she's still so anxious, especially about that monstrous mother of hers. But you've been good to her, Eliza—I can't tell you how grateful I am.'

'She's my friend.'

'You've given her things too, haven't you? She showed me a diamond brooch once.'

'Only *little* diamonds. Nothing, really.' (Now I realise why she never wears it.)

There's a pause and Harry gazes at me. 'This may seem disloyal, but … please don't believe everything Charlotte says.'

I glance at the ruby ring, then the kettle boils and we busy ourselves making coffee. Just before we take it to the guests I say, 'I'll do anything I can to help her, you know. I love her.'

Harry shrugs helplessly. 'Me, too.'

A few weeks later I'm in Freddy's office going through a folder marked *Miscellaneous Investments*. Inside are documents about a company called Air Service Training, based somewhere I've never heard of. 'Where's Hamble?' I say. 'Funny name.'

Freddy looks up. 'Near Southampton. Air Service Training have an aviation school at the airfield. They teach flying, navigation, wireless and engineering. I think they have a future.' He absently rubs his moustache. 'In fact, more of a future than any of us might prefer.'

'Granddad?'

'Darling, the German economy is collapsing and a gang of thugs calling themselves National Socialists have taken over.

They plan to re-arm and make no secret of their territorial ambitions.' He sighs. 'It's as if the Germans learnt *nothing* from the Great War. Sometimes I fear they're even mad enough to start another.'

'Oh?' I say faintly.

Freddy looks at me suddenly. 'But many things would stop that happening. Please don't worry, dear child. Just the forebodings of an old man who's seen too much conflict over the years.'

He seems so concerned I jump up and go around the desk and hug him. 'It's all right, Granddad. It can't possibly happen again. Look how we all banded together and stopped them in the Great War.'

'Took rather a time, darling, and exacted a dreadful toll. I hope —' Freddy shakes his head. 'Lord, I'm a fool, of course it can't happen again. Now, young lady, have a read through that file and tell me if you think those Air Service Training wallahs are worth the investment.'

'I know who'd have a very good idea,' I say. 'My brother Pete.'

'Excellent!' he says. 'Please send him copies of the documents, and ask whether he thinks they're on the right track. Well done, my dear.'

A little later he hands me a paper. 'Here's something for you to file with the *Inverley* records. The account from my share of her purchase in 1922.'

'Only a thousand pounds, Granddad? I know barques were going cheap after the war, but that's ridiculous. And she's made such fine profits over the years.'

Freddy nods. '*Inverley*'s been good to us all. Who'd have thought those obsolete barques would get a new lease of life in the bulk trade?'

He smiles slowly. 'But did you know, my dear, foreigners like me aren't allowed to buy into Finnish ships?'

'Then how did you manage to get hold of a share?'

'Our old friend Captain Nilsen quietly sold me some of his holding. The other investors didn't like it, but they have their own creative practices to hide and could say nothing. You'll see for yourself how they cope when we visit the Ålands. I'm certainly looking forward to it.'

'To the trip or how the other investors cope?'

Freddy chuckles. 'Both, dear child. Both.'

Summer 1932 arrives and we prepare for the Ålands. Freddy takes me to the offices of Clarksons shipping agents to meet his broker Mr Weatherall, who looks rather like a harried bank-clerk until you notice his clever eyes. To my surprise, Freddy introduces me as his representative in all matters concerning *Inverley*, and Mr Weatherall calmly nods.

Afterwards we visit the Baltic Exchange, the famous meeting-place for merchants and brokers to barter their cargoes and vessels and knowledge: especially their knowledge.

On the great trading floor, with its marble columns and gilded lights, people gather and murmur with their heads bent over documents. Again Freddy introduces me with that puzzling formal air, as if he wants everyone—including me—to be certain of my role as his agent.

A little later I stroll to the end of the great room to see the famous lead-lights that depict the Virtues—Hope, Fortitude, Justice, Truth and Faith.

Above them is a glowing stained-glass half dome to commemorate battles of the Great War. The names take me back to my childhood: Ypres, Passchendaele, Cambrai, Gallipoli, Mézières, Arras.

I remember one night on the ship, when Felix had drunk too much and said, 'Was bloody Arras did for me, *third* damned time around. Australians did well, battle of Mont St Quentin, good show, in fact. Not much comfort to me, though. Christ, *Arras*.'

Poor Felix. Thank heavens his wounds and shellshock are behind him now. He and Izabel have bought a dazzling, glamorous flat, with round windows and chrome banisters like an ocean liner.

When Izabel showed me around it a few months ago, she opened a door to a white and gold room with a beautiful child's cot. I gasped, 'Izabel, *congratulations!*'

She laughed. 'Not so fast, darling—more in the way of hopeful anticipation. But I desperately want a baby now and so does Felix. Fingers crossed!'

Soon after she got a role in a Hollywood film, and they left for America, where her dashed-off postcards tell me they're having a wonderful time. They'll be back when we return from the Ålands and I wonder if she'll be pregnant by then with the child they want so much.

Freddy, Min-lu and I leave London on a small passenger ship in August 1932. We stay overnight in Amsterdam then sail through the North Sea. The weather is warm, the water calm and the days pass easily. I begin to feel the old sweet sense of moving with the sway of the ship.

At dinner one evening I meet Bob, one of the ship's radio officers, and flirt a little. He takes me to the radio room and introduces me to the man on duty. Bob is proudly pointing out items of equipment when a message arrives. The duty officer starts noting it down, and Bob, smiling, places another set of headphones over my ears so I can hear the dit-dah of Morse.

'Ah,' I say. 'Weather report. Tyne … Dogger southeast … veering … southwest … two or … three.'

Bob stares at me. 'How the hell?'

I laugh and hand back the headphones. 'As children my brother forced me to learn Morse with him. I didn't realise I remembered it.'

Bob looks at me oddly and when we return to the moonlit deck he doesn't take the obvious moment to kiss me. As he disappears into the distance I think, that's curious.

He wanted me earlier, when he thought I was just a silly young thing, but now it seems he finds a woman with skills, especially in his own field, rather less attractive. I shrug.

Next stop is handsome Copenhagen, then we pass a couple of easy days aboard until Stockholm, where we disembark and stay overnight at a grand hotel.

At dinner the waiter tells us the sun won't set till nearly midnight, so we linger on the terrace over coffee and chocolates throughout the long pale evening. Min-lu yawns and leaves to have a rest.

I watch her go and idly ask, 'How did you and Nanna meet?'

'Oh, I was a young fool at a Hong Kong bank, 1879. Min-lu's family were sophisticated merchants and her father had educated her as thoroughly as his sons—her English put mine to shame.' Freddy leans forward. 'Eliza, I was thunderstruck. She was nineteen and I'd never seen anyone so beautiful.' He smiles. 'And by some miracle she rather liked me too.'

'I've seen photos of you, Granddad, and I doubt you needed a miracle.' Freddy had been tall and broad-shouldered and soulfully handsome.

'We fell in love and were utterly happy. Then I heard my father was dying. He wanted me to come home and marry the Honourable Edith, a woman I'd once had an understanding with. I promised Min-lu I'd go back and end it, and return to her.' Freddy gazes at me. 'But I didn't, Eliza. I simply abandoned Min-lu like a cad. I will never forgive myself. Never.'

He cannot speak for a time and I cover his large hand with mine.

'I had no idea she was pregnant with your father and she, proud woman, refused to inform me. Such regrets child, such *regrets.*'

He takes out his handkerchief and wipes his eyes. 'I finally learnt about Sam when he was five. But Min-lu declared I was not to meet him, nor her, ever again. She wished me joy in my marriage.'

'*Joy?*' He laughs sadly. 'It turned out my wife had no fondness for men, so there was precious little joy. But I endured. Then, of course, Min-lu married Leo Peres and had Filipa and Izabel. I knew Peres slightly from Macao, a good man. I was sorry when he died.'

He sighs. 'Over the years Min-lu wrote to me of Sam's progress, his schools, his ships. I paid for his education: she allowed me that at least. She told me of his marriage, of the births of you children.' He takes a ragged breath. 'And then she told me of his death, my only son's death. The son I'd never seen.'

'Oh, *Granddad*,' I say, tears in my eyes.

He clears his throat. 'Edith died of a growth—mercifully, she was in great pain—and after a time I wrote and asked Min-lu to let me see her, and you and your brother.'

'And that's when we met you in London!'

'The instant I saw her again, how happy I was,' Freddy gazes fondly at me. 'Believe me, child, life rarely offers second chances like that. So here I am, your foolish old grandfather, fortunate beyond my wildest dreams. And if I died tomorrow it'd be with a smile on my face.'

'Granddad, don't *say* that.'

'True, though. Come on, let's take Min-lu a few of these chocolates, what do you reckon?'

Next morning we board a ferry for the Ålands, that bizarre province of six thousand tiny islands lying between Sweden and Finland. By evening we're steaming into the Western Harbour at Mariehamn, past low rocky isles and distant pine trees.

To my delight I can see seven great deepwater sailing ships around the harbour, and one of them is my dear *Inverley*.

Maria and Captain Nilsen are waiting at the wharf, both looking well. They drive us a few miles through pine and birch forests to their farmhouse. I give Maria the gift I bought her, a floral silk scarf from Liberty of London, airy as a cobweb. She drapes it around her neck and says, 'Oh, Eliza, you bring me nice scarf,' and we giggle at our old joke.

Next morning Maria shows Min-lu over the property, while Captain Nilsen drives Freddy and me into Mariehamn. It may be the home port of the last of the world's merchant sailing ships but Mariehamn is not a city—more a prosperous village sprawled across a mile-wide peninsula, with a broad esplanade connecting the Eastern and Western harbours.

We stop at the waterfront where three ships are berthed— elegant *l'Avenir*, magnificent *Herzogin Cecilie* and massive *Pamir*. Out on the harbour are *Viking, Lawhill*, and small three-masted *Killoran*. Anchored a distance away from the others is *Inverley*.

I shade my eyes and gaze. 'I wish she were closer in.'

'Ah,' Captain Nilsen says, 'but *Inverley* is not an Erikson vessel, and Gusta' makes certain it is only his vessels that get the prime moorings.'

Of course I know who Gusta' is—Gustaf Erikson, the greatest of all the Ålands shipowners. His fleet, twenty or thirty strong, comprises not only most of the four-masters, but also the three-masters, schooners and barquentines still busily engaged in trade all over Europe.

'Erikson is actually one of our shareholders too, Eliza,' says Freddy. 'He has an interest in every Ålands vessel afloat. But I fear he much dislikes the fact that his share of *Inverley* is so small compared to ours.' He and *Kapten* exchange grins. 'Now, my dear, are you ready to beard the fearsome Gusta' in his den? We've organised a meeting at eleven.'

'Are you sure you want me along, Granddad?'

'Of course. Didn't I say you'd enjoy seeing how the other investors cope?'

We drive a few miles south through more birches and pines, and over a causeway with reeds swaying in the ripples, to a small island called Styrsö where Gustaf Erikson owns an estate with a handsome white house.

He greets us, charming and hospitable, and ushers us into his office, where the walls are covered with so many paintings of ships there's hardly any space left between the frames.

On his desk is the famous Grain Race trophy, a silver globe on a stand, and I try to pretend it doesn't fascinate me.

Two other men, minority shareholders, are already seated and Erikson shows the three of us to a large leather couch. He's short and bald and inclined to stoutness, but when he looks us over his eyes are as flinty as the sailing master he once was.

Captain Nilsen says, 'Let me introduce Mr Freddy Havers and Miss Eliza McKee.'

Erikson introduces the other men and one says jokingly, 'You do not need to bring your secretary to an informal discussion.'

Freddy says, 'This is not my secretary. This is my granddaughter, who manages my interest in *Inverley*. In time I will deed my shareholding to her.'

He hasn't mentioned that before, but I'm careful not to show surprise. Erikson gazes at me as if he's caught me dropping tar onto a clean deck, then his eyes flicker to Freddy.

'Such things are not to be made light of, Mr Havers. A shareholder must understand at every level what is involved. I fear that Miss McKee, however charming, is not at all a suitable person to make decisions affecting the lives of men or ships.'

Captain Nilsen says, 'In fact, Miss McKee worked as a *jungman* in the 1929 season aboard *Inverley*. She understands very well what is involved.'

Erikson smiles coldly. 'A passenger playing at sailor is not a *jungman*.'

I'm inclined to agree, but *Kapten* says, 'She worked harder than many others in her watch. She understands the ship and Mr Havers informs me she has a good head for business. As the majority shareholder I am in agreement with this plan.'

'Well,' says Erikson, 'How times change. But of course, we must change with them. Welcome to our discussion, Miss McKee.' He means not a word of it.

I listen as they discuss repairs, a dry-docking in Copenhagen, the many gallons of paint required for next season, and the rise in the cost of new canvas, which brings tuts of disbelief.

Freddy clears his throat and says, 'It so happens I have a contact at the Baltic Exchange who can offer me a very good deal on a large quantity of Dutch sailcloth.'

He mentions a price that makes Erikson's eyebrows rise. 'If you secure that contract I would be very happy to take the excess off your hands. At cost, naturally.'

'At a small margin over cost,' says Freddy calmly. 'Miss McKee will handle the transaction and keep you informed of progress.'

Erikson glances at me. 'We will need it within six weeks, you understand.'

'Of course,' I say. 'It will be here before the first ship sails. Will that be *Herzogin Cecilie*? I saw her this morning—she's fine form.'

'Yes,' he says shortly. 'She will be first out for Australia, but *l'Avenir* is departing on a Baltic voyage next week.'

'With *l'Avenir* away it frees up a place at the wharf,' I say. 'It would be useful if *Inverley* could take that berth for her refitting.'

'I had plans to bring *Lawhill* in there.'

I shrug. 'If our costs for *Inverley*'s refitting are a little lower—as they would be, at the shore—it might mean greater flexibility in our price for the canvas.'

Erikson jots down some figures, then says to Captain Nilsen, 'Bring *Inverley* to the wharf, *Kapten*, when the berth is free.' He looks at me, expressionless. 'Perhaps you have a solution to our paint supply problem, Miss McKee? No? I am greatly surprised.'

'I'll see what I can do,' I say evenly. I can feel Freddy's delight.

The discussion veers to other matters, gossip about people and vessels I don't know. I sip my coffee, and slowly get the odd sense Freddy is unhappy about something—he seems to be breathing deeply—but I assume he'll tell me about it later.

The meeting comes to a close and Erikson shows us to the door, once more full of charm. As we walk to the car I notice my grandfather is flushed and frowning, then I suddenly realise he's sweating heavily too.

I ask quietly, 'Are you all right?'

Freddy loosens his tie and collar. 'Just need some air—'

He groans and spreads his hand wide over his chest. His knees buckle and he collapses, wheezing. We manage to get him onto the back seat of the car.

Erikson says urgently, 'I will phone the hospital so they know you are coming. *Go*.'

We drive to the small hospital at Mariehamn, where the nurses get Granddad onto a stretcher and take him away. I stand there, my hand over my mouth, then sit down suddenly.

'I will get Maria and Mrs Havers from the farm,' says *Kapten*.

Soon he's back with my grandmother. She sits beside me, holding my hand, until some unmeasurable time later a doctor comes through the door and we stand up.

He says, 'We believe Herr Havers had heart attack. We give him oxygen and medication. For pain he has nitro-glycerine tablets. We keep him here for two days then he must rest at home.'

'But we're not *at* home,' I say stupidly.

Maria says, 'With us you are at home *always*.'

'Fru Havers may see him but no other visitors now,' says the doctor. He takes Min-lu through the doors and we sit down again.

I remember Freddy's light-hearted words: *if I died tomorrow it'd be with a smile on my face.* I groan and cover my eyes.

Freddy stays at the farm for six weeks, slowly improving. I'm able to organise the Dutch sailcloth via telegram, as well as an excellent deal on a bulk order of paint.

When I report the news to Erikson I don't let my face show any hint of my pleasure, but Freddy's delight at the successful trade makes it even more satisfying.

Maria holds an afternoon tea a few days before *Inverley* is to sail and I see my old friend Artur and some of the crew again. The boys sit nervously in the living-room with dainty cups and saucers, but when *Kapten* leaves the room everyone relaxes. Mr Pölönen, now first mate, is there and tells me shyly he was recently married.

I ask, 'Shall you still be going to Australia this year then?'

'Of course. My wife understands. She is an Ålands woman.'

'Is your house kept cleverly and carefully, Mr Pölönen?' I tease.

His gold tooth twinkles. 'I am very happy, *jungman*.'

Artur is now third mate and responsible, at the age of twenty, for the lives of ten boys. I congratulate him, but he flushes and says earnestly, 'You understand, Elias, even though I will soon be twenty-one I am very sorry I cannot marry you, as I promised— I now have a fiancée.'

'I'm so glad for you, Artur. It was always a comfort to know someone might marry me but I never planned to hold you to it.'

He laughs, relieved, and we chat about old friends, including Niilo, now on *Olivebank*.

Later that night as I lie in bed, I think about Liam and Niilo and Jack and Angus, the men whose lives have intersected so briefly and memorably with mine. Yet I've formed no long-lasting bonds with them, or anyone else, and it puzzles me.

Others seem to make such bonds easily: Izabel and Felix, Harry and Charlotte, my grandparents, my mother (more than once), Maria and *Kapten*, Mr Pölönen, Artur—everyone I know.

What's wrong with me? Am I fated to be left, a spinster, on the shelf? I remember the radio officer on the ship whose interest evaporated as soon as he realised I was not empty-headed.

Do men only love women who know nothing?

In mid-September we stand on the wharf at Mariehamn and wave goodbye to Captain Nilsen and Artur and my watchmates as they manoeuvre four and a half thousand tons of steel under sail as lightly as a yacht. In three months *Inverley* will be back in the Australian heat, while here in Mariehamn the snow will be up to the eaves.

Soon autumn arrives. The fields are golden and the orchards lush with apples, and I can feel the change in the air as the days become shorter and cooler.

In October Freddy is finally well enough to take a steamer to London. Our farewells to Maria are painful, as we've all become close over these anxious days, but we wave, we weep, we turn for home.

19. Pete: QM Air

God knows how, but I scrape through my degree like a complete fraud. But I'm free, I tell myself. Only I'm not. Billie closed down the company six months ago and it feels like an amputation.

She left without giving me a forwarding address and when I ask Frank, employed now by West Australian Airways, he says he hasn't the foggiest.

I've come into my inheritance, enough to support me for quite a few years, but I only want to work on aeroplanes and it just sits in the bank. I could buy myself a Gipsy Moth or even one of the new Tiger Moths, but without Billie to share the fun it seems pointless.

I keep up my flying hours and perhaps even improve, but without Billie to say so, how can I know for sure?

Mama and Anton and Liam tolerate me hanging around. I do some gardening but it doesn't give me much satisfaction. I get drunk with old friends, all settled into their new professions and new marriages. They say they envy me my freedom but I know they're just being kind.

Eliza's letters lighten the gloom, though there's been a lot about weddings lately. Our aunt Izabel married some lawyer who was on the ship with Eliza—so he must be eccentric—and Eliza's best mate Charlotte, apparently a paragon of all the virtues, married that sailor Harry we met at Port Lincoln. Oddly, he's also some kind of boffin, so he's probably even more eccentric.

And for months it's been Ålands this and Ålands that, then out of the blue she sends me a package of papers about Air Service Training and wants my opinion on their prospects.

Well, of course I've heard of AST. If nothing else they've been in the aviation news lately, with Amy Johnson doing their blind flying course.

So I start reading and after a while feel almost sick with envy. Here, people learn to fly from just about anyone who can get a bird off the ground (even Billie doesn't have the full set of instructor licences), but at AST they get a long, rigorous education.

They've got students from all over the world lining up to take their courses, with dozens of different types of planes to learn on. Oh Billie, this is what we should have become. What a missed opportunity.

Oh, *Billie*.

I study the AST documents into the night, taking notes on exactly what they cover, what planes they have, what wireless equipment, navigation gear, and more. When I get up next day I work through my notes and summarise them.

I get on the Norton and race out to the airfield. I find Frank half-inside an engine and say, 'Frank, we need to talk. Now.'

He lifts his head and scowls at me. 'What about?'

'You know where Billie is, I *know* you do.'

I'm lying but I've suddenly realised he must—she needs her mail sent on, if nothing else. He climbs down the ladder wiping his hands. 'Why? She doesn't want a bar of you.'

'I've got something she'll be interested in, a real *opportunity* for her. Please, Frank, would you just send her this?'

I hold out an envelope with the summary. He doesn't take it.

'For fuck's *sake*, Frank, I'd never do anything to hurt her. When that bastard beat her up I helped her, she must have told you that at least.'

'Maybe you were just trying to take advantage of her.'

I laugh. 'Take advantage of *Billie*? She'd have killed me.'

He gazes at me. 'Give it here, but if she doesn't want to read it, not my problem.'

One evening a couple of weeks later I'm at home by myself. The doorbell rings and there she is, wearing trousers and a trench-coat tight around her narrow frame, drizzle sparkling in her hair and drifting past the streetlights behind her.

'Oh, God,' I say.

'Nah, just me. How're you going, kid?'

'Fine, come in, come in.'

I make us tea, my hands shaking, and we sit in the warm lounge-room.

'So where have you *been*, Billie?'

'Where no one'd find me.' She smiles. 'At my parent's place.'

'I thought you weren't supposed to darken their doorstep anymore.'

'That's why I thought no one'd look for me there. Oh, we managed to make it up, we're family after all. I made them promise not to tell anyone where I was.'

'Anyone being me.'

'Just anyone, Pete.'

After a silence I say, 'Are you all right now?'

'Yeah, surprisingly.'

'And … the documents I sent you?'

'Certainly food for thought.' She sits back and stretches out her long legs and absently flexes her feet. 'So what's your plan here?'

'Not entirely sure—but go to England, both of us. Learn everything we can at AST, then set up our own flying business. Concentrate on wherever the greatest demand is, civil or military.'

'How do we know where the greatest demand's going to be?'

'Have to keep our eyes and ears open all the time, stay one step ahead. We'd have to plan, meet people, follow politics, not just fly for fun—but plenty of time for that too,' I add hastily.

'You say you have family over there who might help?'

'My grandparents are well-connected and have lots of business experience. Even my sister's interested in that sort of thing, though all she cares about is boats. Sorry, ships.'

'Is there a difference?'

'Damned if I know. If they haven't got wings who cares *what* they are?'

She grins. 'Oh, flyboy. It's a hell of a plan.'

I nod, my heart thumping. 'So—are you interested, Billie?'

'First we need to discuss how we'd do it.'

'I've got the money, we can do it.'

'So what would I bring to the party?'

I spread my hands in amazement. '*You*. All your experience and knowledge. And yeah, it won't hurt you being a woman.'

She nods. 'More's the pity. Anyway, I've got a bit of money now too. Reconciling with my parents has opened the coffers.'

'Won't they close up again if you keep on flying?'

'Nah. I think at last we understand each other.' She sits forward, elbows on her knees. 'So when would we leave?'

'As soon as possible. I've been keeping an eye on the shipping schedule.' I take a breath. 'There's a liner in three weeks. What do you reckon?'

'A whole three *weeks*? Jeez.'

'Oh. Well, perhaps—'

She puts her arms behind her head and says, 'Don't fret, kid. Everything I've got is in a couple of bags. I could go tomorrow if I felt like it.'

I can't stop grinning. 'That's, that's, oh, *Billie*.'

'Hey,' she says. 'What'll we call ourselves?'

'Um, McKee-Quinn?'

'Come off it. Quinn-McKee, if anything,' she says. 'Quinn-McKee Aviation Training?'

'A mouthful. Air Services Quinn-McKee?'

'Nah, too much like Air Service Training.'

'Quinn-McKee Flying School?'

'We want to be flexible—not just a school, we might want to deliver mail. Or become an *airline!*' She laughs at the absurdity of it.

We toss around another dozen possibilities then I say, 'What about our initials? Something QM? QM something?'

'*Yes.* QM Air. Modern, flexible—we can be anything, do anything with a name like that.'

'Then QM Air it is,' I say, dazed.

Sometimes I look back through my life, the ups and downs, the joys and sorrows; and I wonder if the single happiest moment I will ever experience was sitting by the fire that night, the drizzle outside turning to a downpour, tossing around names for our new company with Billie.

If so, I have no complaints.

I send a letter to Eliza telling her the great news and giving her my excellent opinion of AST. I'm puzzled I haven't heard anything from the famous Ålands but she's probably too busy gawping at ships to write.

Maybe they don't even have postcards there. It's in Scandinavia, I vaguely recall—fjords, perhaps? Reindeers? Who knows? She won't get my letter until just before we arrive, but at least she'll have some warning.

Billie and I are sailing on the *Oronsay* in September, Fremantle to London, a four week passage. When I casually suggest to Billie we share a cabin she mutters, 'Idiot.' (Turns out single men and women aren't allowed to share.) So I book us into adjoining cabins on C Deck's Promenade—portholes, washbasins and wardrobes, all very civilised.

I sell my beloved motorcycle to a cricketing mate and rush around getting a passport. Luckily Billie already has her papers from a trip with her parents or we might have been delayed.

It may be all of 1932, but single women still have to be interviewed before getting a passport, just to make sure they aren't running off to join the white slave trade.

I tell Billie she's safe from any such suspicions and she smiles and says, 'You *really* need to see a bit more of the world, kid.'

She's right. Out of her flying overalls, and elegant in wide-legged crepe trousers and a narrow jersey sweater, she cuts a sophisticated figure. I can easily—far too easily—imagine some sultan wanting her for his harem.

The day of departure arrives.

We throw coloured paper streamers to our parents in the crowd on the Fremantle wharf. The siren blows and the ship eases away from the land, and one by one the streamers break apart and flutter into the water. As the gap grows wider we wave and wave until our old lives are far behind us.

And we turn and look towards the new.

We explore. The topmost level is set up for games, shuffleboard, deck tennis and miniature golf, while the lounges have poker, bridge and bingo, and Billie says if she starts playing any games *at all*, I'm to shove her overboard as an act of human kindness.

B deck has a cafe, smoking room, dance-floor, lounge, bar and promenade. Our own C deck has a pool and kids' playroom, and D has another pool. E has another dance-floor and a cafe, and F holds two dining halls and a smoking room.

I spend a lot of time losing my way and consulting the deck plan, but Billie knows where everything is in half an hour.

Our first port of call is Colombo in Ceylon, nine days away. We brought books with us to study—aeronautics, engineering, navigation, even a tome on accounting, but the days are so sunny and the waves ripple so hypnotically to the horizon, neither of us feels much like reading.

Instead we lie for hours by the pool in the sun.

Billie turns a freckled caramel while I become as brown as a berry. Pretty girls climb in and out of the water, giggling and making eyes at me, but for the first time in my life I don't much care. All I can see is Billie.

I always thought I liked lush, buxom girls like Laura, but now Billie's whippet-like frame lying on the towel beside me seems the most beautiful thing I've ever seen. Her narrow feet and slim legs, her thin hard arms and long flexible fingers, her fine-boned face and graceful neck arouse me absurdly. The tan on my back becomes two shades darker than the rest of me because I have to spend so much time lying on my front.

After dinner every night there's dancing. To my surprise I discover Billie loves dancing, but I hate it, I'm so clumsy. Once, when she isn't besieged by (apparently) every man on board, we go for a spin around the floor, but that's enough for me.

My cabin-mate is leaving at Colombo, and I fantasise that perhaps one night Billie will turn up at my door in a lace negligee and cling to me. A mouse, perhaps, or some sort of peril. Then I sigh. Billie isn't scared of mice, or peril of any kind. And even I have to admit the odds of a lace negligee are close to zero.

But one evening it seems all my fantasies might come true. We're walking tipsily back to the cabins, admiring the moonlight on the water. Billie stumbles and turns her ankle, the one she hurt when she jumped out of that bastard's car. She takes off her shoes and I drape her arm across my shoulder and help her hobble back to her room.

She unlocks the door and turns to me, saying, 'Thanks, kid,' and I gently cup her face and kiss her mouth. She starts to respond, then draws back saying, 'No, Pete.'

'Why not, Billie? You know I'm mad for you.'

'Mad's the word for it. You're too young.'

'You can't keep saying that forever. I'm nearly twenty-two now.'

She sighs. 'It's not your physical age. It's your ... lack of worldliness.'

'But you're all I want, Billie.'

'That's the problem right there. I don't yearn for fidelity and happily-ever-after with one man. I need to be free to be with whoever I want, whenever I want.'

'You'll have to settle down eventually, though.'

'No. Marriage would be a prison sentence for me.' She tilts her head and gazes at me with rare compassion. 'Come on, Pete. You honestly don't want a woman like me. You'd never know where I was, who I was with. It'd drive you insane.'

'But how can you live with that sort of—promiscuity?' (She may be right about my lack of worldliness.)

'It's something I've always believed in. Free love. Love without limits or possessiveness.'

'Good God, *is* there such a thing?'

She smiles. 'I think so, and not just me—writers and philosophers believe it's possible too. Not easy, but possible.'

'But if you never marry, Billie, who'll look after you when you're helpless or old?'

She shrugs. 'I'll look after myself. I always have.'

Her courage. Her vulnerability. Oh, Billie.

'So you don't need anything from me, then,' I say sadly.

'Yes I do, you blithering idiot. I need our friendship, I need our plans for QM Air. I need you, Pete, but not as a lover. It'd mess everything up.'

I sigh and ask jokingly, 'Hey, not even a little bit tempted?'

She laughs. 'Burnt on one side, lily-white on the other. Who'd fancy that? Night, kid.'

Three weeks later we berth at London. It's been a painful time, seeing Billie smiling and dancing with ship's officers and languid chappies on their way home from the colonies.

One moonlit night in the Suez Canal I even thought I saw her kissing someone at the far end of the deck. We stop at Colombo, Aden, Suez and Port Said. I remember nothing much, just a sense of heat and sadness and poverty that seems to echo my feelings.

Then the ugly Mediterranean ports, Naples, Toulon, Palma and Gibraltar—or so the itinerary tells me.

Still, by the time we reach Plymouth I'm feeling a small sense of anticipation. I might not have Billie's heart (or body) but I have our plans for the future. That'll be enough, it has to be.

My sister and grandmother meet us at the London docks on an autumn day. Billie is wearing trousers and a trench coat, her short coppery hair conveying her usual electric air of impatience.

Nanna and Eliza give us the sobering news of Freddy's recent illness. When we enter the drawing room he struggles a little to get up to hug me, but I'm glad he still looks much the same, the dear old codger.

Over afternoon tea we explain more about our grand plans.

Min-lu says, 'Our solicitor will be able to help you set up your flying company—the legalities are probably a little different from Australia.'

'That'd be a big help, thanks, Nanna.'

'You can stay at my farm on the South Downs, too,' says Freddy. 'It's not far from Hamble.'

'Great, Granddad,' I say. 'And I want to hear more about how you run the farm as well.'

'You haven't told us much about the trip,' Eliza says. 'Was it lovely and luxurious?'

'Certainly was,' says Billie. 'We sun-bathed and swam and danced so much.'

I blink. *She* danced so much, and did God knows what with God knows who as well.

'We must hold a welcome party for you,' says Freddy.

'Not while you're still so sick, Granddad,' I say. 'We don't expect that.'

'Nonsense.' He smiles at Min-lu. 'I'll sit quietly in a corner.'

'Well, so long as you do, darling.' She thinks for a moment. 'Izabel and Felix will be home from Hollywood soon, so we could make it a joint affair.'

'Gosh, haven't seen Aunt Izabel for years. That Winnie woman she played in the movie seemed awfully different from how I remember her,' I say with mock innocence.

'It's called *acting*, Pete,' Eliza scoffs.

I grin. 'Ah, Lizzie, how I've missed your sisterly jibes.'

I throw a cushion at her and she throws it back. Despite feeling glum about Billie, it's great to see them all again.

20. Izabel: Mummy

'Do hurry, darling, the taxi's here.' I try not to sound irritated. Felix has been sulking ever since someone called him 'Mr Peres' at the hotel in California. Dear Lord, men and their egos.

I've already told Basil my agent I want to be billed as Izabel Malory from now on. He whinged of course, but at last I'm a big enough star to demand it. Anyway, Malory has a fine British ring to it. Peres is a little *foreign*, after all.

I smooth my dress and glance in the mirror. That shade of gold certainly suits me, and my belly is still as flat as a penny. I haven't told Felix yet—I only found out for certain today—but he'll be over the moon. To hold his own son is his greatest ambition, he once said.

Even if it's a girl I'm sure he'll be happy too. I could try again for a boy after that but I'd have to be careful with my figure. I bite my lip, then stop before I smear my lipstick. What a juggling act my life is. Famous film star, supportive wife and now … doting mother! Can I do it?

Of course I can.

Felix comes jauntily down the staircase, buttoning a cuff and glancing at me with that incendiary smile. All my irritation disappears. He kisses me and says, 'Sorry, Izzy darling, just wanted to find those anniversary cuff-links you gave me.'

Well, who could find fault with such an excuse?

We set off in the taxi and Felix takes my hand. 'You look wonderful, darling. I'll look forward later to …' He whispers a delicious suggestion in my ear that makes me wriggle with delight. 'Stop it, you beast,' I murmur. 'We're almost there. But I'll hold you to that.'

'You'd better,' he says with a grin.

I sigh, pleased. Oh, Felix, my love.

Thank God that difficult time in California is over. It was all my fault really. I know he's bored with his legal career, but it was unfair to take him away for so long with nothing to do except be 'Mr Peres'. Well, I won't make that mistake again.

Thank God I fired that strumpet of a maid before it went beyond a kiss—the little bitch obviously led him on. I didn't even realise he liked blondes either, I think with a touch of unease, but then remember I'm playing a Swedish princess in my next film. I'll just have to make certain I'm blonde where it matters too. He'll like that.

We arrive at Mother's place, and I wonder for a moment how poor old Freddy is going after his heart attack. I always find him a ghastly bore but I know he means a lot to Mother.

Felix gets out and opens the door for me. A couple of photographers (my agent's doing) are waiting and we pose for the obligatory shots. Mother is standing by the door and I hug her lightly and say, 'Min-lu, how delightful to see you again.'

I sense rather than see her slight flinch when I call her Min-lu. Well, nothing much I can do about that. She knows our cover story is necessary in public. We enter and it's not a large gathering, perhaps twenty or thirty people.

I exclaim over my little nephew Peter, all grown up and surprisingly dark and dishy, and his girlfriend—or not, I quickly realise. This Billie is quite an extraordinary creature, tall, thin, mop of red hair. But she's got lovely skin and fierce green cat eyes, and I rather like her. (I have a part as a girl explorer coming up and she'll come in handy for inspiration.)

Little Eliza is beautifully groomed, as usual—I've taught her well. I remember her kindness when I told her about my lost pregnancy to Gideon and hug her more warmly than usual, thinking, I have a secret, Eliza, a lovely *baby* secret, and soon I'll tell you and everyone else the marvellous news.

Felix calls me over to say hello to his doctor friend who came to our wedding, Harry something-or-other, and his blonde wife Charlotte, who was also apparently there.

As she greets me, demure and amused, I recognise her type and think, you're a clever little piece, aren't you? What's your game? She's Eliza's closest friend it seems, and I wonder if Eliza realises she's not to be trusted. I doubt it.

That girl is simply too nice about everyone. She even thinks the best of me, which is hilarious. But I'll be a good person when I'm a mother. Or at least a better one.

I greet Freddy, who's seated on the sofa near the fire. I'm feeling a little faint on my feet—that's happened a few times lately—so I sit down beside him. 'Glad to see they've given you a large whiskey,' I say, sipping my own champagne.

'Watered down, damn it,' Freddy says. I glance at him. He isn't as hale as usual and there are dark circles under his eyes. I feel a twinge of disquiet.

'How have you been, Freddy?'

'Oh, this and that, my dear.'

He grins, his moustache curling with his smile, and I suddenly think, I hope you'll be all right, old man—my mother's loved you her entire life. Heavens, you might even have been *my* father if she hadn't married Leo Peres. But then I wouldn't be myself—and who would I be instead?

The philosophical complexity of that gets too much for me so I take another sip. Then I have a sudden, desperate urge to tell someone my news, I can't keep it to myself any longer.

'Freddy,' I whisper, 'I'm going to have a *baby*, but not a word, I haven't told Felix yet.'

'My goodness,' he says quietly. 'You clever, *clever* girl, Izabel. I'm so proud of you.'

I flush with pleasure. It's so unfamiliar to have a man approve of me for myself, not because he wants to sleep with me or make money out of me. Is that what it's like to have a father?

Leo Peres died when I was only two. As a child I wanted to believe I remembered him but my older sister Filipa would mock my memories. He left me a porcelain-faced doll which I adored, and one day Filipa, in a fury, threw it on the fire. (I have *never* forgiven her.)

No one could understand my grief then, but it was all I had left of that magical being, my father. Yet now I have Felix to love, and soon I'll have our wonderful baby.

'You've always been very dear to me, Izabel,' Freddy says. 'I couldn't be happier for you. And your mother, my goodness, how *pleased* she'll be! What a gift. *Bless* you, child.'

Astonishingly, tears come to my eyes. I kiss him on the cheek, saying, 'Thank you, darling Freddy,' and I mean it.

He squeezes my hand and says, laughing, 'Tell that young devil of a husband of yours soon, won't you? I'm not sure I can keep such a good secret to myself for very long.'

Still smiling I return to the party. Felix is chatting to a couple of fellows he knows, not far from a small group from the film world I can't be bothered with.

I stand with Eliza, Harry and Billie, making mental notes on the red-head's posture and air of concentration, as Harry says something dull about disease and air travel. Odd fare for a party, I think and my interest drifts.

Not far away my nephew Pete is chatting to the blonde, Charlotte. I watch amused. I played a character like her once and recognise the wry smile, the come-hither air. But she's pretty good, I have to give her that, and in minutes she's simply reeling him in.

I approach them and Pete says, 'Aunt Izabel—'

'Just Izabel, darling.'

'Izabel, Charlotte's got the most fascinating hobby. She studies horse-racing and does very well at it, I hear.'

'How lovely, Charlotte. I had no idea *anyone* could win against the bookies.'

'Oh, it's ups and downs really, Mrs Malory, swings and roundabouts,' she says demurely. 'But I do enjoy the excitement. I was just telling Pete he should come out to Ascot one day while he's still in London. It's so amusing.'

Ah, there it is.

'Sounds lovely, darling. Oh, someone I must speak to. Do excuse me.'

I draw Eliza away and say quietly, 'Your friend Charlotte— she's trying to get Pete to bankroll her at the horse track. I'm not sure that's an awfully good idea.'

Eliza pales. She clearly knows what's up.

'I'll leave it to you then, shall I?' I say and pat her shoulder.

My mother is speaking to one of the waiters, then sees me and smiles. She's looking pretty tonight, in a green silk gown that suits her silver hair.

'Hello, Izabel,' she says. 'Are you settled in at your flat now?'

'Yes, and it's *wonderful* to be home again,' I say, remembering with a thrill the white and gold nursery waiting for my secret baby. 'And I just had a lovely chat with Freddy. How do you think he's going?'

She looks surprised to hear me say that as I usually avoid Freddy—and perhaps she's even a little surprised I express interest in his well-being. (Honestly, people give me no credit at all for sensitivity!)

'I don't know,' she says. 'He seems to be recovering slowly, but of course whatever damage remains … well.' She shakes her head.

'I'm sure he'll be all right in the end,' I say automatically, as I suddenly notice Felix has gone to join Pete and Charlotte. Pete doesn't look pleased, but Charlotte certainly does. And Felix?

My mother says something, but I can't hear for a ringing in my ears.

Felix touches the woman's arm and gazes at her with his buccaneer smile. I see Pete's disappointment as he realises he's lost her attention, and I see Charlotte lift her face and smile, sultry as an orchid, into my husband's attentive eyes.

'Izabel, are you all right?' asks my mother urgently.

I realise I'm shaking. I put my glass down and says, 'Sorry. I feel a little unwell.'

'Come into the next room, darling, and rest. I'll get you some tea. Shall I call a doctor?'

'Of *course* not,' I say lightly. 'But I'll sit down for a moment.'

Call a doctor? I almost laugh. No doctor on earth could ease this pain.

Holding a cup of tea on the sofa in the next room, I gaze at the fire. I don't cry—really, what is there to cry about? Felix is a flirt, I always knew that. Most men are, you have to be realistic. My God, in my industry who ever hoped for—let alone expected— faithfulness?

I did, I mourn. I did. I meant every word of my vows, Felix.

After a time I think, well there's only one way to deal with this. Even if he strays I must make certain he still comes home to me. I must take on my greatest role: the loving wife choosing to remain blind to her husband's foolishness.

Anyway, whatever might happen he'd come back to me, of course he would. There's never been a woman like me in his life and he knows it. I've been fatally distracted that's all, with work, with my pregnancy.

He must know at some fundamental level he's been sharing my attention, and of course he wants that thrill of sole possession again. God, *men.*

I put down my tea—it's gone cold—and rest my forehead on my hands. My head aches and I slowly realise my body does too. I suppose it's the shock, but all my muscles hurt.

I must have been clenching them. I remember some acting class where we systematically worked muscle clusters to experience their associated visceral emotions. Or something like that. My arms, my thighs, my shoulders, my back—I'm so *uncomfortable*.

Oh. That isn't an ache, that's a stab. I move a little and rub the small of my back. Have I twisted a muscle? These brocade shoes are new and have rather high heels. Perhaps they've thrown out my spine—

Ugh. That one really *hurt*, the same spot too. Oh dear. Perhaps I need to see a doctor after all. I had a bad back in a production a couple of years ago but the masseur was marv—

I grunt, bending forward. Jesus, that was nasty, but it's only my back, not my abdomen, thank God. The stabs of pain are coming in a few places now.

I whimper as they spread like a sheet over the small of my back and deep down inside my hips—

I gasp and almost cry. I've never felt such pain before. I hope childbirth isn't this bad. No, it couldn't possibly be.

I groan aloud, a long low keen. I can't help myself. When I can get my breath I say loudly, 'Min-lu? Darling, are you *there?*'

But the door is shut and the noise from the party drowns out my words. I have a respite of a few moments then the pain descends again and I whimper.

When I get my breath back I call out, 'Is anyone there? *Please?*'

No one hears. Music blares from the gramophone, people are dancing. I lie down on the sofa, I have to, and start to weep. The pain comes back and this time it does not leave me.

I cry out, '*Somebody help me!*' and sob like a child through the waves of agony.

I don't know how long I'm lying there, but finally there's a spreading warmth in my belly and between my legs and I think, oh I need a pad, my period's arrived. Then I'm puzzled. But I'm pregnant, that's not possible.

After a time I lift my head. I can see blood on the sofa, on my gold dress, on my silk stockings, on my new brocade shoes.

And I scream *Mummy, Mummy*, and finally she hears.

Min-lu rushes in and gasps, and calls out, 'Harry, come here! Felix, Eliza!' She bends over me. 'There, there, my darling.'

'Mummy,' I whisper. 'It hurts so *much*.'

She puts her hand to her mouth. 'Oh, my baby, we'll fix it, don't worry here's the doctor.' She looks up. 'Harry, help her!'

I'm seeing everything through a sort of fog now and Felix's boring medical friend looks rather like an archangel. He holds my wrist and says crisply to someone, 'Ring for an ambulance immediately.'

Eliza, a young saint, is holding my mother who is crying. Crying?

Then beyond them all I see Felix, who appears to have a glowing halo.

'Oh, darling,' I murmur. 'Seem to have gotten myself into a bit of bother …'

But my beloved doesn't rush to my side. I see him stare at the blood, the red, red blood, and go pale and stagger back and vomit.

Men, I think wearily.

21. Eliza: The Little Gang

After the welcome party, poor Izabel loses the baby she'd yearned for, the baby we didn't even know she was carrying. She is ill for a long time, but at least her life is spared.

But far worse is to come that year. Granddad Freddy begins to fail and must return to hospital, several times. We greet each small rally with relief, but every day he slips away a little more.

I spend as much time with him as possible—there's a peace to it, an intimacy beyond the everyday. We talk together about ships and people and loss and love, and I reveal more of my heart to him than I've ever shown anyone.

He gives Pete and me a small packet of letters from our father, Sam, who'd write to Freddy from his boarding school. His shy, boyish words make me love both of them even more.

Despite everything the doctors can do, Freddy dies just a few weeks before Christmas. We're all with him and it's a peaceful end with loving embraces, but that doesn't ease the grief.

Nanna is devastated. Oddly enough it's Izabel, still recovering in hospital, who helps her the most, and Nanna finds a deep consolation in her daughter's need of her after so long.

My grandfather was loved by a larger group of friends than I ever imagined, and at the funeral I recognise many faces famous in politics, the arts and academia. We even receive a surprisingly kind letter from Gusta' Erikson himself.

Granddad knew what was coming and left his affairs in order. His Irish estate reverts to a relative, but there are bequests for my family, and Lucy and Danny. He left Billie the funds to do her aviation courses at Hamble, Pete the shares in Air Service Training, and me the *Inverley* holding, just as he said he would.

He'd already told me he was leaving the South Downs farm to Pete—so there's something to ground him when he's up in the air, Granddad said with a laugh—so that wasn't a surprise. What is a surprise is discovering he's left the Kensington house to me.

'Why?' I ask Nanna. 'Surely it's more yours than anyone's.'

She shakes her head. 'It was Freddy's long before I re-entered his life, and he badly wanted to set you and Pete up with something substantial in your lives. You're his grandchildren, remember. He never imagined he'd even meet you, let alone know you and love you.'

'But don't you care about the house, Nanna?'

'I am rather fond of it, and must assume you won't immediately turn me out into the street,' she says wryly. 'But I've lived in many places, Eliza. I was fond of them all and will be equally fond of wherever I go next.'

'Oh, *Nanna*. This is your home for as long as you want,' I say laughing, then weeping a little, as I now so often do.

The old year comes to an end and 1933 begins, but we have no reason to celebrate. Pete and Billie's studies at Hamble don't begin for a month or two, so they stay on in London and I'm grateful they're around.

While the rest of us are lost and bewildered, Billie is a fount of common sense and keeps the household ticking over like one of her flying machines.

She recognises how distressed the staff are, so she and Pete take the cook, Penfold the maid and Spencer the chauffeur out one night to the pub for a private wake. Next day I can see Penfold is more content and the cook almost her old self again.

Later, Billie tells me she thinks Spencer has a tenderness for Penfold. I hope so—Penfold deserves some happiness. By now I've lost any sense of trepidation around Billie. Her sharp tongue is only a shield and her sardonic ways make me laugh.

But poor old Pete! He clearly adores her but she keeps him at arm's length. He makes half-hearted attempts to flirt with other women—and I think he's rather attracted to Charlotte—but it's Billie who clearly matters most to him.

We start going out several times a week, to cafes or pubs—Charlotte, Harry, Billie, Pete and me. It's a welcome distraction from our sorrows at home and we soon become a close little gang. Billie and Harry have similar quick minds, Charlotte and Pete like to play the careless youngsters, while I'm somewhere in the middle.

Still, Harry and I seem to have a particular bond from our *Inverley* days. Sometimes our eyes meet when Billie says something delightfully biting, or Pete flies off into one of his clouds of enthusiasm, and I love the private unspoken pleasure we share.

One evening Harry and I both arrive a little early at our favourite pub. It has coloured glass windows, open fires, cosy nooks and wintery swirls of fog through the door whenever it opens.

We sit in the saloon in a quiet corner with a lamp above the table. Harry buys us half pints of bitter and we clink glasses.

'Where are the aviators this evening?' he asks.

'Went off to do something vaguely aeronautical, but Pete said they'll be back later and meet us here,' I say. 'Where's Charlotte?'

'Not sure.'

'The track?' I say tentatively.

'Probably.'

'Oh, Harry. Is she ever going to come to her senses?'

'I used to hope so, but I'm starting to doubt it. She's still having those godawful quarrels with her mother and claiming the stress makes her gamble. But I think now that's an excuse. She just loves the thrill of taking risks—she calls it *playing with fire.*' He stops and takes a drink.

'Is she handling the expense of it any better?'

He shakes his head.

'But what does she do when she has debts and can't pay the bookies?'

'Most won't take her bets anymore, so that's a relief,' he says. 'The others? In my darkest moments I fear she pays them in kind.'

'In kind? What do you—' I stop.

'Christ, no, not really.' He rubs his eyes with his palms. 'No, she probably just persuades them black is white and winter is summer, as she always does with me.' He looks up, his lean face desolate. 'Sorry.'

'Perhaps ... if she had a baby she might settle down,' I say.

'No. Charlotte is adamant she is not having a baby in the foreseeable future.'

'But you once told me you wanted lots of children.'

'I did, didn't I? No, she didn't quite clarify her stance before we married,' he says dryly. 'She doesn't want a child, nor me much either, except as a shield of respectability. She says she needs excitement in her life because I'm so dull.'

'I'm terribly sorry, Harry.' I don't know what else to say. 'What about work? Is it going well?'

'Yes, we've had some amazing breakthroughs recently—might save millions of people's lives if we're on the right track. How can Charlotte matter in that scheme of things?'

'She matters to you.'

After a pause he says, 'Enough of my gloom and doom. What's happening in your life?'

'Nothing much. Mourning for Granddad. Looking after Nanna.'

'Seen anything of Angus lately?'

I shake my head. 'Long gone, and there's no one in sight to replace him.'

'You do realise, Eliza, if I stood up in this pub and said you're available, I'd be killed in the ensuing stampede?'

I smile. 'Lately I've been thinking relationships seem too complicated to cope with.'

'Sometimes they're worth it,' he says, but I hear the doubt in his voice.

I sip my drink. 'By the way, I saw Izabel yesterday at the hospital.'

'How's she going?'

'She'd have died that awful night without you, Harry.'

'She's a strong woman but, yes, I'm glad I was there.'

I lean forward. 'I arrived just as her doctor was leaving, and she was terribly upset. He'd just explained that the miscarriage did her serious damage because of scars from a—procedure— many years ago.'

He nods and I see he understands exactly what I mean.

'Harry, he said she can't have a child now, not *ever*, and they both wanted one so much. But Izabel said she's not going to tell Felix! She made me swear I wouldn't either, though I said nothing about you. You're bound by confidentiality, anyway.'

'She's got to, some time or other,' says Harry, drinking his beer.

'She says she'll keep trying and perhaps a miracle will happen, so it wouldn't be fair to break Felix's heart when God might prevail.'

'I had no idea she was so religious.'

'She's not—or not till now, at any rate. I suppose if it gives her hope …' I shrug.

'You don't embrace the faith yourself?' Harry says.

'Not really. I observe the proprieties, Christmas services and so on,' I say. 'You?'

'I'm not, but my mother's a devout Catholic, which rather complicates things. You see, to comfort her when my father died I promised her that I'd always follow Church teachings. Such as not divorcing, for instance.'

'Oh,' I say. 'The papers report the ending of so many marriages nowadays I thought if things were too difficult with Charlotte—'

'Sadly, not while my mother's still alive.' He smiles wryly. 'And she's that tough-as-nails Scottish stock that goes on forever. No, Charlotte and I are stuck with each other.'

'Would a psychiatrist help, perhaps?'

'She did see one for a few sessions, but then she persuaded *him* to go to the track with her! No, Charlotte doesn't want to understand her problem and all I can do is endure with good grace. Bury myself in work. Put on a civilised face.'

'I'm so sorry, Harry. For both of you.'

He gazes at me. 'Don't look so sombre, *jungman*. Worse things happen at sea.'

'Perhaps they do, *matros*, but that doesn't stop dry land being something of a trial as well.'

'Very true,' he says, and we both laugh.

A moment later Pete and Billie come in the door, with Charlotte just behind them, excited because she's had a win and wants to shout us all drinks.

Pete and Billie depart for Hamble and their letters are full of happy tales of prangs and near misses and delight in their achievements on various sorts of machinery. I'm not sure what any of it means but I'm glad for them.

For myself I'm finding the reality of inheriting the Kensington house more daunting than I'd expected—the legalities, the repairs, the expenses. Nanna helps of course, but despite my buffer of capital in the bank I'll need to get a job at some time. I can no longer afford to go on playing the lady of leisure.

But what can a girl like me do? I'd asked Harry that night we were nursing Maria on the ship, and I still have no idea. I envy Billie her passion for flying, yet that's something she can do by herself. But I can hardly sail a square-rigger alone—and at heart I know my time on *Inverley* was a unique and unrepeatable experience.

With Freddy's death I've changed too. No longer a girl but not a woman either. I'm twenty-five now and it's surprising how rarely I meet men who interest me, or who are interested in me in return. Perhaps one day I'll find a lover, a husband, settle into a marriage.

But oh, how I wish I could be brave *jungman* Elias once more, or that confident Aphrodite of *West-End Winnie* days, or even a child again, safe behind my coolness and distance and clear secret gaze.

And I wonder instead how I've come to this.

Izabel, pale and thin, has taken on a part in a new West End production, playing a secretary tormented by an evil doctor. She's billed everywhere now as Izabel Malory, not Peres, which pleases Felix. He often mentions their hopes for a future pregnancy and Izabel echoes him. It worries me, but I suppose it's her choice to maintain a thread of optimism. Or delusion.

The reviews of Izabel's play are excellent, so Harry, Charlotte and I go to see it one night. It's a packed house, probably because people have come to gawk at Izabel so soon after her illness. But they're quickly won over by her character's wit and sensitivity, her triumph over the evil doctor, and of course, her handsome detective lover waiting in the wings.

Afterwards we go to a nightclub. Charlotte is in indigo satin and looks wonderful. I'm in my favourite deep red silk dress, but I don't wear the ruby ring that matches it—I've put that safely away, haunted by Harry's expression when he said to give it to his daughter if he had one. Now I know he believes he'll never have a child.

Charlotte seems to know quite a few people at the club, smiling and waving her champagne glass at them. A man comes over and asks her to dance and when she returns, flushed and happy, my bare hand catches her eye.

'You're not wearing the ring I gave you, Eliza,' she says teasingly. 'Are you sick of it?'

'Not at all, it's beautiful.'

'But?' Charlotte laughs. 'Sweetie, don't *worry*. Harry told me you'd quite misunderstood—fancied I'd said it was my grandmother's ring when it was really *his* old granny's. Too much champers, I expect.' She shrugs carelessly. 'Still, it was mine to give away if I felt like it.'

'Of course, Charlotte.'

But I hadn't misunderstood her. My friend had lied to me.

Another man comes over and she goes to dance with him. I meet Harry's pained, patient eyes and we smile ruefully.

'I do love the ring, Harry,' I say. 'And I'm certain you'll have a daughter one day to inherit it.'

'Perhaps. But I can't imagine anyone but you wearing it now, Eliza,' he says, with an odd intensity. I'm pleased, but not quite sure what he means.

After a pause he says, 'I saw Izabel the other day. I suggested she tell Felix the truth about her infertility, but she still refuses to. I also tried to explain to her the damage *he's* still suffering from the war, but she wasn't much interested in that either.'

'Is Felix still suffering? I thought it was all behind him.'

He shakes his head. 'I have an old friend who specialises in shellshock who'd say it will probably never be behind him. That kind of trauma can recur under stress. Eliza, always be a little careful with Felix, won't you?'

'He's my *uncle*. I can't imagine he'd hurt anyone.'

'He's unreliable under pressure, especially if he feels threatened,' says Harry. 'Remember how viciously unpleasant he could be on the ship?'

'That was ages ago and he's been fine ever since. And he was *so* kind to Izabel when she was ill.'

Harry nods and shrugs. 'Perfectly true. I probably just worry too much.'

The music ends, and Charlotte and her partner sit down with a rowdy group at another table.

Harry says, 'Now Izabel's better, what do you think Min-lu is going do? Any plans?'

'She's decided to return to Australia at the end of the year to see Filipa and Lucy and their families again.'

There's a long pause. 'Ah.' There's an odd tension in his voice. 'Does that mean you're going back with her?'

'No, I like it here, Harry,' I say, sipping my champagne. 'I'm happy to stay put.'

I look up and he's gazing at me, his grey eyes steady, his intelligent face still. 'Good to hear,' he says.

And something shifts—shockingly—in the world. For the first time I understand that I could not bear to leave London: I could not bear to leave Harry.

I would miss him terribly, this man I once so lightly assumed was not for me. I would miss Charlotte's husband more than I could possibly endure.

Light glances off the glass in his hand and I yearn to hold those dear fingers against my cheek and kiss them. My throat tightens with regret and anguish and love.

How on earth did I not *know*?

Later, sleepless in the early hours, I scold myself. Of course I didn't know, because there's nothing *to* know. I can't trust these feelings—I'm in mourning, I'm vulnerable, prey to infatuation. This is simply an old friendship grown sentimental with loss. The madness will pass like a sudden storm, forgotten when the sun emerges.

But the storm doesn't pass.

I read yet another yet interview with Izabel and Felix in the paper, and am intrigued to see that Felix says he's giving up his law practice: he has patriotic plans to do more for his country.

I sigh. Soon we all may have to do more for our country. Exactly as Granddad had feared, the resurgence of Germany has been fast, violent and terrifying. Herr Hitler is now dictator and rearmament has began.

Every day I see worrying reports, but to my astonishment most people simply disregard them. Some even claim the stories are planted by 'agitators' or 'communists.' Harry is the only person I know who's as concerned as me, but we rarely have a chance to talk.

Perhaps in rebellion against her famous father, Charlotte gets annoyed if anyone mentions those *tedious events* in Germany. Her father may be Jewish but her mother isn't, so she's not a Jew herself, she says, and glad of it. Really, people should just stop *complaining*.

But I see dreadful patterns emerging. In just a few short months, political parties and trade unions are banned, prison camps set up for Jews, Gypsies and homosexuals, and books burnt like witches in savage celebrations.

War is suddenly no longer a thing of the distant past, but an ominous storm roiling dark in the offing. And today's glittering weapons and ships and planes are triumphs of lethality that make the Great War look like a quaint, muddy relic.

Yet like everyone else I hope the Germans will come to their senses, or that the world, struggling with the Depression and extremism and unemployment, will find a way to avert disaster.

It will all work out I tell myself. And like everyone else I prefer to focus on my own ordinary life.

But even that is diminished.

Pete and Billie are away at Hamble, and there are few reasons for our little gang to get together. And when we do, I don't know what's more painful—not seeing Harry at all, or having to pretend he's simply a friend when I do.

I also fear that Charlotte has realised my feelings towards her husband have changed.

She's flirtatiously happy when Pete and Billie come to London, but when it's just the three of us alone she's cold to Harry and sarcastic to me.

She makes it clear she finds our chat unbearably dull, especially if it concerns ships, old friends or the situation in Europe. We don't even meet for afternoon tea together as we used to. She's *awfully* busy, she says.

One day when I'm browsing in a bookshop in London, I look up surprised, thinking I see her outside in her favourite cornflower-blue coat.

But the woman is turned away and walking arm in arm with a good looking man. He bends his head and kisses her, so it couldn't have been Charlotte.

PART III: THE *HERZOGIN* SUMMER

22. Pete: Free Love

I'm glad Billie and I came over to England when we did. Now, when I sit by Freddy's bed, he tells me tales of spices and silks and intrigues in the East, when he was young and in love with Min-lu.

He says gruffly the years after her were pretty dull, at least until she came back into his life, but I suspect they weren't all that dull. He's always been a fine figure of a man.

Sometimes he talks about his son, my father Sam. Of course I knew Freddy married someone else not knowing Min-lu was pregnant, but I hadn't thought about how it was for him. Missing out on Sam's life is his greatest regret, he says.

He wants Eliza and me to have a precious dog-eared packet of letters Sam sent him from boarding school. When I read them later I see what a nice little kid my father was, and his words give me a lump in my throat.

Billie sits with Granddad too and always makes him laugh, even when he's in pain. He fades slowly and we have enough time to say our farewells, but it's still a kick in the guts when he finally goes. Afterwards Billie is a gem, while the rest of us are useless with grief.

Eliza is fairly knocked about by the loss too, and we all start going out for meals or a drink a few times a week. I think it helps her. She doesn't seem to have much of a social life, which is odd, because she's a bit of a stunner when she wants to be.

During this time I get to know her mate Harry Bell, the mosquito boffin, who I thought was such a bore in the pub at Port Lincoln all those years ago. Turns out he's a great bloke after all. And Charlotte, charming Charlotte. What can I say?

I'm still head over heels for Billie but I don't have a chance—she's made that clear enough, often enough, till even someone dimmer than me could understand. Golden Charlotte is so different from Billie: feminine, sweet-natured, alluring. How could I not find her attractive?

But she's a married woman so I keep a firm rein on the old impulses. Speaking of reins, she certainly has a bee in her bonnet about horse-racing!

Eliza tries to warn me off but I go to the track a few times with Charlotte and it all gets rather expensive, rather quickly. Even the pleasure of her company doesn't quite ease the pain of my empty wallet, so I back out of that particular amusement pretty smartly.

One bitterly cold morning in February 1933, Billie and I leave for Hamble. Spencer the chauffeur drives us the eighty miles to Hampshire, and I can't stop myself staring at the rolling fields that look like something out of my childhood story-books.

I'm pretty curious to see this farm my grandfather has left me. It's two hundred acres or so and carries sheep and cereal crops. I'm not sure how I'll juggle being a farmer and a pilot, but expect I'll figure it out. Spencer was raised in this part of the world so I can get a few tips from him.

We drive along a winding road up to the old stone farmhouse, which has a courtyard and barns to one side and looks out over green hills. A fire is burning in the sitting-room grate and we rush to warm our icy hands and feet.

There are four comfortable bedrooms upstairs, mine and Billie's respectably separated by a bathroom.

That evening the housekeeper, Mrs Warren, produces a great spread for dinner. Afterwards I stretch and say, 'Reckon I could get to enjoy the life of a country squire.'

'What about flying?' says Billie. 'You'll have to concentrate, Pete. No mucking around.'

I nod. 'Don't worry, I want this as much as you do.'

Next morning we drive the old farm car the ten miles or so into Hamble. The car's no racer but it'll be useful for getting around. When we reach the town even Billie is charmed by the quaint houses.

We can see the waters of the Solent glimmering ahead, so I realise we've passed the airfield and need to go back half a mile. Finally we enter the Air Service Training grounds, a long road with clusters of sheds and buildings on either side.

I stop beyond the buildings. In front of us is a big hangar and a dozen planes lined up on the airfield.

'We're here,' I say. 'We're bloody *here*. I can't believe it.'

Billie says haltingly, 'Thanks, Pete. Thanks for everything, especially for making me get off my arse and come along.'

'Couldn't have done it without you, crazy lady.'

AST is booming. It has squash courts, tennis courts, a sailing club, and sports fields for cricket, hockey and soccer. It also has a large dormitory for students: but not for Billie.

The ex-RAF Commandant says, 'Of course, we *welcome* the interest of the fair sex in aviation, but I'm afraid we don't actually have the facilities for women to, ah, live in. However, we do provide a female lavatory not too far from the training rooms.'

'I'm sure Lady Bailey, Countess Frijs and Amy Johnson found that of enormous comfort,' Billie says, and the Commandant's moustache anxiously twitches. But he finds her lodgings at a nearby cottage, which she likes, especially as it's warmer than our rooms.

The Commandant tells us that this year there'll be students attending from twenty different countries. Our own particular cohort includes a Siamese prince, an exiled Russian, two Germans, a Chinese, a Pole, an Iraqi, three Indians, and a Peruvian, as well as a dozen British lads from posh schools.

Few have even as much experience as me, and of course none have as much as Billie, the lone female student. Some of the men are scornfully dismissive: at least until they see her fly. Then they go rather quiet.

Many students are doing just a single course, like the private pilot's A or commercial B, or Navigator, Ground Engineer or Wireless Telegraphy licences. Those here for the full three years do all of these, plus AST's own blind-flying and instructor courses.

Since I already have the pilot's A and an engineering degree, and Billie has A, B and instructor endorsements, we'll do the full course over only two years.

Billie's greater experience should have reduced her time even further but, as she says, she clearly has to train for longer because she doesn't pee standing up.

New students fly Avro Avians, Cadets and Tutors, rugged little biplanes like the Moths I'm used to. Advanced training is on Armstrong-Whitworth Atlases, a Siskin, a few seaplanes and flying-boats, and a powerful, triple-engined Avro Five. Billie says she can't wait to take that out for a spin.

I start studying towards my B licence, and Billie works on endorsements for AST's unfamiliar birds, but much of our time at Hamble isn't actually flying.

First we do a parachute course, then start the longer Ground Engineer's A and C licences, plus Navigation (to my own relief it turns out I'm quite good at that).

We study the unfamiliar Avro and Armstrong-Whitworth planes, their engines, construction, rigging, electricals. It's hard work, but wireless telegraphy is fun—as a kid I was obsessed with Morse, so I only need the short course. Billie does the long course, but of course she picks it up faster than anyone else.

We learn to fly blind, on instruments only. In class we use a mock-up of a cockpit covered with a hood and I 'crash' a sobering number of times before getting the hang of it.

That's followed by real flights, with a hood over the cockpit and an instructor in the seat behind to keep us out of trouble. It's hair-raising.

Through the spring and long summer of our first year at Hamble we make friends and study and fly and play sports.

I find a place on the cricket team while Billie's a demon at hockey. We spend weekends at the farm and even Billie enjoys the quiet. We're blissfully happy.

Well, perhaps not blissfully.

I still yearn for Billie and she still yearns for anyone but me. She has a few flirtations—the Russian, an Indian, a public-school boy—but that summer she seems to fall hard for one of the Germans, Herr Heinrich Hell.

'Herr *Hell*?' I say. 'You've got to be joking.'

He not only has a stupid name, he's a cold-eyed bastard too, like his equally unpleasant compatriot, short, dark Franz. Herr Hell himself is tall and blond and smooth and, beyond my own selfish desire to consign him to hell—I worry about Billie.

Of course she reckons she can take care of herself, but she seems more caught up in this bloke than usual. And because men speak unguardedly among themselves I know Herr Hell has little but contempt for women, and Billie in particular.

One day I tell him calmly if he opens his mouth about her one more time I'll do something to his plane and he'll never get home to his Nazi mates again.

He shuts his trap, at least in my hearing, but then I really start worrying when I realise she's teaching herself German from a book. At the farm one afternoon I try to bring it up casually but she sees through me.

'Spit it out, Pete,' she says. 'You don't like Heinrich? I'm not surprised. He knows how to treat a woman.'

'What, I don't?'

'You know how to charm them into bed but I doubt they have a very good time there,' she says. 'You always go for the easy targets, the barmaids, the shop-girls, but never for someone you'd actually have to care about.'

'But Billie, I care! About *you* if you haven't noticed.'

'Puppy-love,' she says. 'You don't care about what's going on in the world.'

'And your little Nazi does? Prison camps for anyone his stupid dictator doesn't like? Burning *books*, for Christ's sake? What kind of civilisation does that?'

'A sophisticated civilisation trying to create a better future for all of us,' she says loftily.

'For all of *them*,' I say. 'The rest of us don't have much to look forward to.'

'You don't know anything about it, Pete.'

'Golly, Heinrich's prick has taught you that much?'

She throws *Teach Yourself German* at me and doesn't miss.

'Do you ever wonder what he says about you behind your back, Billie?' I say, rubbing my throbbing head.

'Yeah? Do tell, Pete.'

'It's not quite what you'd call *sophisticated*. He's planning to hand you over to his malignant mate Franz to screw you sideways when he's finished fucking your tits off. And I quote.'

She's very still. She's worked among men for years and she knows I'm not lying.

'But then, you've always believed in free love—without limits or possessiveness, wasn't it?' I shrug. 'Going great guns by the look of it. Old Heinrich's certainly not possessive.'

She walks out.

This is all rather awkward, as we're going to a wedding tomorrow. Min-lu's maid Penfold and Spencer the chauffeur have decided to tie the knot.

Penfold's a dear but I can't for the life of me see what she's hoping to get out of the marital bed. She must be at least forty.

My housekeeper Mrs Warren wants to retire, so the plan is for Spencer and the new Mrs Spencer to move into the housekeeper's cottage and look after the farm. It's a great idea because Spencer is a fount of knowledge on farming matters.

Eliza and Min-lu are driving down from London tomorrow morning for the wedding, and bringing Harry and Charlotte with them.

I've been looking forward to having a nosh-up and seeing the old gang again, so I hope the argument with Billie doesn't put a dampener on the day.

That evening I have a couple of beers. Herr Hell drives up in his racy red sportscar (another reason to dislike him) and Billie leaves with him without a word. I've calmed down now. I know there's truth in what she said—not about Hitler and his thugs, of course—but about me.

> *You know how to charm them into bed but I doubt they have a very good time there. You always go for the easy targets, the barmaids, the shop-girls, but never for someone you'd have to actually care about.*

I haven't had as many conquests as Billie thinks, but I know full well I turn on the charm to get my way, then turn it off when I want out. And yes, the girls are often easy targets. Lately I've been laying siege to a barmaid at the local, and anticipate a quick victory.

Do girls *not* have a very good time in my bed? I've noticed they don't seem to lose themselves in the moment as I do, and I feel a bit awkward trying the old fingers-and-mouth trick I'd hoped might be the key to female delight.

I sigh. Basically it's all still a bit of a mystery. But if I were with someone I cared about—someone being Billie of course—I'm certain it wouldn't be such a mystery.

Later I hear her return. Herr Hell drives off without his usual infuriating flurry of beeps on the horn and Billie goes upstairs without her usual greeting. Have they argued? I bloody hope so.

After she's had time to get ready for bed I finish my beer and go upstairs. I fall asleep quickly but have to get up again because of the beer. Not wanting to disturb her I'm as quiet as possible in the bathroom.

When I turn to go I hear a soft noise. She's weeping.

I haven't the foggiest what to do. I wish I had the guts to go in and comfort her but don't think I could survive another scalding rejection. Instead I go back to bed and try to forget the sound of Billie's grief.

The day of Penfold and Spencer's wedding is hot and scented with hay. Eliza, Nanna, Charlotte and Harry arrived at eleven, and I'm gobsmacked to see *Eliza* behind the wheel of the car.

'Now Spencer's coming to live here I want to be able to get myself around,' she says, cool as a cucumber. 'Driving isn't all that hard, you know.'

I hug Nanna, whose gaze is calm and affectionate. I hope the pain of Freddy's death has eased for her; it's been over six months now, after all. (Later I realise, in a lifetime of stupid thoughts, that would have to take the absolute cake.)

Harry looks well. I joke about the small gold-rimmed spectacles he now wears and he grins. Charlotte, delectable as always, kisses me on the cheek. Her perfume makes me think of sex but most things about Charlotte make me think of sex.

Of course it's Billie I love, but Charlotte is unique, a law unto herself. I can look, can't I?

At the wedding Billie wears an olive green dress, sophisticated and flattering, and she's got extra make-up on her eyes. We sit beside each other in the pew and the only sign she gives of yesterday's quarrel is the tension in her hands.

I murmur, 'You look really nice, Billie,' but she ignores me. Maybe that's a sign too.

Penfold comes down the aisle on her father's arm. To my surprise she has a good figure, previously hidden by her maid's uniform.

As she takes her place beside Spencer they gaze deeply into each other's eyes, and I realise that not only is Penfold going to have fun in the marital bed, but she may even have had a romp or two in the pre-marital bed.

The wedding breakfast is held at the farm. We've set out tables in the courtyard so there's room for everyone to toast the speeches and enjoy the lavish spread, and I have fun catching up on what's happened over the last six months.

Eliza tells me she's still at a loose end and I get the feeling she's oddly distracted by something. Harry's apparently going great guns with his research, though he's a bit distant too. Probably thinking about his beloved mosquitoes.

Charlotte says she finds life a little dull away from her teaching job, and I wonder why she doesn't just have a kid or two. She says she's had some marvellous wins lately at the track, so clearly she's still mad for the gee-gees.

I search for Billie after the meal and finally run her to earth in the little sitting room, curled up on one of the sofas sipping a drink.

She glances at me then looks away. I sit down beside her—at a distance, I'm not that stupid.

'Billie, I'm sorry,' I say. 'I truly didn't mean to hurt you, but you needed to know Hell really is a bastard. He just wants to screw you and boast about it. He doesn't care for you.'

'Thanks heaps, Pete,' she says calmly. 'Now fuck off, will you?'

I can't think of a witty riposte so I do, then go upstairs to the bathroom—too many beers as usual.

When I come out Charlotte is leaning casually against the wall.

'Oh, sorry,' I say. 'All yours.'

She smiles with that amazing combination of sweetness and lust, and before I can even grasp what's happening she puts her hands on my shoulders and pulls me towards her.

Then she kisses me. Charlotte *kisses* me.

Part of my mind says, Billie, remember Billie, you fool. The other part doesn't say anything, it just falls and falls into a timeless, dark, sweet moment where everything in the world at last makes some kind of sense.

I hear someone coming up the stairs.

Charlotte steps back—I'd have killed to keep going—and gazes at me. As whoever it is almost reaches us she says, 'I *do* love playing with fire, don't you?'

She slips past me into the bathroom and I see Eliza at the top of the stairs.

'Great party, Pete,' she says. 'I'm enjoying it.'

'No thanks to me, Sis, it's Penfold and Spencer's big day,' I say, amazed at how steady my voice sounds. 'See you downstairs.'

23. Harry: Playing With Fire

It's Penfold and Spencer's wedding day. When I answer the door Eliza says happily, 'Spencer's down at Hamble helping with the preparations, so I'm going to be your chauffeur today!'

As she gets in the car Charlotte says, 'What a little *adventurer* you are, sweetie.' I put our bags in the boot and sit in the back seat beside her, greeting Min-lu in the front.

'Spencer says he's taught her everything, so I assume we'll get there in one piece,' says Min-lu.

Eliza grins at her then releases the brake and off we go, weaving neatly through the streets then onto the main road to Hampshire.

Eliza drives well but that doesn't surprise me—she's always tackled everything with a fierce sense of focus. That's why I'm puzzled she's seemed so lost lately, although Freddy's death was probably enough to throw anyone off course.

I glance at her. She's wearing a jaunty red hat, her soft dark hair falling to her shoulders. I can just see the line of her cheek, her eyelashes, her strong small hand changing gears.

'Oh, do look, darling,' says Charlotte, gazing at Eliza. 'Some sort of *cow.*'

We pass a herd of what are indubitably cows and I wonder if anyone else can hear the venom.

I wonder how she knows. I didn't. Not until that evening at the nightclub six months ago, when Eliza and I were chatting about my grandmother's ring.

It crossed my mind how wrong it had looked on Charlotte the few times she wore it—woefully old-fashioned she said—and how perfectly the dainty, intricate richness suited Eliza.

Without thinking I said, *But now I can't imagine anyone but you wearing it now, Eliza.*

We went on chatting about ordinary things; but my pulse was pounding and I didn't understand why. And then when she spoke of going away, at last I did. The sense of loss hit me like lightning.

How did I not *know* what she means to me, what she's meant to me since *Inverley?* Of course I've always loved her fierceness, her kindness, her wit; but the shifting sands of Charlotte's excesses have left me cautious and full of self-doubt.

When Eliza said she was happy to stay in London I could only mutter *Good to hear,* like a bloody fool. I actually felt like leaping up and kissing her forever, but of course I didn't. Sensible, boring old Harry won out, and the moment was lost.

Strangely, Charlotte realises. She knows something has changed in my tired acceptance of her risk-taking, even to the lovers I have every reason to believe she takes. Acquiescence has shifted to indifference and she doesn't like it.

When we were arguing once she said she'd never divorce me, everyone would think her immoral. *Immoral?* Sounds like her ghastly mother's favourite rant. She also said I'm too useful to her and, yes, I suppose a meal-ticket always comes in handy.

But Charlotte has the upper hand.

Just as I began to consider divorcing her, despite my promise to my poor widowed mother, my young sister Tina wrote to say that Mum is well at the moment, but the doctor fears her heart might not be able to cope with any sudden shocks.

Charlotte found Tina's letter and read it aloud at the dinner table, and smiled.

It's a relief when we finally reach the farm. Pete seems his usual cheerful self then I realise he's rather distracted, and when Billie gets in the car to go to the wedding I suspect she's been crying.

Perhaps things aren't as smooth sailing—or flying—here as I'd assumed.

At the small church Penfold looks most attractive and Spencer is bursting with pride, and I'm happy for them both. Their vows are touching but they make me feel old and cynical.

At the wedding breakfast I find Eliza has been seated on one side of me and Charlotte the other. After a time Charlotte gets up with her drink and wanders away. I have a few words across the table to Billie, as sardonic as ever, but then she goes inside. Pete chats for a while but keeps looking around, for Billie I suppose. Then he disappears too.

I've mostly kept my distance from Eliza in recent months, it seems the wisest thing to do. Perhaps I'll get over what I feel for her—though I suspect not—but I don't want her to be any more of a target for Charlotte's malice than she already is.

But I'm relaxed with the food and wine and we fall into our usual easy ways. She tells me about recently visiting *Inverley* at the London docks, when Clarkson's agent Mr Weatherall took her to authorise some supplies for the layup in Mariehamn.

'Captain Nilsen was so happy,' Eliza says. '*Inverley* came third in the Grain Race this year—can you believe it?'

'No,' I say laughing.

'But *Parma* won with eighty-three days, a record. Ruben de Cloux was master.'

'Not surprising then. He had all those fast passages with *Herzogin Cecilie* a few years ago.'

'Speaking of the Duchess, she was there too! Captain Nilsen took me aboard and, my goodness, she's magnificent. I almost blushed for *Inverley*, not in the same class.'

'But be fair, no ship's in *Herzogin*'s class,' I say.

'And her master, Sven Eriksson, so tall and solemn, served us wine. The saloon is beautiful too, all panelled timber and red velvet.' Eliza grins. 'Marred a touch, perhaps, by the portraits of grim Gusta' and his wife Hilda on the wall.'

'They're mandatory on all of Gusta's vessels. Keeps everyone on their toes,' I say, gazing at her smiling eyes. 'Do you think, if you could, you'd ever go to sea again?'

'Yes, but now I think I'd find it hard to feel there's a place for me there. You?'

'The same,' I say. 'I'd love it but you have to be born to the life, like the Ålanders. Anyway, I'm too old and creaky now to be scampering up ratlines.'

She laughs. 'You're only thirty-one, Harry. I reckon you could still get to the topmast without too much effort.' She shakes her head. 'Heavens, I used to think thirty was ancient. Now, at twenty-five, it's staring me in the face.'

'Not yet, *jungman*. Enjoy your wild, carefree youth for now.'

'Hah,' she says. 'Nothing very wild or carefree about it.'

'How's Min-lu going?'

'Her usual dignified self, but she's still suffering.'

I nod. 'She and Freddy were lucky. Happiness like that in a marriage is rare.'

'Is it, *matros*?'

I don't know what to say and there's a pause. Eliza looks at her glass. 'You said once you'd tell me how you and Charlotte got back together again.'

'Well, I went to a talk at the Fabian Society and she was there helping her father Otto, who'd broken his ankle.' I shrug. 'I don't know. Sometimes you just can't stop yourself. Like you and that fool actor. Oh, sorry—'

She says, 'Yes, me and that fool actor,' and we laugh quietly.

After the wedding, the Spencers leave for their cottage down the lane and we all help clean up. Well, not all. Charlotte has a headache and goes to rest upstairs.

In the warm sunset I stand on the flagstones outside the kitchen and gaze at the golden hills. I deliberately turn my thoughts to a phase of the *Plasmodium* life cycle and a new staining technique I'm experimenting with.

It almost stops me thinking about Eliza.

Pete, somewhat the worse for wear, is sitting inside at the kitchen table. Through the open window I hear Eliza saying, 'Heavens, Pete, you really do need some coffee.'

There's a clinking of cups. 'There. So what on *earth*'s going on with you and Billie?'

Pete sighs. 'Just a stupid argument, Sis. She got herself involved with some bastard and didn't take kindly to me pointing out that's what he was.'

'Is that all?'

'It was a pretty savage argument.'

'And upstairs?'

'You saw?' His voice is startled.

'I know your guilty look.'

'She was only flirting. Playing with fire, she said.'

'Pete, don't grin. How *could* you?'

'It was just a silly moment, that's all. You know I wouldn't— she's *married*, come on, Lizzie.'

I close my eyes in despair.

That night I can't sleep in the unusual warmth. Everyone goes to bed, Eliza and Min-lu at the end of the hall and Pete and Billie in their own rooms. Charlotte and I have the large front bedroom and I can hear her slowly breathing beside me. She's drunk too much as usual.

The house is silent. I get up, put on a cotton dressing-gown and tip-toe downstairs. Through the kitchen, the flagstones pleasingly cool under my feet, and out into the scented night. I light a cigarette and lean against the wall.

I think for a moment about Charlotte but that's too painful, so I try not to think, but I'm overwhelmed with memories instead. Glimpses of soft lips and the curve of a cheek, slim hands and warm unguarded eyes.

After a time I sigh and light another cigarette. The door opens and my heart thumps as Eliza comes out, a cotton kimono tied around her narrow waist. She's gazing ahead at the hills, silver in the moonlight, then sees me.

She says shyly, 'Oh. I'm not the only one awake.'

'It's certainly warm tonight,' I say, like a fool. There's a silence.

'Didn't know you smoked, Harry.'

'Now and then, under stress. And when on watch, of course.'

'Rolf used to share his smokes with me then, too.' She smiles. 'Not much more than butts.'

'Here you are. Better than a butt.'

I offer her the cigarette and she takes a puff, but it makes her cough and she hands it back. 'Too much for me nowadays.'

'Me too. Just an excuse to come out here, really,' I say.

'It's lovely tonight.'

Silence falls again. I stub out the cigarette. 'Can't sleep?' I ask.

'Not very well.' She sighs and says, 'Oh, Harry. It's just … I wish I could find myself again. I'm still not off that lee shore.'

'It was only nine months ago you lost Freddy, don't forget. You're still bereaved.'

'Not as simple as that, I fear. I've probably got to grow up,' she says. 'Accept my lot in life, settle down, get married. Everyone assures me that's the path to happiness.'

'Well, everyone may not be entirely correct in that regard,' I say dryly.

After a pause she says, 'Are you all right, Harry, *really*? Charlotte's so unkind to you, and it must be painful.'

'Oddly enough, it doesn't hurt anymore.' I shrug, gazing at the silvery hills. 'No, what really hurts is yearning for something that's completely … impossible.'

'Yes,' she says. 'I know that feeling.'

She glances at me then looks away. I hear a dog barking in the distance, and through my light dressing-gown I can feel the heat of her body beside me.

But she's not standing that close, I think, then I realise she is. And I'm lost.

'I should go back to bed,' she murmurs.

I turn and we gaze at each other. 'Oh, my *dear*,' I say helplessly.

I reach out and run my fingers down her cheek, and she sighs and her eyes close. I can hardly breathe as I stroke her warm neck and shoulders and small pointed breasts.

She puts out her hands as if to fend me off, then they fall to my hips and I can feel them trembling. She says my name and pulls me against her, and I fold my arms across her slender back.

Her nipples are warm on my chest. Her hair is perfume and silk, and I kiss her face, her mouth, as if she's every desire I've ever known in my life. She whimpers deep in her throat, and I'm as hard as a lad, and she moulds herself around me—

'*Charming,*' says Charlotte.

The shock is indescribable. We painfully move apart.

Eliza says quietly, 'We didn't mean …'

'No one ever does, do they, Harry?'

My heart is pounding in rage and frustration. 'Stop it.'

'Stop what? Fancy *that*—Elias the deckhand and my long-suffering husband. Didn't think your tastes ran to boys, Harry.'

'Charlotte, don't make it worse—'

'—than it is?' She laughs. 'People who play with *fire* …'

'Funny,' Eliza says shakily. 'Pete quoted those words earlier. Those words exactly.'

'Oh, *that's* your knock-out punch, dear?' Charlotte flings back her hair. 'Guess what, Harry? I smooched this bitch's brother today.' She steps closer. 'But unlike you, *I* didn't mean it.'

Eliza whispers, 'Please don't.'

Charlotte turns on her. 'Fuck off, Eliza. But keep this in mind —Harry's institute couldn't possibly have a divorced man on their letterhead. Even a *hint* of scandal might bring an abrupt end to his career. Wouldn't want that, would you, sweetie?'

24. Pete: A Small Flying Boot

They all leave next morning, everyone saying they had a wonderful time. I kiss Min-lu and she says, 'Dearest Pete, I hope you find happiness at Hamble.'

'It's great there, Nanna, but I just don't know about Billie. She's such an enigma.'

'You'll work it out. She's an extraordinary woman.'

'Too extraordinary for me, perhaps,' I say sadly.

Nanna smiles. 'You must give each other time.'

'But what if someone else is more suitable for me?'

She looks at me curiously. 'I suppose you'll find out one way or the other.'

I hug Eliza, who's pretty quiet this morning. Harry is too—hung over, I expect. Mind you, I was blotto myself too. I recall seeing them laughing together about something, probably their silly ships. My poor old sister, practically a spinster, and Harry, such a good bloke. Why is he with a wife who take risks with strange men? Well, I'm not *that* strange, but still.

And *la belle* Charlotte herself? She makes everyone feel the centre of her golden regard. Penfold becomes teary when she kisses her goodbye and Mrs Warren packs her a basket of goodies to take back to London. Everyone loves Charlotte. How could they not?

It's a grim drive into Hamble that morning. I try to make conversation but Billie stares wordlessly out the window. In desperation, I say, 'Billie, I can't bear you being so sad. I love you, truly, I love you. Please talk to me.'

There's a long silence.

I'm just about to give up when she says, 'I know you do, but you're too young.'

'For Christ's *sake*, Billie, I'll soon be twenty-three. Are you going to keep on about this till I'm thirty-three? Forty-three?'

'It's not the age. It's the cold young man you are. I'm just a fantasy to you.'

'*Cold?*'

I can't say anything more. I pull over and rest my head on the steering wheel. I certainly have something of a hangover but this is painful beyond endurance.

She says, 'I'm sorry, Pete. I don't want to hurt you. You've been a good friend, even with your clumsy attempts to save me from Herr Hell—who by the way is more talk than action.'

'It doesn't matter.' I sigh. 'If not him there'll always be someone else, won't there? You'll chase after any strutting fool as long as it's not me.'

She turns away and we drive into Hamble in silence.

I'm glad I won't see Billie much around the airfield today, we have separate classes. This afternoon she's taking a long flight, a navigation circuit test in one of the powerful Atlases.

The air is brilliantly clear, and when she takes off I watch until she's just a speck above the distant hills, gaining altitude quickly in one of the dizzying climbs she loves.

I go to the workshop, but a few minutes later hear a noise— not a bang, just a distant, horribly *wrong* noise.

I dash outside and beyond the hills is a thin, rising column of smoke. I drive as fast as I can, faster than the AST fire engine and ambulance, and get there within fifteen minutes.

By then of course there's nothing I can do. Nothing anyone can. The Atlas is still burning, a twisted skeleton, black against flames and fierce embers.

I get as close as I can—next day I find my eyebrows are singed off—but even if I'd plunged into the heart of the pyre itself it's obvious nothing could remain alive to be saved.

The fire engine arrives and pumps water until gradually the flames die down. It'll be a day or so before the ashes are cool enough to sift for fragments of bone, or a melted watch, or the zip of a small, surprisingly small, flying boot.

Other students and local farmers arrive and stand watching in silent horror. There's nothing for the ambulance men to do so they drive away, followed soon after by the fire engine.

One student comes over and says I should go back to the aerodrome but I just shake my head.

Eventually everyone leaves. I walk up a hill nearby and sit in the grass, and try to comprehend what has happened. Just this morning, this *morning*, Billie was sitting beside me, the arch of her neck as graceful as a wing.

Her fine, clever hands were alive, and they buckled her helmet and started her engine and worked the melted controls of this ... inferno.

None of it makes sense. I simply sit while time passes and discover that the phrase *aching heart* isn't a metaphor after all. Or perhaps I've been shot in the chest and hadn't noticed.

Farmers and local villagers drive along the lane below, stop and get out and stare at the embers, murmur to each other, then leave. A few come up the hill to check on me and sit down and try to say sympathetic things, but I send them away.

Later I see a pair of swallows swooping high in the sky and they make me think of her. I start crying in harsh sobs and cannot stop, but that eases nothing at all and eventually I fall silent in the rosy twilight.

What a beautiful day it's been, just the kind she loves.

Loved.

It's almost dark by now and I should make a move. But I don't know where to go. The airfield? The farm? Why would I bother going anywhere at all if she isn't there? Perhaps I'll just roll over onto my side and sleep right here in the grass.

Sounds reasonable, but I'm not sure I know how to fall asleep anymore. It hits me that this is the start of my new life—my *before* and *after* life—and I've no idea how to even begin.

Yet another car stops in the lane and I feel sick. A farmer in a hat goes over to the dying embers and stands there outlined against the glow, while another comes towards me and sits down, grunting. Fuck off, you old creep, I think. Just leave me alone.

'Pete?' says the figure beside me. I realise despair has finally driven me into madness.

The figure grabs my wrist and says, 'Pete, it's *me.*'

I look at the hand, the arm, the face. The face half-covered in shadow. In blood. The fragments of the impossible reorganise themselves, and for the second time that day I feel as if I've been shot in the chest.

'I parachuted *out*, Pete,' she says. 'But I got stuck at the top of a tree.'

'Why didn't you undo your harness?' I say stupidly.

'Hit my head and hurt my wrists. The harness was jammed, took ages to cut through. I was so dizzy climbing down, and had to walk miles through the fields to find a farmhouse. I didn't think I could make it but I knew you'd be worried—'

'Yeah, a bit,' I say. My face is raw, swollen and tear-stained.

'The farmer couldn't get his car started for ages. He didn't have a phone, I couldn't ring to say I was safe. I was nearly screaming with frustration.' There are tears running through the dried blood on her face. 'Pete, I'm so *sorry.*'

She rests her head on my shoulder and sobs. I put my arms around her but I don't weep. I can't, not anymore. I remember my fantasy on the ship, Billie in danger so I could rescue her.

But she was in danger today and I couldn't do a thing. She looked after herself, just as she always said she would.

Finally she rubs her wet, bloody face on my shoulder and says, 'Let's go back to the farm. I need a bath.'

'Doctor first.'

She stands, grunting in pain again. We walk down the hill and thank the farmer who brought her. He says he'll drive to the airfield and tell them she's safe, so I can get her to a doctor as soon as possible.

I do so, and a nice old bloke stitches up the cut on her forehead and bandages her sprained wrist and tells me how to check her for concussion.

It's late when we get back to the farm. The stars are a stream of silver, brilliant in the clear night, and Billie stops to admire them as she always does.

'Come on,' I say. 'You need supper. I do as well. Haven't eaten all day.' The newlywed Mrs Spencer has left sandwiches out for us and retired to her cottage with Mr Spencer, and I think longingly of such simple happiness, so far beyond my reach.

We eat the sandwiches and they taste like nectar.

'Go and have your bath,' I say. 'I'll make a pot of tea.'

Later, both freshly washed, we sit by the fire.

'Must have been an oil blowout,' she says. 'A black spray burst all over the windshield, then the engine stopped.'

'Yeah, that plane was leaking last week, but the workshop said it was repaired. So have you got any double vision? Headache?'

'No, my head's okay. Tired, though.'

'Not surprising. Me too.'

She hesitates. 'Pete, I can't *tell* you how sorry I am—'

'Then don't. Let's turn in.'

I'm about to switch off my bedside lamp when the door opens and Billie, in a cotton nightgown, enters.

She pulls back the sheet and lies down beside me. I move over to give her room, then stop.

'Billie, *no*. What the hell is this—sympathy sex? I don't want it.'

And it's true. For the first time my ever-dependable body, ready to spring into action at the merest thought of her, simply couldn't care less.

'No. Not sympathy.'

'What, then? I don't speak German, you know, and after all I'm only a *kid*.'

I lean up on one elbow, exhausted and pissed off. She has a plaster on her forehead, her short copper hair is in disarray on the pillow, and she's gazing at me.

'It's too late, Billie, I don't want to *care* about you anymore. Today's cured me of that.'

'Did you ever wonder why I wouldn't sleep with you before, Pete?' she says.

'*Why*? You didn't want to. Obviously.'

'No, you idiot. Because I *did*, but I didn't trust you. Remember this morning when I called you cold? You are, you know.'

'Oh, that was just this morning? *Christ.* Yes, I do recall you calling me cold. That'd be why I was bawling like a baby when I saw swallows that reminded me of you, why I wanted to *die* when I thought ...'

My throat closes. I lie back with my hand over my eyes and stupid tears trickle into my ears.

Billie curls against my side and whispers, 'Pete, it's all right.'

'It's *not* all right. What if you'd really been *killed*? How the hell would I have even gone on?'

(I think of my blithe assumption Min-Lu would get over losing Freddy in just a matter of months and even from the depths of my sorrow I feel shame.)

'You said this morning you loved me, but this is love,' says Billie. 'It's not dancing and romance, it's *this*. Did you have any idea this morning you could feel something so deeply?'

I rub my eyes. 'No, and quite frankly I'd rather not have found out, either.'

'I'd rather not have found out myself, too,' she says. 'It's been a fucking horrible day.'

That makes me smile. 'So you didn't crash the plane on purpose just to teach me a lesson?'

'Idiot.'

I turn sideways to look at her. Daringly, I stroke the side of her face and trace the line of her lip with my thumb. I say quietly, 'This has been the worst and best day of my whole life, Billie. Losing you and finding you again.'

She nestles into my shoulder. 'No it's not. It's after midnight now, so *today* is actually going to be the best day of your whole life.'

She stretches her long thighs against mine and caresses my face, and very slowly kisses my mouth. And my ever-dependable body suddenly remembers what it's supposed to do should I ever have the amazing, unbelievable good fortune to find Billie Quinn in bed beside me.

Later, dozing, bedazzled with joy, I think, she's mine, she's *mine*. And I fall into the profound sleep of the very young and very foolish.

25. Eliza: Kittikins

Next morning Charlotte's contempt poisons every word she utters during that excruciating drive back to London, but I remains silent at the wheel. Min-lu is clearly puzzled at the atmosphere, while Harry stares out the window, his face rigid, his heart probably aching like mine.

Next day the phone rings.

'How are you?' Harry asks, his deep voice so familiar my whole body flushes.

'Um, fine. You?'

'I'll live. I'm sorry, Eliza. It was completely my fault and I've told Charlotte that.'

'Does she believe you?'

'I haven't the faintest idea what she thinks,' he says dryly.

'But it wasn't all your fault, anyway. I wanted it to happen too.'

'I'm glad of that.'

After a pause he says, 'Still, if I hadn't upset the applecart we might have been able to go on as before.'

I gasp in pain. 'No, Harry, we couldn't. It was already too hard, it still is. We can't meet anymore. Shouldn't even talk like this.'

There's a long silence.

He takes a ragged breath. 'Will you be all right?'

'Christ, I don't know! Will you?'

'No.'

'Your institute—Charlotte said even a hint of disgrace—'

Harry laughs. 'It's a slightly more sophisticated place than she imagines. The departmental chairman lives with a nice young chap. The eminent lady scientist is divorced and lives with a nice young chap—'

'Not the same one, I hope.'

'And the Managing Director is in a ménage à trois.'

'Really? Who does the washing-up?'

'The Managing Director.'

I laugh, then groan. 'Oh, Harry, we can't do this. We mustn't—'

'I know. I just wanted to hear you laugh.'

After a pause I say, 'For the last time.'

After a longer pause. 'Probably.'

'I hope you'll be happy,' I say. 'Perhaps Charlotte will be too, with you all to herself. Maybe she'll even decide to have a baby— that might help.'

'No. There won't be any babies in this marriage.' His voice is rough with regret.

There's a silence.

'I should go. Nanna will be back soon.'

'Yes, I suppose so. Eliza—'

'No,' I whisper.

After a few moments he says, 'Goodbye then, shipmate. Fair winds and following seas.'

A few days after that final telephone call with Harry, Nanna sits me down and says, 'What on earth is going on, Eliza?'

I look at her in despair. 'The other night, at the farm ... Harry kissed me. Charlotte saw.'

After a pause Nanna says, 'Did you plan it?'

'No! I just got up in the night, didn't know he was there ... we didn't mean—I've been avoiding him in case this happened. I realised ages ago I cared more for him than I should.'

'Ah.' She nods. 'You've always been close.'

'As friends. I didn't expect it to come to this.'

'What will you do now?'

'I don't know.' I look up and sigh. 'Not see him, of course. Try to forget him. Oh, *God*.'

'More easily said than done, but it can be done.'

I nod. 'I suppose you had to forget Freddy when you were young.'

'Indeed, and I did. My marriage to Leo Peres was a very happy one.'

'But then Freddy came back into your life ...'

'Child, it was *forty years* later. Don't wait for that, all you'll know is disappointment. Freddy and I were fortunate, but most people find only bitterness and despair in such straits.'

'Yes.' I take a shuddering breath. 'Yes, of course I must forget, all of it.' I sigh. 'And Charlotte, too. We've grown apart but she's still my friend.'

Nanna hesitates. 'She's not your friend, Eliza. She's not anyone's friend, not even her own.'

Those few lost moments haunt me over and over—the heat of Harry's mouth, the scent of his skin, the delight of his body— and I discover time heals nothing much at all.

Drinking helps, but the consequences are too unpleasant, so I don't find much solace there.

Months pass. Life drags on and I still don't have a job or the slightest idea of what to do.

Sitting by the fire, just before Christmas, Nanna says, 'Eliza, you know I had planned to return to Australia, but now I'm not sure I should go.'

'Of course you should!' Anxiety flutters under my ribs. 'I'll miss you, but it's the right thing to do. You haven't seen the rest of the family for ages.'

'But I'm worried for you. You horizons seem to have greatly narrowed.'

'Maybe I'm just getting old, Nanna. A venerable twenty-six, after all.'

'It's not age. Remember Freddy's interests his whole life long.'

'Courage, then?' I sigh.

'Of course you've been hurt, my dear, but I think the real problem is that you're *bored*. You need something challenging. Remember how good you were at mathematics in school?'

She looks at me over her glasses. 'And I was perfectly aware you hardly even tried.'

'Were you?' I smile. 'Nobody else was.'

'You were clever at hiding away, being *unremarkable*, you once said, but you always had such a restless, curious intelligence.'

I shrug. 'I liked solving puzzles. I wonder if I love ships because they're such a puzzle? So many complex parts that have to work together to make the whole.'

She looks at me fondly. 'If Freddy were here I'm certain he'd agree with you.'

I sigh. 'Oh, Nanna. When do you think you'll go?'

'Not immediately. In a few months.'

Anxiety flutters again in my chest.

Some weeks later Izabel invites me to dinner at her glamorous apartment, and greets me, laughing.

'You're looking very well,' I say as I kiss her.

'Marvellous news, darling—a new film! *Hollywood* at last. Gable and, my God, *Cooper*.' She shivers with delight. 'Months of shooting too—the utter *luxury* of it.'

I hug her. Dear Izabel: selfish, funny, kind, tough as nails. She deserves her big break.

'She's abandoning me, I'll have to be a bachelor again,' Felix says grinning. 'But needs must. New job, you know.'

He hands me a cocktail. 'Regarding your plans to do more for your country, Felix?'

'*Absolutely*. You know I've been concerned about goings-on in Europe, damned nasty stuff. Still, I might have pottered along as before, except the most extraordinary thing happened.'

Izabel offers me a plate of canapés. 'It's *terribly* secret and thrilling, darling.'

'I was tapped on the shoulder, Eliza,' Felix says proudly. 'The Powers That Be are on the lookout for bods who speak Japanese and my accomplishments came to their attention.'

'Japanese? Why?'

'For keeping tabs on the blighters, that's why. Monitoring transmissions, deciphering codes, making sure we can read their messages when we need to. Good God, they say they want to be the Great Britain of the East!' He snorts in derision.

'And who's actually performing this monitoring?'

'That's the secret bit, young lady. King and country, you know.'

I'm intrigued. 'I can speak some Japanese too, Felix, and I'm actually at a loose end.'

Felix laughs. 'Dear child, this is man's work and they only hire ex-military or boffins. Girls'd be too busy filing their nails! But I'll keep you in mind if they need a typist.'

Buttering my toast next morning I say, 'Felix has a new job, something hush-hush to do with Japanese codes. It sounded fascinating, but he clammed up about his employers and said girls couldn't work for them anyway.'

Nanna looks exasperated. 'Lord, that man's a fool sometimes. I know who he's working for. Izabel mentioned something and I put two and two together. It's a department of the Secret Service, the Government Code and Cipher School.'

'*Spies?*'

She laughs. 'Not quite—simply modern diplomacy. Britain needs to know what the Germans say, what the Japanese think, even what those rather unreliable Americans are up to.'

'Heavens, how do you know all this, Nanna?'

'One of Freddy's friends was an Admiral in that department. We used to have wonderful dinner parties—lovely man.' She smiles wistfully. 'But for once Felix may be correct. They don't welcome women into their ranks.'

'I didn't expect it anyway.'

She nods. 'But think about this, darling. It won't be easy to monitor my interests from Australia. How would you like to manage Pearlshell Ltd for me here in London?'

'Your *company*, Nanna? Are you sure? You'd trust me to do that?'

'You know the background, you've got the mind, and some of the skills—my people could teach you the rest. You'd be paid according to your success, of course, but you might enjoy it.'

The anxiety that's been haunting me eases a little. 'Goodness. Yes, I think I would.'

'But I'm still worried you'll be lonely, Eliza.'

'Nonsense,' I say. 'I'll be too busy to notice.'

'I had another thought, darling. You shouldn't hold on to this big empty house if you don't want to. Freddy would have hated that. If you sold it you could buy a nice flat like Izabel's.'

'I do love this house, but it's old-fashioned and hard to keep warm. Izabel's place is certainly comfortable.'

'I'm not over-fond of chrome myself,' says Nanna. 'But perhaps something with more blues and greens might suit the part-owner of a deepwater ship?'

Despite my brave words I feel forlorn as I wave farewell to my grandmother as her liner leaves for Perth in March 1934. Don't be silly, I tell myself, just keep busy.

Although we've chatted happily about the possibilities of a new flat, I'm not in any great hurry to sell the big house right now. First I want to get to know Nanna's business properly.

I spend time with her solicitor, Mr Oswald, cynical and formal as an undertaker, and the accountant, Mrs Terry, who moves numbers about with the ruthlessness of a chess grand master: even in these difficult days of the Depression they manage to bring Pearlshell Ltd a small profit.

The Clarksons shipbroker, Mr Weatherall, is also a great help with my Inverley shareholding, and over the next few months I find I'm becoming more confident and enjoying my work.

That's why it seems bizarre when I begin to sleep so badly.

My earlier anxiety returns, and it's more intense. I wake from horrible dreams, my heart pounding, and can't fall asleep again. The large quiet house saddens me with its memories of Nanna and Freddy and happier days.

The only staff I have now are a daytime cook and cleaner, so I tell myself I'm anxious because I've never lived alone before, but it doesn't help.

I take the train to visit Pete and Billie at Hamble, but they're in a haze of joy at their blossoming new relationship, which just makes me childishly envious.

I suppose the truth is I *am* lonely. Izabel is tied up in her plans for Hollywood, Felix is getting sillier about his secret job every day, and I deliberately go out of my way to avoid people I met through Charlotte and Harry.

Of course, Harry himself haunts my dreams. Sometimes I reach out to him in joy but then he's gone, his back turned as he leaves me behind. No matter how I try I cannot find him and, devastated, I know I am utterly alone.

A few months of this is exhausting, but then another grief awakens, one from long ago. In those dreams I sense the spices of my father's gentle presence, but when I raise my arms to be lifted to his comforting shoulder, he too turns away.

And just when I think I cannot bear any more, the true nightmares begin.

In the darkest of hours the spectre of Gideon Meade looms above me, taunting me, beating me, molesting me. I come abruptly awake and lie there, rigid with horror, sobbing dry-throated, my mind thick with terror.

Without much enthusiasm I visit Izabel just before she leaves for Hollywood. She's giddy with excitement, showing me her new dresses and hats, then takes me into her study to give me a list of things for me to do, especially events to occupy Felix.

'I'm not your assistant anymore, Izabel,' I say as evenly as I can. (I'm bad-tempered with exhaustion.) 'What's happened to your latest girl, anyway?'

'Let go. Of course I can't have her in the flat when I'm not here.' She doesn't say why, but I remember Felix's wolfish grin when he said, 'I'll have to be a bachelor again.'

Izabel gazes around the white and gold study and sighs. 'This was going to be the *nursery*, do you remember, Eliza?'

'Yes.' Even through my tiredness I feel pity for her.

'If I hadn't miscarried, the child would be a year old by now. Heavens, if I'd had Gideon's baby she'd be fourteen.' Izabel smiles sadly. 'You know, I always imagine it would have been a little girl. If only Lucy hadn't interfered—'

'Izabel, *don't*,' I say. 'Gideon died of the flu like millions of others. A doctor told me that it's unlikely hospital would have saved him. His death had nothing to do with Lucy.'

'We'll just have to take your doctor friend's word on that, won't we?' she says coolly. '*I'll* certainly never have the chance to know what kind of life we might have had together.'

My grief and fatigue overwhelm me. 'Dear *God*, Izabel, I know what kind of life! Gideon was a cruel, evil man. If you'd had a little girl I'd have feared for her well-being.'

'What on earth are you saying? He was a good man—'

'*Good* man? Does a good man beat a little girl?'

'Of course not! Are you saying Gideon was capable of that?'

'He was my *stepfather*, Izabel,' I say bitterly. 'Yes, he was perfectly capable of it. That's exactly what he used to do to me.'

'You're lying. Utter nonsense. Why would you say such a terrible thing?'

'Because it's true.'

'How dare you. If Gideon were here to defend his good name–'

'Stop *deceiving* yourself!' Suddenly I can't stop. 'All the time he was busy screwing you, he was trying to force Lucy into bed and making life *hell* for me with his wandering hands!'

'Lucy? Are you mad? When he had me?'

'He should have been content with you, Izabel, but yes, he wanted Lucy too.'

She is pale. 'But you haven't the slightest proof of that. And, surely I misheard–wandering hands? You're not implying a man like Gideon would … *interfere* with a child? How can you say such a thing, Eliza, have you no shame?'

'Shame? *Shame? He* was the one sneaking around, lifting my dress, pushing his fingers into me, calling me his little *kittikins.*' I sit down, trembling. 'And when I'd try to resist he'd beat me in places where the bruises wouldn't show.'

I begin to sob, my face in my hands.

Izabel leaves the room. I think, dear God, what have I *done?* After a time she returns, holding two glasses of whiskey, and hands me one. I sip, grateful for the heat.

I say, staring down, 'I'm sorry, Izabel. I didn't *ever* mean to tell you. I'd never want to hurt you or shock you, but you can't go on believing that *fantasy*—'

'I suppose not.'

I look up and she shrugs. 'You've seen the world I work in, Eliza, there's nothing under the sun could shock me. And hurt? I know you're not malicious.' She takes a drink. 'But are you quite sure? You're not lying?'

'I don't lie to you, Izabel.'

She nods slowly. 'You don't, do you?'

There's a very long silence then she wipes her eyes. 'It was such a comfort, you see. No matter how badly a man might treat me—and by God some did—I could tell myself Gideon once loved me. But … I was only *eighteen*. And I've had to suffer the consequences ever since.'

Izabel takes another slug. 'And today. This? Why didn't you tell me before, Eliza?'

'Would you have listened?'

'Probably not.'

'Then why do you believe me now?'

'A turn of phrase,' she says bitterly. '*Kittikins* is sadly familiar.'

A week later Izabel leaves for Hollywood, confident and bright-eyed, and I understand more than ever how courageous she is.

After that day of revelation between us, it's as if a weight has lifted from my heart, and Gideon's malevolent presence disappears from my dreams.

Sometimes I even wake up feeling almost content, warmed by memory-fragments of spices and Broome's gemstone light. And now, when I think of Harry, it's with regret, not anguish.

Nearly a year has passed since Penfold's wedding and I start forcing myself to look to the future. My work once again is satisfying, and at last I have time to consider the formalities of selling the big house and buying a flat.

With solicitor Mr Oswald, I also begin setting up QM Air, Pete and Billie's aviation company. They'll be graduating in six months and I want it to be ready for them.

This means I have to travel to Hamble often to discuss details or get papers signed. But I like the train journey to country Hampshire, and slowly Pete's farm becomes a second home.

At Hamble I share the laughter and long summer evenings. I wear floral dresses and broad-brimmed hats and let myself enjoy the light-hearted friendships.

I flirt outrageously with the flying students, most of whom are younger than me, but that's good: there's no chance of taking anyone seriously.

Billie flings herself down on the picnic blanket, laughing. 'Did you see my goal, Lizzie?'

'Spectacular! But isn't the Commandant limping now?'

She shrugs. 'Deserves it, the old sod. Keeps saying there'll be more facilities for women in the new admin block, but I'll believe that when I see it.'

I smile and hand her a glass of lemonade. We're easy friends now. Of course she's got a rough edge to her tongue, but after *Inverley* I can hold my own. I taught her some shipboard curses too, and she loves being able to swear in Swedish.

'Can I get a lift to the farm with you later?' I ask. 'Can't see Pete anywhere.'

'Yeah,' she says. 'You'll enjoy the drive more with me anyway.'

This is true. Billie bought Herr Hell's little red sportscar when he went back to Germany and she drives it as skilfully as she flies a plane.

'Where is Pete?' I ask.

'Don't know,' she says. 'Off sulking somewhere, I expect. He's cross at me because I bought the red car, and he thinks it means I want to sneak off and meet other men.'

'But why would he think that?'

She settles herself cross-legged on the blanket.

'A long time ago I told him I believe in free love.'

'You mean having lovers even if you're married? That's rather Bohemian of you, Bill.'

She smiles. 'It's the ideal of not letting love for one person stop you from loving another.'

'And do you? Love someone else, I mean.'

She shakes her head. 'No, I'm happy with Pete, but he still worries. I think it's actually his own guilty conscience—he's attracted to someone else, so he assumes it's the same for me.'

'Who?'

'The *perkele* cow.'

'Charlotte?'

'He sees her occasionally. Drinks in London, race track—just mates, he tells me. But even if he loved someone else I wouldn't be jealous, I've told him that. I only care about us. If he wants another woman, then that's between them.'

I shake my head. 'You're so brave, Bill, I had no idea. But what if someone you love really prefers someone else?'

'It's no good hanging onto a relationship if it's not honest.'

'Perhaps you should mention that to Charlotte at some time.' I try not to sound bitter.

'I never said you have to *like* the other woman, Lizzie. Especially if she's a *förbannat* bitch.'

I look up. 'But I thought you two were so happy together. When did this start?'

'A while ago. I told Pete I wouldn't marry him. I've always said I'd never marry, but he thought it didn't apply to him.'

'Never *marry*? But I rather hoped you'd be my sister-in-law one day,' I say wistfully.

'I'm surprised *you're* surprised. I thought you didn't want to marry, either.'

'Well not just for the sake of it. But if I really cared about someone… Still, that's all theoretical—I'm not in any danger of having to make up my mind in a hurry.'

'Lot of blokes here, Lizzie,' Billie says looking at the cricket field, where a game is in glacial progress. Something goes thwack to a murmur of 'Good show.'

'Flyboys? Got to be kidding.'

'I'm with you there,' she says. 'Pub later?'

'Yes, why not? I'm back to dull old London tomorrow.'

In the long clear evening we walk to the local pub and sit outside on timber benches. The air is grassy-scented, the sky fading to a rosy haze. Pete turns up a little later with a bunch of mates and seems happy enough.

Maybe this is just a bump in the road for them. My brother couldn't be so stupid as to let Billie go, not for Charlotte.

Oh, Harry, I wonder if you know she's flirting—perhaps more than flirting—with other men. From the pain in his voice that night at the farm he probably does. Don't think about it.

I've met most of the boys with Pete before, apart from one or two Royal Air Force Reserve pilots. In fact, most of the new students lately have been RAF trainees. Oh God, *Germany*. Don't think about that either.

'Lizzie, this is Stefan Sadler. Stef, this is my sensible sister, Eliza.'

I smile and hold out my hand. He's a nice-looking man, in his late twenties I suppose—most of the RAF Reserve students are older, more experienced pilots.

'And this is Billie,' says Pete, pride in his voice. 'Best flyer in the whole place.'

The other students murmur in agreement. They'll be all right, I think, he loves her so much.

The new man, Stefan, sits down. Dark hair, green eyes. Medium height, pleasant face.

I say, 'Stefan? Unusual name.'

'My mother's Polish,' he says. 'It's not as bad as my middle name—people can actually pronounce it.'

I smile and we chat about why we're both here at Hamble. He's doing the long Navigation course so he'll be around for the next five months. Rather a pleasing prospect.

The jokes and gossip and laughter fly back and forth through the long soft twilight, just like any other happy evening at Hamble: significant only in hindsight.

Next morning Pete takes me to the station to catch the London train. Driving along in his uncomfortable old farm car I can appreciate why Billie loves her little red motor.

'Billie mentioned you'd seen Charlotte lately,' I say.

'Yeah, had a few drinks, caught up at the race track.'

'I thought you didn't like racing. Too expensive, you said.'

'True, but Charlotte always makes it fun.'

'Are things all right with you and Billie?'

He doesn't say a word. I keep gazing at him and he shrugs. 'Dunno, Lizzie. We're crazy about each other, but half the time I'm worried she'll find someone else. I mean, look at her! Brilliant, beautiful. I'm not in her class and she's got to realise that one day. And then?'

'She told me she believes in being honest in relationships. I don't think she'd lie to you.'

He grins. 'Doesn't hide her opinions, that's for sure. But I thought once we were together everything would be easy, and it's not.'

'So *Charlotte* is your backup plan?'

'Christ, no. She's fun, but I told you I wouldn't get involved with a married woman.'

'She's made it crystal clear to me there's no chance she'll ever end the marriage,' I say, trying to speak steadily. I've told Billie what happened with Harry, but no one else.

'Aha!' he says. '*Thought* you two had a falling out—I can tell from your voice. Harry's quite fond of you and I bet that puts Charlotte's nose out of joint. Is that it?'

'More or less.'

'Can't imagine her ever having to worry about you as a rival. Sorry, Sis.'

'True. Anyway, here we are. Thanks for the lift, Pete, and look —trust Billie a bit more, she loves you. And trust yourself too. You're all right even if you are just my little brother.'

He grins, takes my bag out of the boot and kisses me goodbye.

I settle myself in the carriage and get out my new book, Mr Villiers' *Last of the Wind Ships*, his tale of the grain race won by *Parma* a year ago.

I don't pay attention to the latecomers boarding the train, then a figure says, 'Miss McKee, isn't it? We met last night.'

It's the pilot, Stefan Sadler. I smile and say, 'Please have a seat.'

He puts his bag in the rack, sits down with his own book and asks, 'What are you reading?'

I tell him and mention I once worked on such a ship myself. I've discovered this is a good way to weed out those tedious chaps (like Mr Villiers) who are firmly convinced women have no place aboard ships.

Fortunately Stefan is an enthusiastic yachtsman and his book is Joshua Slocum's charming *Sailing Alone Around the World*, so we spend the trip deep in conversation.

Stefan's eyes are impish, his dark hair unruly, his hands expressive, and the time passes so quickly I'm surprised when we pull into Waterloo.

Before we part he asks if he might take me to dinner one evening, and I'm happy to agree.

After a sensible period of acquaintance we become lovers, and I'm happy to agree to that too. Stefan is warm, skilful and engaging company. Best of all, there's nothing about him reminds me in the least of Harry.

In August 1934 a problem arises with *Inverley*, docked in Northern Ireland. I could probably sort things out from London but I yearn to see the ship again.

Mr Weatherall can't come, so I catch the train by myself to Liverpool, then take the night ferry to Belfast.

The problem is fixed with the usual application of money, but Captain Nilsen says there are greater hurdles ahead. Work on the hull demands a dry-docking, the steel mizzen-mast needs replacing and the donkey-engine is on its last legs.

I notice handsome *Herzogin Cecilie* is also berthed nearby, unloading wheat from Wallaroo.

Captain Nilsen tells me the Duchess brought a female passenger this year, one who worked like me as a *jungman* during the voyage.

We go aboard and are greeted by solemn, nice-looking Captain Eriksson. He introduces us to the passenger, Pamela Bourne, and I like her immediately.

She's a journalist, tall, attractive and strong, with a wicked sense of fun. I notice she and Sven Eriksson seem rather fond of each other, although they try to be discreet.

Pam and I chat over drinks in the saloon, and find we have much in common. She was re-christened Nils, as I was Elias, and we laugh at the absurd ways male crews cope with female sailors. She's written a book on her travels too, and I promise to read it when it's published.

As we're leaving she says, 'Elias, come and see our beautiful Duchess.'

On the wharf we gaze up at the figurehead I remember from Port Lincoln. During their passage Pam repainted it herself, and now the Duchess is serene and sweet-faced again.

'Oh, Nils, she's *lovely*! I wish I'd thought to do that with *Inverley*'s figurehead.'

'Do it next voyage, then.'

'Probably won't be a next for me.' I sigh. 'Seem to have swallowed the anchor. You?'

Pam smiles. 'Perhaps one or two more passages lie ahead.'

Captain Eriksson's eyes suggest he rather hopes that's the case.

Back in London, at last I'm moving. I've sold the Kensington house and bought a three-bedroomed flat in Cartwright Gardens, a crescent in Bloomsbury.

It's not far from Izabel and Felix's place, but is a safe distance from Keppel Street's School of Hygiene and Tropical Medicine: and Harry.

I redecorate my flat with cream-coloured walls and green and blue curtains, while one bedroom becomes a study with shelves for my many books. There's a tiny balcony which catches the sunlight and overlooks a garden square full of trees.

My lover Stefan is an engineer at the de Havilland aircraft factory at Hatfield, north of London, where he also keeps a flat.

When we drive to Hatfield we pass near Borehamwood and I remember filming West End Winnie there four years ago, when I was besotted with caddish Jack Brandon. Am I besotted still, with Harry this time? Don't think about it.

My relationship with Stefan deepens. We go out on a friend's yacht and he's a good sailor, calm and careful. He's a gently amusing man who suffered one of those frigid British upbringings, sent away to boarding school too young.

Thanks once more to my education in the starboard watch, I'm not shocked at what he tells me of the fate of small pretty boys, but the place sounds as if it was an abyss of loneliness.

Still, one good thing to come out of Stefan's schooling was a friendship with the author Toby Fenn, whose books about his travels in Asia Minor enchanted me a long time ago.

Toby is immersed in his first novel now, and loves to pick my brains about women's attitudes for his characters. Toby is witty, blond and good-looking, so I wonder why he doesn't just ask some girlfriend, then I realise he's not much interested in women—nor, apparently, men.

Stefan tells me Toby's heart was broken long ago and he's never quite recovered, which frightens me. Surely everyone recovers from heartbreak eventually?

Like Toby, Stefan's social set are a creative and welcoming group, and I makes friends with Stef's cousin Sofia, a classical musician, and her friend Klara, a poetess from Finland who shares my love of the Åland Islands.

It's been a long, hard few years, but at last I feel as if the pains of the past are behind me.

Perhaps I'm even becoming reconciled to the loss of Harry, although I'm careful not to ponder too deeply about that.

As time passes I fit contentedly into Stef's civilised world. He'd like to marry and have a family one day, and that's quite a pleasing prospect. Something in the offing, perhaps.

26. Pete: My Bohemian Mates

Of course I lied to my sister. Charlotte and I haven't actually bedded each other but we've certainly enjoyed a few kisses, and they always transport me to that dark sweet place where everything seems to makes sense.

Nothing much does now with Billie.

Charlotte told me what happened at Penfold's wedding and I was gobsmacked. Apparently Eliza tried to seduce Harry, although I must say it's hard to imagine my sister as a *femme fatale*. Charlotte's forgiven Harry—it wasn't his fault, after all— but she says he's cold and hard now and impossible to live with. She's lonely, poor girl.

Strangely, she doesn't gamble much anymore. Her mother Ilse died some months ago and Charlotte inherited quite a packet. I joke because it's her money now she's a bit more careful with it, but she never seems to find that very funny.

So yes, I'm a fool and playing with fire. And I know Billie's the other half of myself, but Christ, I'm pretty sure I'm not as pig-headed as she is.

All right. Truth is, I'm trying not to think about what I've done. You see, I've always had a soft spot for Kingsford Smith's partner Charles Ulm. A good solid flyer, I rather identified with him (my workaday Ulm to Billie's brilliant Smithy, perhaps).

Anyway, poor old Ulm disappeared a week ago on a flight near Hawaii. It made me feel bleak so I went out and got blotto. Well, we all do *that*, but this time I didn't stop drinking till dawn.

Then I took the triple-engined Avro Five out for a spin. Since I wasn't exactly qualified for that particular bird, it's probably not surprising I ran into trouble.

The Avro was a write-off, but at least I came down safely. Came down, in fact, about fifty yards away from the Commandant, who smelt my breath and expelled me there and then. (Perhaps he was a bit cranky about one or two earlier misdeeds of mine as well.)

So now I can't finish my last two courses, Instruction and Navigation, which is bloody annoying. I'll never get those tickets unless I start all over somewhere else. But the Commandant said he'd make damned sure I wouldn't get into another flying school anywhere in the country.

So that's put a bit of a crimp in our plans for QM Air.

Understandably, Billie isn't happy. But we could still do something—I've got other licences, Ground Engineering for instance. But I suppose if I haven't got that Instructors' ticket I don't have much to offer.

We might have been able to somehow weather this disaster, but then Air Service Training offered Billie a job as one of their own tutors. Good pay and all the fun of a flying school, without any of the business risk. She'd be mad not to take it.

I'd tell her that too if only she was speaking to me.

Billie's moved out of my farmhouse into new digs in Hamble, and I hear through the grapevine she's taken the job with AST. The farmhouse is empty without her, so I go to London for a few weeks to stay with Eliza.

She's pretty cranky with me too, but her nice boyfriend Stefan invites friends of his to dinner to cheer me up. They're certainly a bit different from the pilots I'm used to.

There's writer Toby, a witty bloke, brunette Sofia who plays the cello (Toby's girlfriend, I think), and Klara from Finland, a long-haired blonde poetess.

We all start going out to the pub regularly and have a lot of fun. Not that I'm looking for a new girl.

I write to Billie and she replies formally, so I haven't given up all hope. Still, I must say it's a comfort being with people who don't really care, one way or the other, how spectacularly I've screwed up my life.

Now it's the new year of 1935 and I haven't the foggiest what to do. I've returned to the farm but don't like going into Hamble village itself. It's hard seeing other pilots wandering around carefree as larks.

One part of me yearns to run into Billie and the other is terrified I might, and then I'd—what? Break down? Beg her to come back?

I don't have any financial problems. Amusingly, I even have those shares in AST I inherited from Freddy. They yield a good dividend: the place is doing very well, with or without me. Still, I'd like to be employed and have some routine to keep me busy.

Mrs Spencer cooks and keeps the house warm, but can't do anything about how empty it is without Billie. Spencer tries to get me interested in our plans for spring, the crops we'll plant, the sheep we'll breed. And I do care about it all.

But not enough to stop my heart breaking whenever I see a distant plane and wonder if it's Billie there in the cockpit.

So I go back to London. Stefan's mate Toby is looking for a flatmate to share the rent, so I take the second bedroom. It's good to know someone else is around in the middle of the night, otherwise I might break down, and that would never do.

I get on really well with Sofia and Klara—Toby calls them the terrible twins, though they're nothing alike. Fair Klara is small and dreamy, while Sofia is nicely buxom with direct, dark eyes.

But I'm surprised to find out she's not Toby's girlfriend after all, and in fact neither girl seems to ever stay over with him. I worry I might be cramping his style and suggest one night I could sleep at my sister's occasionally.

'Why?' asks Toby.

'You know. So you can spend some time with the terrible twins. They're both really nice.'

He looks up from his typewriter. Toby works surprisingly hard, writing notes then typing, typing, typing. He's got a book being published in a few months so there's a good reason for it, but he seems fairly driven anyway. I envy him his passion.

He sits back and lights a cigarette and says, 'You don't know much about the world, do you, Farmer Pete?' (They like to call me that.)

His words remind me painfully of something Billie used to say, so I shrug and busy myself with the ashtray. 'Much the same as anyone else, I suppose.'

Toby smiles. He's got a good smile—with his blond hair and blue eyes he must cut a swathe through the ladies. He leans forward and says, 'Then you might have noticed those girls aren't much interested in me. Or you.'

That's true. They're fun to be with, but I never get that sort of *twinkle* I get from Charlotte.

'Fact is, Pete, they're only interested in each other. They're lovers. Lesbians.'

'Oh. Guess that explains it.'

'Guess it does.'

Golly.

I try to see if I can tell just by looking at them, but can't. Klara's a little sweetheart, while Sofia is hilarious, makes me double up laughing. All right I think, this is the Big City and these are my Bohemian mates. In fact, being with them makes me feel amazingly sophisticated.

I wonder if I dare ask them what they do in bed? Maybe not, Sofia's pretty strong from lugging around that big cello. It's a pity she doesn't like men, though—she played for us once and the way she gripped the instrument between her thighs was, well, *mesmerising*. And I liked the music too.

Later that night, Toby and I are having a final drink before turning in.

I say, 'Thanks for setting me straight, Toby. Guess I haven't met many girls like the terrible twins before. Hanging around engineers and pilots limits your horizons a bit.'

'That's fine, Farmer Pete.'

'Offer still stands though. I'll get out of here if you want to bring someone home.'

Toby smiles. 'I don't bring people home. I'm not interested.'

'But what if you fall in love?'

He looks at me, startled. 'I am in love. Thought you knew. I've been in love for oh, ten years now. But if I can't have him I don't want anyone.'

Golly.

Charlotte comes to the pub a few times with us, but she doesn't like Toby's lack of interest in her, she thinks Klara's boring, and she wasn't at all happy the time Sofia tried to play footsie with her under the table.

I can't take her to dinner with Eliza and Stefan either, she's very unfriendly towards Eliza. So this means we have to go out by ourselves, without the safety net of other people. I tell myself I'm a big boy, I can be responsible (I seem to hear Billie laughing hollowly at that). Still I'm sure Charlotte and I can go on nice sociable outings without crossing the line.

Like tonight, a pub by the river, lovely spring evening. After a few drinks Charlotte says she's dying to see the flat I've told her so much about. Seems safe enough—Toby was tapping away at his typewriter earlier—so I throw open the door and find he isn't there after all.

I make coffee and try to keep everything on an even keel, but somehow it all ends up like my last flight in the Avro Five. Everything spinning madly out of control.

I try to resist, I really do.

Lying on the carpet after the first time I say, 'We can't do this Charlotte, it's madness!' The second time, against my bedroom door, I pant, 'What about Harry? Such a good bloke—'

The third time, on the bed, Charlotte riding above me in shameless golden glory, I manage, 'But…' before being overcome with a tidal wave of such agonising pleasure I expect to die of it but don't much care.

When I come to, with Charlotte's hair tangled in my mouth, her bites tingling on my shoulders, her moans echoing in my ears, I'm rather glad I didn't, in fact, die.

I'm a bit worn out now, but oh God I want more of this.

At last I'm initiated into the mysteries of female delight. Charlotte is perfectly happy to demonstrate to my heart's content, with fingers, tongue and tackle.

Like music she says. Set the theme, build up to a nice rhapsody, ease back for a pastoral twiddle, then go for an oompah-oompah climax. Makes lots of sense and I'm sure Herr Beethoven would agree.

Our affair continues nicely and I'm getting over Billie. I buy a little Tiger Moth and keep it at Eastleigh airfield, near Southampton, and go flying again.

I buy a fast car as well and zip back and forth between London and the farm. I'm learning a lot from Spencer now—this year the harvest and shearing goes well and I think Granddad would be pleased.

And our affair seems to make Charlotte surprisingly happy too. Sometimes I dream she'll get divorced one day and I can have her all to myself. When I mention it, she says Harry's *very* religious and would never divorce her. But I'm still optimistic.

27. Izabel: A Touch of the Tarbrush

Rugged up in my furs, leaning on the rail of the liner, I watch the coast of England approaching after our five-day passage from New York. I ask myself, is there another actress in the world as lucky as me?

Probably not. Obviously my talent and looks have helped, but to have had this marvellous break? *Thank* you, dear Lord.

What a time I've had. I've missed Felix terribly, and was away a little longer than I'd planned, but I've been so busy the time just flew. Gable and Cooper were delightful to work with as well. Professional and considerate, and (mostly) kept their hands to themselves.

Best of all, the director was sensible and the script superb, a poignant comedy of two old friends chasing the same girl, with that clever twist everyone's been raving about. *The Bride's Secret* was released a month ago to acclaim, and I'm already hearing whispers about the Oscars.

But my God, promoting it's been hard work. Still, it's almost over except for the big premiere in London. I can just imagine the night and the red carpet, me in a wonderful gown and Felix, devilishly handsome, on my arm.

Oh, darling. I've missed you absurdly and hope you've missed me too. Let's just go straight home to bed and I'll show you how much.

The press conference at the dock is a great success. I wear an adorable little hat and my red suit with the tiny waist, and pose on a pile of luggage for the photographers.

Then the reporters leave and the pleasant lady publicist who accompanied me on board also says goodbye.

Some officials from the shipping company have their photos taken with me, then escort me to a limousine. I smile, my arms full of flowers, and wave merrily as the driver pulls away, but my mouth is dry.

Where's Felix?

In his last letter he said he'd meet me. Surely he hasn't had an accident? My heart thumping, I jump out of the car as we arrive and dash upstairs to the flat.

'Felix, are you *here?*'

The flat is stuffy and tobacco-smelling, and very quiet. I stand, confused. The driver lugs my bags up the stairs in five or six trips then goes, thank God.

What should I do? I suppose I could ring his office, but *surely* he isn't at work on the day I get home!

He is. 'Sorry, darling. Bit of a flap on, balloon's gone up.'

It's not the bloody Western Front, I think, gritting my teeth. You couldn't take the time to meet me, or have the wit to leave me a *message?*

'I'm tired anyway, darling,' I say. 'Think I'll have a bath and a nap. See you tonight.'

'Ah. Bit of a problem there, I'm afraid, Izzy. The bigwigs want me at a dinner, some confidential pow-wow. Won't be home till late. Awfully sorry.'

I can't speak for a few moments, then say, 'All right, darling. See you when I can.'

After a time I stop staring into space and go to make a cup of tea. It has to be black because there's no milk in the refrigerator. There are, however, empty bottles of gin in the rubbish bin, and in a dusty corner of the bathroom, a hairpin.

Not one of mine, the sort used by blondes.

In my red suit and adorable little hat I sit down at the kitchen table and cry.

Felix comes home, tipsy, at two in the morning. In bed he turns away from me and starts to snore. I've had witch-hazel compresses on my eyes to try to keep the swelling down, and tell myself I'll look better in the morning anyway, but it's little comfort.

I rise early, ring for a delivery of groceries, make Felix's bacon and eggs the way he likes, then put on my prettiest negligee and take him food, coffee and a light-hearted greeting.

We share a flirtatious breakfast and a subsequent passionate homecoming that leaves nothing to be desired. Flushed and laughing we embrace, and I tell myself that yesterday was simply a storm in a teacup.

Storm in a bloody *teacup*? I don't know what it is, but Felix still isn't himself. He's apparently not getting on with the old duffers at work who, he says, might have written a Japanese-English dictionary but don't know quite as much as they think they do.

Correcting his accent, his grammar—when he studied at Oxford, for God's sake! I bite my tongue and don't remind him he did Japanese for only one year, while those old duffers worked in Tokyo for decades.

But one evening he comes home in high spirits, opens a bottle of champagne and hands me a glass saying, 'Cheers!'

'Heavens, darling,' I laugh. 'What's this in honour of?'

'Got called in to see the Head of Department today—was a bit nervous I can tell you—but he's offered me a *promotion*. Wants me to move into administration, says I've got a real flair for it, simply wasted on the language side.'

'Oh, congratulations!' I'm pleased for him, and glad too he doesn't quite understand why they're moving him.

Felix grins bashfully. 'Sorry I've been such a bear with a sore head lately, Izzy. You've been an absolute brick. I've just been, well, a bit worried.'

'Of course, darling. Cheers to *you*! I couldn't be happier.'

'One tiny fly in the ointment though, my love.' He gives me his wry smile. 'They want me on deck at their new Bureau.'

'And how is that a problem?' I laugh as I pour us more bubbly.

'It's called the Far East Combined Bureau.'

I'm suddenly rather sober. 'East of where, precisely?'

'The *Far* East, darling. Hong Kong, actually.'

'How can you work in a Hong Kong bureau from here?' I say.

'Can't, got to be there, keep an eye on things, punch the old time-clock. You know.'

'But—but what will *I* do?'

'Anything you like! Pop over to Hollywood, come back to London to do theatre now and then. Sky's the limit, old girl.'

'But Felix, I have to be *here*. Auditions, interviews, publicity. In any case, I couldn't *bear* to live in Hong Kong.' I shudder. 'All those ghastly Asians. The noise, the smells, the gibberish. I can't go, I simply *can't*. Surely there's some way around it?'

'Ah.' He looks at his glass. 'Well, I suppose—the Head did mention another position. Not as big a promotion of course, but here in London.'

'Oh, darling, *please* take that one. I'll make it up to you, I promise, and in a year perhaps we can think about it? Not just now, not yet. Give me time.'

He's silent for a few moments then nods.

'Of course. I'll tell them I need to postpone it.' He shrugs. 'The Japanese threat certainly isn't going away and even the London job's still rather a good prospect.' He holds out his arms. 'Come here, darling Izzy. We'll sort it out.'

The premiere of *The Bride's Secret* is held in January 1935, a triumph I'll never forget. I wear a low-cut silver sheath and diamond slides in my hair. Felix is beside me, amusing and loving and absurdly attractive in his tuxedo.

I relish every moment. The flashbulbs, the flowers, the applause, the eyes—so *many* eyes—gazing at me in adoration. After fifteen years of achingly hard work such recognition is sweet beyond measure.

A few weeks later I drop in to see my agent, Rupert Grimstone, who's effusively welcoming. He damned-well should be too, I've made him much richer than he ever was before.

We drink tea and chat, and he tells me a new film is on the cards, a drama that sounds thrilling.

Then Rupert clears his throat and asks, 'Izabel, darling, had a look at today's paper?'

'A bad review?' The critics have been complimentary, but my insecurity is never far away.

'No, a *fabulous* review. That's not it.' He hesitates. 'The syndicated gossip column. It's hinting at something quite absurd. Of course it won't stick, but you probably need to be prepared.'

I do not have the slightest premonition.

He winces apologetically. 'They're saying—I'm sorry darling, I *know* it's ridiculous—that your exotic looks aren't actually European in origin, but from somewhat, ah, further East.'

'My father was Portuguese, Rupert.' My voice is steady.

'They're suggesting, perhaps, on the, hmm, maternal side—?'

'My mother was a Gypsy who died when I was born, Rupert, you know that. Then my father died as well, when I was only two years old.'

I sigh. 'My sister Filipa and I had no one else in the world, so my darling Chinese nanny Min-lu brought us up. I've never hidden it! Someone's just got the wrong end of the stick.'

I shrug. 'God, *reporters*.'

'Of course *we* all know that, dear, but they've somehow got hold of an ancient clipping about a ball in Melbourne.' Rupert grimaces apologetically again. 'Celebrating a Mr Sam Lee's marriage to a Miss Rosa Fox.'

My heart seems to slow. *A warm night, a ruffled white dress. My sash is pink. Fili's is blue. Lucy is looking after us in a sitting room and we're watching the grown-ups waltzing in the perfumed air and flickering candlelight.*

'The, um, guest list. You, Miss Izabel Peres, your sister, Miss Filipa Peres ... and Mrs Min-lu Peres, your widowed *mother*. Highly regarded in business circles as prosperous Chinese merchant, Min-lu Lee.'

I call upon every skerrick of fifteen years of art and artifice, and laugh. 'Hilarious! Yes, Min-lu became a successful merchant, and of course she cared for us like a mother. That fool of a reporter simply assumed she was. He got it wrong, Rupert.'

'Naturally it's nonsense, but you do need to know what they're *saying*, darling. I suppose you've heard the gossip about Merle Oberon?'

'Rupert, I've been away for eight months,' I say evenly. 'Do tell.'

'Half-*Indian*, not Tasmanian or whatever she claims, and with rather a juicy past.'

Suddenly I'm exhausted. 'What does it matter, Rupert, what does it fucking *matter*?'

He's startled. I rarely swear.

'Well, it's box-office poison, Izabel dear,' he says coolly. 'You know how the Yanks are about race. A touch of the tarbrush? Career-terminating.' He smiles at me with his big yellow teeth. 'But nothing to worry about, eh? *I'll* put the record straight.'

'Thank you, Rupert.'

'My job, after all, darling.'

Thanks for nothing, you old shit. I descend the stairs from his office, my throat tight, my mind blank, my heart pounding.

I remember the eyes at the premiere, so *many* eyes. Gazing at me in adoration, or so I thought. But were they really gazing at that other me instead, that hidden, shameful me? Were they seeing a snub nose made aquiline, a slanted eye carved into roundness, a yellow complexion under my porcelain makeup?

There's a noise in my ears and I simply cannot think. I hail a taxi and recite my address. My back straight, my hands clasped in my lap, I serenely watch the passing London streets and see only opium addicts, Shanghai whores, rickshaw peasants, all that jabbering, filth and confusion.

A tiny sound comes from my throat. If my jaws weren't clamped shut it would be a moan.

I smile adorably and pay the driver and get out of the taxi and find my key and step, step, step, up I go and I'm at my own front door. I unlock it and walk into the bedroom and put a pillow against my face.

And then I scream and scream and scream.

Hollywood is a much *blonder* place than it used to be (with the bloody gold hairpins to match). Harlow, Lombard, Dietrich— even the brunettes are going a few shades lighter nowadays. I play that game too of course, but stick to reddish tones, they suit me better.

Game? Of course it's a game.

I lean back on my pillow and light a cigarette. I'm absolutely numb now, feeling nothing. This life was always a gamble I suppose, but my God I played it brilliantly, I sustained the role for so long. Still, the truth had to come out at some time.

The studio bigwigs could have quashed this story but they haven't. I always thought they'd protect their investment in me, but apparently my tainted blood is too much of a risk. Safer for them to throw me to the wolves and find themselves a *blonde* instead. Yet I'm hardly any better. After all, I dislike my mother's race as much as any bigot.

I roll over and stub out my cigarette, then drift back into the memories that almost overwhelmed me in Rupert's office. The night of the ball for Sam and Rosa, my handsome big brother and his new wife.

That was the night I first met Lucy, Rosa's sister. She was only sixteen then, but she seemed so grown-up to seven-year-old me.

I can feel the smoothness of my pink satin sash, the crisp muslin ruffles of my dress, the soft hair of the doll that was all I had of my father Leo.

Fili said I couldn't possibly remember him, but Lucy said she could remember things from when she was very little. (I'd forgotten, too, how kind she was to a lonely child.)

We nibbled at the refreshments and sat on a couch before a fire and talked about dogs and cats, and I fell asleep content, while the orchestra played and the perfumed guests waltzed around and around, their jewels and silks and brocades glimmering in the candlelight.

After a bath and more witch-hazel on my eyes I'm almost presentable. Felix comes home and I tell him calmly what's happened, and he understands. Rupert may plaster over the cracks today but this story will never be forgotten. Whenever the newswire is quiet it'll be pulled out of the filing cabinet and slyly revisited. My career is over.

'No, darling Izzy, don't you *say* that.' I'm sitting on the rug before the fire, my head against Felix's knees. 'You're too talented to give up. This will blow over. And my God, the way things are going, we'll all soon have more than rubbish like this to worry about.' He sighs.

Dearest Felix. What a selfish bitch I've been about his intelligence career, so vital to the world, while mine is just prancing around in stage makeup.

God, I wish I could just crawl into a hole, go somewhere I'm unknown. Perhaps one day I can return—the studios might find they miss me, financially if nothing else. But where could I go?

Oh. I lift my head. 'Darling, I've just had a marvellous idea.'

Felix looks down and strokes my cheek.

'That job you were offered in Hong Kong,' I say. 'Could you still take it? Suddenly getting away to the ends of the earth sounds rather attractive.'

'But you *hated* the thought of it, Izzy.'

'I hate the thought of living here more.' I shrug. 'If I'm away this might blow over sooner.'

'That's true. They haven't filled the position just yet—hard to find another chap with my skills, after all. Are you *sure*, darling?"

I take his hand and kiss it. 'We'll just have to make it our very own adventure, Felix.'

He beams. 'There'd be so much you could do in Hong Kong. Perhaps a Chinese studio you could do films for.' (I wince.) 'Or teach acting to kids, plenty of English families there. Or you could just rest in luxury, you've been working so hard.'

I do need a rest, I do need a change. I do, Lord knows, need to get away.

I get up and sit beside him and he holds me and murmurs loving words. I put my head on his shoulder and watch the flames in the fireplace and feel oddly at peace.

Eliza invites me around for lunch to admire her new flat, and I certainly do. She's developed a good eye (I've taught her well). I notice a framed photo on the mantelpiece, her beau Stefan, dark and attractive.

There's an ease between Eliza and me now, as if we've survived some great disaster together. As much as I can I've put away my regrets over Gideon and our unborn baby, and even let go of my anger at Lucy, choosing instead to recall her kindness to me when I was small.

'Some amusing news, darling,' I say over coffee. 'Felix and I are off to Hong Kong in a few months. He's had a promotion in his hush-hush job, whatever it is they do.'

'He'd be pleased.' Eliza hesitates. 'But what about you, Izabel?'

'Oh, I'll be glad to get away, let all this nonsense blow over.'

'The papers have been *horrible* to you,' she says. 'I don't know how you can bear it.'

'Needs must,' I say, shrugging. 'Still, new frontiers and all that.'

'Will you be seeing your mother's family in Hong Kong?'

'Are you joking? Certainly *not.*' I shake my head. 'My God, Eliza, that would be madness after all the hue and cry about my shameful Oriental background.'

She smiles. 'Sorry. Does Min-lu have family there now, anyway?'

'Oh, just a brother I think, Bao-lim. He lived with us in Melbourne when I was young, and had a long grey queue down his back which fascinated me.'

Eliza refills my cup and I take another of the dainty biscuits she's set out.

'These *are* delicious,' I say. 'One good thing about stopping work, I can eat more. Not too much of course, but at least the iron discipline can be cast aside for a while.'

'And think about the food you'll be able to have!' says Eliza. 'Remember Min-lu's amazing cook? Those dumplings. The noodles. The *duck.*' She groans. 'I do envy you Hong Kong, Izabel. I'll have to visit so you can ply me with banquets.'

We laugh and I feel almost cheered. Eliza's such a dear, always makes the best of a situation. Getting on a bit though—needs to nab that dishy Stefan as soon as possible.

Later, rummaging through my cupboards and thinking about what I need to pack, I suddenly decide I *will* go and see Mummy's brother after all.

Bao-lim was surprisingly kind to me. He had a seamstress make a small silk gown for my beloved doll and we'd walk in the kitchen garden and look for strawberries to eat. I'd chatter endlessly to him, but he was always patient.

I stop rummaging. Good heavens—we used to speak together in *Chinese*. After Bao-lim left I insisted on using only English at home. The girls at school were calling me cruel names.

Language is my stock in trade, of course. I'm passionate about nuance, tone, timing, the subtle potential of every single syllable.

And as Bao-lim's words return to me—elusive, witty, poetic—I sit down, overwhelmed. How *exquisite* is that long-forgotten language of my childhood?

After a time I mentally shake myself and think, heavens, what a lot of bizarre things have happened to me lately just because a gossip columnist stumbled across an old newspaper clipping.

I get up to make a cup of tea then stop and think, but that's rather odd, isn't it? Did the columnist leg it down to Melbourne to thumb through the press archives, looking for a clipping from twenty-eight years ago?

Not very likely. In fact, as far as I know, the only copy of that clipping is in my mother's scrapbook.

I feel an odd disquiet.

I walk into the white and gold study, the once-upon-a-time nursery. The scrapbook takes a while to find because it's tucked at the back of a drawer and not on the shelf where it usually is. That's odd too—I can't imagine who's moved it, as only Felix and I come into this room. The cleaner perhaps?

The book is full of snippets of old newsprint and the smell of paste takes me back to my childhood. To memories of Mummy at her desk, keeping a record of her rise to prominence: to as much grudging prominence a Chinese woman merchant might be permitted in rigidly White Australia at the turn of the twentieth century.

Everything seems in order as I turn the pages to the year 1907, to the date of Sam and Rosa's ball. But there's an empty space where the clipping used to be. I'm strangely unsurprised.

It's July 1935, a rather lovely summer, but soon to be replaced by the fierce humidity of our destination. We stand at the ship's stern and watch England recede.

I try not to think of my homecoming last winter, returning in triumph from Hollywood. I do try.

I'm wearing a floral silk dress, flattering and expensive, but this time there are no photographers at the docks. Felix, in his white shirt and linen trousers, turns to me grinning.

'What a rush, eh, Izzy? But all tickety-boo now. We can just enjoy the cruise.' A distant look comes over his face. 'Though I'm not the world's best sailor. Get seasick rather easily.'

There are bags under Felix's faded blue eyes. His narrow moustache, once so dashing, looks rather dated, his skin is slightly pockmarked near the jaw and there's grey in his hair.

But he's still a fine-looking man, and God knows I've always been susceptible to male beauty. Naturally, our bond runs much deeper than appearance: we have intimacy and love and trust.

I try not to think about trust. I do try.

Harry Bell, the doctor who was so kind the night I lost the baby, tried to warn me how damaged Felix was. Of course I didn't understand then.

I do now. Shallow, *faithless* Felix.

But you see, I need him, I won't pretend for a moment I don't. And I'm an actress, one of the best. I concentrate on the role I must play, take a deep breath, let it flow out smoothly and hit my mark.

'Darling, I'm so looking forward to everything!' I squeeze my husband's arm and laugh. 'What *fun*.'

28. Pete: Identity Crisis

It's March 1936, fifteen months after Billie and I parted. I go into her old bedroom and gaze at the hills outside the window. Lately Charlotte's been moody, and I've been—I don't know—a bit glum.

Perhaps it's because good old Smithy finally bought the big one, India to Singapore last November, gone without a trace. Happens to us all one day, I suppose.

I sit down on the bed and sigh. Why does everything keep changing? And ending? And how the *hell* did I lose Billie?

I'm overwhelmed with memories of us entwined, whispering, laughing, caressing. The copper waves of her hair, the copper curls of her slim body. Breakfast on spring mornings, beers on summer evenings, late winter nights at the airfield, frost crunching under our feet and stars sparkling forever in the dark sky above.

It's not that I don't love Charlotte, I do, but it's an easy love built on light-hearted pleasures. We're not together long enough to resolve our differences and we don't share books or furniture or belongings (I stroke my hand across the bright bedspread Billie bought when we were together).

And my dreams of marrying Charlotte are receding further into the distance every day.

At the back of the cupboard is a box of small things Billie forgot to take, but I've never had the resolve to face her and give them back. Now I decide I must.

I leave a message at her digs asking her to meet at Hamble teashop on Saturday to return some of her belongings. I turn up at the appointed time and Billie walks in a few minutes later.

She's as tall and slim and electrically impatient as ever, dressed in flying overalls and a sheepskin coat. The waitress brings us tea and sticky buns.

'Some of your things,' I manage to say, nodding my head at the box. 'You left them behind in the cupboard.'

She opens the flap and says, 'Ah, *there*'s that bloody compass, and my books. And the satchel, too. Thanks.'

I eat some bun. 'So how are things?' I say. I seem to be having trouble swallowing.

'Good. What about you?'

'Good.'

'How's the farm going?' she asks.

'Yeah, good. And the job at AST?'

'Fine. They finally built that womens' bathroom they always promised, too.'

'Good.'

A silence descends.

I close my eyes and before I can stop myself I say, 'I miss you so much, Billie.'

After a few moments she says, 'I miss you too, Pete.' I open my eyes. She's gazing at me with a familiar mix of affection and exasperation.

'I'm so *sorry*, Billie,' I say. 'I'm so sorry I messed up and ruined all our plans. I don't understand why it happened.'

'I expect it was because you wanted it to happen, Pete. I imagine you weren't ready to be a grown-up, but since I'm not a psychiatrist I suppose we'll never know.'

Another long pause.

'Are you going out with anyone?' I ask.

'Yes. You?'

'Mmm.'

'Charlotte?' Billie takes a bite of bun.

'Um, yeah.'

'And how does Harry feel about that?'

'He doesn't know.'

'Then why would she bother?' Billie says. 'The whole point is to hurt Harry.'

'Sorry?'

She shrugs. 'She hates the way Harry has that deep, constant love for your sister. And respect too—something Charlotte will never get from him or anyone else, she's such a lying *hora*.'

'*Hora?*'

'What it sounds like,' she says. 'What does Eliza think?'

'She doesn't know either.'

'Not quite declaiming your love from the rooftops, are you?'

I say desperately, 'We weren't carrying on while you and I were together, you know.'

'I told you, Pete, if you were honest I wouldn't have cared.' She finishes her bun and licks the sugar off her fingertips. 'No, it was more your annihilation of years of my hard work that pissed me off, not who you might have been screwing.'

'No possibility you'd give me a second chance is there, Billie?'

'No possibility.' She stands, picks up the box and says, 'Thanks, Pete. Bye.'

I drive back to London and go to see Eliza straight away. I desperately need to talk to someone who knows Billie, and of course I should also tell her about Charlotte.

It's pretty stupid to have kept her in the dark for so long—nearly a year, for God's sake.

When my sister answers the door I'm surprised to see she's still in her dressing-gown. It's a glamorous quilted satin thing, but it's unusual for afternoon wear.

'Hello, Pete,' she says evenly. 'Come out to the balcony. I've just made tea.' Her little balcony overlooks a garden square planted with rare trees by a Victorian botanist. When I visit I often go for a wander around, but not today.

Eliza pours the tea, offers me a cigarette and lights one herself. I notice the ash-tray is almost full and joke, 'Didn't know you were such a smoker, Sis.'

She gazes at the trees and says to herself, as if recalling poetry, 'Now and then, under stress. And when on watch, of course.'

The penny drops. 'Are you *okay*, Lizzie?'

She pauses. 'Oh, Stefan's having something of an identity crisis. Not very easy to live with.' She ashes her cigarette. 'And what have you been up to, Pete?'

'Just back from Hamble. I saw Billie this morning, first time in ages. She's looking wonderful. Still pretty cranky at me, though. I told her I missed her horribly and begged for a second chance, but she wouldn't have a bar of me.'

'And you're surprised?'

'Suppose not.' I sigh. 'Anyway, she scolded me because there's something I haven't told you about, I've been keeping it quiet till I knew what was happening.'

I take a deep breath. 'Fact is, Sis, I've been seeing quite a bit of Charlotte lately.'

'Seeing?' Eliza stares at me. 'Really? You mean an *affair*?'

'She's pretty lonely, you know,' I say. 'Old Harry's not very kind to her.'

'I wonder, Pete, if that's because you're just the latest in a high-stepping chorus-line of her boyfriends?' Eliza says coldly.

I suddenly remember a bloke once who seemed annoyed with Charlotte, but she gave me some half-plausible excuse. Another time a man in the street went to hug her and she coldly pulled away. Were they old boyfriends?

Feeling miserable I say, 'But Lizzie, you're probably not very objective.'

'Oh, *really*, Pete?'

I'm cross now. 'Look, Charlotte told me all about Penfold's wedding and you deliberately trying to seduce Harry.'

Eliza stares, then laughs. 'Is *that* what she says?'

She grinds out her cigarette. 'One stupid little kiss, and by God I've made amends. We've kept well away from each other ever since, and *still* she tortures him.'

'But—but she says Harry won't give her a divorce.'

'No, Pete. Charlotte won't let *him* go—a public divorce would give her little game away. Remember her mother's snide moralising? Charlotte adores her fun but she's terrified of anyone knowing. Your sly girlfriend's not letting Harry go. Not for you, not for any man.'

After a long pause I say, 'All right, Lizzie. Sorry.'

I don't know whether it's true or not, but I feel sick and want to change the subject. Lying on the table is a framed sketch and I nod my head towards it. 'Nice. New?'

'Birthday present.'

I look more closely. 'But isn't that *you*? On your ship?'

'Yes. Tarring some lines with a boy called Rolf, and he's just told me one of his terrible jokes.'

'But it's caught you *exactly*,' I say, sitting forward, surprised. 'The line of your head, your laugh, your hands. And Rolf looks like a nice kid too.'

'He was, Pete. He was the one who died, remember? Died in a fall.'

Oh God. With shame I vaguely recall her telling me about it.

'Lizzie, I'm sorry, I forgot,' I say. 'But it's a great sketch anyway. Who did it?'

'Harry.' Her eyes are stricken. 'I can't talk now. Another day.'

Back in my car I check the time and rub my eye-sockets. Jesus. I'm supposed to be meeting Charlotte at our favourite pub by the river now.

I stop at a flower-seller to buy her some roses, all golden and lush like her, then gun the engine and get there only about ten minutes late.

But she's not cross with me, she's waiting calmly at a table, gazing at the river. She breathes in the scent of the roses and says, 'Darling Pete.' Then she looks up. 'Let's take a walk.'

I carry the flowers for her and we wander along the river footpath in the afternoon sun and I relax. This is Charlotte, after all. Yes, she's flirtatious and too imaginative for her own good. She's run poor old Harry ragged, but that's *her*. Of course Billie and Eliza have their own reasons to dislike her, but this is my own lovely Charlotte.

She stops. 'Pete. I've got some news.'

I turn to her and kiss her forehead. 'Mm?'

'Bit awkward, actually, sweetie.' She takes a breath. 'Turns out I'm pregnant. It's the last thing I ever expected.' Her mouth is bitter. 'I've done everything possible to avoid motherhood for years, but even the best-laid plans, as they say.'

'*Golly*. Are you all right? How far along?'

'Four months. I was a bit moody there for a while. Sorry.'

'Hardly noticed it,' I fib, then suddenly I can't stop grinning. 'My God! This means we can get *married*! I'll look after you forever, I promise, darling Charlotte.'

I hug her, laughing, then realise she isn't responding.

'Charlotte?'

She steps back, her hands in her pockets, and sighs. 'Thing is, Pete, I'm not leaving Harry.'

'But it's *my* child, isn't it? You said you and Harry don't—'

'We don't. Yes, it's yours.'

I can't make sense of her words. 'But Harry won't want to raise another man's child.'

She shrugs. 'He'll have to. He knows perfectly well I won't divorce him, and he certainly can't divorce me, it'd upset his frail old mum too much. He'll accept it.'

'But what about *me*?'

The pulse is beating so hard in my throat I think it must be audible.

'Pete, you know the only legal grounds for divorce are violence or adultery. Pretending Harry is violent would be absurd, and I couldn't possibly stand up in court and ...' She lifts her chin. 'And of course everyone knows children should always be born in wedlock.'

I'm shaking my head in disbelief, the hollow in my gut agonising. 'But you can't just tell me this, Charlotte, and then— what? Never *see* me again?'

'Afraid I have to. I'm truly sorry. It's been odd, but you've make me happier than anyone else ever has.' She smiles sadly. 'Darling old Pete.'

She kisses me on the cheek, and turns and walks away.

I stand there unable to move. I remember Granddad Freddy telling me on his deathbed that his greatest regret was missing out on his own child's life. I remember, too, how I'd hoped such a thing would never happen to me.

Charlotte is out of sight now and I'm still holding the golden roses. Their lush scent sickens me and I throw them into the river. They drift away, but I wish they'd disappear, just plummet to the bottom and lie deep beneath those cold heavy ripples.

I wonder what that would feel like? Just a few moments of agony I expect, then surely some peace.

But I doubt I could bear a single extra instant of pain, so I go home.

It's evening now. I let myself into the flat, and in the firelight I see Stefan and Toby sitting together on the couch. Their hands are clasped, and Stefan's head is on Toby's shoulder.

Oh. Guess that's what Eliza meant about Stef's identity crisis.

I say, 'Hello,' and go into the kitchen and sit down at the table. They come to the door and Toby turns on the light and gasps.

'Christ, Farmer Pete, what's happened?'

I look at him, dazed.

Well, Toby, there's Billie my beloved, whose dreams I shattered through my idiot carelessness, and my sister, broken-hearted over a sketch of a poor dead boy. A sketch by Harry, the most decent man I ever met, a man whose trust I've betrayed for a year without a qualm.

And here's my friend Stefan in obvious pain, and you, good Toby, who's loved him without hope for ten long years. And of course there's cold, cold Charlotte, who's simply walked out of my life with our child. Our child unborn, unknown, and lost to me forever.

But I can say nothing.

I can only put my hands over my face and sob.

29. Eliza: The Sketch

Pete always had his excuses for drinking too much, driving too fast and flouting the rules at Hamble. But when he got drunk, crashed a plane he couldn't fly and got thrown out of aviation school it was beyond forgiving, even for flexible Billie.

Pete drifted then between Hamble and London, utterly lost, until kind Toby took him under his wing. Although Toby loves his solitude and didn't need the money, he still asked Pete to move into his flat to 'share the rent.'

Sometimes I think it's Toby who's the true heart of our social set. He's christened us the *avant-garde gang*, and Stef's cousin Sofia and her lover Klara are certainly modern and creative forces. Elfin Klara produces her poetry by hand on a printing press, hour after laborious hour, and the shimmering, eerie worlds she builds out of her simple verses enchant me.

Amusing Sofia gets the occasional job as a classical cellist, but not with the big orchestras—as official policy they don't hire women, no matter how talented. She plays for us sometimes, her music fierce and engaging and tender.

So I'm happy to see Pete start to find his feet here in London, with the avant-garde gang to help take his mind off the past. Although Sofia says if he 'casually' puts his hand on her knee again she's going to punch him in the nose.

Pamela Bourne and I stay in touch. I read her light-hearted memoir about her travels aboard *Herzogin Cecilie*, and love it. She doesn't give much away in the book about her feelings for Sven Eriksson, but writes to tell me when they become engaged.

In October 1935 I receive a happy postcard—Pam and Sven have just been wed in Finland and are setting sail that night on the Duchess. By the time I get the card they're far away, so I send my congratulations to their destination, Port Lincoln.

In January 1936, when they arrive at Port Lincoln, the newspapers trumpet the spectacle of the annual gathering of great barques. Not only *Herzogin Cecilie* and dear old *Inverley*, but *Olivebank* too, with *Viking*, *l'Avenir*, *Winterhude*, *Pommern*, *Penang* and *Archibald Russell*.

The papers also print a photo of Pam and Sven in the ship's elegant saloon. Sven sits in a large leather chair with Pam perched beside him, leaning on his shoulder. His arm hugs her hips, she lightly encircles his neck.

They smile, contented, as if they've just arisen from a rumpled bed, bonded in heart and body and soul. It's a beautiful photo. I don't understand why it makes me cry.

But of course I do.

The unravelling is so slow it's almost unnoticeable. Stefan becomes remote, distracted by tight deadlines, the demands of his parents, the sad, lingering illness of a friend. I don't understand it and talk to Toby.

He tells me Stef's sick friend is an old schoolmate of theirs, although he says he has no idea why it's hitting Stef so deeply. That's surprising, because Toby usually knows what's going on.

Then in November the poor schoolmate dies, and after the funeral Stefan falls into a deep depression. It's around the anniversary of Freddy's death, so I feel a little raw myself.

Toby says he thinks Stefan is simply shocked at the realisation of his own mortality, as it's the first death our circle of friends has experienced.

One night Stefan opens up a little, saying he's recognised his life has taken him along pathways he didn't choose.

He's tried to live up to the wishes of his parents, his schools, his colleagues, but didn't understand until recently how far those wishes had diverged from his own.

'But if you want to change what you do, Stef, I'll do anything to help,' I say. 'Would you like to study something new, or travel overseas, perhaps?'

I carefully do not suggest marriage or babies. Amusingly, I have now come to yearn for the simple things I once scorned. I have become the *kapten* Harry teased me about, the *kapten* who would one day want the responsibility of others.

But the man who used to speak so joyfully of our future together, now avoids such dangerous waters. He doesn't want to study or travel. Not with me at any rate, though he has an old running joke with Toby about Venice in spring one day.

It seems so unfair. Stef is gentle and sensual. It was hard at first to open my heart, but almost as an act of will I taught myself to love him and look forward to our life together.

But sheer will cannot prevail over feeling: not for Stefan, and not for me. I find that out for myself when I open the large envelope that arrives on my birthday.

I ran across my old notebooks and thought you might like this. I haven't done any drawing for a long time, unless you count some rather terrifying Anopheles gambiae mandibles that were a great hit with the editor of Nature. This is the only picture I ever did of Rolf—he never kept still for long enough—but it captures something of him. Not of you. No pencil could capture your quicksilver being. I hope you are happy.

I look at the sketch once then put it aside as I cannot bear to contemplate it. Rolf's laughing face and child's frame and braced bare feet; my hair tied back with a scrap of rope, my narrow hands, the joy in my eyes. No, Harry, I am far from happy.

The sketch arrived a few months ago. The other day, trying to keep my foolish pain in perspective, I showed it to Stef. Of course he knows of the loss of Rolf, but I told him more about the ship and its people and my joy of being, for a time, simply deckboy Elias. Without saying anything, Stef took the sketch and had it beautifully framed.

This evening he presents it to me. I thank him, although I'm not sure I'll be able to bear the sight of it on my wall every day. I pour us drinks and we sit in the armchairs by the fire.

Stef clears his throat. 'Darling, I want you to know how much I've appreciated your strength over these difficult months. I've been unfairly preoccupied.'

Outlined by the firelight, his profile is that of the fine quick man he was before this long period of withdrawal, and I feel a surge of affection.

'I know it's been hard for you too, Stef, but perhaps we can be happy again.'

He shakes his head and I stop.

'Eliza, I can't keep pretending to be the person you believe I am.' He turns to face me. 'Do you remember, at the beginning, when we talked about the people from our past?'

In our early days, as lovers do, we confided our old entanglements to each other. I'd mocked Jack Brandon and spoken calmly about Harry, and Stefan told me ruefully of several women who'd left their marks upon him.

'There was someone I never mentioned.' He takes a deep breath. 'The man who died last year. It happened so long ago and I'd always told myself it was just a passing phase. Now it's hit home what he really meant to me.'

'Why—why didn't you stay together?'

'Confusion, inexperience, too many parties. He played around with another boy and I left him. I went back to what my parents wanted, what everyone expected of me.' He shrugs. 'Obviously I like women well enough too, so it didn't seem a problem.'

'I never felt short-changed,' I say as lightly as I can.

He smiles and takes a drink, gazing at the fire. After a moment he sighs and says, 'There's someone else, too. Someone who's loved me for a long time.'

I'm puzzled, then suddenly comprehend. 'Ah. Toby.'

'Toby. I've denied him and tried to be the man I'm not for years, and now I can't hide what I really want any longer. I'm sorry, Eliza. You're a dear woman and we might have made a good life together, but my heart just wants what it wants, without wisdom or reason.'

'There's always a sort of wisdom to it,' I say helplessly. 'Just not much reason.'

After a pause he says, 'And you—what about you and Harry? Do you think, if we weren't together, you might work something out?'

'No, there's no possibility of that. He can't change his own situation.' I take a drink. 'Does Toby know what you're thinking?'

'Not yet.' His voice wobbles a little. 'And after all this time he may not even want me.'

'I'm absolutely certain he does, dear man, just as he should,' I say. 'And if you hurry up you can see Venice in spring together at last.'

Stef smiles at the old joke as I'd hoped. 'Oh, *darling*. I wish—'

I shake my head. 'We've been happy together and who knows, perhaps we'll even stay friends. I'd hate to lose you and Toby from my life.'

'You won't, Eliza, I swear it.'

We speak gently a little longer, and he leaves. Then I cry, mostly from the deep and terrible relief of understanding.

Next day I sit around in my dressing-gown and smoke too much, and wonder what on earth will happen now. The doorbell rings and Pete is there, his hair messy, his eyes worried, and tells me of his heartbreak over Billie. And his affair with Charlotte.

I'd believed him when he said he and Charlotte were simply friends, so I'm shocked at my gullibility, Pete's naïvety and Charlotte's deceit.

Her self-centred allure reminds me a little of Mama and, like Mama, she has a rigidly conventional side. I wonder if that's what attracts Pete?

Then again, who bloody cares?

I'm so *sick* of having to cope with Charlotte in my life. I gaze at Harry's sketch and wish I were far out on the ocean once more. Beyond the offing, beyond the horizon: beyond even the four quarters of the earth.

I ring my brother a few days later to apologise for being so distracted when he visited.

'Think nothing of it, Lizzie. Probably the best part of the whole day anyway.'

It takes me a moment to realise he isn't joking. 'Why, Pete? What happened?'

'Ah, I was a bit premature telling you about Charlotte, that's all. She left me that very afternoon. Said she's staying with Harry.'

My heart thumps and my eyes sting. 'Did she?'

'That wasn't everything—but, well, you'll hear soon enough, so I'll skip the gory details.' He takes a breath. 'Anyway, I'm going back to the farm and getting a job. Stef told me about an engineering firm in Southampton that needs someone with my background.'

'Sounds interesting. What do they make?'

He laughs sadly. 'Aircraft.'

'Oh Pete, I'm so *sorry*. About Billie and flying and Charlotte too. You've had a rough trot.'

'Nah. Brought it on myself. Time I grew up.' He clears his throat. 'What about you? A bit under the weather the other day.'

'You've seen Stef since then, so I expect you know why.'

'Yeah. Sorry, Sis, but I guess ...'

'He's happier with Toby?'

'Looks like it.'

'Then that's good for us all. I hope the new job goes well, Pete.'

I put down the phone and sit staring at nothing.

Charlotte has gone back to Harry. For a brief moment hope had glimmered—perhaps she might leave him for Pete? But no, Harry will never be free and I must go on accepting that.

Strangely, I start to feel a new peace. Discovering the cause of Stefan's unhappiness has helped because now I know there's nothing I can do about it.

Sometimes I have meals with Klara and Sofia, kind and undemanding company, and I spend a lot of time on the phone with Billie. Her wit and good sense keep me grounded.

She got on well with Stef at Hamble, so she's glad we're staying friends, and when we talk about Pete she calls Charlotte the *perkele* cow, and worse, and that helps me laugh a little.

But there's still pain in her voice when she says my brother's name and I wonder how long it will be before she's over him. She sees other men, but no one serious.

She's increasingly angry, too, at the way she has to push back against the prejudices of the cocky new RAF recruits. They find the mere idea of a female instructor hard to accept, even though hundreds of women already have aviation licences.

'Everyone loves a girl flyer, Lizzie,' Billie says. 'Except the boy flyers.'

Some weeks later, she rings me and says she's coming to London, and wants to meet at our favourite pub. When she arrives we hug, and I feel a touch of concern. She's always been thin, but surely not as thin as this?

I've already bought her a shandy—she's never been a big drinker—but she shrugs and goes to the bar to get herself a gin.

When she sits down I say, 'Bill—what's wrong?'

'Ah, Lizzie. Turns out it's not a good move to threaten a tutor if he doesn't get his hand off your arse. Turns out it's an even worse move to knee him in the balls when he doesn't.'

She grins painfully. 'I was fired.'

I squeeze her hand. 'Bill, I'm so *sorry*. Fancy firing you when it was his fault!'

'Oh come on, Lizzie, it's always the woman's fault. You know that.' She rubs her face with her hands. 'Don't worry, though, everything's all right. Got another job—Stott's Flying Display.'

'The big aerial circus?'

'Yeah. I do *Miss Billie's Daredevil Handkerchief Stunt*. Swoop past the crowd in a Tiger Moth and hook a hanky off the ground with one wing. Takes a bit of concentration.'

She smiles. 'But the other pilots are a professional bunch, the clowning around's just for the customers.'

'Don't you have to move all over the country?'

'Yeah, new town every few days, but it's a well-oiled machine —trucks go ahead and set up the tents, workshops, seating. We fly overhead to excite the crowds, then give a couple of shows. But the big money's in taking people up for joy-rides. We've got a nice big Clive that seats ten.'

She finishes her gin. 'Of course, I don't do that. Customers wouldn't get in a plane flown by a woman.'

Nearly two months after parting from Stefan, I go out one morning to get a newspaper. As I put on my coat in the lounge-room I gaze around and feel content.

I've spent the last few weeks repainting and rearranging the flat, and it's been satisfying. Propped on the mantelpiece is the final touch—a handsome etching of Venice, a gift just arrived from Stefan and Toby in Italy.

The newsagent and I chat about the mild spring weather as he hands me the paper and I tuck it under my arm.

I don't even glance at the headlines until I'm walking along the footpath: and then I stop short in horror.

Windjammer Runs Ashore In Early Morning Fog
World's Fastest Sailing Vessel Doomed
The proudest, the largest, and the fastest of windjammers, the Herzogin Cecilie (2672 tons), met her doom on the fog-bound rocks at Sewer Mill Cove in the early hours of Saturday morning. With the Channel blanketed with a thick, swirling mist, she struck a reef at 3.50 a.m. on 25th April. Her steel hull was pierced and water poured into the holds.
The four-masted barque sent up flares and rockets and the Salcombe lifeboat was immediately launched. This week the Herzogin Cecilie arrived at Falmouth after a voyage of 86 days from Port Lincoln, South Australia. Captain Sven Eriksson, the Master, and his wife, formerly Miss Pamela Bourne, who had just completed their honeymoon trip, steadfastly refuse to leave the vessel and remain on board.

30. Harry: Bolt Head

Charlotte, thank God, is out. It was bad enough she was spending so much time with Eliza's brother, but after she coolly informed me a few weeks ago of the consequences of her fling, and the role she expects me to play in her poor mite's future, I don't have a word to say to that selfish bitch.

When I open the newspaper I see the headline, *Windjammer Runs Ashore In Early Morning Fog*. I read quickly, then grab my atlas and look up Salcombe. It's a small town in Devon, two hundred miles away, and the train runs from Paddington.

I pick up the phone, notice my hand is trembling, and dial Eliza's number. I've never rung her new flat, but I memorised the number long ago.

I wonder briefly how much she knows about Charlotte and Pete but then, compared to what's happened to the Duchess, she probably couldn't give a damn. I certainly don't.

At the sound of her voice my mouth goes dry, but I say, 'Have you seen the news about *Herzogin Cecilie?*'

'Yes, just this minute,' she says, her voice shaky. 'I'm going down to Devon on the 11 a.m. train.'

I say simply, 'I'll see you at the station,' and hang up.

While I'm throwing things into a small bag my mind is in a daze. What am I doing? What will I say to her? But another part of me is thinking, at last! At last this bitter stalemate is ending. At last I'll see her again.

The taxi drops me off and I rush into the station, buy a ticket and wait at the barrier near the train, my heart thumping. A few minutes later I see her stopping at the ticket window, then she turns and comes towards me. Dear God, she's lovely.

I say, 'Let's go!' feeling like a truant schoolboy, and we dash to the nearest carriage door. Inside I lift our bags and put them in the luggage rack.

'Want the window seat?' I ask.

'Don't mind,' she says, breathless.

In a few months it will three years since since we last met. I always remember her birthday, and when she turned twenty-eight I sent her the sketch of her and Rolf on the ship.

It's one I particularly like, not simply because it's of Eliza, but my hand was looser, freer then. If I draw anything now it comes out boring and pedantic—just like me, as Charlotte says.

The train starts with a jerk and we almost fall onto the seats. Eliza and I gaze at each other, smiling. I know I've got lines beside my eyes now and my hair is receding at the temples, but she's more beautiful than ever.

'You haven't changed a bit,' I say.

'That's kind, Harry, but not entirely correct.'

'Well, we're all older, and I expect you're wiser.'

'You're not?' she says. I shake my head ruefully.

'But why are you coming to Salcombe?' she says. 'You don't know *Herzogin*'s crew.'

'To talk to you. A few hours on a train seems a good opportunity.'

Eliza takes a breath and says, 'All right. About what?'

'Charlotte and your brother, for one thing. Did you know they were seeing each other?'

'He mentioned it but said they'd broken it off.' She glances at me. 'Would you have wanted me to tell you?'

'Of course not. I knew in any case—she always made certain I did, whoever the man was.'

'Harry, I'm so sorry about Pete. He's a fool and knows it, but that doesn't excuse him.'

I nod. 'Is that all he said about Charlotte?'

She nods, then it hits her. 'Don't tell me there's *more*—'

'Of course there's more!' I laugh. 'Excruciatingly, absurdly more. Just when I think Charlotte has reached a whole new level of dreadful behaviour she surprises me yet again.'

'Harry, *what?*'

'Have you ever wondered about becoming an aunt, Eliza?'

'An aunt? For that my brother would have to father a child.'

'Correct.'

She stares at me. 'Charlotte's *pregnant*? To *Pete*?'

'But she's kindly granting me the honours of putative fatherhood.'

'She's going to *pretend* it's your child? Couldn't she just be lying again? Perhaps it's really yours after all.'

'Well, if a child could survive a whole three years in the womb, there might be some chance of that. Failing a medical miracle there's no possibility it's mine.'

'Oh.'

She knows what that means. How long it's been since I touched Charlotte, and why.

'What will you do?' she says.

'In any sane marriage we'd get a divorce, but she's adamant this child will be born within wedlock. But Charlotte has gone one amazing step further. To rule out the slightest possibility of me even considering divorce, she's sent tickets to my family for a cruise to Britain, so they're here for the happy event.'

'I know you promised your mother—'

'Worse than that. My mother's heart is weak, and now she mustn't be exposed to any shocks at all. I can't even *mention* the word divorce. I'm utterly hamstrung.'

Eliza laughs, horrified. 'My God, that's devious. If Charlotte ever took up politics she'd rule the country in short order, and probably the world soon after that.'

'So there we are.' I shake my head. 'I simply had to talk to someone, and who but you, Eliza, would believe a word of it? I feel such a bloody fool.'

'Then don't, Harry, don't you *dare*. If we're talking foolishness in relationships I'm right at the head of the queue.'

'But I thought you and Stefan were happy.'

'So did I. However, I stupidly overlooked the long-suppressed passion between him and his best friend Toby, despite being aware of their torrid upbringing in an English boarding school. And now they're on what amounts to a honeymoon in Venice.'

I'm incredulous. 'I'm sorry, Eliza, how could *anyone* choose someone else if they already had you?'

'I suppose it just comes down to love, Harry.'

'And you love Stefan.'

'I tried—but no, in the end I didn't.'

'So you don't love Stefan,' I say, a glow of joy in my chest. 'And I don't love Charlotte. And they don't care about you and me.'

'That's right,' she says, smiling.

I take her warm slim hand in mine. 'Then it's just us now.'

We have three years to catch up on, but the carriage fills up so we must be restrained. She rests her head against my shoulder and we murmur to each other.

'Work's been a consolation,' I say. 'We're so close to understanding malaria in humans now.'

'Will you be able to treat it then?'

'One day. We'll save millions of lives, and it's such a privilege to be involved. But I don't want to bore you with all that.'

'*Bore?*' she says. 'Darling Harry, you could recite a train timetable and I wouldn't be bored.'

I stroke the sweet curve of her cheek. 'And you? How's dear old *Inverley?*'

'Next year's looking bad. Charter rates have collapsed and the deepwater ships are being scrapped. Remember *Mozart*, the last barquentine left in the world? Broken up, like beautiful *Grace Harwar*. And record-breaking *Parma*? Scraped a dock, barely damaged, but off to the breakers. And now the poor, stranded Duchess. What will it mean, Harry?'

'We know what it probably means, love. One by one they'll go. It has to happen.'

'And soon no one will even remember their names,' she says sadly. 'But they embody so much knowledge and wisdom and experience. Onto the scrap heap, the lot of it.'

I squeeze her hand. 'Will it be the end for the Duchess?'

'I don't know,' she says. 'It's a cruel equation—the grain cargo is insured but she's not. If Gusta' can't salvage the cargo then he won't pay to salvage the ship.'

Far too soon the train arrives at Totnes, fifteen miles from Salcombe. I hire a car and drive us to Sewer Mill Cove where, according to the afternoon papers, the famous four-masted barque *Herzogin Cecilie* is now awaiting her end.

We walk through the fields to Bolt Head, the cliff above Sewer Mill Cove, among masses of curious people. Finally before us is a scene of such terrible incongruity we can only stand, shocked into silence.

The air is misty with spume from the violent sea below. Not far from shore, perhaps a quarter of a mile, is the grey ridge of the Ham Stone, the great rock that holed the Duchess. Before us, stranded on a reef so close we can see the details of her rigging, is the wallowing white ship.

Every line of her is yearning forward, yearning to sail away—if only the reef would let her go. But the ship's holds are heavy with thousands of tons of grain and she cannot float free. Every breaker thundering against her hull tells of the brute reality: *Herzogin* will never be let go.

A tripod has been set up with cables carrying a breeches buoy that runs out to the ship. Someone is in it right now, coming jerkily ashore, a tall, dark-haired woman. People help her out of the buoy and carry bags to a pile of gear. The woman stands staring at the desolate scene before us, her shoulders slumped.

Eliza murmurs, 'Pam,' and goes closer and touches the woman's arm. She turns and they hug.

'Nils, thank *God* you're safe!' Eliza says.

'Little Elias! Damn it, I'm not going to cry.'

'Nor me,' says Eliza, though that's clearly a lie. 'Are you all right? What happened?'

'The helmsman said the compass went mad just beforehand,' says Pam in despair. 'We can't understand—' She takes a shuddering breath.

'And Sven?'

'Dealing magnificently, but most of the crew have simply gone —only the mates and a handful of men are left, but they're working like demons.'

'Pam, this is Harry,' Eliza says. 'He was a sailor on *Inverley*.'

Pam quickly smiles at me. 'A friend. Good.'

'Can we help?' I say.

Pam sighs. 'Bloody Gusta' wants the sails and valuables off, doesn't give a damn about the ship. Will you watch over our things for a while? We've been sending them ashore in case she sinks but people have been stealing, *stealing* our few—' She almost sobs with rage.

'Of course we will,' says Eliza.

'I must get back. A truck is coming later from Salcombe to pick all this up.'

The breeches buoy has returned with kitbags, so we help unload them onto the pile. Pam is soon in the air on her way back to the ship, while Eliza watches anxiously. The lifebuoy wouldn't be much help if the line gave way above rocks, but I tell myself firmly they're pretty safe contraptions.

Men are unbending a sail on a foreyard, but there aren't many of them to help with the work, poor bastards. When the buoy returns with more bags, I say to Eliza, 'Look, I should go out and give them a hand. Will you be all right?'

She nods, her eyes large.

I climb into the circular buoy, fitting my legs through the 'breeches' dangling down, and I'm soon whizzing through the air. It's much less frightening doing it myself than watching someone else.

I land on the ship and it's good to be able to help. My hands are pretty soft nowadays but the first mate, Elis Karlsson, finds me some leather gloves and I work with a will, stowing canvas and loading it on deck. The dank grey afternoon continues.

Finally we get the word the man from Salcombe has arrived. Karlsson and I go ashore and, with Eliza's assistance, carry the crew's belongings to a small truck. It's getting dark now. Karlsson, exhausted and grim, says to Eliza, 'We have enough food on board, Elias, but tomorrow, perhaps you might bring us fresh bread and coffee?'

We shake hands then he goes back to the ship, looming as pale as a ghost in the gloom.

Subdued, Eliza and I drive into town three miles away, and park outside the Salcombe Hotel. I look at her beside me, unable to utter a word.

She gazes back, her eyes gentle. 'Of course, Harry,' she says and, absurd as it is for a doctor to say, my heart turns over.

At the desk I register us as Mr and Mrs Bell. We take our bags upstairs then go to the dining room. I haven't eaten since this morning but I barely notice what's on our plates.

Back in the cold bedroom our conversation ceases and we stand quietly, side by side at the window. Like most places in this hilly town the hotel looks over the estuary, but now at night all we can see are the glimmer of distant lights.

'Would you like the first bath?' I ask and Eliza nods. She takes her bag into the bathroom, then says, 'Oh no! It's freezing and I left my nightgown in London in the rush.'

I hand her my pyjama top around the door. A little later she emerges shyly, wearing the flannelette top and some large woollen socks.

'My God, you utter minx,' I say. 'Do you always torment men in this way?'

'Only the scientists. So hurry up and have your bath.'

I don't take long, then I get into bed bare-chested and shivering, and we snuggle together, laughing and kissing. My feet are warm so she takes off her socks. My arms and mouth and chest are warm too, so I remove her top and caress her sweet small breasts.

Undoing my pyjama pants she returns the favour, stroking me slowly and deliciously. By then we don't care about the cold, or the sad day, or our complicated lives.

All we want is each other. All that gives us joy is each other.

And all we know, at long last, is each other.

Next morning we take breakfast in the dining room, murmuring and smiling and occasionally yawning. We buy food for the ship and drive back to desolate Bolt Head.

The waters are calmer today and we both ride the breeches buoy out to *Herzogin*. Eliza helps Pam while I work with the crew, loading foresails and spare canvas onto a small boat to go ashore.

When we stop for a cup of tea Pam says she's been writing dozens of letters, to brokers, agents, newspapers and Gusta' himself.

She tells us angrily that a salvage tug arrived when they were stranded and might have saved them, but the crew refused to take on the job, saying the return on an uninsured four-master wouldn't be worth it.

We gaze at each other, the bitterness almost tangible, then go back to work.

All day long, motor-boats bring journalists and sightseers on board. Pam loathes the sightseers, who are openly stealing small items as souvenirs, but tries to be helpful to the journalists.

She wants *Herzogin Cecilie*'s plight well-known, as she thinks only public pressure will force Gusta' to try to save the ship.

Carloads of people and streams of cyclists and hikers clog the narrow lanes, and awed crowds stand watching on the cliff. The local newspaper reports:

> *It is safe to say that during the weekend 20,000 to 30,000 people visited the Cove to gaze upon the spectacle of the world's finest ship of her class impaled upon the deadly rocks, waiting for her end.*

Eliza and I stay at Salcombe for two weeks, through days of grim labour and nights of great joy. The days are quickly forgotten, but the nights are the most glorious I've ever known.

Finally the time comes when I must return to work in London, but by then the initial emergency is over. Despite the predictions of the reporters, the ship will not dramatically sink.

The gear is ashore and Pam is receiving hundreds of letters, many with small sums of money. A salvage attempt may even be on the cards as well—firms are now quoting more reasonable charges.

But water is still surging over the stranded Duchess and trickling through her breached hull. And her thousands of tons of grain are rotting and starting to swell.

31. Eliza: Vivian

Harry and I return to London on the train. I'm foolish with joy to see his lean, contented face, so changed from the defeated man I met at the station just a fortnight ago.

Of course he's still married to Charlotte, and Charlotte is still pregnant to my feckless brother Pete, but my heart is light when we kiss each other goodbye at Paddington.

The phone rings as I open my front door.

'Hullo, Mrs Bell,' says Charlotte. 'Enjoy your fling in Devon?'

'*Christ*, Charlotte. You've interrogated Harry already?'

'No, he's not speaking, the utter bore. I simply rang the largest hotel in Salcombe and they told me the charming Mrs Bell had departed this morning for London. With my husband.'

'Charlotte, let Harry *go*! Just divorce him—the people at the hotel can testify to our adultery. Look, I wouldn't wish you on my worst enemy, but you'd be happy with Pete. He adores you and he'd be a loving father. *Please.*'

'Amusingly, sweetie, you're probably right. Perhaps we will be together one day. But at the moment I am *not* bringing this baby and my own good name into public disrepute.'

'Think you're managing to do that all by yourself, Charlotte,' I say through gritted teeth.

'Oh, *catty* Eliza. By the way, Harry's mother and sister are arriving in a month—would you like to meet them? I'm planning a darling soiree.'

'Of course I'd like to meet them, but not with you, Charlotte. Are you mad?'

'Don't know, dear. Depends how much you want to protect your darling Harry.'

'Fuck off, you *förbannat* bitch.' I slam down the phone.

At the soiree a month later Charlotte wears a gown that flatters her pretty face and rounded belly. She introduces me to Harry's mother Jessie as his shipmate and her very dear friend.

Jessie has her son's wise grey eyes and I like her immediately, while young Tina is a cheerful seventeen-year-old with blonde curls. Harry himself is beyond joy at seeing them again.

Despite my misgivings the night is an odd success. Charlotte is wryly charming and says she'll show Jessie and Tina the sights of London, and would love me to come along too.

So over the next few weeks I cautiously accompany them to the Zoo, the National Gallery and shopping in the city. It all seems to go surprisingly well.

'I can't bear it,' Harry says. We're in bed at my flat. My head is on his chest and his voice rumbles pleasingly against my ear. 'Seeing you and Charlotte together, knowing how dreadful she can be. I keep waiting for some other—appalling—shoe to drop.'

I laugh. 'Me too, but she's being so nice whenever we go out.'

'And at home too. Mum and Tina think she's wonderful.'

I lift my head. 'Well, what about next week, then?'

Two months after the shipwreck we've had a letter from Pam, saying tugboats are ready now to try to get *Herzogin* off the reef.

'Charlotte said she doesn't mind in the slightest if we go down to Devon again. She even announced to my slightly startled mother she'd be delighted to have us tedious ship-lovers out from under her feet for a while.'

I shrug. 'Then let's go.'

Pam says they've been pumping water and rotting wheat out of the holds for weeks to try to lighten the Duchess. This is their second go at pulling her off the reef. Apparently the local farmers are becoming prosperous from charging sightseers sixpence a time to cross their fields.

On a clear day, Harry and I wait in the crowd at Bolt Head. Two tugboats tie up to the ship, then start churning the water, engines growling, pumps thudding in the background. Nothing happens. They try again without success. People murmur and my eyes start to sting.

Suddenly the four-master shivers.

She rocks a little and lifts, ponderously, from the reef. The towlines grow taut, the engines roar, and slowly, slowly, Herzogin begins to move.

The tugs toot their whistles and everyone cheers, and soon the ship is gliding through the sunny blue water, followed by a noisy fleet of yachts and motorboats celebrating the great moment. Harry and I hug, laughing in relief.

The Duchess is towed along the coast to an anchorage in calm, sandy-bottomed Starehole Bay, where *Kapten* Sven hopes to discharge the rest of the rotting wheat, get to the hull and finally make the desperately-needed repairs.

That evening we share a meal at Salcombe Hotel with an overjoyed Pam, Sven and the mates, and it seems as if everyone in town stops by the table to celebrate.

And that night in our room, Harry and I celebrate in our own sweet way. We're learning a lot about each other.

Life continues as before in London, but Charlotte's sunny mood becomes darker, her words sharp. Perhaps it's the strain of keeping up appearances before Jessie and Tina, but I wonder if she's anxious about the birth as well.

A month after the triumphant salvage of *Herzogin Cecilie*, I'm hurrying out to dinner at Charlotte and Harry's, and pick up a letter just arrived from Pam Eriksson.

While we're having cocktails I glance at it quickly. Shocked, I show Harry, but we don't have time to talk. Charlotte claps her hands irritably and calls us to table.

Over dinner she drinks more than usual. Harry tries to tell her it's bad for the baby, but she's petulant and unrepentant. She's cold to her husband and sarcastic to me, and nothing can disguise the venom. I yearn for the evening to come to an end.

Then Jessie asks innocently, 'Have you any family in England, Eliza?'

Pete is a dangerous topic, so I say off-handedly, 'Oh, a brother in Southampton. Haven't seen him for ages.'

'I have,' says Charlotte, very deliberately. 'Pete's *awfully* excited about some new planes called Spitfires. Rather aggressive name, but given the situation in Europe ...'

We all sigh about the situation in Europe. Then I wonder just when Charlotte saw Pete.

Charlotte is watching me. 'Oh, didn't I *tell* you, sweetie? While you and Harry were gallivanting around your shipwreck, I took the train to Southampton and dropped in on Pete at the farm. You remember the *farm*, of course.' She turns to the others. 'Such a lovely place, so romantic, especially at night.'

Jessie glances at Charlotte, then asks me, 'And what *is* the latest on your dear old Duchess?'

My head starts throbbing and I take a breath.

'Well—as it happens, I've just received some awful news. They were unloading the grain in what they thought was a well-protected bay, but an intense gale struck them unexpectedly last week. The ship is even more badly damaged.'

'But can't they just mend it?' says Tina.

'No, not now. Repairs will cost too much.' I swallow. 'Our friends Sven and Pam have been ordered to strip everything. The owner has decided to sell the ship for scrap metal—for a trivial *two hundred* pounds.' I stand up, my eyes filling. 'I think I'll leave now.'

'Harry'll go with you, won't you, darling?' says Charlotte. 'Make sure Eliza gets home safely. Oh *do* go, Harry, don't dither.'

He stands. 'I'll take you down to get a taxi, Eliza.'

'Take her down to get a *taxi*?' Charlotte says. 'Just take her home and get her into bed. As *usual*.'

I whisper, 'Goodnight,' into the stunned silence and leave.

At the front door, Harry hugs me. 'I'm so sorry, love.'

'I'm all right, but what if she's upset your mother? No, I'll get home by myself. You stay here and see what you can retrieve from this disaster.'

'And I'm bloody sorry about the Duchess too,' he says sadly.

I nod, unable to speak, and kiss him and leave.

Next morning my doorbell rings and I answer it, my eyes red and hair in a mess.

Harry's young sister Tina says, 'Here, Eliza, box of chocolates. Best thing in an emergency.'

I try to smile. 'Thank you. Come in, I'll put some coffee on.'

I wash my face and we sit on my balcony, summery perfumes wafting from the garden square. We drink coffee and eat chocolates and I say, 'You're absolutely right. They should carry these in first aid kits.'

Tina gazes at me, her head to one side. 'Charlotte isn't having a baby with Harry, is she?'

'Um. You'd have to—ask her about that.'

'Eliza,' she says solemnly. 'I'm not a child, I know something of what goes on in the world.' She takes a chocolate. 'And that just confirms my suspicions. So who's the real father?'

'Tina, I can't—'

'It's your brother *Pete*, isn't it?' she says, her eyes sparkling. 'I *knew* it. And has he abandoned Charlotte?'

I give up trying to be discreet. 'No, Charlotte left him. She doesn't want any sort of scandal about the birth, certainly not divorce proceedings. That's why she arranged for you two to come over here. To force Harry to go along with the charade.'

'Force?'

'She knows your mother can't cope with any shocks, so Harry doesn't dare say a word. Oh—is Jessie all right after last night?'

'Yes, Mum's a pretty tough old bird.' Tina leans forward. 'Look, Eliza, she's not nearly as religious now as Harry seems to think. She's changed since Dad died. You see, a friend of hers was trapped in a violent marriage, and she killed herself and it was *awful*! Mum says priests might call divorce a sin, but she reckons there are far greater sins take place in this world.'

I'm suddenly light-headed. 'Tina, are you saying ... if Harry wanted a divorce it wouldn't be a shock to his mother after all?'

'Shock? She says if *he* doesn't start the bloody proceedings soon, she'll do it for him! Look, Harry's tried his best, but he's only himself when you're there. And Mum knew straight away —she says you're both hopeless at hiding your feelings.'

'Oh.'

'She's not just tough, she's a wise old bird, too.' Tina smiles. 'Anyway, we're changing our tickets and going home. Mum says we're not hanging around for some poor little cuckoo's birth. And if Harry wants to try for divorce, we think he can't be rid of that dreadful woman fast enough.'

Jessie and Tina return to Australia, and Harry and I wave goodbye to them at the docks. Charlotte isn't there, of course— now she no longer has any hold over Harry she starts spending all her time with Pete again. Pete doesn't care. He just wants to be near her, and drives back and forth between Southampton and London, utterly happy.

Harry moves into a room at a colleague's flat, a place conveniently close to mine. I take his grandmother's ruby ring out of the box where I've kept it safe for four years, and wear it on my middle finger.

Harry says he's looking forward to the day he can ask a jeweller to make it smaller so it will fit my ring finger instead, but of course it's not that simple. Charlotte refuses to sue Harry for adultery, and he can't sue her without formal evidence.

Yet infidelity, real or play-acted, may not be the usual way out of an unhappy marriage for much longer. Recently legislation was proposed that would permit divorce after three years of desertion, so we'll just have wait for it to become law.

In September, we take the train to Devon for the last time and meet Pam Eriksson in Salcombe. Together we walk the river path to Starehole Bay, to a cliff above the small beach.

Half-submerged, the great stranded ship lies with her bow pointing towards the horizon. She leans a little, her decks are barren, her once-white paintwork filthy with rust. Pam's letters had told us they'd removed everything, down to the panelling and cornices of the elegant saloon, but the reality is shocking.

Herzogin Cecilie's beautiful figurehead and most of her yards are gone, as well as the leather armchairs, paintings, rugs, tables, anchors, compasses, bunks, marlin-spikes, chronometers, lamps, pulleys, chains, ropes and companionways. Even the portraits of Gusta' and Hilda have been loaded onto a motor-ship for Mariehamn.

'We were doing so well at offloading the grain, but suddenly one night a dreadful gale hit,' says Pam. 'The rivets were popping like gunshots, then the sand shifted and she broke her back on the rocks beneath. We all knew it was the end.'

'Couldn't she go into the estuary for protection?' says Harry.

'We *begged* to be allowed, but they wouldn't let us, damn them. Yet everyone profited from her—the hotels, the shops, the farmers, the newspapers,' Pam says bitterly. 'Around here they call it the *Herzogin* summer, you know. The summer they all got rich while they watched her die.'

We walk back to the hotel where Sven is resting, and buy them both dinner. It's a subdued meal at first, then lit with unexpected happiness. Pam tells us she is pregnant and already a surprising five months has passed.

'We think it happened somewhere in the westerlies as we approached the Channel,' she says, and exchanges a pleased glance with Sven.

'Heavens, Nils,' I say. 'And you've been working like a demon without saying a word.'

'Our congratulations to you both,' says Harry, raising his glass.

'Not just both,' says Pam, laughing. 'I suspect this child will be born of three parents—the two of us and the Duchess.'

Sven smiles for the first time that evening. 'Death and life. We are returning to Pellas, to my family's farm, to have the baby. And then, who knows?'

Next morning we help Pam and Sven pack to leave at last for the Ålands. Harry and I wave them goodbye, then in the afternoon return to Starehole Bay to farewell the Duchess.

Gulls mewl and swirl as we walk the two miles or so along the winding river path to the cliff above the bay, while soft clouds cast sunlight and shadows over the fields.

We sit on the grassy hill as the evening approaches, and watch the sea washing against the barque's scarred hull.

'Her bow's turned to the open sea,' I say. 'She'll never move again, she'll rust away to nothing right here, yet she'll always be yearning for the offing.'

Harry leans back on his elbows. 'I was thinking about the deepwater ships being lost one by one, and that day—you remember, that astonishing day on the train?—when you said, *soon no one will even remember their names.*'

'That *was* an astonishing day, wasn't it?' I lean over and kiss him. 'Yes, once they're sunk or wrecked or broken up, they're gone as if they never existed.'

'But think of it another way, Eliza. This loss has been in full view of the world. Never before in history has a shipwreck been so well-witnessed. How can it possibly be forgotten?'

I shrug. 'There must have been thousands of stories printed and photographs taken—to say nothing of the hordes of day-trippers who paid their sixpences to thrill to the gruesome spectacle.'

Harry strokes my hair. '*Jungman*, I believe as long as sailing ships are loved, no one will ever forget the summer of *Herzogin Cecilie* and the terrible pity of her passing.'

'But dearest *matros*—now it's autumn.'

As evening falls, the pale hull of the Duchess is slowly shadowed by the cliffs. We watch until only the tips of her empty steel masts remain lit by the last of the day. Then they too are gone.

We walk hand-in-hand back to town along the river path, while high above us the seagulls cry, just as they did in the amethyst skies of my childhood.

A week later my doorbell rings. Charlotte is due to give birth any day, so I'm surprised to find it's her standing there.

'I want to talk to you.' She walks in. 'What's that you're offering?' she says, wide-eyed. 'A cup of tea? Well yes, Eliza, I'd love a cup of tea.'

'All right,' I say ungraciously.

I take the tea-tray out to the balcony, where Charlotte is sitting, her belly enormous.

'How are you?' I say.

'Awful. No husband. No waist. No sleep. Never become pregnant, Eliza, it's hell.'

'Is Pete around at the moment?'

'No, he's working. In stupid Southampton.'

'Will he be here with you for the birth?'

'Are you insane?' she says. 'Of course not. What woman wants a man around then?'

'I've no idea, but I believe some do.' I pour the tea in silence.

'Actually,' Charlotte says, clearing her throat, 'Actually, Eliza, I was wondering ... if *you*'d perhaps come with me. To the hospital.'

'What?'

'For the birth. I don't have anyone else. Mother's dead, no aunts, not many women friends. Well, not any, really. There's just—you.'

'But Charlotte, you can't stand me.'

'I can stand you a little bit,' she says in a small voice.

Another silence.

'Really?'

She nods.

'You have no one?'

She shakes her head. For the first time since I've known her I see real tears in her eyes.

I put out my hand and take hers. 'All right.'

'Don't have to be so smug about it.'

'Okay, you ungrateful bitch, I won't.' I shrug. 'So when do you want me there?'

'Today—now—I think it's started. Oh, God, this *minute*.'

Charlotte is magnificent, raging like a lioness throughout the whole sweaty ordeal. At its peak she swears like a foc's'l hand, and the midwife says, 'Now, now, Mrs Bell.'

'I'm not Mrs fucking Bell,' Charlotte whispers venomously. 'This fucking bitch stole my fucking *husband*—' Then she groans again, a long keening moan, clutching at my hands till they're scratched and numb.

I mop sweat from her face and whisper words of encouragement, and finally sob like a baby myself when a tiny black-haired being is lifted mewling into the light.

'She's beautiful, oh God, Charlotte, she's *beautiful*!'

Charlotte holds the small body against her own and presses her face to the warm, moist head. 'Sweetie, there,' she whispers. 'Oh, there, there.'

The nurse takes the child away to be weighed, then brings her back and Charlotte holds her again, dazed. The baby gazes up at her, blinks several times, then closes her eyes and nestles into her mother.

'Vivian,' says Charlotte, the baby asleep in her arms. 'Means alive —she was so vivid to me, as if she was giving off light, invisible light. That doesn't make any sense, does it?'

'Nothing made much sense by then,' I say. 'If you saw invisible light, who am I to argue?'

'It hurt terribly at one point—that's why I was so brutal to your hands.'

'I think there were possibly more points than just one,' I say. 'See all the plasters?'

'I certainly do,' Charlotte says. 'Nice ruby ring, by the way.'

There's a silence.

'Well, I'm glad you were there anyway.' She laughs lazily. 'Even though I was pretty rude to you—and about you.'

'You had your reasons.'

She sighs. 'All right, Eliza, you didn't actually *steal* my husband. From the day he first said your name I knew he was gone. The rest was just a matter of time.'

'But that's not so! You were both happy for years—remember when you got married? You can't say Harry wanted me then.'

'He always kept his feelings hidden, but I knew. That's probably why I gambled,' she says airily. 'I'd take the risk he might leave me, and when he didn't I'd be comforted. Until I felt anxious again.'

'Charlotte, don't you *dare* blame your gambling on Harry! Or I'm leaving this minute.'

'No need to get huffy, sweetie. All right, it was *my* fault, all mine. There, see how contrite I can be? Anyway, you might think you can walk away from me, but you can't. Never again.'

'Of course I can.'

'Look at Vivian,' Charlotte says. 'That face. Those eyelashes. Those tiny hands. You're her aunt, Eliza—you're able to leave *her*?'

'Well ... I suppose not.'

'So you can't leave me either. And even if that stupid desertion Bill becomes law, you'll still be stuck for three years waiting for Harry's divorce.'

'*Christ*, Charlotte. I was hoping motherhood might make you a tiny bit nicer.'

She smiles and stretches a little. 'Well, perhaps it has. You see, I've decided I *will* sue Harry for adultery after all. He'll have to go to a hotel and be caught with some brazen harlot, but I expect you'll fit the bill perfectly, Eliza.'

I'm stunned. 'Why the change of heart?'

'Well, adultery means we can be divorced in six months. Now I've got Vivian I want to marry your brother as soon as possible, not in three long years. See, Eliza? I *can* be nicer.'

Charlotte yawns and holds out the baby. 'Please put your niece to bed, sister-in-law. I must get some sleep.'

Dozing Vivian barely stirs as I tuck her into the cot, and gaze at her rose-petal face, her lavish eyelashes, her tiny starfish hands. I remember how she mewled at her birth like the seagulls high above the stranded Duchess.

Death and life. My throat aches with love.

I say crossly, 'I'm not your sister-in-law yet, Charlotte,' but she's already asleep.

Thank You, Readers

Thank you for reading *Testing the Limits*. If you've enjoyed it, please recommend it to your friends and give it a review or rating on your favourite book site.

This is the first in the Tempo series, but the foundation novel of the series is *Silver Highways*, which introduces Eliza's aunt Lucy and her mother Rosa in Broome in the early twentieth century. Eliza's life on a sailing ship is drawn from my award-winning biography, *Alan Villiers*.

seabooks.net provides links to the books, reviews, extracts, images and background information. *Testing the Limits* is followed by **Embers at Midnight**, set during WW2 in Britain and Asia. **See the following pages for an excerpt.**

About the Author

I grew up near Lake Macquarie, NSW. My background is in science and technology, but in 2000 I ran across the story of the charmed life of an old Broome pearling lugger, and discovered the joys of historical research and writing. My first book, *Redbill*, won the Western Australian Premier's Book Award for Non-Fiction. My second book, *Alan Villiers*, won the Mountbatten Maritime Award, and my novels include *The Turning Tide*, *Atomic Sea* and *Silver Highways*, *Embers at Midnight* and *Harbour of Secrets*. I live in green South Gippsland, Victoria, Australia.

Acknowledgements

As always, I'd like to thank my Wofl friends, Alison Shields, Gillian Clarke and Ruth Carson, for wise editing and great company, and my sons, Alex and Joe, for their thoughtful feedback.

Excerpt, Tempo 2: *Embers at Midnight*

In the sunny peace of 1937 Britain, a group of friends and lovers cannot imagine the storms that will soon engulf them.

Fierce female pilot Billie has only one prospect, but the only problem is the job's in some little dust-up in Spain. Newlywed Eliza is drawn into the world of intelligence and sent to work in Singapore. She thinks it's probably safer there than in London.

Fireman Toby must face a city-wide inferno while his lover's Spitfire battles enemy planes in the skies above. Yet nothing compares to the role actress Izabel must play when fortress Singapore is reduced to embers.

And when the friends reunite in blitzed London, how can they prepare for the loss and betrayal to come? Some things are beyond imagination.

1. Eliza: A Confidential Path

Golden Charlotte always gets what she wants. In this case it's my brother Pete swearing his life unto hers, here at the Registry Office. (Even the bride's famous charm could not convince the local vicar to let a divorcée wed in his church.)

The bridal bouquet is heavy, a mass of lilies as lush as Charlotte herself, and I'm tired. Any day with Charlotte can seem long but this one started particularly early.

Yet Pete is so happy. My feckless baby brother is a man now, dark-haired, rangy, strong. He's a farmer at heart and an engineer by profession, although once, in another life with another woman, he was a pilot. But now he's landed his beloved Charlotte, and they kiss and turn to the wedding guests as the organ rings out in triumph.

Eight-month-old Vivian gurgles in the arms of the housekeeper and waves her small hands at her parents. The polite fiction has it she's from Charlotte's previous marriage, but those bright brown eyes mark her unmistakably as Pete's daughter. Vivian, laughing, flutters her hands at me too. I feel as if my heart is being squeezed and wave back to my tiny niece.

I hand the bouquet to Charlotte and follow the newlyweds along the aisle. Pete's best man, Toby, falls in beside me and we roll our eyes at each other in relief. He murmurs, 'Dear God, I need champagne.' He's had a long day too.

It's May 1937 and chilly in the spring sunlight. We arrange ourselves for photos, then climb into cars and return to Pete's farmhouse for a wedding breakfast. Toby delivers a witty speech, although twice he comes perilously close to mentioning Pete's previous love, Billie.

We toast the happy couple and eat. Seated to my right is Charlotte's father, Professor Otto Fischer, as burly, bearded and committed as Karl Marx. On my left is Harry, Charlotte's ex-husband, grey-eyed behind his gold-rimmed glasses. Now and then he strokes my thigh deliciously beneath the table.

As I argue with Toby about who's had the most exhausting day (I win), I notice Harry and Professor Fischer are deep in worried, private conversation. I know it's not about the wedding.

Once Charlotte was my friend, and I tried earnestly not to fall into Harry's arms. But a year ago I did, and high time too — Charlotte was already pregnant to Pete. But she was terrified of the scandal of divorce and refused to let her marriage go: until the birth of baby Vivian gave her the courage.

So Harry and I went to a hotel and expressed amazement when the detective burst into our unlocked room, and the divorce came through in six months. Since then Charlotte and I have rebuilt a wary friendship, based mainly upon my love for small Vivian and Charlotte's love of ordering me around.

That evening, when the newlyweds have retired and only a few close friends remain, we dance in the sitting room to the gramophone. It's great fun, especially when the avant-garde gang — Toby, Stefan, Klara and Sofia — do the Charleston, now absurdly outdated.

Then Stef and Toby sit down at the piano, their heads together, laughing and playing snippets of Noel Coward songs, and pale Klara waltzes, her eyes closed, in the arms of red-lipped Sofia.

Later, Stefan and I dance too, his slim body pleasingly familiar. We were lovers once, until he realised Toby meant more to him than any woman could. It was a painful time, eased now by new happiness: this marriage and baby Vivian and of course, Charlotte's ex-husband.

Stef goes to the kitchen for more champagne, refills our glasses, then stands at the gramophone chatting to Harry about the music. I gaze at them both, such fine-looking men, and smile to myself.

Harry and I survived these long years of believing we could never be together, and now at last we are. A waltz begins and we dance. He nuzzles my neck, and I caress his back in a place I know brings him particular pleasure. Then we go upstairs to bed.

Lying sated and content, Harry murmurs, 'Did you miss Billie today?'

I kiss his warm shoulder. 'Terribly. She should have been here despite everything.'

'Jealous of Charlotte, perhaps?'

'Doubt it,' I say. 'Remember it was Billie who left Pete.'

'Where did you say she was living now?'

'All over the place really, wherever the aerial circus is performing,' I say. 'Poor thing.'

'I suppose she'd still prefer to be teaching RAF recruits at Hamble aerodrome.'

I laugh. 'The "snotty-nosed, public-school types"? Don't think so.' I roll onto my other side and Harry cuddles me from behind.

'What were you and Otto Fischer talking about?' I say. 'You seemed rather intense.'

'The civil war in Spain. He's appalled at what's happening.'

'Oh, *matros*, surely it'll work out somehow. You mustn't worry.'

'I try not to, but really, it's unbelievable. A Fascist coup against an elected Republic, in *this* day and age?' Harry sighs. 'Otto wants Billie's opinion on some planes his group would like to send to the Spanish government.'

'Hope he doesn't expect her to *fly* them. Why not ask Stef or Pete, they're pilots too?'

'They don't have her experience with so many different old crates.'

I nod. 'Well, she might need the work, she said the aerial display could be closing down soon. No one wants to see planes for fun any more — just reminds them of the Guernica bombings.'

'And who could blame them?' says Harry. 'Anyway, I told Otto to speak to you in London. So sleep now, *jungman*. We've got cleaning up to do in the morning.'

'It's bloody Charlotte's home now. She can clean up.'

'Unlikely,' he says. 'Bet you she has a headache and everyone else has to do it.'

'You terrible cynic. Anyone would think you know her well.'

'Oh, far too well. I'd love to forget.'

I turn to face him, and stroke him slowly from nipple to belly to groin. 'Again? I can do my best.'

'Yes please, my darling.'

A week later I'm sitting on the small balcony of my flat in Bloomsbury, reading in the spring sunshine. I put the book down and gaze at the leafy garden square across the road, thinking about the wedding and my brother Pete.

He's resigned himself at last to his manager's job in an aircraft factory, and leaves his small plane stored at a nearby airfield. With all the demands of Charlotte and the baby he doesn't have time for flying.

I wonder how much he misses it. Or how much he misses Billie too.

Of course he adores Charlotte, most men do. She's wry and seductive and restless, while fierce Billie couldn't be more different. Pete used to call her a red-haired Amelia Earhart — a sarcastic, scowling Earhart.

He and Billie had planned their own aviation business, but Pete sabotaged everything by getting thrown out of flying school and flinging himself into Charlotte's arms.

Billie picked herself up and tutored for a time at Hamble (which welcomed the air-mindedness of the fair sex they said, yet took forever to provide any women's bathrooms), but finally even she couldn't bear the casual, constant prejudice any longer.

'Everyone loves a girl flyer, Lizzie,' she said. 'Except the boy flyers.'

Oh, *Billie*.

Just then the bell rings, and standing at the door is Charlotte's father, Professor Fischer. Though he and Harry have been friends for a long time, we've never spoken much before. I make us coffee and we go to sit out on the balcony.

'Miss McKee,' he says formally, 'Harry Bell has mentioned to you my request regarding Miss Quinn?'

'Yes, he did. But Professor Fischer, surely you don't expect Billie to fly aeroplanes in Spain?'

'No, not at all! And please call me Otto. I will take the liberty of addressing you as Eliza, since that is how Harry has spoken of you from his heart these many years.'

'Of course.' I'm amused at the Professor's old-fashioned charm.

'I must ask, Eliza, do you understand what has happened in Spain?'

I sip my coffee. 'Not really. I know civil war broke out last year after General Franco's right-wing rebels staged a coup against the Republican government, but it's all been a bit confusing ever since.'

Otto leans forward, his eyebrows drawn. 'Then you should know, Eliza, if the rebels do defeat the Republic, Fascists all over Europe will believe they are invincible. Another war will almost certainly begin.'

'Oh, surely not, Otto.' I smile. 'This isn't the Middle Ages. An elected government should be able to crush some raggle-taggle rebels.'

'Eliza, those rebels are very powerful. They are supported by the richest landowners, the Catholic Church, the Italian Fascist and German Nazi governments. Even our own conservative British rulers wish them well.'

'But aren't the Republicans supported too? I thought volunteers from around the world were helping them.'

'Indeed, but they *must* be volunteers — their own conservative countries loudly proclaim neutrality. Eliza, the rebels are powerful and wish us all to return to the Middle Ages. We must stop them now. Or soon it may be the Nazis we have to stop.'

'Oh.' My chest feels tight. 'I've read about them doing terrible things to their Jewish people.'

'*Ja*. Even my own family —' He swallows. 'Now. I work with a committee that wishes to send old aircraft to Spain for the air force. They are loyal to the Republic but do not have enough planes to fight the Condor Legion. You have heard of the Condor Legion?'

I nod. 'The German pilots who bombed Guernica.'

'Indeed. War should take place on battlefields, or so civilised people have always assumed. It should not descend from the sky onto market-towns full of innocent people. Now there is nothing to stop such a thing happening everywhere. Even here in quiet London.'

Bombs here? I gaze at the sunny garden square and shiver.

'Our committee has located some unregistered planes, but we have no idea if they are airworthy, and their owners want a lot of money for them. So Miss Quinn could help us decide if we should buy them.'

'But how would you get them to Spain?' I say. 'Aren't all the ports blockaded?'

'We can ferry them legally to France, then,' Otto shrugs, 'not quite so legally into Spain. The Republican pilots would do the fighting and your friend would not be involved in the slightest. Of course we would pay for her advice.'

'Well, Billie's still touring, but I'll give you the number for head office. After that it's her you'll have to convince, and she has no interest in politics.'

'Ah, but she has interest in flying, and we all know the aerial circuses are finished. I doubt anyone needs persuading what extraordinary inventions aeroplanes have become,' he says drily.

He leans back and stretches a little. 'A good wedding last week, *ja?*'

I'm relieved to change to easier topics. 'You must be pleased Charlotte is so happy. And baby Vivian too —' I smile to myself.

'What joy she brings. The image of Charlotte's mother Ilse, gone these two years now,' he says, his eyes suddenly bright with tears. He clears his throat. 'Still, my work is a consolation.'

He looks around and sees my book on the table. He picks it up, puzzled, stroking his beard, and gazes at me from under his eyebrows. '*The American Black Chamber?*'

I laugh, a little shyly. 'I read anything that interests me.'

'Indeed. Cryptography interests you?'

'I've always loved mathematics — and in application like that it's fascinating.'

'For me too, of course,' he says slowly.

'But aren't you a professor of philosophy?'

'My philosophical research is based upon the concepts of the Vienna Circle, now of course devastated by the Nazis.' He sighs. 'But mathematics is essential to that work. Connected, in unexpected ways, to cryptography.'

He gazes at me for a moment and I think he's seeing me properly for the first time. He carefully puts down the book. 'When you have read this, Eliza — and only if you are interested of course — I have one or two introductory papers you might enjoy. I would be happy to discuss them, but they are highly confidential. Still, perhaps that is too much of an undertaking.'

'No, *no!*' I say. 'I'd love to see your papers, I'd *love* to talk about this, it's always fascinated me. But as a woman I've been told pretty often that such things are not open to me.'

'But now at this time, in this place,' he says, 'everything is open — *must* be open — to all.'

We walk to the door and he shakes my hand. 'I will send you the paper, Eliza, then let us talk. But please remember they are secret, for you only.'

'Thank you. I'll look forward to it, Otto.'

'Of course, this is unconnected to your friend Billie Quinn, quite a different matter.' He shrugs. 'But perhaps not. Many things may help preserve civilisation in this increasingly gloomy world.' Then he laughs sadly. 'I am a romantic fool. Civilisation is already lost.'

I'm curious to see Otto's papers, because lately I've been at rather a loose end. Harry is a doctor, a researcher in malaria, so the many and varied species of *Plasmodium* parasite are a common topic at our dining table. My own interests are odd too, but they don't occupy me in the same way.

I run a small company for my grandmother in Australia, importing pearlshell from Broome for the jewellery trade. But recently overfishing has damaged the market, so business is quiet.

The other interest doesn't demand much of my time either: it's a shareholding in a cargo ship, *Inverley*, left to me by my late grandfather. But *Inverley* isn't the usual sort of ship with an engine — she's a massive steel windjammer, a four-masted barque.

There are very few of her kind left afloat nowadays, and if I mention them most people are puzzled. '*Steel* sailing ships?' they say. 'But aren't those clippers or galleons or whatever, made out of wood and they race to China and back with tea ... or something?'

'No,' I say, 'these are modern vessels, well, modern forty years ago — and they're gigantic, hundreds of feet long. Only a dozen or so still exist and every year they bring the grain harvest from Australia to Europe. They're owned and sailed mostly by the Finns.'

Usually at this stage, say at a party, people give me a look as if I'm teasing them and go to talk to somebody else. But I'm not teasing.

Square-rigged *Inverley* may be an anachronism in this era of engine-driven vessels, yet she certainly exists. And I love her. Eight years ago she brought me from Australia to England, and on our four-month passage I was grudgingly permitted to work with the crew.

They rechristened me Elias, and under their rough tutelage I grew strong and confident and a little wiser in the ways of the world.

All the square-riggers are growing old now, and one by one going to the breakers, so I'm lucky to have known such a life. *Inverley* is the wellspring of my happiest memories.

And of course I love her most of all because Harry and I first became friends upon her deck.

True to his word, Otto sends me a large envelope by first class mail with three of his papers. The formal language is intimidating but, little by little, the logic unfolds, along with a surprising sense of beauty. I also buy a textbook he suggests will help, and slowly this new world draws me in.

We meet every few weeks for a chat over coffee, and Otto guides me towards what he calls the wider view. Not only of the work itself but how it's applied in real life: especially in the intelligence services, about which he seems to know a surprising amount as well.

Conversations with Harry at our dining table about *Plasmodium* research are now interspersed with my excited insights into the realm of codes and cryptography. I read at my desk when it rains and out on my balcony in good weather, and sometimes I look across to the trees in the garden square and feel utterly content and absorbed.

It never occurs to me to wonder where this fascination will lead. I don't ask myself why Otto is being so helpful, why he is clearing a path before me, a confidential path, one I would never have discovered for myself.

I don't question what it might mean for me, or Billie, or Harry.

The Great War passed so long ago it's easy to assume today's peace will last forever. I cannot for a moment imagine these sunny days will pass, and soon an eyewall of thunderclouds will slowly engulf the sky.

I cannot imagine, either, how carelessly I will stray into that stormfront.

Perhaps some things are beyond imagination.

2. Billie: Kites in Spain

Miami, Saturday, 31 May 1937: Mrs. Amelia Earhart Putnam announced tonight she hopes to restart her world flight tomorrow. Noonan, who will act as navigator, will accompany her on the entire journey. She will fly to South America and then across the Atlantic and the Channel to Aden, Karachi, Darwin, Lae, Howland, Honolulu and from thence to Oakland, California.

I put down the newspaper and sigh. Lucky cow, wish it were me instead. Pete always said I was like Earhart, but she's calm and patient and good natured — I'm just a cranky bitch, as Pete wasn't too slow to point out, either.

I look up and realise there's someone hovering at the opening to my tent. Wilfred Bettany. I really don't want to deal with his anxious politeness — polite anxiety? — this afternoon.

Sometimes I think I should take out a newspaper advertisement: *Miss Billie Quinn would like to apologise to all the men of Planet Earth for making them nervous because she can fly aeroplanes better than they can.*

'Ahem, Miss Quinn?' he says, taking off his hat.

'Hello, Wilf. What's up?'

'The meeting, Miss Quinn, remember? Major Stott's come from London to address us.'

'Reckon he's got good news, Wilf?'

'Doubt it.'

We walk together to the large tent where everyone else is assembling. Wilf's not that bad really, but I've told him often enough not to call me Miss Quinn. If he didn't annoy me so much, he'd be almost attractive in a puppy-dog sort of way.

We move towards the rear of the tent as the Major stands up to speak. He took over the business a couple of years ago, but unfortunately it was when the novelty of human flight was wearing off and the unpleasant reality of aerial warfare was emerging.

Not a good time to try to charm the paying public with a flying circus, but at least he doesn't beat around the bush. Tight economic conditions, blah blah, poor weather, blah blah, reduced takings, blah blah. Terribly sorry, old chaps. When you finish today it's for good. Thank you.

'Do you think we'll get paid out for the month?' says Wilf as we leave the tent, everyone murmuring around us.

'I'll be surprised if we get paid out for the week.'

'Will you be all right, Miss Quinn? What will you do?'

'No idea, Wilf. And for Christ's sake call me Billie. What about you?'

He shakes his head. 'Family's disowned me and I never finished my studies. Not many civilian aviation jobs around now.'

'Air Force?'

'Well, it's a pay-packet. And they're desperate for men —'

'Not much use to me, then.'

He grins. 'Suppose not. Couldn't have girls —' He goes red. 'Sorry.'

Something simmers over, as it does all too often nowadays. 'You know how many women hold pilot's licences in England now, Wilf? Close to *two hundred*. You don't reckon there's a few of them might be some use in the air? Especially if ... when ...'

I run out of steam.

Wilf gazes at me. 'I'll be sorry not to see you every day, Billie.'

'Yeah.' I'm surprised to find myself thinking *me too*.

'Will you come to the pub with us later? I know you usually don't, but it's the last night.'

I shrug. 'Maybe.' He smiles and I think, okay. Nice skin, broad shoulders, slim hips. And I'll never see him again after this. Why not?

Wilf goes to check his plane. I can see people already lining up for tickets at the gate, even though the afternoon show doesn't start for an hour. Maybe they've heard this is going to be the last one.

As I get to my tent I'm surprised to see a large bearded man in an overcoat waiting by the entry. He takes off his hat as I approach, and steps forward.

'Miss Quinn?'

'No, Queen of bloody Sheba.'

He smiles politely. What an utter shit I've become.

'Sorry. Force of habit. And you are —?'

'Professor Fischer, Otto. You would know of me as Charlotte's father.'

'Oh, okay. How did the wedding go?'

'It was very pleasant. I was sorry not to see you there, but I was able to prevail upon Miss Eliza McKee to help me track you down.'

To my amusement I'd been sent an invitation to the wedding. I'd ripped it up, not out of pique, I just couldn't be bothered to go. After all, Pete didn't dump me for Charlotte — it was me who left him after he stupidly threw away all our years of hard work.

I don't even hate Charlotte either, although I'm perfectly aware of the barbed steel spine beneath all that sweet lushness. At my kindest, which isn't very often, I sometimes pity her, though could never have said why.

She has Pete, she has their child, she apparently has everything she ever wanted. But I'll be mildly curious to see if that's enough for her in the years ahead.

And Charlotte did one good thing at least: she released poor Harry Bell from their bitter shell of a marriage and made Lizzie's life complete. My dear friend Lizzie, who has her own spine of steel, but hers is flexible and far from barbed.

'Miss Quinn?'

'Sorry. Just thinking how delightful the wedding must have been.'

To my surprise he says wryly, 'I rather doubt that,' and I can't help but grin.

We sit on folding stools in my tent and he says, 'As I explained to Eliza, we hope to buy several aircraft to send to the Republicans in Spain, but we need a professional opinion on their airworthiness. It must be confidential of course, as it is technically against the law. The Non-Intervention Committee has some very peculiar ideas, and we prefer not to attract their attention.'

'The Non-who?'

'A government body preventing anyone sending arms to Spain, but in reality stopping only those who would aid the Republicans. No such restrictions hinder Fascists in their support of the Nationalists.'

'Okay. And the Nationalists would be —?'

He smiles kindly. 'The rebels who carried out a military coup against the elected Republican government.'

'Oh, the baddies.'

He stops smiling. 'In any war both sides may behave culpably, but yes, there have been extraordinary barbarities ...' His jaw clenches. 'Yes, the baddies. And if they win, German aggression will be unstoppable. You would know that many British volunteers — soldiers, nurses, drivers — have already joined the International Brigades to support the Republicans.'

'Not really, I only read the aviation news. So why do the Republicans want these old kites?'

'The Spanish air force is loyal, but the pilots are poorly-trained and have few working planes.'

'Poorly-trained?' I say slowly. 'Well, I need a job and I'm a qualified instructor.'

'Spain is a *war* front, Miss Quinn, not suitable for —'

'I think that's for me to decide, Otto.'

'Ah.' He hesitates. 'Certainly, a number of foreign airmen were hired last year to help protect Madrid. They did well, although most have now left, forbidden by their own countries to take part.'

'Hired? What were they paid?'

'I believe it was something like two hundred pounds a month.'

'That's pretty good. What would they pay for a flight instructor, do you reckon?'

'I do not know.' He frowns in concern. 'Miss Quinn —'

'Call me Billie, for Christ's sake.'

'Billie, please understand that half the country is now held by the Nationalists, and they are ruthless and very well armed. And by 'ruthless' I mean they visit atrocities upon civilians on an almost inconceivable scale. Women especially are targeted for —'

He stops and rubs his face with both hands, his eyes sad. 'Spain is not a place for innocents of any kind, Billie. Political or personal.'

'I'm thirty years old, Otto, and I've worked with men as an equal since I was seventeen.' I shrug. 'Okay, maybe I'm a political innocent but I'm not interested in all that argy-bargy.' I lean forward. 'I just need *work*, this job's finished. Why shouldn't I train Republican flyers?'

'The Russians are setting up a school at the moment to instruct Spanish pilots, so the job would not last for long — months at most.'

'Any paid work suits me. Those Russian planes are mainly Polikarpov I-15s and I-16s, aren't they? I've flown an I-5, it's a good bird.'

'I have no idea at all about those machines. It is why I am here in the first place.'

'Come on, Otto, I need a job. Do it for the Revolution.'

He closes his eyes. 'Billie, it is the legally elected *government* we are supporting.'

'Oh that's right, it's the baddies who are doing the revolution.'

'Indeed it is.' He sighs. 'Very well. I will enquire.'

'Great. Now, those planes you wanted me to check, what are they?'

He gets a notebook out of his coat and shows me a list of names, and I have to smile.

'Sorry, Otto, I don't need to see any of these. If even one of them could get off the ground I'd be surprised. They were slow and obsolete twenty years ago. You'd be wasting your money.'

One of the assistant riggers calls from outside the tent, 'Final checks, Miss Quinn. Don't be late.'

'All right,' I say, scribbling on a page of the notebook. 'Here's my phone number in London. Ring me when you know more.'

Miss Billie's Daredevil Handkerchief Stunt goes off as usual, but I can't say I'm sorry it's for the last time. Swooping past the crowd in a Tiger Moth and hooking a hanky off the ground with one wing may not be quite as terrifying as it looks, but getting it wrong would leave a large and bloody hole in the ground.

Afterwards I help strip down the planes and load them into the trucks. Everyone's subdued but careful, as always. There'll be plenty of work ahead for the mechanics and riggers and pilots — the Royal Air Force can't get enough men — but the women who sell the tickets and cook and keep the whole shebang ticking over don't have any such guarantees, and I see a few red eyes.

By evening it's all over. The sleeping and mess tents will stay till tomorrow but everything else is packed. I go to my tent, have a quick wash and change, then head along the path through the wheatfield to the pub.

The other pilots are already sitting around a table in the courtyard, so I get half a pint and sit beside Wilf, who goes red. The pilots are pretty easy company. They gave me some shit at first but we've learnt to get along.

There was one creep who thought I'd fall into his bed with a sob of gratitude, but I enlightened him. He departed a few months ago, still sulking, but at least he never touched me again.

Night falls and most people leave for their tents — it'll be an early day tomorrow. Finally it's just me and dear old Wilf, who's run out of conversational gambits and has a faint air of desperation.

'Would you mind escorting me back through the field?' I ask, as if I haven't safely negotiated paths through fields and lanes to our campsites for months. He nods, speechless.

We set off in the dark but luckily Wilf's brought a torch. Halfway back I stop and look up to the sky.

It was hazy earlier, but now there's a quarter-moon and the stars are brilliant in the mild night air. I love them, even though these northern skies aren't nearly as beautiful as those of my Western Australian childhood.

'Switch off the torch, Wilf. I can't see properly.'

He does so, and after a time gazing upwards I turn to him, and step close and put my hands on his shoulders. I rest my head lightly on his shoulder too, surprised at how tired — of just about everything — I suddenly feel.

But he smells of young, healthy male and I nuzzle his cheek and nibble my way to his nicely-shaped mouth, and he obliges me with a kiss that's rather more pleasingly experienced than I'd expected. I tilt my head back and smile at him in the faint moonlight.

'Billie,' he says, breathing deeply. 'God, that's …'

I take his hand and draw him away from the path and we sit down among the soft green wheat. He puts his arms around me and kisses me again, as delightfully as the first time.

I suddenly regret I didn't try this with him before, but it wouldn't have been wise in the gossipy world of the aerial circus. But tomorrow we're going in different directions.

He leans over me, and I reach up to his amazed face and bring his mouth to mine again. I guide his fingers to my buttons and he opens them and I shrug off my shirt. I'm so slim I usually wear just a camisole beneath and, as he pulls it off and his tongue finds my aching nipples, that seems a particularly good idea.

I groan and his mouth comes back to mine and his hands are doing marvellous things — everywhere — but the rest of my bloody clothes are getting in the way.

I undo my trousers and kick them off, along with my knickers and shoes, and don't even have to suggest to Wilf he does the same. Efficient lad, I think, as the stars waver above us and stalks of wheat slide smooth against my back.

Exquisitely, wickedly naked to the air, I wrap my thighs around his hips and pull him deep into me: then I don't notice the stars above or anything else. I haven't had a man in quite a while, so it's not very long before I'm arching in pleasure, waves throbbing through me, softening and glowing and easing away.

Wilf comes too, hot on my belly, then we doze for a few moments.

He wakes, cups my face and whispers, 'Oh, *Billie* —'

I put my hand on his mouth. 'Shh. We'd better get back before anyone notices.'

We dress, Wilf finds his torch, and we walk calmly back to the camp. No one is about so I kiss him quickly and push him towards his tent. He goes to say something and I shake my head.

'Night, Wilf.'

Next morning he's shy and pleased, but I'm glad to see there's no swaggering or significant looks.

At the breakfast table the chat is of future prospects. Ours was the last of the civilian flying displays and now only the RAF, with its promises of power and protection, draws the crowds.

'What you going to do then, Billie?' asks one of the mechanics.

I shrug. 'Might be getting work in Spain, training pilots for the Republicans.'

'Who, the *Reds*?' says a man named Jones. 'Better get paid in advance. Haven't got a hope — the Krauts and Wops are walloping them.'

'They're not Reds,' says Wilf, surprising me. 'They're the government, elected to modernise the place and bring in some of the freedoms we all take for granted.'

'Ha! Fellow traveller over here, boys,' says Jones. 'Give it up, Wilf, they're just Commies, and the Krauts'll show 'em what for.'

'And then?' asks Wilf. 'They'll try to show us what for as well.'

'Doesn't matter — we've got the RAF,' says another pilot proudly.

The head mechanic says, 'Don't be so confident, laddie. The Germans are miles ahead of us, *miles*. Christ, what I'd give to get my hands on one of those Messerschmidts.' He grimaces. 'But Jones is right, the Republicans don't stand a chance. Trying to take on the Condor Legion with a few old kites?'

'Well, not me personally,' I say. 'But if they'll pay me to teach them flying, why would I turn down the job? Not much else available.'

'Maybe they'll start up a women's RAF just for you, Billie,' says someone, snorting with laughter and the others join in.

I grin, but oh, how sick I am of the same old jokes.

I know I can outfly any of these smug bastards, and I know they'll never acknowledge it. And they'll always have work handed to them on a plate, they'll always get the newest, sleekest birds.

And me? Clapped out old kites in Spain.

3. Toby: Whitfield Street

Stefan drives us back to London. I'm tired, but mainly glad that ghastly wedding's over. Poor old Pete was terrified something would go wrong at the last minute (which it has fairly often in the dear boy's life), but now at last he's happy. Even the terrifying Charlotte seemed content, and she's never been what you'd call a serene soul.

Klara is beside me in the rear seat and she dozes, her head on my shoulder. I gaze at Stef and Sofia in the front.

They're cousins, two peas in a pod as they say, both dark-haired and green-eyed; although Sofia is buxom while my love is slim and entirely beautiful under his well-cut clothes.

Their mothers were the Naughty Diamant Twins, dancers who came from Poland at the turn of the century and found themselves generous and compliant husbands.

I suppose we're really rather a mixed bunch. Klara, slight and fair, is from Finland — I believe there was a brief marriage to some oaf in Cambridge, then she met Sofia and that was that.

Me? I'm the mundane one. Tall, blond, English, and my accent as anonymous as I can make it.

I watch the trees flickering past the window and return to thinking, what *will* I do about that bloody house? My darling old aunt Maude died recently and bequeathed me her London terrace in the bohemian district of Fitzrovia.

Some might rejoice at their good fortune, but I used to visit her in the ghastly old pile and my heart sinks.

The Depression may be easing off but it's left a lot of good property going for pennies. It would be hard to even give the house away right now, let alone find a willing purchaser — it's shabby and Victorian and hopelessly unfashionable.

In any case I know Maude wanted it to stay in the family. She was always kind to me, even paid for my education, so I do owe her that, and it's not as if Stef and I couldn't do with more space.

My desk is in a corner of the sitting room in our small flat and, although he says it doesn't bother him, my tapping on the typewriter must be irritating. But I've got to get a manuscript to the publishers in the next few weeks so I simply can't avoid it.

Maude's place has four storeys plus an attic and cellar. It might be possible for us to live on a couple of floors, but the cold, decrepit remainder? Rent it out perhaps? That could be tricky. I'd have to do it up and I'm not very handy that way.

Tricky in other ways too — who would we share the house with? There are rather a lot of loud and unpleasant individuals out there who'd love to see me and Stef in gaol simply for being who we are. Even at our current lodgings we have to be ludicrously discreet, yet the landlord is still spitefully watchful.

I say lightly, 'Sofia, want to live in my rotting inheritance?'

'What would the rent be, dear one?'

'Only joking, blossom. I wouldn't impose that slum on anyone.'

Sofia turns around. 'No, honestly, Toby. I've been to your aunt's — remember when we took her a hamper last Christmas? It's not that bad. And our landlady has just given me and Klara notice.'

'Why?'

'You know why. For being us, despite always paying our rent on time and putting up for years with her ghastly cats.'

Beside me Klara murmurs, 'And the minister wants my printing press out of the church cellar. Your new house has a cellar?'

'It's not a *new* house, Klara, it's a horrible, disgusting old one. And you'd have to clean it and paint it and repair it —'

'We could do that,' says Sofia.

She's correct. Unlike me, they both maintain their surroundings simply and competently.

'Tell you what, old chums,' I say, laughing. 'You do the repairs around the place and you can have a floor to yourselves for free.'

'I want the cellar for my press,' says Klara sleepily. 'And an attic room for a study.'

'You drive a hard bargain, darling. God knows, I had plans to bury bodies in that cellar, but if it's what you want —'

Klara claps her hands. 'Toby, that would be excellent indeed.'

'Are you serious? Stef, what do you think?'

He keeps his gaze on the road and nods. 'It's rather a good idea, Toby — could protect all of us.'

Sofia says, 'Of *course*. Two men, two women. As far as the busybodies are concerned that's how it's supposed to be. Our real lives can remain our own business.'

'I suppose it *could* be something of a haven,' I say doubtfully.

'Plenty of space, too,' says Sofia. 'I desperately need a rehearsal studio with good acoustics. One of those big empty rooms would be perfect.'

'Are you sure?' I say. 'You do realise how much work it needs?'

'Ha!' says Klara confidently.

She's rather less confident the day we go to see the house in Whitfield Street: a vulgar Victorian interloper in a row of elegant Georgian residences. The rain doesn't help much, but even a sunny day wouldn't flatter the garish red bricks beneath their layers of London soot.

I unlock the front door and a dreadful smell hits us in the face.

'Just needs an airing,' says Sofia briskly. She looks into the front room and says less briskly, 'Oh God, poor decomposing beastie. Those rugs'll have to go, *then* an airing will work wonders.'

Downstairs the walls of the two reception rooms are covered in acres of printed brown agapanthus, and at the rear is an old-fashioned kitchen and bathroom. Being careful not to catch our feet in the worn runner, we climb the staircase to the first floor. It has a sitting room, two bedrooms and its own small kitchen and bathroom.

'This was where my aunt lived,' I say. 'She was converting the upstairs floors into flats to rent out, but became unwell and stopped. So they weren't finished off, although the basics are there.'

'It might do us rather nicely, Toby,' says Stef. 'What do you think?'

I have to agree. Maude's rooms are musty-smelling but not in bad condition, and they also have a few good sticks of antique furniture. We climb the next flight to the second storey, laid out like the first, but needing a little more work to make it livable.

'One of these rooms would make a good music studio,' says Sofia.

Klara says, 'I like this place, Toby, but I still want a study in the attic to look out at the sky.'

'Let's hope the roof is sound, poppet, or you'll be closer to the sky than you might prefer.'

'Really, the whole place does have potential,' says Stefan slowly.

'If you overlook the squalor,' I say as we reach the third floor, where we stand, astonished at the mess. I shudder and say, 'Beyond redemption,' and the others murmur in agreement.

Klara dashes up the last flight of stairs to the attic. She calls out, 'There is a good view over the rooftops and I do not see the sky through the ceiling. I think I will have my attic, Toby.'

'It's not bad, you know,' says Stefan. 'The mould is only superficial.'

'Hopefully.' I shrug. 'All right, let's have a think about how on earth we might do this.'

Aunt Maude left me some money and I have a small income from my books, Stefan is gainfully employed, and Sofia plays her cello in elegant hotels. Klara is perhaps the least prosperous, but still manages to get by, selling her hand-printed volumes of poetry to devotees and bookshops.

None of us is as poor as perhaps it sounds, but we're all in our late twenties and certainly don't want to ask our parents for help. And while Stefan and Sofia's families are well off, Klara's are rather less so. And mine, I always fib, are long since departed.

Sofia and Klara start on the house immediately and we hire a man to help them. They labour happily at Whitfield Street throughout the rest of that long summer, while I argue with my publisher's copy-editor and wrestle with successive drafts of my manuscript.

This is my first novel, a light-hearted detective story. My two earlier works were non-fiction, based upon my travels in the Middle East as a wide-eyed innocent. They were well-received, even garnered small literary prizes, but I'm finding fiction rather harder to write.

It's a relief to be able to skip the reference lists, but I'm not a slap-dash author and even fiction, no matter how light-hearted, still needs research. I sometimes discuss my female characters with Eliza, although she's such an odd little thing I'm not certain she's a reliable exemplar of womanhood.

She laughs when I say that, and insists females are very different from each other, and most of them want more than marriage and babies in their lives. That's not what the ladies' journals tell me and Eliza herself can hardly talk: she's absurdly fond of babies, and marriage to gorgeous Harry is certainly on the cards.

But her women friends certainly sound like a rum lot, especially Billie, the girl flyer. I'd love to meet her one day, although she does sound rather fearsome.

Stefan is a pilot too, and an engineer at an aircraft factory. He's also a member of the RAF Reserve, but I'm not quite certain what that entails, apart from him having to attend dull lectures or go away on aviation courses.

Lately he's been bored with his work, and speaks longingly of the Supermarine works at Southampton where they turn out those new Spitfire planes. That's where Eliza's brother Pete works too, and when they get together it's as if they're speaking a foreign language.

Pete used to share my flat. I took him in when flygirl Billie decided she'd had enough of him, and it was there he finally fell prey to Charlotte's sheathed claws. Pete used to feel sorry for me because I'd never bring girls home, but I didn't have the faintest idea how innocent he was until he tried to pair me off with Sofia and/or Klara.

I had to break it to him gently they had no interest in me and equally, I had no interest in anyone but the man I'd loved hopelessly for a decade. At that, he nearly ran terrified for the hills. But then he decided being part of our little avant-garde gang made him a sophisticated chappie of the world: dear old Farmer Pete.

By then I'd long given up any hope of Stefan. I still had lovers of course, I won't pretend that men don't find me attractive.

And I'd go cottaging when lust became too much, despite the astonishing hypocrisy of the law: peers of the realm soliciting in dark corners, judges taking their pleasures in parks, and most infuriating, members of Parliament condemning us all as monsters then creeping out at night for blow-jobs.

Of course it's part of everyday life for a queer man in modern England: terror that the next moment of joy might also mean the pantomime of arrest for *persistently importuning*, the condemnation of court, the brute violence of prison. I know poor chaps who've been flung into gaol, and afterwards were denied jobs or places to live.

Still, there's nothing I can do to change society or myself. I've loved Stef since we were at school, and when he fell for other boys I accepted it, and when he played with women I pretended not to care.

In fact I like women, but to me they're an interesting, separate species — I could no more want to make love to one than, say, to a friendly zebra.

Yet Stef has always yearned to fit in, and when he began a

relationship with Eliza a few years ago I truly hoped he'd be happy. In the end he couldn't keep pretending to an orthodoxy he didn't feel, and he turned, thank God, to me at last.

The house at Whitfield Street is livable by November 1937, the agapanthus wallpaper gone, the ceilings painted and floors waxed, the lights repaired and chimneys swept.

By some miracle of modern plumbing we have working kitchens and bathrooms on each floor. We fit a new runner to the staircase and Stef's parents give us a few old Turkish rugs for the living areas.

Moving in is hard, but Pete drives to London with his farm truck and, with Eliza and Harry's help, we manage to shift all our books and clothes and beds and desks and wardrobes, even Sofia's fragile cello and Klara's *infernally* heavy printing-press.

At the end of that long day I'm in Aunt Maude's old bedroom unpacking some of our things, and notice an object wrapped in brown paper at the back of the wardrobe.

I undo it and discover a framed oil painting, a portrait of Maude as a young woman, her blue eyes brimming with laughter, blonde hair in a loose knot, a gauzy wrap around her bare shoulders.

Until I was eleven I didn't know my aunt very well, but then she'd visit me at my boarding school, a quiet presence overshadowed by her glum banker husband.

When the husband died a few years later Maude blossomed in an endearingly eccentric way and I became very fond of her. I can barely recall my own mother, so Maude was always the most important female in my life. I'm gazing, charmed, at the portrait when Stef comes in with another suitcase.

'Remember Aunt Maude?' I say. 'She'd visit our school on open days.'

'Vaguely. That's rather a good painting though, isn't it?'

We take the canvas downstairs and hang it above the fireplace in the sitting room. Klara says solemnly, 'To have Aunt Maude up there is like thanking her for this house.'

'It's *perfect*, Toby,' says Sofia, stepping forward to level the frame slightly. 'She's so like you, especially around the eyes.'

'Well, my mother's sister, after all.'

'Did your mother look like Maude?' asks Klara.

'No idea, poppet. She died when I was very young.'

'But don't you have a photograph?'

'Sorry, no.' I quickly change the subject. 'Who's for a cup of tea?'

By Sunday evening the move is done and Stef and I return to our old lodgings to give the nasty little landlord his key. We wait in the hall until he shuffles to his door, then he rudely snatches the key from my hand. I'm tired and have had more than enough by then.

'By the way, you old bastard,' I say. 'Here's what you've been hoping to see all these years.' I kiss Stefan slowly and pleasurably.

The landlord's eyes bulge. 'You *perverts*, how dare you?'

'Oh, we dare, and I bet you wish you did too, darling. Can't keep it hidden forever, you know.'

As we leave Stef murmurs, 'You don't really think he's secretly queer, do you?'

'I always thought he was just a little *too* fascinated by our every move. I expect we've just made his day.'

Laughing, we saunter down the road to catch the underground back to our new home. Our haven. Whitfield Street.

See <u>seabooks.net</u> for more on *Embers at Midnight*.

Fiction by Kate Lance

HARBOUR OF SECRETS — Kate Lance, Seabooks Press, 2022

The war is over. The reckoning is not.

Tempo Book 3: It's the hip 1950s on Sydney's shimmering harbour, but how do you reconcile a past that gave — and stole — so much?

Tina runs Tempo jazz club at shady Kings Cross, keeping secrets with, and from, her beguiling boss Jimmy. And from her lonely husband.

Harry yearns to forget his days in a Singapore prison camp, yet his friends won't let him. Nor will his conscience.

Ex-pilot Billie now works at the flying-boat base. When her old lover Pete turns up with a new wife there's a lot she prefers to conceal. Even from herself.

Yvonne rebuilds a life by the harbour with her beloved Klara. But secrets emerge when she publishes Harry's wartime memoir, then no one can postpone the reckoning.

EMBERS AT MIDNIGHT — Kate Lance, Seabooks Press, 2021

"The writing is beautiful and haunting. The characters are drawn with razor-sharp precision. It's compelling reading of the highest standard, full of evocative triumph and tragedy."

Tempo Book 2: In the late 1930s, a group of old friends at a sunny wedding could not imagine what storms are about to engulf them.

Fierce pilot Billie is glad she's got a job at last — only trouble is it's in some little dust-up in Spain. Secretive Toby has no wish to volunteer for anything. Till he finds out for himself what *blitzkrieg* means.

Newlywed Eliza is posted to Intelligence at Singapore — safer than London, she thinks. But when fortress Singapore is reduced to embers, it is actress Izabel who is forced to play the role of her life.

SILVER HIGHWAYS — Kate Lance, Seabooks Press, 2018

"A beautiful and poignant coming of age romantic tale that kept me reading from start to finish."

Foundation of the Tempo series: Lucy Fox is sailing to Melbourne in 1906 with her sister Rosa, when a tragic landfall leaves her life entangled with three seamen: gentle Sam, cynical Danny and beautiful

Gideon. After Rosa's scandalous elopement, trader Min-lu shows Lucy a new world of silks, spices and the silvery pearlshell of Broome: a place where breaking the rules is a way of life. The Great War begins, and Lucy's beloved must go to sea, where ruthless U-boats stalk the last of the old sailing ships. But when peace returns the influenza pandemic comes too—and Lucy, far from home, discovers how cruelly she has been betrayed.

ATOMIC SEA — CM Lance, Seabooks Press, 2016

"Brilliant! Every chapter holds a twist you can't see coming. Fast moving and worth the reading ride."

Radiation Book 2: Chernobyl, the nuclear power station that contaminated Europe. Fukushima, smashed into radioactive rubble by a tsunami. And now ... Broome? Worm Turning nuclear waste plant is fast-tracked on sacred ground near Broome. A certain Great Power says it'll take all responsibility. Sadly it's lying.

Life ashore becomes surprisingly threatening for scientist Lena and hacker Jessie, and their only refuge is Simon's old lugger. Sadly he's lying too. An eerie blue boat turns up with a glowing cargo, the grand opening of Worm Turning is just days away, and a cyclone called Cyril is on the move.

And Lena discovers being stuck on a committee isn't her worst nightmare after all.

THE TURNING TIDE — CM Lance, Allen & Unwin, 2014

"It took me about two pages to fall in love with this beautiful Australian book."

Radiation Book 1: Mike Whalen trained as a commando in 1942 at rugged Wilsons Prom and fought in East Timor. Now a widowed academic in his sixties, and more damaged than he realises, he meets Lena, the granddaughter of his glamorous old friends Helen and Johnny. When Johnny died in the war he left Mike with a burden of secrets, and as Lena draws him back into her family he discovers more secrets existed than he ever imagined. From the Prom to devastated Hiroshima, this is a saga of adventure and passion.

Non-Fiction by Kate Lance

ALAN VILLIERS: VOYAGER OF THE WINDS

2nd Edition, Seabooks Press, 2020. Fully revised and with over 100 photos. **Mountbatten Maritime Award 2009**

> *"A delightful warts-and-all biography of one of the world's most notable chroniclers of seafaring life."*

When Australian journalist Alan Villiers sailed on the last of the giant merchant windjammers in the 1920s and '30s, his writings and photographs made him famous.

Villiers crewed on beautiful *Herzogin Cecilie* and tragic *Grace Harwar*, took tiny *Joseph Conrad* around the globe, sailed on Arabian dhows, led wartime landing craft, captained *Mayflower* II across the Atlantic, and inspired sail training and ship restoration projects.

Drawn from his personal diaries, this award-winning biography of the author-adventurer reveals both his mythmaking and his achievements. It is a tribute to the greatest sailing ships ever launched —and to the extraordinary man who loved them.

REDBILL: FROM PEARLS TO PEACE

Fremantle Press, 2004.

Western Australian Premier's Award 2004 for Non-Fiction

> *"Lance has presented the biography of Redbill with quiet passion and exquisite detail."*

Redbill is the true story of a sailing boat's voyage through a century of history. She began life as a Broome pearlshell lugger owned by the buccaneering Captain Gregory, then became naval vessel HMAS *Redbill*, bombed in Darwin during WW2. After the war *Redbill* went pearling in Papua, then worked for Greenpeace in Tahiti, and raised funds for refugees.

Redbill also filmed a Bass Strait voyage, *If It Doesn't Kill You* and reunited a young Aboriginal man with his long-lost family. Finally she took on an epic voyage around the coast of Australia, to return to the North-West to face her greatest challenge yet: Rosita, the most powerful tropical cyclone to strike Broome in ninety years.